Sinful Desires

Complete Series

By

M.S. Parker

This book is a work of fiction. The names, characters, places and incidents are products of the writer's imagination or have been used fictitiously and are not to be construed as real. Any resemblance to persons, living or dead, actual events, locales or organizations is entirely coincidental.

Copyright © 2014 Belmonte Publishing LLC
Published by Belmonte Publishing LLC

All rights reserved. Without limiting the rights under copyright reserved above, no part of this publication may be reproduced, stored in or introduced into a retrieval system, or transmitted, in any form, or by any means (electronic, mechanical, photocopying, recording, or otherwise) without the prior written permission of the copyright owner.

The author acknowledges the trademarked status and trademark owners of various products referenced in this work of fiction, which have been used without permission. The publication/use of these trademarks is not authorized, associated with, or sponsored by the trademark owners.

ISBN-13: 978-1505349511
ISBN-10: 1505349516

Table of Contents

Sinful Desires Vol. 1 7
Chapter 1 7
Chapter 2 15
Chapter 3 25
Chapter 4 29
Chapter 5 44
Chapter 6 51
Chapter 7 60
Chapter 8 66
Chapter 9 75
Chapter 10 85

Sinful Desires Vol. 2 90
Chapter 1 90
Chapter 2 95
Chapter 3 104
Chapter 4 114

Chapter 5 124
Chapter 6 136
Chapter 7 150
Chapter 8 157
Chapter 9 164

Sinful Desires Vol. 3 169
Chapter 1 169
Chapter 2 175
Chapter 3 181
Chapter 4 193
Chapter 5 208
Chapter 7 223
Chapter 8 231
Chapter 9 246

Sinful Desires Vol. 4 252
Chapter 1 252
Chapter 2 264
Chapter 3 276
Chapter 4 290
Chapter 5 296
Chapter 6 311

5

Chapter 7	315
Chapter 8	328
Chapter 9	338

Sinful Desires Vol. 5	344
Chapter 1	344
Chapter 2	350
Chapter 3	358
Chapter 4	369
Chapter 5	375
Chapter 6	385
Chapter 7	392
Chapter 8	404
Chapter 9	411
Chapter 10	421
Acknowledgement	429
About The Author	430

Sinful Desires Vol. 1

Chapter 1

The first time I felt his clammy hand on my tits, I chalked it up as a slip. After all, he'd been stuffing a dollar bill into my almost sheer bra. The second time, however, the bastard actually squeezed one of my boobs.

"Ricky!" I yelled over the music.

A massive man with no neck, and arms the size of my thighs lumbered over. I never knew how he heard us over the pounding bass, but Ricky never missed one of us girls calling for help.

"All right, buddy." He grabbed the guy by the scruff of the neck and gave me a nod as he dragged the drunk away.

I made a mental note to thank Ricky after my set was done and then went back to shaking my tits and ass. That's what this was, after all. It wasn't dancing, not for real. It was getting away with pasties and g-string instead of full nudity just so I could call it exotic dancing rather than stripping. It was a thin line, I knew, but it helped me look at myself in the mirror with a tiny bit less disgust.

As I peeled off the last item of my clothing – my barely-there bra – I heard the familiar cat-calls as my breasts came into view. I wasn't as big as most of the other girls, since at least seventy-five percent of them had gotten their busts enhanced to reach the in-demand double D's, but I was natural. I had an athlete's body with just enough extra on top to be annoying. Fortunately, it also meant that I had big enough boobs to work as a dancer when I hadn't been able to find anything else.

Dancer... right.

I bent down and gave the room a view of my swaying breasts and basically bare ass, and then flipped my hair up, letting the spotlight make the bright red waves look like dancing flames. Most everyone thought I dyed it to get that color, but it was all natural. I'd inherited it from my mother.

The music ended as I reached my final pose and the men cheered, some simply yelling while others shouted propositions and what I supposed they considered compliments.

"How much to fuck that ass?"
"Damn, baby, you got me so hard."
"Shake it some more!"
"Come give me a lap dance!"
"I got a pole for you to dance on."

8

I smiled and gave them the 'oh baby, you make me *so* wet' look, then rolled my eyes as I walked off stage. Once I was out of sight, I pulled the tight blouse back on just to give me coverage until I got to the locker where I'd left my real clothes. Aurora shook her head as she walked past me towards the stage. None of the others understood why I didn't just walk around half-naked like they did. I wasn't mean enough to tell them it was because I wasn't like them.

"Good set." A tall blonde dressed like a naughty nurse called over as I stopped by my locker.

"Thanks, Tammy." I started taking off what little was left of my costume. It had taken me two months to get used to changing in front of the others.

"I noticed that you had a problem with one of the audience," Tammy said.

I nodded, grimacing as I pulled off the daffodil pasties I'd been wearing. I appreciated not having to bare all, but those things chafed the hell out of my nipples. I almost laughed. How pathetic that a couple half-dollar sized stickers and a piece of dental floss made me feel superior to anyone. I was just like all the other girls who'd come to Vegas with a dream and ended up shedding her clothes instead.

"That's the third time this week Ricky's had to throw someone out for getting handsy."

"Really?" That was a bit surprising. The Twilight Room had a reputation as being one of the safest places for a girl to work. That had been my main reason for choosing it when it had become painfully obvious my dream of becoming a real dancer wasn't going to happen.

Tammy came over to stand next to me as I pulled on my jeans. "There are some rumors going around that one of the other club owners is sending in people to stir things up."

"Who'd do that?" I asked as I pulled my t-shirt over my head.

"Danny Whitehall, for one," Tammy said.

"Right." I scowled. Danny owned a club a bit further down the strip and even though his girls did everything including the audience, he struggled to keep his doors open. Everyone knew he blamed The Twilight Room for ruining his business. Apparently, there was some history between him and Gino, the man who owned this club.

"You coming out with us tonight?" Tammy asked.

"Not tonight. Thanks." At the end of every shift, she asked the same thing, and I always said the same thing back. I felt bad for never taking her up on her offer, but I wasn't exactly friends with any of the other girls, not enough to want to go get drinks.

"Be safe," she said as I walked away. I could feel her eyes on me and wondered, not for the first time, if Tammy had a crush on me. I knew she was a lesbian, but so were Faye and Deedee. They never stared at me like they were wondering what I tasted like.

I grimaced as I stepped outside. We were in the middle of a heat wave that made the Nevada night unbearably oppressive. I would've been more comfortable in shorts or a skirt rather than jeans, but I'd learned early on that coming out of a strip club wearing something even the slightest bit revealing invited more comments from the men going in and out. With my hair in a sloppy ponytail, wearing regular clothes, they rarely noticed me, too intent on whatever they wanted to see or had already seen.

I walked briskly down the brightly lit street, heading towards the apartment I called home.

Home.

Until two years ago, home had been Philadelphia, the city where I'd been born and raised. The city where I buried my mother after four years of illness. I'd waited tables for seven years, four during high school, three after, saving every penny I could to pay for dance school. Two years into my mom's illness, the job that had provided her health insurance finally figured out a way to fire her and my savings had been all we'd had to live on.

I'd moved out here after she died, thinking a fresh start on the other side of the continent would be a good idea. I should have known better, nothing in my life had ever worked out and this grand plan wasn't an exception. So here I am, stuck, barely making rent, much less earning enough money to move back, even if I'd wanted to.

And I didn't want to. Philadelphia may have held a lot of great memories, but it also held painful ones.

I was almost to my place when my phone rang. I sighed, hoping it wasn't the club calling me to work a double. Maybe it was just my roommate, Rosa, letting me know she wouldn't be home tonight. It wasn't either one.

"Anastascia?" I didn't try to hide my surprise. Anastascia Galaway had been my best friend in Philadelphia, my only school friend really. She was the only person from back East who bothered to keep in touch since I moved. She'd also been the one who'd given me strength during those four terrible years. Especially the last few, even worse, weeks.

"Hey there, stranger!" Chipper as always. "I just got back from Paris and had to give you a call."

If it had been anyone else casually dropping that they'd been in Paris, I'd have said they were bragging. Anastascia wasn't like that though. She'd never been like that. My first day at St. George's, a very expensive private high school in the Chestnut Hill district, had been miserable up to my last class when I'd met her. I'd endured the whispers and the not-so-subtle stares, refusing to give any of them the satisfaction of seeing me cry. By the end of the day, I'd been ready to crack when a stuck-up blonde bitch made some comment about taking out the trash. I'd almost lost it when this tall girl with caramel-colored skin and wild black curls came over and saved my life.

"You sound like you enjoyed your trip," I said, snapping back to the present.

"It was amazing. You really have to come with me to Europe sometime."

"Sure, as soon as pigs fly and hell freezes over," I replied. "I can barely afford my rent." I changed the subject before she could offer to loan me money. I loved that she was generous, but I hated feeling like I owed anyone anything. "What are you doing up this late?"

"Still on French time, darling," she said. "I'm a combined seven hours ahead, which means it's almost eight in the morning for me."

I laughed. "All right then. What are you doing calling me at eight in the morning?"

"I just wanted to make sure you were planning on coming to our reunion this weekend."

I sighed. I'd completely forgotten about it. No, that was a lie. I'd made myself forget about it. "Why would I want to go back to a place where no one wanted me in the first place?"

"Come on, Piper, it'll be fun," she begged. I could almost see the pouty look she'd be trying to use to guilt me into coming. "We can see who didn't lose the freshman fifteen and who's already divorced."

"You can do that reading the society section," I reminded her.

"Well, you don't have a choice," she said.

"Excuse me?"

"I've already bought you a ticket. You leave Friday evening and I'll pick you up at the airport."

I stopped in front of my apartment building. "What? No. But," I stammered, then sighed. "I don't really have a choice, do I?"

"Nope."

Even as much as I hated the idea of seeing all those people again, I couldn't help but smile at the thought of seeing my best friend. I missed her terribly, the one person in the world who really cared for me. I realized I would ensure just about anything to see her again.

Plus, it wouldn't be hard to get a few days off. I could pull some double shifts to cover the missed time. Before thinking too much about it, I agreed, "I'll be there."

Anastascia was still squealing when I hung up.

Chapter 2

My chest was starting to tighten as I stepped into the terminal. I scanned the waiting crowd, looking for a familiar face, but wasn't really surprised when I didn't see one. My flight had actually arrived on time and Anastascia was chronically late. I decided it would make more sense for me to get my bags, then head toward the entrance and wait for her. I could call her on the way and let her know to look for me there.

I'd only gone a few steps past the next gate when something hard ran into me, almost knocking me to the ground. I heard a deep voice utter an oath and then a pair of strong hands caught me. It all happened so fast I'd barely started processing the fall before I was in some stranger's embrace.

I tilted my head back to get a better look at who was holding me. He was tall, well over six feet, with messy, golden blond hair and a pair of eyes so dark they almost appeared to be black.

I knew those eyes.

I absorbed the rest of his features. Handsome, with features that toed the line between pretty and masculine. Lips almost too full for a man, but not quite. A small, thin scar ran through the bottom one. A scar he'd gotten three weeks into my freshman year at St. George's.

Reed Stirling was three years older than me and, aside from Anastascia, had been the nicest person at school. I'd watched him step between a bully and his victim, and I'd never forgotten it. He'd even talked to me once or twice, though only to say hello. I'd had a crush on him for years even though I'd known I'd never had a chance.

The Stirlings were old money, the kind who'd had an apartment in the city worth millions, as well as a house in Chestnut Hill near the school. They'd also owned a vineyard in Italy and a villa in France, or something like that.

"I'm so sorry."

Reed's voice brought me back to the present. Under his tan, I could see his cheeks turning red. I took a step back, taking a deep breath to regain my composure.

"It's okay," I said. "No harm done."

I looked up at him again, unable to stop the twinge of disappointment when I saw no recognition in his face. It wasn't surprising, not really. The two of us hadn't had any classes together and we hadn't been friends. His sister and I hadn't been friends either...

"Reed!"

I winced as I heard an all-too familiar squeal. I took another step back as my former classmate threw herself into her brother's arms.

I loathed Rebecca Stirling.

As she released her brother, I turned to go, but I was too late to avoid being recognized.

"Piper?" She sounded surprised.

I fixed a fake smile on my face and turned back towards her and Reed. "Rebecca." She didn't look any different. Same dyed light blond hair and cold hazel eyes. She was taller than me by a couple inches, nearly twice that with her heels. If anything, she looked even thinner, bordering on skeletal. She'd always been slender, but I knew that starved look wasn't natural.

"Piper?" Reed looked puzzled as his gaze went from me to his sister and back again.

"Piper Black," Rebecca said promptly. "She went to St. George's with me." Her lips pursed. "She was a scholarship kid."

"Well, Piper Black from St. George's, let me apologize again for almost knocking you down." Reed held out a hand without acknowledging his sister's last comment.

I shook it, trying to ignore the little tingle through my hand and up my arm. I wasn't going to act like some smitten schoolgirl. I'd all but forgotten about Reed over the years. I wasn't about to revert simply because he'd shaken my hand.

"Back in town for the reunion?" Rebecca asked.

Before I could answer, I heard the voice I'd been waiting for.

"Piper!"

I breathed a sigh of relief as Anastascia threw her arms around me for a quick hug. When she stepped back, she gave Rebecca a dismissive look, nodded at Reed and then linked her arm through mine. I didn't even have a chance to say anything to either of the Stirlings as Anastascia led me away, keeping up a steady stream of chatter about how much she'd looked forward to this and how much fun we were going to have.

By the time we reached the baggage claim and she'd paused to catch her breath, I'd regain my composure enough to tell her about bumping into Reed and then seeing Rebecca. I kept my tone casual, even Anastascia hadn't known about my crush. That secret had been for my mother only. While my friend wasn't anything like the other rich kids in class, I wasn't sure how she would've reacted if I'd told her I had a crush on a guy like Reed.

"Well, at least you've gotten that out of the way," Anastascia said. "Now, let's forget about that bitch and start talking about what we're going to wear tonight."

I smiled, but my heart wasn't in it. What had I been thinking, coming out here like this? What was I supposed to say when everyone asked what I was doing in Vegas? And what about clothes? I hadn't even thought about that when I'd packed my bag. I'd grabbed some jeans and a couple nice shirts, and borrowed a cheap red dress from Tammy. I didn't own anything that would even compare to what I knew the other girls would be wearing tonight. I had exactly one dress and it was the stiff black one I'd worn to my mother's funeral, and then to various job interviews. Well, except the last one. Funeral dresses didn't exactly advertise a body that men would pay to see nearly naked.

"Earth to Piper," Anastascia teased. "If you're not careful, you're going to get left behind."

I look around, startled. I hadn't even realized we'd reached the train station. I gave her a puzzled look. I would've thought we'd be taking a taxi to her apartment.

She smiled, most likely guessing what I was thinking. "I moved out after graduation."

"Seriously?"

Anastascia had gone to Columbia for their paralegal program and I knew the law firm she wanted to work for was just a few blocks away from her family's place.

"Mom and Dad bought me a place in Fishtown."

My eyes widened. "Are you kidding?"

She shook her head as she stepped onto the train. I followed, taking the aisle seat next to her.

"I'm still at Masters and Griffin, but I wanted a place of my own. One of their friends was selling their place so my parents asked if I wanted it."

She kept gushing about her new place as the train started to move. I was happy for her, but at the same time, I couldn't help but be jealous. I shared a tiny two-bedroom apartment with another stripper and could barely make rent while her parents had bought one of those brick row-houses for what was probably just under a quarter of a million dollars. I looked out the window as we started to pass my old neighborhood. It hadn't changed in the past two years and as I saw kids playing basketball as we passed, I wondered if I knew any of them.

"I bought you something," Anastascia said suddenly.

My eyes narrowed. "Why?"

"Because I missed your birthday and Christmas twice these last two years." She was still smiling, but I could see the sympathy on her face. I was right. She knew things weren't going well for me. Her voice softened and I could see compassion in her deep brown eyes. "And because I knew you'd be thinking about not having anything to wear tonight but you'd be too proud to ask for help."

"Ana," I started to protest.

She put her finger over her mouth just like she used to do when we were younger and I'd start telling her she was being too generous. "It's your birthday and Christmas gifts, as well as an 'I'm glad to see you' present. Besides, I can't return it and we don't wear the same size."

That was true. I was about five-six and nothing to be ashamed of in the bust department, but Anastascia was five-eleven without heels and somewhere in an E cup. I'd borrowed a couple t-shirts when we were younger – and wore them as nightshirts. Whatever she bought me would end up going to Goodwill if I didn't accept it, and considering that was where I bought most of my clothes, I nodded.

"Thank you."

She beamed.

When we got off at Fishtown, I was surprised at how quickly it all came back. I might have been in Vegas for the past two years, but this city was in my blood. I wasn't sure if that meant I'd come back permanently some day, but it did mean I felt at home even though this wasn't my neighborhood. I smiled at the fishes decorating the doors and sidewalks.

"This way." She led the way, telling me about her job as a paralegal for a civil rights law firm.

I'd never been a very talkative person, so it was just like old times as she let the conversation flow from one topic to the other. She'd occasionally ask questions, but when I'd only offer a short answer, she didn't push it. Talking on the phone with her had been different. I'd forgotten how much of our friendship was intuitive. She knew when to move on and when I wanted to talk but was reluctant to do so. A lump formed in my throat as she showed me to the guest room. The pain I'd been expecting at seeing the city again wasn't coming from memories of my mother, but rather from how much I missed having someone around who cared about me.

She left me alone to clean up and by the time she returned with my dress, I'd gotten my emotions back under control. I would enjoy this time with her, but I wouldn't forget why I'd left or why I was going to stay away.

"I was really hoping you hadn't gone through any extreme weight loss or something," she said as she handed me a hanger with way less fabric than I'd expected. I glared at her. "Trust me, Piper."

I sighed. It wasn't like I had much of a choice. I took the dress and wondered what I was going to wear underneath it. All of my underwear was nice enough, but I'd never had the money for fancy lingerie. Not that I needed it. What I did need, however, was a strapless bra and a thong because there was no way anything I'd brought with me would work with this dress.

"I got these with it."

As if she'd read my mind, Anastascia held out lace panties and a bra that both matched the dress. She gave me a grin and practically skipped out of the door, leaving me alone to change. I didn't even glance in the mirror as I put on the bra and panties, or as I wiggled into the impossibly tight dress. Only when I'd gotten everything adjusted and in the right place did I finally look up. And gasped.

Anastascia had done an amazing job.

The dress had only the thinnest of straps and the neckline was cut low. Combined with the bra, it actually gave me a decent amount of cleavage. Nothing as impressive as my friend would be sporting, but enough to accentuate my figure. The cut of the waist showed off the little bit of hips I had without making my muscular legs look like tree trunks. Most people don't realize how hard it is for athletes to find something that makes their legs – and arms for some – look nice. The hemline was mid-thigh, long enough to show off some skin, but not so short I was uncomfortable. The dress, and everything that had come with it, was a dark, rich emerald color that made my own dark green eyes glow and my hair shine. I didn't bother to see if the cheap, faux leather shoes I'd brought with me would match. I was sure Anastascia would have a pair of heels that would look fabulous. Since my feet were a little bigger than average for my size and Anastascia had small ones, we met in the middle with the one thing we could share: footwear.

Anastascia let out a whistle as she stepped back into the room.

"Right back at you," I said as I took in her dark red dress that highlighted every one of her curves.

"What do you say we show up Rebecca and her snobby friends?" Anastascia asked with a grin.

I nodded. I still wasn't feeling particularly enthused about the reunion, but at least most of the dread had gone away. I looked like I fit in now, and if people asked how I could afford living in Vegas, I could always tell them I was working while studying dance. No one had to know the details. It's been five years, and maybe most of my classmates could be grown up enough to put aside social status and we could have a pleasant evening.

Chapter 3

I hadn't been back at the school for more than ten minutes before I realized how foolish that hope had been. After half an hour, it was painfully obvious that nothing had changed since high school, even if my wardrobe had improved. There was no doubt in anyone's minds that Anastascia had bought me the dress, confirmed by the multiple conversations I overheard regarding being my friend's charity case.

I was already fuming when a tall, skinny young man with dark hair and a prominent Adam's apple approached. I didn't need to look at the name-tag to know it was Eddie Rancid, a kid with a last name so awful he should've been less popular than me in school. Not the case.

"Hey, Piper."

He still had the same sleazy smile.

"Hi, Eddie." I kept my tone polite. Eddie had been picked on mercilessly in school for his sci-fi obsessions and bad complexion, but those weren't the reasons I hoped he'd keep walking.

"Looking good." His eyes ran over me and I could feel him mentally undressing me. Considering what I did for a living, the fact that I had to stop myself from shuddering spoke volumes about how creepy I found him.

"Thank you."

He edged closer, invading my personal space. "You know, I wanted to ask you to prom senior year."

"Really?" I crossed my arms and tried to make a single word convey how not-interested I was.

"I mean, I figured if anyone was going to put out, it'd be you."

Really? Had those words really just exited this dick head's mouth? I gritted my teeth and could feel my temper start to rise as I ground out, "Is that so?"

Either Eddie was a moron when it came to reading people's body language and inflections or he simply didn't care. I was willing to bet it was a little bit of both. Either way, I shouldn't have been surprised when he kept talking.

"Everyone knew girls from your neighborhood were easy. What are you doing aft—"

Raising a hand to interrupt him, I inhaled slowly and then let it out. "I'm going to walk away now, Eddie, and if you know what's good for you, you're going to let me go."

He had the audacity to look shocked at my response. I caught a glimpse of the surprise on his face before I turned and headed towards the memorabilia display. I didn't really have anything I wanted to remember, but it was as far from

Eddie as I could get while still being inside the building. I stayed there for a couple minutes, putting up with more sly glances and not-so-subtle comments, but then I couldn't take it anymore. I needed some air.

"I'm going to take a walk," I said, leaning close enough to Anastascia to be heard over the music without raising my voice.

"Do you want me to come with you?" There was concern in her eyes.

I shook my head. "Stay." She'd been subjected to some prejudice in school due to being mixed race, but most of her isolation had been self-imposed, choosing me over the shallow rich kids who were now fawning over how great she looked and all of the wonderful things she did. She deserved her time in the spotlight.

Before she could argue, I hurried away. No one stopped me and only a few even looked my way. I cut a wide path around where I saw Rebecca and her gang of friends chatting. They probably all still lived in the city and met for brunch every Sunday, picking at salads that cost more than a full meal at some places and sharing the latest gossip. I wasn't entirely sure I'd be able to keep myself from slapping that smirk off her face if she said something, so I figured it was better to steer clear. I didn't want to be the girl who got kicked out of the reunion for fighting. Despite my current occupation, I had too much self-respect for that.

I took a deep breath as I stepped out into the chilly evening. It wasn't quite freezing, but there was a bite in the air that said winter hadn't quite relinquished its grip despite it being early May. I rubbed my hands over my arms as I looked around the school grounds and tried to figure out what I was going to do while I waited for the reunion to end.

"Are you cold?"

I froze, and not because of the air. I didn't have to turn towards the voice, however, because the owner of it was stepping around so I could confirm what I already knew.

"Rebecca insisted I bring her tonight when her date canceled, but as soon as she got here, she went off with her friends." Reed flashed a charming smile. "I was trying to think up an excuse to leave when you came out. Looks like you're as bored as I am. Want to take a walk with me?"

Chapter 4

It had been almost three years since I'd walked down Germantown Avenue. Those last couple years with my mother, I hadn't gone anywhere but home, work and the hospital, but before that, when I'd been at St. George's, I'd walked down here often. I'd hated the school, but the neighborhood, with its cobbled streets and little shops, was beautiful. I'd walked it in the morning, afternoon and evening. I'd walked it with Anastascia as well as alone.

But I'd never dreamed I'd be walking it with Reed Stirling.

"I always preferred Chestnut Hill to the city," Reed said suddenly, breaking the surprisingly comfortable silence between us. He didn't look at me, but I risked a sideways glance at him. His hands were in his pockets and he looked completely relaxed. "It's one of the reasons I asked my parents to sell me our family home out here rather than buying an apartment in the city like they and my sister have. I got my fill of city living when I was at Columbia getting my MBA."

Like with Anastascia, I didn't hear any arrogance as he spoke about his family's wealth. I appreciated that he didn't try to downplay it either. That was a mistake people often made, thinking that those of us who had less money would want them to act as if their money was shameful.

"It is beautiful here," I admitted. "I remember the first time I came here, when my mom brought me to do the testing to get into St. George's, and I thought about how amazing it must be to live here."

"But you left the city," he said.

"I did." I waited for the next inevitable question about what I'd been doing since graduation.

It didn't come.

"I remember you."

"What?" I looked over at him, startled.

He gave me that smile again. "I'll admit it. I didn't recognize you at first, but once my sister said your name, I remembered you."

I raised my eyebrows, letting my expression show my skepticism.

"I swear." He held up his hands as we started back up the hill. "Believe it or not, even the juniors heard about the freshman who told Professor Kirkwood that Ernest Hemingway was a drunken misogynist with an ego the size of Spain and a writing style reminiscent of a sleep-deprived toddler."

My face grew hot. I'd forgotten about that. Needless to say, Professor Kirkwood and I hadn't gotten along very well after that. I'd gotten the impression that if he could've flunked me, he would've. My scores had just been too high.

"I can't believe you remember what I said," I mumbled.

"Are you kidding?" He grinned. "Kirkwood was a pompous windbag everyone had wanted to see taken down a peg or two."

I laughed, my cheeks flushing at the admiration in his voice, and started to cross the street. My heel caught in one of the trolley tracks and I stumbled. Reed's arm wrapped around my waist, keeping me upright. Without breaking his grip, he bent and gently pried the heel of my shoe from where it was wedged. When he straightened, there was barely an inch between us.

He looked down at me, his dark eyes searching my face as if he was trying to read my mind. Then a car horn honked, only two soft taps, but enough to break his gaze. I took a step, expecting him to relinquish his hold. He didn't. His arm stayed around my waist as we made our way to the other side of the street, his thumb stroking up and down as we walked.

He was only worried about my safety, I kept telling myself, only wished to avoid another near-accident. But when we reached the sidewalk, he didn't pull away, only seemed to hold me closer to his side. My heart was pounding and it didn't have anything to do with the walk.

"By the way," he said. "I'm sorry my sister was such a bitch to you earlier."

"Yeah, well, I'm used to it." The words popped out of my mouth before I could stop them.

He gave me a sideways glance and I could see he was debating whether or not to ask. If he didn't, I'd let it go, but if he did, I'd tell him the truth. I wasn't going to sugar coat it. Instead of blowing it off or pushing further, he said the last thing I expected.

"I always hoped she'd outgrow it, but sometimes I think she's a bigger bitch now than she was back then, and I know that's saying something."

I laughed. I couldn't help it. I thought he'd try to defend her or at least pretend to be offended.

"Rebecca's my sister, so I love her, but I don't like her very much."

"Me either," I admitted.

"And I have a feeling, if she saw you tonight, she'd be even worse than usual." He gave me a slow once over, his gaze heated. "You look amazing."

I flushed, suddenly aware of the electricity racing across my skin from where we were touching. "Do we have to keep talking about your sister?" I asked.

"Nope." He grinned at me. "I'd prefer we didn't."

"What'd you want to talk about then?" I regretted the question as soon as I'd asked it. I'd just given him an open invitation to ask about anything, including what my life was like now. Telling him I was a stripper would definitely send him running.

"Didn't you used to work at the trolley car diner?"

I looked over at him in surprise. "Yeah, I did."

"I thought so." His eyes sparkled with humor. "They did a whole retro day where you ladies had to wear fifties clothes, right?"

I groaned and shook my head. Of all the ways for him to remember having seen me, a poodle skirt and pink cardigan that clashed with my hair was not what I would've chosen.

"I'd come home for summer break," he continued. "And I'd been craving those amazing cinnamon buns they had."

"The ones with the cream cheese icing." I nodded in agreement. I actually hadn't minded my job, especially the food part. The customers, on the other hand, hadn't always been so delightful. "Your sister used to come in..." I let my voice trail off.

"We're talking about her again," he said and looked at me, a determined expression on his face. "Let's see if I can do something about that."

When he yanked me towards him, I gasped and he took advantage of my parted lips to cover my mouth with his, running his tongue along my bottom lip before darting it inside.

There was an edge to the playfulness, a desire that made my stomach warm. His arm slid around my waist as I leaned into him, my fingers gripping handfuls of his shirt. His lips were soft, moving with mine with an unhurried laziness. When he finally raised his head, it was only far enough that we could meet gazes. His eyes truly looked black now and I shivered.

"I can walk you back to the reunion and the kiss stays a kiss." He tucked a strand of hair behind my ear. "Or we can go to my place and..." His lips sank into mine, finishing his sentence for him.

Need stroked through me like a knife and I realize the choice wasn't a choice at all. I would go with him, be with him; I'd be greedy for the first time in my life.

"Yes," I whispered into his mouth and he moaned, his hands fisting in my hair. Then he turned, pulling me behind him and we walked the quarter mile in silence.

I tried not to think about how his house cost more than my entire apartment building back in Vegas, and then he was shutting the door behind us and leading me towards what I assumed was his bedroom. I quit caring about how rich he was.

We were in darkness for a moment, and then a light came on, filling the room with a soft, warm glow. I registered a bed, nightstand and dresser, but didn't get any details before Reed was pulling me into his arms.

When his mouth came down on mine this time, there was none of the humor that had been there before. This was all wanting. Lust. Need. One hand slid down my spine to the small of my back, his fingers on the swell of my ass. The other hand moved up until he was cupping the back of my head, those fingers buried in my hair. My hands went around his neck and I pressed my body against his. I ran the tip of my tongue along his bottom lip and he opened his mouth wider, letting me slip inside. I could taste the champagne they'd been serving at the reunion mingled with the sharp tang of fruit from the buffet. His tongue curled around mine and I moaned.

As a teenager, I'd imagined what it would be like to be kissed by Reed Stirling. My imagination hadn't done him nearly enough justice. His teeth nipped at my bottom lip and I pulled back. Concern filled his face and I knew he was worried that I hadn't liked it. I slid my hands under his jacket and pushed it off of his shoulders.

"Too many clothes."

My words washed away the worry and he smiled as my fingers tugged his shirt from his slacks. I quickly undid the buttons, secretly thankful that the one thing my job had taught me was how to undress quickly. Moments later, his shirt was falling to the floor and I was running my hands over his chest.

He had a lean build, but there was nothing thin about him. Every inch was cut and defined muscle beneath tanned skin. I ran my fingers down his flat stomach and hooked them into the waistband of his pants.

If I was going to finally get to sleep with Reed, I was going to make this one to remember. I'd head back to Vegas with at least one positive memory from my reunion and we'd never see each other again. That thought made me sad, knowing this was it, but I refused to let it take root. I hadn't come here looking for anything and I was going to get something I'd dreamed about for years. What came after didn't matter.

I pulled him toward the bed and gave him a gentle push. He looked surprised but didn't say anything as he sat down. I'd spent almost two years taking off my clothes for men I despised. Now, I'd at least put my skills to good use.

There wasn't any music, but I didn't need it. I wasn't exactly dancing, but his eyes watched my every movement as if I was in the spotlight. I slowly pulled off my dress, making a mental note to thank Anastascia for the underwear. When I stepped out of the garment, Reed reached out and grabbed me around the waist, pulling me onto him. We fell back on the bed and he rolled us over, his body pressing down on mine.

"You are so damn sexy," he murmured as he began to kiss his way across my collarbones and then further down.

He pulled down the cups of my bra, his hands catching my breasts as they came free. His touch was rougher than I'd expected after that first kiss, but I arched into it, loving the feel of his fingers kneading my flesh. He ran his tongue around my nipple and I moaned. When his teeth scraped over it, I hissed, running my nails down his arm. My eyes closed as his lips wrapped around my nipple and began to rhythmically suck. Each time Reed's teeth touched my skin, a new bolt of electricity went through me and I found myself wetter than I'd been before and we'd barely gotten started.

"I could spend hours doing this," Reed said, looking up at me. "But we don't have a lot of time."

I nodded, feeling a pang of regret. There was so much I wanted to do, but he was right. Anastascia was bound to get worried if I was gone too long.

He ran his hand over my stomach and slid it beneath the elastic of my panties. I swore as his fingers made their way between my legs and chuckled as he circled my clit for a moment before moving down to where I wanted him most. His laughter died away as he pushed a finger inside me.

I shuddered as a ripple of pleasure washed over me.

"You're so tight." He pressed his lips against my stomach as his finger moved in and out, preparing me for what I knew was coming next. Suddenly, his head jerked up, something very much like panic on his face. "You're not..."

I shook my head and he relaxed. I wasn't a virgin, but I was pretty close. I'd only had one lover and while Luc been a nice enough guy, he'd never managed to get me off. Now, I was about to come just from Reed's finger. I could feel the pressure building inside me and it reached the breaking point as he slid another finger in alongside the first. Then he crooked them, and everything exploded.

Dimly, I was aware that my phone was ringing, but I couldn't think of anything but the pleasure coursing through me. I cried out as my pussy tightened around Reed's fingers, stopping their movement and letting me ride out my orgasm without additional stimulation. When my muscles unclenched, Reed removed his fingers and I made a sound of protest, earning a laugh.

I was still blinking the haze away when I heard the sound of a foil packet ripping. That was good. I wasn't entirely sure I was coherent enough to have thought of protection. A moment later, I felt him pulling aside the crotch of my panties and I forced my eyes to focus, locking with his as he entered me. My thigh muscles trembled as he slowly inched his way inside. He was so thick, stretching me until it was just this side of painful, but I never considered asking him to stop. I didn't know where he was on a size scale, but as he came to rest all the way inside me, I did know I'd never been so full.

He lowered himself over me until our bodies were touching, but his arms kept his full weight off of me. His lips came down on mine as he began to move, drawing whimpers of half-pained pleasure from my throat. He swallowed each one as he thrust into me, each stroke rubbing the base of his cock against my clit until I was writhing beneath him. I was going to come again and my entire body trembled in anticipation.

"I'm not going to last long," Reed confessed, his voice barely a whisper. I could hear the strain. "You're too tight. Feel too good."

I slid my hands down his back and over his ass. I hadn't realized until then that he'd taken his pants off, or at least pushed them down. My fingers ran over the firm muscles and I dug my nails in, encouraging him to move harder, faster.

He pushed himself up, grabbing onto my hips. The change in angle dragged the head of his cock across that spot inside me and I cried out. I wrapped my hands around his wrists, feeling the tendons and muscles there moving as he began to slam into me, pushing himself deeper than before. His fingers dug into my flesh and I rode the line of pain and ecstasy as he drove me toward my second orgasm.

He groaned as he buried himself, the muscles in his body twitching as he came. Still, even as he climaxed, he rotated his hips, rubbing against me exactly the way I needed to push me over the edge. I wrapped my arms around him as he slumped down, my body moving against his as I drew out every last drop of pleasure, wanting to savor the moment I knew would never happen again.

When he finally rolled off of me, I felt a pang of loss. But he pulled me close, kissing my hair and whispered, "I'll be right back."

I rolled onto my side, curling into a ball of contentment just as the memory of my phone ringing suddenly came back to me. I groaned as I stretched out to snag my purse from the floor. I moved onto my stomach as I pulled out my phone and saw that I had a missed call from Anastascia.

"Shit," I swore quietly as I listened to the voicemail.

"Piper, where the hell are you? You went out for some air and now I can't find you and you're not picking up your phone? You better hope to hell you've been kidnapped or I'm going to kick your ass."

I quickly hit the call back button and closed my eyes as I waited for the inevitable scolding. She answered on the first ring and didn't even bother with a greeting, launching into a lecture about how I'd scared the shit out of her and I'd better have a good reason for leaving and not telling her where I was going. I waited until she paused for air before I spoke.

"I went for a walk and lost track of time."

"Are you kidding me?"

"I'm so sorry. I'll never do it again," I promised, letting my voice take on a teasing note. As I'd hoped, it defused her anger.

"Well, where are you? I'll come pick you up."

I stifled a laugh, picturing the expression on her face if I told her I was currently in Reed Stirling's bed. "I'm taking a taxi back. Wait for me. I'll be there in a few."

"All right." She sounded reluctant, but I didn't waste time trying to convince her.

I said my good-bye, hung up and shoved my phone back in my purse, pushing myself onto my knees as Reed came back into the bedroom. He slid his arms around my waist and my body hummed from the contact. He pressed his lips against the hollow spot under my ear. I shivered and closed my eyes, resenting the fact that I had to go.

"I have to get back. Anastascia's worried about me."

"Is that who called earlier?"

"Yeah. I'd told her I was going out for some air." I reluctantly removed myself from his embrace and set about collecting my clothes. "Needless to say, I've been gone a bit longer than I'd planned."

I heard a hint of pride in his voice as he said, "I'll call you a cab."

I managed to get dressed before he finished, but he was still naked when he wrapped his arms around my waist and pulled me against him. His mouth came down on mine and I was helpless to do anything but kiss him back. My

41

arms wrapped around his neck and I pressed my body against his. He groaned as my hips ground against his cock and I knew he must still be sensitive. The thought made me push my hips harder against him as I tangled my tongue with his. I wanted him to remember this, to remember me.

His hands cupped my ass, squeezing and kneading the muscles and sending a rush of desire through me. I was still wet from before and now I was practically dripping. Just as I was beginning to think it might be worth Anastascia being mad to have another round with Reed, a car honked outside.

I broke the kiss but stayed in his arms a moment longer. "That's my ride."

He cupped the side of my face. "Are you sure you can't stay longer?" He brushed his knuckles down the side of my face.

"I really have to go." I took a step back and headed for the door. By the time I reached his front door, he was only a few steps behind me, dressed in a pair of pants, but still shirtless.

"I'd come with you," he said as he followed me down to the sidewalk. "But I can only take my sister in small doses, and I've had enough today to last a while."

I smiled, trying not to show my combination of relief and disappointment. Part of me wanted to show back up at the reunion with Reed, just to see the looks on everyone's faces, especially Rebecca's. Another part wanted to keep all this secret, something private just for me. His decision saved me from having to make that choice.

I paused before climbing into the taxi, unsure how I was supposed to end this. He reached out and pushed back some hair from my face.

"When can I see you again?"

My heart twisted and I leaned forward to brush my lips over his. I couldn't tell him the truth, so I settled for a vague lie. "Let's let fate decide."

I got into the backseat and closed the door before he could respond. As the driver pulled away from the curb, I leaned back in the seat and resisted the urge to turn for one last look. I wasn't planning on another return to the city, so I knew this would be the last time I'd ever see Reed. And I knew it was for the best. I hadn't come back looking for love and I didn't want it. Not with someone from Philadelphia. My life was in Las Vegas now and that wasn't going to change.

Chapter 5

As I climbed out of the cab and looked up at my apartment building, I sighed. Everything that had happened in the past few days seemed like some sort of dream.

The rest of the reunion had gone about as well as expected, with me dodging more bitchy comments and hateful stares. Finally, Ana had taken mercy on me and declared it time to go. I'd never been so relieved to exit a room in my life.

The following day was much better, just the two of us enjoying each other, laughing at old times and sharing our hopes and dreams. We'd eaten in, ordering take out since neither of us wanted to cook. We'd shared a bottle of wine, and then another, laughing and talking into the wee hours of the morning.

Next morning, at the airport, I'd been close to tears as I hung onto this beautiful girl. As much as I'd wanted to be home, I hadn't felt like leaving.

I was definitely glad I'd slept with Reed. Maybe that was the problem, I thought as I trudged up the dark and dingy stairs. Apart from the actual reunion, things had gone so well that coming back here just made my real life seem drab and miserable by comparison.

I opened the door to my apartment and wrinkled my nose. Rosa had been trying to cook again. The stench of burnt something-or-other was still fresh. My roommate was three years older than me and had been stripping in Vegas since she was sixteen. Ten years later, she still worked at The Diamond Club, and it was even more sleazy than it had been when she'd started. She was nice enough, but we weren't close. She hadn't just accepted her life... she liked it. And she knew I didn't, which could make things a bit tense at times.

"You have messages," Rosa announced as she came out of her bedroom.

"Thanks, Rosa." I put my bag down and picked up the first one from Tammy.

As I read, I sat down, unable to believe my eyes. The note after Tammy's was from one of the other girls and said the same thing. Each one, some from co-workers, two from managers, was nearly identical. I needed to come down to The Twilight Room to pick up my last check and then go to the police station to give a statement about whether or not I'd ever been ordered to have sex with a patron.

"What the fuck?" I stared at the stack of papers.

45

"Sucks." Rosa adjusted her bra, then reached for a coffee mug. "I heard some girls talking about it. Seems like The Twilight Room was a front for sex trafficking."

I shook my head, unable to believe it. They didn't even make us get completely naked. How could that mesh with forcing women into being sex slaves?

She shrugged. "We got a couple spots open if you want a job."

"Thanks, Rosa, but I'll be fine." Even as I said the words, I wasn't sure they were true. The knot in my stomach said what my brain didn't want to recognize that soon I'd have to take her up on her offer. I cringed, hoping it would never come to that.

*****

Six days, twenty-seven applications and no calls later, I was forced to admit that Rosa's offer was the best I was going to get. Girls willing to take off their clothes were a dime a dozen in Vegas and while I may have had better dancing skills, the clubs were more interested in tits and ass. Desperation finally overcame what little pride I had left and I went in for an interview. With Rosa vouching for me, I got the job and was able to start right away.

If someone had told me I'd miss The Twilight Room, I would've laughed at them, but The Diamond Club made my previous place of employment seem like a dream job.

My first indication was the so-called interview manager told me to strip down in the middle Granted, there'd only been a cleaning crew there at the time, but it was still awkward, and it had gotten worse while he'd circled me, not touching but close enough to have made me even more uncomfortable than I'd already been.

I wasn't ashamed of my body, but being treated like a piece of meat wasn't something I enjoyed. I did my work at the club, taking off everything but a tiny g-string that could barely count as covering. We wore those during the shows, but I knew most girls stripped to nothing in the back room or during a private party. It was the unspoken rule that as long as the club got its percentage, it was up to the girls to decide how far they were willing to go. Rosa did the parties as often as she could and I never asked what she did to earn the tips.

Still, I declined the invitations for private performances and kept putting in applications wherever I could. The problem was, legit places looking for employees would always ask where I'd been working since coming to Vegas as my employment history clearly had a gap. As soon as I'd tell them The Twilight Room, I could see the interview was at an end. The places where I'd filled in my full history didn't even bother to call.

Still, I was managing to find a sort of rhythm with the work and that made blocking out the clients and wearing a niling face much easier. It was harder when I was home, lying in the dark, staring up at the ceiling, and wondering what my life would've been like if I'd stayed in Philadelphia. It was then that the memories would come back. Sometimes it was my mom, other times Anastascia, but most often it was Reed and our night together. I knew it was stupid, but I clung to that memory, playing it over and over again.

I was dreaming about him when a noise woke me, raised voices coming from the other room. It took me a couple disorienting seconds to register that it was Rosa arguing with someone. A man. I sat up. It sounded like our landlord, Mr. Fenton. I climbed out of bed and threw on a t-shirt, heading for the living room.

"Like hell we will!" Rosa was yelling.

"What's going on?" I asked, trying to keep my voice as polite as I could.

"Fenton's saying we have to give him fifteen hundred dollars by the end of the week," Rosa answered.

"For what?"

"Fixing some electrical problem." Her dark eyes were flashing.

"According to my electrician, the issue was caused by improper usage," Mr. Fenton said. "And since there's no way to tell where the problem started, each tenant will be providing me with compensation."

I wondered what slick-ass lawyer had written that for him. Not that it mattered. Rosa and I would have to pay or Fenton would find some excuse to kick us out. He'd done it to Tyler and Mickey down the hall when they wouldn't sleep with him. Fortunately for Rosa and me, Fenton was strictly into dick. He might shake us down for money, but he'd never ask us to fuck him.

"You have until the end of the week." He stormed off before either of us could argue more with him.

"Well, we're fucked," I said without looking at Rosa.

"Maybe," she said slowly.

Now I did turn toward her. "What'd you mean, maybe?"

"Godfrey got a call about a private party Friday night, a bachelor party. Guaranteed two thousand dollars, with the possibility of extra."

I didn't need her to explain what the extra included.

"That's great," I said. "I'll see if I can pick up an extra shift or two to help pay for my half."

"I couldn't take the job."

"Why not?"

"They asked for two girls and everyone else was busy Friday night." She gave me a pointed look and I immediately knew what she was not-so-subtly hinting at.

I thought about what she wanted me to do, and about the zeros in my checking account. I thought about Mr. Fenton and how he wouldn't hesitate to kick us out. My only other option would be to ask Anastascia for the money. I knew my friend would have it and she wouldn't even hesitate to help me out. I also knew I couldn't ask for her assistance. I was out of choices.

I nodded. "All right," I heard myself say. "I'll do it."

Chapter 6

Rosa assured me that my usual work outfit would be fine for the private party in Astoria's fancy penthouse suite. The guys hadn't requested any sort of specific costume. That, at least, was good. I couldn't imagine what I'd do if they'd wanted me to be some kind of biker chick or naughty nurse.

A handsome guy with sandy-colored hair answered the door to the penthouse suite. He gave us each a quick once over and I could see that he was wondering why we weren't wearing something slutty.

"You got a bedroom where we can change?" Rosa asked.

"This way." The man gestured for us to follow him.

As we walked through the enormous suite, I heard laughter coming from the main sitting area, but we didn't go that way, instead heading for another hallway that kept us from getting a glimpse of the men we'd be entertaining. That was fine with me. I didn't particularly want to see them yet anyway.

The guy left us alone to get ready. While we took off our street clothes and changed into our costumes from work, Rosa explained how things were going to go. We'd do a shortened number of the club's opening routine, both of us wearing our masks, and then I'd step back to let her do hers. Once she was finished, it'd be my turn.

"The thing you have to remember," she said as she adjusted her breasts. "Is that while you're here to entertain everyone, the opening dances are for the groom. We do our routines and focus on him. Once we're done, we take a couple minutes, then head back out to dance. Not routines, but actually dance with the guys. Depending on how friendly you get, that's when the tips start flowing."

I nodded and tried to pretend I wasn't nervous as hell. Someone knocked on the door and a man's voice asked if we were ready. Rosa opened the door to the same sandy-haired guy who'd let us into the suite and we followed him back down the hallway and into the main sitting room. It was huge, with glass walls along the far side, high ceilings and carpet so thick it was going to make dancing in heels dangerous.

I didn't have much time for details though as the music was starting, which was our cue to move. The first dance went smoothly, though I was concentrating more on not falling than I was on paying attention to the men cat-calling, and then I stepped back to let Rosa take center stage. I watched her as she zeroed in. I followed her gaze.

A handsome man with unruly dark curls was laughing and leering, clapping another man on the shoulder; a man who Rosa was clearly focusing on. That, I decided, must be the groom. I shifted as Rosa moved and saw the groom's face for the first time.

My heart almost stopped.

Reed.

What the fuck?

It had been less than a month since he and I had slept together, and now he was getting married?

My hand went to the mask on my face. The opening dance had all of the girls in disguises and the first thing we did when we went on for our individual sets was to toss the mask aside, letting the men see our faces for the first time. Did that mean he hadn't yet recognized me or had he found out my secret and called The Diamond Club on purpose? Even as I thought it, I realized it was ridiculous. The groom didn't plan his own bachelor party. This was just some very bizarre coincidence. One that was about to get even more awkward.

Before I was ready, Rosa's music ended and it was my turn. I knew I had a choice to make. I could either walk out and probably lose my job or I could do what I came here to do and damn the repercussions. I lifted my chin. I hadn't done anything wrong. Either Reed had met, dated and proposed to someone in a very short period of time or he'd fucked me when he'd been engaged. I hadn't known. I had nothing to be ashamed of.

I walked toward the center of the room, facing the couch, and pulled off my mask, tossing it aside.

His jaw dropped and his eyes widened, but I didn't acknowledge him. Instead, I did what I'd been paid to do, although I couldn't bring myself to make eye contact. When I finished, I flashed a fake smile at the whistling and cheering men, then grabbed my shirt from the floor and put it back on. The rest of our dancing could be done half-clothed, as long as we were showing more flesh than we were hiding and we were willing to take the clothes off again. I buttoned the middle two buttons as Rosa told the men she and I were going to take a couple minutes to freshen up. She promised them we'd be back.

She went back to the bedroom we'd come from, but I went in the opposite direction, not wanting to explain to her why I was freaking out. A party in a penthouse suite at the priciest hotel in the city had some advantages, there were several bathrooms to choose from.

I splashed cold water on my face, keeping my eyes closed even after I dried my face.

"Piper?"

My hands flexed on the sink and I looked up, making eye contact with him through the mirror.

"Fancy meeting you here." The words came out more snidely than I'd intended, but I didn't apologize. He didn't deserve it.

"I can explain." He took a step into the bathroom, then stopped.

I saw the hesitation on his face, but I didn't do anything to help him. I made my voice as flat as possible. "You don't need to. There weren't any expectations. We both knew that. We don't owe each other anything."

My heart twisted at my words and I knew I'd let myself care too much. If I'd never seen him again, I could've handled that. I could've cherished our time together. Instead, every moment of that night was tainted now by the knowledge that he'd used me to cheat on his fiancée. He wasn't the good guy I remembered from school. I didn't tell him any of that though. I just brushed past him, ignoring the way my stomach clenched at the scent of his aftershave.

"I have to work."

For once, I welcomed the pounding, pulsing music and let it take over. I spotted Rosa already grinding on one of the men and I made my way over to her side. In two years, I'd gotten very comfortable dancing with women when we were both half-clothed. I didn't have any sexual attraction to women, but I could dance like I did without getting overly friendly. Some of the women made out – or did more for all I knew – but I wouldn't have to worry about that with Rosa. She'd never cross that line. She let me set how far things went.

The two of us danced with each other and with the men, fending off wandering hands with flirtatious laughs that sounded hollow in my ears. Normally, I would've just been the responder, but the anger simmering inside me pushed me further than I usually went. I let hands linger longer than usual, sometimes pressing into them as they brushed against my breast.

I tried to ignore Reed, maneuvering Rosa so that she was always closer to him, but I could feel his eyes on me no matter where I moved. The other men were watching me too, eyes glued to the places where the shirt lifted and parted, giving them all an eyeful of what they'd paid to see. That wasn't where Reed was looking, however. The one time I permitted myself a glance, I found his eyes searching for mine. I was wearing only a partially-buttoned, practically see through white shirt and he was looking at my eyes.

I turned to Rosa and began dancing with her, needing something else to distract me. I saw surprise flit across her face and then she was all business. She let me lead, mirroring my movements so that when I ran my fingers down her arm and then looped her arm around my neck, she did the same. I let our bodies close in until we were practically grinding against each other.

I could see the tip bucket we'd set out filling up as Rosa and I danced, but I didn't care as much about that as I did about pissing Reed off. As one song changed into the next, Rosa and I broke apart and moved back to dancing with the other men. I saw her trying to get Reed up and moving, but he just glared until she went back to the sandy-haired man we'd met first. I kept myself surrounded by a few different men, letting them press their bodies against mine until I could feel their arousal. A part of me was yelling at myself to stop, that I was going too far, but I didn't care. I wanted Reed to see that he wasn't the only one who wanted me, desired me. I wasn't some desperate street trash from the wrong side of the tracks who'd fuck anyone who gave me a kind word.

Before I could get myself into real trouble to prove something to Reed, Rosa leaned over and told me one of the groomsmen was going to give her something extra for an exclusive dance. I nodded and said I just needed a couple minutes to get some air, then I'd be back and she could go... dance. She jerked her chin towards the balcony and then turned her attention back to a handsome blond.

I stepped outside, breathing in the cool night air. It was the perfect temperature, warm enough that I wasn't cold, but still refreshing. I leaned against the railing, closing my eyes and enjoying the breeze. I didn't have more than a few minutes of peace before I heard voices. I opened my eyes and saw a couple on the balcony next to me looking my way. I looked down and straightened, realizing the way I'd been standing had caused my shirt to ride up. I was essentially flashing anyone who happened to look. At least in Vegas, the chances being arrested for indecent exposure were slim. I sighed as I took a step back. I needed to go back inside.

I heard the door slide open behind me and I froze, hoping it wasn't Reed again.

"Thirsty?" It was a man's voice, but not one I recognized.

I half-turned and saw the dark-haired man from earlier holding out a bottle of water. He had a handsome face, though more rough and chiseled than Reed's, and his eyes were light, a pale blue color that was almost gray.

"I'm Brock, by the way." He seemed to be choosing his words very carefully, but none of them were slurring so he couldn't have been that drunk.

"Thanks." I took the bottle. Rule number one of stripping: never accept a drink in a glass from a stranger. Bottles, however, were fair game. I opened it and took a drink. I hadn't realized how thirsty I'd been.

"I've been to The Diamond Club quite a few times and that's why I requested Rosa, but I've never seen you there." He took a step toward me. "Why's that?"

"I just started," I confessed. "Not dancing in general, but at the club. Before that, I was somewhere else."

He reached out and brushed his fingers over my arm. "How do you feel about a private lap dance?" His eyes left no doubt as to what he was actually asking for. "I pay very well."

I started to take a step back but a wave of dizziness washed over me and I staggered. Brock caught my arm and I heard him say something, but I couldn't make it out. The edges of my vision started to go gray and the ground rushed up to meet me.

Chapter 7

A hand inside my shirt groped my breast.
My legs pushed apart.
A hand over my mouth.
Shouting.
Someone's arms around me.
A strange rocking movement.
Darkness.

It was still dark when I opened my eyes later. I wasn't sure how much time had passed or where I was. All I could tell was that I was in a bed I didn't know and someone was sitting next to me.

"Hello?" The word sounded fuzzy, blunted, and my tongue felt too thick.

"Shh. It's okay."

Reed.

His hands covered mine. "You drank too much and passed out. Go back to sleep. You'll feel better in the morning."

I wanted to tell him I hadn't drank anything but water, but the darkness was calling again and I couldn't refuse it.

As I slipped under, I thought I felt arms wrapping around me, holding me, but I knew that was just a dream because the sensation of being held melted into a half-memory, half-dream of a childhood trip to the zoo.

When I woke up, this time I knew I'd been asleep for hours. The sun was peeking in through the gap in the curtains and it was morning. My head hurt and when I tried to remember why I was in a strange bed wearing only a half-buttoned shirt, I drew a blank. I looked around, trying to find some clue as to what had happened.

A soft knock at the door made me grab the blankets and pull them over me. I almost laughed, considering whoever's room this was had already seen me naked, but I still kept the blankets where they were.

"Breakfast's here." Reed stuck his head into the room.

I stared at him, wracking my brain and trying to figure out why I was in his room. We hadn't... again, had we?

"Piper?" He sounded concerned.

"What?" I snapped more sharply than I'd intended.

"I ordered room service."

He didn't seem perturbed by how I'd spoken to him, but I could see a hint of something in his eyes, something I might've thought was sadness. The idea that he might be sad about me being rude to him annoyed me enough that I no longer cared that I wasn't wearing much. He had no right to act as if I'd hurt him, not after what he'd used me to do.

Without being invited, he stepped further into the room, carrying a tray loaded with breakfast. Toast, butter, strawberries, syrup, pancakes and whipped cream. That was a lot of food. Far more than I'd ever eat, even if I'd had an appetite.

"I have to go," I said, swinging my legs over the side of the bed. "My roommate will be worried about me."

"If your roommate is the girl you were dancing with last night, she isn't looking for you." Reed sat on the edge of the bed. "She's in Danny's room."

Oh. I sat back and eyed the food, feeling foolish. My stomach growled, betraying me. Okay, maybe I was hungry. I took a piece of toast, avoiding his gaze as I took a bite. I didn't just want to look at him. I wanted to demand an explanation, demand he tell me why he'd done that to me. If he'd just wanted to get laid, he could've fucked anyone else at that reunion. Why did it have to be me?

I could feel his eyes on me as I ate, but I refused to raise my head. I didn't want him to see how bothered I really was by what had happened. But then he spoke and I had to look up.

"Let me take you to dinner tonight."

My eyes narrowed as I looked at him. What was he playing at? "No thank you." I kept my voice cold and even.

"Look, it's my way for apologizing for what happened last night."

Now I was just confused. "What are you talking about?"

He rubbed the back of his neck, an embarrassed expression on his face. "You don't remember?"

I shook my head.

"I came out on the balcony to make sure you were okay and found my future brother-in-law pawing at you." He shook his head. "You were passed out and Brock was drunk – not that it excuses him. I told him to go sleep it off and then brought you back here."

I frowned. "The last thing I remember is going out for some air." I was also pretty sure I hadn't had anything to drink, but that route had implications I didn't want to deal with, especially since nothing had really happened.

"Well, I feel bad about what happened, even if you don't remember it," Reed said. "Let me at least take you to dinner and make it up to you."

I was torn. On one hand, I wanted to tell him to fuck off. I wanted to believe he'd lied to me, he'd used me and that he'd walked away as if it was no big deal.

Then there was the logical part of me that reminded me of the practically empty cupboards back at the apartment and the ten packets of ramen noodles Rosa and I had eaten as our main meal this past week. If I went with him, I could get a real meal, the biggest they offered, and the leftovers would keep us for a day or two. Rosa wouldn't have even hesitated.

Still, there was a part of me that knew the truth. I wasn't thinking about agreeing for those reasons. I wanted to go to dinner with him because I enjoyed his company. That night back home hadn't just been about sex. I'd felt comfortable with him in a way I'd never felt with a guy before. The talking had come easy and even the silence had been comfortable. It was nearly impossible to find someone to talk to, to be quiet with and who could do such amazing things in bed. Women would kill for a guy like Reed, even if for only one night. Was I really willing to give up at least a couple hours of someone to talk to just because I was pissed at him?

"All right," I agreed.

He smiled. "Great! What time should I pick you up and where?"

I held up a hand, silencing him. That was sounding way too much like a date, and I needed to nip that in the bud. "How about we meet for dinner?"

"Oh. Okay."

I wasn't sure if it was my imagination or if he really sounded disappointed, but I wasn't going to think about it. Instead, I asked, "Where are we meeting?"

"Alizé."

I blinked. Alizé was one of Chef André Rochat's restaurants. It served the best French food in the city, had a huge wine selection and offered the most spectacular view from atop the Palms Casino Resort. Or so I'd heard.

"You already have reservations?"

Reed gave me a sheepish grin as he shook his head. "I know people."

Of course he did. Well, I definitely wasn't going to turn down that. I was just glad I still had my dress from the reunion. I didn't have anything else that would even come close to being appropriate for a place like that. I tried not to let myself be disappointed at not having one Reed hadn't seen before. That wasn't the point.

"So I'll see you there at eight?"

I nodded as I shoved the last bite of toast into my mouth and climbed out of the bed. I needed to find my clothes, get Rosa and get us home. Being around Reed was more confusing than I liked. I needed some distance if I was going to be able to go through with dinner.

Chapter 8

The appreciative look Reed gave me when I got out of the taxi said he didn't mind that I was wearing the same thing I'd worn to the reunion. In fact, if the heat in his gaze was any indication, he was remembering what it had been like watching me take it off. I wondered if he realized now that I'd been using some of my work skills that night.

"Thank you for agreeing to have dinner with me," he said as he held out his arm. Despite what I'd seen in his eyes, his actions and tone were completely platonic.

I let my arm hook around his and we walked towards the entrance. I could feel the muscles in his arm through the material of his jacket and wondered if he was as aware of me as I was of him. I pressed my lips together and made myself think of other things. I couldn't think of him in a romantic way, not now that I knew he was getting married. My father had cheated on my mother for years and walked out as soon as she'd told him she was pregnant. It was one thing to know there were married men ogling me at the strip club, and something else entirely to entertain sexual thoughts about one I knew was married, or at least partway there.

When we reached the restaurant, I was unable to keep myself from gawking at the view. Everything I'd heard had been true. The skyline was breathtaking, lit up against the deep blue sky. It was early June, so the sun was just starting to go down and the colors popped against the lights from the buildings. Up here, you couldn't see any peeling paint or drunken guests. The sleaziest strip clubs looked as clean and bright as the newest casinos.

Reed led me to our table where I was finally forced to look away from the city. He ordered wine in fluent French, of course, but didn't have a smug smile when the waiter walked away. At least his lack of pretentiousness had been real, even if nothing else had been.

I looked down at the menu, frowning when I saw it was in French.

"Oh, sorry, I forgot," Reed said. "The menu's written in French, but there's–"

"Je crois que je vais poulet," I interrupted.

He stared at me and I couldn't help but laugh at his expression.

"I went to the same high school you did," I reminded him. "Four years of Ms Boudreaux." I couldn't resist adding, "And it comes in handy when I pretend the reason I don't answer some of those assholes at the club is because I don't speak English. You'd be surprised at what idiots say when they think the stripper is foreign."

The tips of Reed's ears reddened.

"Ask it," I said.

"Ask what?" He looked down at his water glass.

"What you've been wanting to ask since you recognized me last night." I'd seen the question in his eyes from that first moment and now I just wanted to get it out of the way. I didn't want it hanging over me all night.

"I-I don't know what you mean."

"You want to know how I got into this, or why I do it. The wording may be different, but it comes down to the same thing." I kept my words clipped and even, unemotional.

The waiter returned with the wine, and I fell silent while he poured. Being matter-of-fact about what I did was one thing. Having someone overhear the conversation was something else. No matter how polite and professional the waiter would be, I knew he'd only see me as a whore. It didn't matter that I didn't have sex with the men at the club. I sold the idea of sex, and for a lot of people, that was enough.

After the waiter promised to return in a few minutes for our orders, I waited until he was out of earshot and then gave him the short version of the story.

"When you move to Vegas at twenty-one with a high school diploma and waitressing as your only skill-set, there aren't a lot of opportunities for employment," I said. "I want to be a dancer – a real dancer – and I thought this would be a good place to try to get my start." I took a sip of the wine, and then added, "It pays better than waiting tables back in Philly."

"There are dance schools back in Philadelphia," Reed said. "And anyone who still remembers their high school French and had such a well-formed opinion on literature as a freshman should've been able to get an academic scholarship. You had options. Why'd you leave?"

I frowned. "That seems a bit too personal for an apology dinner."

"So we can talk about you getting naked for money, but not about why you didn't go to college?" Reed seemed almost amused.

I scowled at him. "Yes, and if you're going to be a jerk, I'll just go home."

"I'm sorry." He immediately backpedaled. "I didn't mean to pry."

I was saved from having to respond when the waiter returned. Once our meals were ordered, Reed started on some small talk that led us safely away from areas that were too personal. He asked about which classes I'd liked at St. George's and we reminisced about teachers we'd shared. We talked about favorite things like food and movies, but we stayed away from ballet and our families.

I found myself enjoying the mundane conversation and relaxing as we talked and ate. As the dinner started to near the end, however, Reed began to appear more anxious. He started tapping his fingers on the table and leaning forward in his chair. Either he was waiting for something to happen or he had something he'd been wanting to say. He was running out of time in which to say it.

"Look, I know we've been keeping things light, but I need to tell you something." The words came out in a rush.

I tensed. What was he going to say now?

"After I saw you at the airport, I couldn't stop thinking about you, and then you came outside at the reunion. I've never been able to talk to someone as easily as I can talk to you," he confessed. "And that night... I can't stop thinking about it." He reached out as if he was going to take my hand. "I want to be with you."

"Are you fucking kidding me?"

He froze, his eyes wide. Clearly, that hadn't been the response he'd been expecting.

All of the anger I'd been feeling since I saw him in that hotel room came bubbling up and out. "You want to be with me?" My laugh was brittle. "You're engaged, you asshole! Isn't it enough that you've already used me once to cheat on your fiancée?" I fought to keep my voice low. There were too many people around who'd love to see a good show. "Maybe you think that because of what I do, or because we slept together before, I'm easy, but I'm not. I had sex with you because I genuinely liked you. I thought you were a nice guy—"

He finally found his voice. "I don't think you're easy."

I glared at him and made a gesture for him to continue. I needed to hear his explanation so when I stormed off, I'd feel justified.

"And I wasn't using you, Piper. I really liked you. I *do* like you."

He touched my hand and I pulled back. I didn't want him touching me, especially when just that little bit had sent a jolt through my entire body.

"Dammit!" He ran his hand through his hair and leaned back in his seat. "This isn't going how I thought it would."

"How you thought it would?" I shook my head. "What, you thought you'd take me out to eat, tell me you want to be with me and I'd just forget you were getting married and fall into bed with you?" I crossed my arms. "And before you say I did it once before, let me remind you that I didn't know you were engaged then."

"I thought you'd at least believe my feelings were sincere," he said. The expression on his face was almost sad and if I hadn't been so pissed, I might've felt sorry for him. "I thought we had a connection. I thought you'd felt it too."

I had felt it, but that didn't mean it wasn't just physical attraction, a need to get laid, the psychological response to all those memories coming home had brought back. None of those were reasons to break up a relationship headed towards marriage.

"Connection or not, you have a fiancée." It didn't seem fair that I had to keep reminding him of that fact.

He nodded. "I know, but it's not... I mean." He blew out air in a frustrated sigh. "I don't have this with Britni." He gestured between the two of us.

"Dinner?" I said dryly.

Not even a hint of a smile. "I don't have anything in common with her. I can't talk to her like I can talk to you, and I've known her since we were kids."

"I'm not sure why that's my problem." My voice was tight and I shifted uncomfortably in my seat.

"I'm going about this all wrong." He rubbed the back of his neck.

"Considering you neglected to mention Britni before you fucked me, I'd say you definitely went about whatever this is the wrong way." I knew I should just get up and go, head back to my apartment and forget all about Reed Stirling. I didn't know what his game was, but I knew that's all it was. I should've known better than to think he was different.

"I don't love Britni."

Yeah, hadn't heard that one before. Still, I raised my eyebrows and waited for him to go on.

"Our fathers went to Brown together. Our families took vacations together. Her parents are my sister's and I's godparents and my parents are godparents to her and Brock." He leaned forward. "She's five years younger than me, but as soon as she turned eighteen, our parents started pushing us together, having us sit next to each other during meals, encouraging us to spend time together, that kind of thing. Then, two years ago, my parents told me that they and the Michaels had basically decided that they wanted our families to join together."

"Like a merger?" I thought I knew where he was going with this, but I wasn't going to assume. Fool me once...

"Exactly like a merger. Except there wasn't a buy-out or a contract. Just wedding vows." His voice was flat, as if he felt nothing about what his parents wanted him to do.

"Why didn't you just tell them you don't love her?" Maybe I was overstepping my bounds, but if he was going to make me into the other woman who ruined his engagement, I thought I had the right to push a bit.

"They already know." He ran his fingers through his hair again and I found myself remembering how it felt to do it too.

"And they don't care?"

"When they first told me what they wanted, I didn't care." He met my eyes and I couldn't look away. "I'd gotten burned, bad, in college and I didn't think I'd ever fall in love."

His eyes were blazing and my chest tightened until I could barely breathe. I refused to let myself think about what he was going to say next.

"But I think I could fall in love with you."

Chapter 9

I couldn't look into his eyes and not believe what he'd said. Or at least believe that he believed, at least in this moment. This time, when he reached for me, I let him take my hand. He was right about the connection. I could feel it, and I didn't want to ignore it. The need to touch him was too strong. He paid the check and laced his fingers through mine as we headed out of the restaurant. Neither of us said anything and I wondered if his brain was as busy as mine.

I had so many questions I wanted to ask him as he flagged a cab. What did it mean that he wanted to be with me? Here in Vegas? Back in Philadelphia? Did he expect me to move back? I'd be able to stay with Anastascia if I needed to, and I could probably find a waitressing job without too much trouble, but what about dancing? Then again, was I actually more likely to make it in Vegas, where I was a stripper, than if I tried in Philly? What would his family say, especially when they found out where I worked? I didn't doubt for a minute that Brock would tell his sister about me being a stripper when he found out that

Reed called off the wedding for me. And what if it didn't work out? Would I be stuck back in Philadelphia?

"We have a choice to make." Reed's statement drew my attention back to him. He looked at the cab. "Is he making two stops, or just one?" He pulled me to him and wrapped his arms around my waist. "I want you, Piper, but I'm not going to ask you to do anything you don't want to do."

I looked up at him. I was doing what I always did. I was over-thinking things, making plans for things that hadn't happened and might never happen.

"Come back to my hotel with me." He brushed my hair back from my face, letting his fingers linger on my cheeks. "Let me show you how much I want to be with you."

It might've been stupid of me, but I couldn't stop the way I felt. I nodded and he lowered his head to kiss me. Our first kiss had been gentle, searching, testing. The second had been full of desire. This was something else entirely. Reed felt like he was possessing my mouth, staking a claim. He thrust his tongue between my lips, devouring with teeth and lips. By the time he released me, my heart was racing and I was gasping for air.

Even though we behaved ourselves on the ride back to Reed's hotel, the cabbie couldn't stop smirking at us. The only part of us touching were our hands, but as his thumb made small circles on the side of my hand, I couldn't help but remember what it had felt like to have his hands on more intimate places and my stomach fluttered in anticipation.

The elevator ride was torture. There we were, this enclosed space, so close that I could smell his aftershave. I'd heard people talking about craving someone's touch, but I'd never truly understood it until that moment. It was like there was this deep, inexplicable hunger inside me and he was the only thing that could satisfy it. I knew I was getting in deep, but I'd been lost from the moment I'd let him take my hand.

When he shut the door behind us, I expected him to be all over me. I wouldn't have been surprised if he'd just done me up against the wall or bent me over the couch. Instead, he just pulled me after him towards the master bedroom. I remembered then that he was sharing this suite with his former wedding party. Having them walk in on us fucking wouldn't be the best way to let them know that the wedding was off.

When he didn't immediately start ravaging me when the bedroom door was closed behind me, I was thoroughly confused. I started to turn towards him, but he slid his arms around me from behind and pulled me back against his body. He pressed his lips against the side of my throat and I shivered.

"When we were back in Philadelphia, we had to rush. Tonight we don't, and I intend to take my time with you."

He slid his hands up over my ribcage and cupped my breasts through my dress as he fastened his lips over the place where my shoulder met my neck. I closed my eyes as he sucked the skin into his mouth, losing myself in the sensations of his hands and mouth. I knew he was marking me, telling everyone that he wanted me, and a thrill went all the way to my toes.

"I'm going to do exactly what I promised, show you how much I want you," he whispered in my ear. "And I'm going to make you come loud enough that no one else is going to doubt how much I want you."

I started to turn but he held me tightly, keeping me facing the bed. I felt his hands in my hair, and then the waves began to fall, one by one from the up-do I'd put them into. When my hair was free, his hands moved to my zipper and slowly lowered it. I didn't move as he slid the dress off of my body. His fingers traced along my spine, stopping at the waistband of my panties, and then moved up again to the clasp of my bra.

He stayed behind me as he removed my bra, his hands running over me from behind. His fingers teased at my nipples, rolling and pinching them until I was moaning, arching my back to push them into his hands.

"I don't like the fact that other men have seen these." There was a possessive edge to his voice that made my breathing stutter. "I don't want anyone else looking at you like this."

I nodded even though he hadn't asked a question. This was a side of him I hadn't seen before.

"Do they touch you?" His fingers tightened until it was almost painful.

"They're not supposed to," I managed to say. "But sometimes..." I whimpered as he twisted his grip.

When he released my breasts, my nipples throbbed and I wasn't sure if I was relieved or wanted more. One hand slid down my stomach and over my panties.

"What about this?" He cupped my sex over the green silk. "Do they touch you here?"

I shook my head. "No."

"Good." He practically growled the word. "I hate that other men have seen you, but if they'd touched you..." His hold tightened almost convulsively. "No more." He ran his tongue along the outer rim of my ear. "From now on, I'm the only one who gets to see you naked."

There were logistics, practicalities, that needed to be discussed, but I wasn't about to kill the mood. That was pillow talk for after.

He released me and his fingers hooked under the elastic at my hips. He lowered my panties, but I didn't realize he was on his knees until I felt him press his lips against my right ass cheek. His hand settled on the small of my back, putting pressure on it until I realized what he wanted and bent over. We were close enough to the bed that I was able to put my hands down on it to steady me, which was good considering what happened next.

Without easing into it, Reed buried his face between my legs and I swore. His tongue twisted and probed, sliding in and out of my pussy until I was spreading my legs further apart, wordlessly begging for more. Luc had always been reluctant to go down on me, and had pretty much only done it for foreplay or because he wanted a blow-job. Reed, however, was applying himself with so much enthusiasm that I felt myself going from practically zero to a hundred in seconds.

As his tongue circled my clit, he slid a finger into my pussy, only giving me a couple strokes before it disappeared. Then his lips were around my clit and I was making a sound I'd never known I could make. I was so close, I could taste it. All I needed was a little more and I'd come.

I felt something pressing against my asshole and started to speak, but whatever word I was going to say turned into a wail as he did two things at once. The suction on my clit increased as his finger slid into my ass. My legs buckled, but he held me up, his mouth never ceasing as my climax crashed into me. He kept licking and sucking on my sensitive flesh even as I came, pushing one orgasm into another until I wasn't sure they were separate anymore and I was certain I was going explode.

"Stop, please," I gasped. My body called me a traitor but I ignored it, my mind needing relief. "Too much."

Then he was gone and my knees were giving out. Before I hit the floor, his arms were around me, lifting me and moving me to the bed. I flopped bonelessly on the bedspread, my muscles still quivering from the force of my climax. I wasn't sure I could move my limbs at the moment, but I did manage to turn my head so I could watch him undress.

Before, I'd only seen his cock as he'd been entering me. I wanted to see it now, see how turned on he was. His eyes met mine and then he slowly started to remove his shirt, revealing that cut body I'd enjoyed feeling beneath my hands. Next came his pants and he kicked them aside, pausing for a moment to let me enjoy the sight of him in just a pair of tight black boxer-briefs that clearly demonstrated just how much he'd been enjoying himself.

Then they were coming off too and I groaned as his cock appeared, thick and long and fully erect. I remember it filling me, stretching me, sinking into me so deep. I pushed myself up on my elbows. Now I wanted to see if it could fit in my mouth.

"Where do you think you're going?" Reed's voice was a mixture of dark and teasing. He reached the edge of the bed at the same time I managed to get myself into a sitting position, which put me exactly where I wanted to be.

"Right here." I smiled up at him as I wrapped my hand around the base of his shaft. My fingers couldn't touch.

I leaned down and ran my tongue along the underside of his cock, tasting salt and something that was distinctly male. He groaned and I smiled. I loved the texture of him and explored him as thoroughly as he'd explored me, licking every inch of him before taking the head between my lips.

"Shit."

I looked up to see his eyes closed and took that to be a good sign. I took more of him until my jaw began to ache and I had to back off. I repeated the movement and then his hand was in my hair, pulling me back.

"As much as I love the idea of coming in your mouth, I need to be inside you." Reed lowered his head and kissed me hard, shoving his tongue into my mouth until I could taste our mingled flavors.

He pressed me back on the bed, crawling over me without breaking the kiss. I heard the rip of a wrapper and had a moment to wonder where it had come from, and then he was pushing inside me and I didn't care. He entered with a single thrust and I cried out. He took the sound, stilling inside me as my body trembled, adjusting to the sudden intrusion. I was wet, but still very tight.

I squeezed my eyes shut, trying to absorb the myriad sensations coursing along my nerves. He rested his forehead against mine, our mouths parting.

"Like a fucking vice." He was panting.

We stayed like that, joined as intimately as possible, our breath mingling, until our body's most basic urges overpowered everything else and Reed had to move. His strokes were slow and deep, making every inch of me feel every inch of him as he thrust over and over again. This was nothing like before when he'd pounded into me, relentless and focused on reaching our release. This was more like I'd always imagined making love would be; though I didn't want to use that particular four-letter word. Still, as he drove forward with a steady rhythm, I knew that this was something more than fucking. He was doing what he'd promised, showing me how much he wanted me.

The pleasure inside me was building differently than before. That had been an explosion while this was a flame being stoked into a raging inferno. I wrapped my arms around his neck and hooked my ankles around the back of his thighs, loving the feel of his muscles moving under his tanned skin. Even as I felt myself reaching the point of no return, I didn't want it to end. I wanted to stay like this forever, our bodies moving together, working to bring each other pleasure.

"Come for me, baby." His voice was strained. "I want to see your face when you come."

He was moving faster now, but still in control, and a roll of his hips was all it took for me to obey his command. I lifted my body to meet his as I called out his name and the movement drove him deep. He cried out as we came together, my pussy tightening around him, drawing out every last drop of pleasure for us both. I clung to him, wanting the moment to last. He rolled us over, putting me on top of him even as he pulled the bedspread around us both, cocooning us together.

"Believe me now?" he murmured the question against the top of my head.

I nodded, not sure I had the energy to form words. Words could come tomorrow. Right now, I just wanted to bask in the afterglow and fall asleep in his arms.

Chapter 10

Wakefulness came slowly and I wasn't sure where I was at first. I only knew that this wasn't my bed or my apartment. It was too quiet, the mattress too soft. Then I felt a familiar ache between my legs and remembered.

Reed.

I smiled and opened my eyes, wondering what this new day would hold. We had plans to make, things to discuss, but first I wanted him and breakfast. In that order.

Then I registered what I was seeing. A suitcase on the end of the bed and Reed putting clothes into it.

"Reed?" I didn't trust myself to say anything more than his name. I told myself not to jump to any conclusions, but that didn't stop my stomach from twisting.

"My flight leaves at ten." He sounded even and calm. "I need to be back in Philadelphia tonight."

I waited for what was coming next. Would he ask me to come with him now or would he want to wait until he'd ended things with Britni? I felt a twinge of guilt that I hadn't asked last night if he'd already called off the wedding. He didn't love her, I reminded myself, so a single day didn't matter. I wasn't sure if I'd believe the lie later, but it worked for now.

Maybe he was going back to Philly to get all of his affairs in order before moving here. Either way, I was sure he'd find a way for me to be able to quit The Diamond Club. He'd already said he didn't want anyone else seeing me naked. I didn't know what I'd do, but I'd find something. Philadelphia or Vegas, it didn't matter as long as we were together. Maybe we'd go somewhere new. A fresh start for both of us.

"I have a couple thousand dollars in cash."

He was talking again and I turned my attention to him, ready to hear what he had planned for us.

"I'll have the hotel keep the room for a couple days. That should be enough time for you to find a nice apartment. I'll set up a joint account and wire money into it as soon as the bank opens tomorrow."

I frowned, pulling the sheet more tightly around me. Something about this didn't sound right.

"I'll make sure there's enough money in it so you can quit stripping and focus on your dancing."

I climbed out of the bed, still keeping myself covered. Suddenly, I didn't feel like being naked in front of him. I swallowed hard and asked the question I needed answered.

"What about you?"

He didn't look at me and that was enough to tell me it had all been a lie. I grabbed my dress and pulled it on, snatching up my underwear as he answered.

"I usually fly to LA every couple weeks for business, and most of the time I stop in Vegas for a lay-over. Adding an extra day or two won't rouse any suspicions."

Suspicions. I felt the urge to throw up. How could I have been so stupid?

"You're still getting married." I picked up my shoes and told the tears burning against my eyelids that they weren't allowed to fall. "You lying, cheating bastard." I spit the last words through clenched teeth and then stormed out, not caring if anyone saw me. I heard Reed say my name, but kept walking. I let my anger take control, knowing the alternative would be to cry. I wished I'd never gone to that stupid reunion. My crush could've stayed sweet and innocent instead of being destroyed by finding out what a true asshole Reed Stirling really was.

I was still fuming when I got off the elevator and started through the lobby, so much so I almost walked right into a solid wall of muscle. I stopped abruptly and looked up into a pair of pale blue eyes.

"Piper?"

I crossed my arms. I was so not in the mood to deal with Reed's soon-to-be brother-in-law. "What?" I snapped.

"I just wanted to apologize for what happened the other night." Brock's handsome face was sincere and I studied it for a moment, almost missing that he was holding out an envelope.

A new flare of anger went through me. What was it with these rich people thinking they could just buy people off? I folded my arms more tightly. "You were drunk. It's not like I don't deal with that every night at work. I don't want anything from you."

I started to step around him, but he took the step with me, still blocking my way.

"Look, I feel bad. Just take it, please." He gave me one of those expressions I was sure had gotten him out of a lot of trouble growing up and, despite my anger, I found myself softening. "I wrote you a note."

I sighed. What the hell. It wasn't like I was at a place financially where I could afford to refuse a tip. I told myself that's all it was when I took the envelope.

"Don't open it yet." Brock smiled. His eyes flicked over my head and then back down again. "I have to get going, but I hope you'll accept my apology and maybe I'll see you later."

I almost told him not to count on it, but then I saw Reed walking through the lobby with the rest of his groomsmen. He stared straight ahead, not even glancing at Brock when the other man fell in step at his side.

I watched them walk out, my fingers tightening around the letter until the paper crinkled. I let out a slow breath as the men got into a limo and drove away. I'd take Brock's money, put the rest of the weekend behind me and get on with my life. I'd survived taking care of my dying mother, survived losing her, survived Las Vegas by myself for two years. I'd survive this too, and I'd never be this foolish again.

After making that promise to myself, I opened the envelope. The first thing I saw was six crisp one hundred dollar bills paper-clipped together with a note saying, "For your ticket."

I frowned. What the fuck did that mean? I pulled out a folded sheet of paper and read it. Then I re-read it because I was sure it had to be a mistake, but no, there it was, in sloppy masculine hand-writing.

"Piper, I would like the chance to prove to you that I'm not the man I seemed to be the first time we met. Please agree to be my date to my sister's wedding. The cash enclosed is for a plane ticket if you agree, but please keep it even if you decide not to come. Should you agree to be my date, you'll receive ten thousand dollars for your services. Sincerely, Brock Michaels."

Ten thousand dollars to watch Reed marry a woman he claimed not to love.

Fuck.

End of Vol. 1

Sinful Desires Vol. 2

Chapter 1

One hour.

That's all I had left to question the decision I'd made, and since I was sitting in the Las Vegas airport waiting to get called to board my flight, I had nothing better to do than second-guess myself. Then I'd have nearly five and a half hours to sit on a plane, worrying, beating myself up and listing and re-listing the pros and cons of going back to Philadelphia.

One of the biggest cons, of course, was the main reason I was going and why my last trip back home had been such a disaster. Mother-fucking Reed Stirling. My gorgeous high school crush and older brother to the biggest bitch at St. George. I'd just never thought he'd turn out to be as self-centered and self-important as his sister.

I stuck my hand in my purse and fingered the envelope there, hoping against hope that I'd find a little money left. There wasn't of course, it had gone to buy this ticket and a few extra groceries. There were only so many times I could eat the same cardboard shit. The reason I'd brought the envelope, however, was because of the promise inside.

Ten thousand dollars.

I'd texted Brock to let him know I'd agreed to be his date to the wedding and he'd sent back a message that had sounded enthusiastic despite the lack of punctuation. He'd told me he'd have a car take me to a hotel where he'd rent me a room, but he still hadn't mentioned anything about what 'services' he was expecting for that payment.

I wasn't just doing it for the money, although that was a big motivation. The other reason was more personal and a lot more vindictive. I wanted to see the expression on Reed's face when I walked into his wedding on the arm of his fiancée's brother. I wanted to watch him squirm, see his face flush with uncertainty. I wanted to see if he could look me in the eye. It might've been a bit petty, but after what he'd done to me, he deserved it.

I felt a twinge of guilt. I wasn't the only person he'd hurt, and if anyone had the right to be angrier than me, it was Britni. She was being pressured into marrying a man she didn't love, a man she knew didn't love her. The least he could've done was be faithful, and he hadn't even been able to do that.

I sighed, leaning forward and burying my head in my hands. What was I thinking, taking Brock's offer? Sure, I was pissed at Reed and wanted to do something that could at least make him uncomfortable. I doubted anything I did could actually hurt him as badly as he'd hurt me. I'd tried telling myself over and over that I'd just gotten caught up in the emotion and that I didn't really care about him the way I thought I did. I'd almost convinced myself of the lie.

I groaned in frustration, thankful no one was sitting close enough to hear. Was I really any better than him, thinking only of myself? What kind of person showed up at the wedding of a guy she'd fucked just a week before? It was bad enough Britni had to go through with this farce of a marriage. Did I really have to rub it in her face that Reed didn't want her?

Then again, I countered. He didn't want me either. Not really. He wanted my body. He wanted to fuck me. He didn't want me. He wasn't interested in who I was as a person, just what was under my clothes. In a way, he was worse than the guys who came to the club, because at least they were honest about what they were looking for. Reed was a liar who thought he could buy me off like I was some whore he could pay for sex.

I could just walk away. Pick up my bag and leave. Brock would understand. I could offer to pay him back for the ticket even though he'd told me to keep the money if I didn't come. I thought about him, how he'd wanted to make things right for something he'd done but had no control over. Reed had just expected me to be grateful for what he could give me and hadn't even tried to apologize.

I straightened. Why was I beating myself up over this? Brock had asked me to a wedding. Why should I let Reed screw up the chance for me to spend time with a nice guy who actually seemed to like me? I ignored the part of my brain that asked why, if Brock was so nice, had he offered me money for 'services'?

Maybe he was just a generous guy who understood what it was like for someone to struggle to pay the bills. Even if I was lying to myself and Brock did want me to sleep with him, I hadn't made any promises. If I did fuck him, it'd be my choice, and not because of money.

I squared my shoulders and told myself I was done trying to talk myself out of going. I'd enjoy my time with Brock and let myself have the guilty pleasure of seeing Reed's reaction. I wouldn't spoil anything and I wouldn't make any expectations of Brock.

"Flight 731 to Philadelphia, will begin boarding in five minutes." A woman's cool voice came over the loudspeaker.

I stood and picked up my bag. They hadn't announced my section, but I wanted to stand. I'd be sitting for hours soon and I didn't like walking around on planes. I didn't like flying, actually. As I passed a pair of screaming toddlers, I checked my purse for the sleeping pill Rosa had given me. It'd be my luck to have those two right behind me. I'd never be able to relax on my own under the best of circumstances, and after the past week, I needed to be able to turn my brain off for a while. Besides, I didn't want to be too tired to appreciate the wedding. I wanted to enjoy every minute of it.

Chapter 2

I couldn't do it.

When Brock and I first walked into the massive, ancient church, I was full of confidence. He'd bought me a dress that made me look like I belonged here and sent me to one of the best stylists in the city. He'd even given me a necklace that matched my eyes. For the first time in my life, I felt jealousy from girls who'd grown up with everything. Then saw Rebecca's face as she came out to speak to her parents, the look on her face was priceless, every emotion she'd ever possessed must have flitted over her expression. The fact that she was wearing a yellow dress that made her look sallow and washed-out made me feel even better.

Brock, of course, had to take his place with Reed, leaving me to sit alone, but even that was okay. I was content to look at the decorations and flowers, all of which cost more than I made in a year, maybe more. The colors were yellow and blue, more spring colors than summer, and I'd wondered if Britni'd had any say in them. I had to admit, I was curious to see her.

Then the groom and his groomsmen had come in and I watched Reed's face when he saw me. The shock, then something that had looked like sadness, before he finally settled on a smile so fake I'd doubted it fooled anyone. I didn't let myself linger on him, instead I searched for Brock, flirting with little smiles even while feeling Reed's eyes on me.

When the bridal march started, I stood and turned with everyone else, but the veil kept me from seeing anything about Britni other than her dark hair. I made it through the opening, but when the priest got to the part of the ceremony where he announced that the couple had written their own vows, my stomach lurched and I knew I couldn't stay.

I hurried out as quickly as I dared, not quite breaking into a run, and now I was wandering around, trying to find somewhere I could wait out the rest of the ceremony until it was safe to come down. Once it was all over, I'd be okay, or at least that was the current lie I was working on. I was still telling myself it when I found myself in the last place I expected.

The bell tower. The wind was brisker up here than it had been on the ground and it cooled my overheated face. I looked out over the city and could almost imagine no one else in the world existed. Right now, that sounded pretty good.

"Piper?"

I froze. I had to be dreaming. There was no way that voice was real. I stayed facing the horizon, closing my eyes as I felt tears burning behind my eyes.

"Piper."

He was closer this time and I couldn't deny who it was anymore.

"I couldn't do it."

I turned then. Reed's previously flawless hair was a wild mess and his face was flushed. I swallowed hard, unable to stop my stomach from twisting at the sight of him.

"I got up there and it was like I could see my whole life stretching out in front of me. Empty. Because it was the wrong woman standing across from me." He walked toward me, until there was less than a foot between us. "I'm so sorry for how I treated you, and I promise I'll never give you a reason to doubt me again."

Despite everything that had happened, I wanted to believe him. The connection we made at the reunion was still there, drawing me to him. My heart thudded a warning against my ribcage, telling me not to be stupid... again. The rest of me was remembering what it had been like to have him touching me, thrusting into me. Consuming me.

He closed the last of the distance between us, as if he knew I couldn't make the move. "Please," he said softly. "Forgive me. I need you. I can't be without you."

I tilted my head back and he took it as my acceptance. His mouth was gentle, his lips moving slowly with mine, as if we had all the time in the world. As if there wasn't total chaos going on beneath our feet as people were trying to figure out what had happened.

He held my face as his tongue slid between my lips, his fingers touching me as if I was something delicate, breakable. When his hands moved down my neck to my shoulders, I stepped into him, pressing my body against his, melting into his warmth. I slipped my hands under his jacket, feeling the heat of his skin through the thin cotton of his dress shirt. My palms slid over his muscular sides and up to his shoulders even as his fingers moved over my back, bare skin burning beneath his touch.

I hadn't even realized we'd moved until his hands were at my waist, maneuvering me as he sat on a wooden bench tucked into a hidden alcove. His hands ran down my ass to my thighs, pulling my legs onto either side of his waist so I was straddling his lap. I could feel him hard beneath me and the knowledge that I caused it made me wet.

His hands moved to the thin straps of my dress and I pulled back, our eyes locked as he slowly lowered my top until it pooled around my waist, leaving my breasts bare to his hungry gaze. My head fell back as his lips made their way down my throat, light butterfly kisses that stirred things deep inside my core. I leaned further back, trusting him to bear my weight as one arm stretched along the length of my spine.

When his mouth closed around my nipple, I bit my lip to stifle a cry. The last thing we needed was to have someone hear us and come investigate. I should've felt guilty about how wonderful he felt against my breast while his bride was downstairs, humiliated, but all I could think about was the delicious pull of his mouth.

I buried my fingers in his hair, holding him against me until the pleasure was almost too much. I tugged on his hair, bringing his face up so I could cover his mouth with mine, sucking his tongue into my mouth until he groaned. My stomach tightened and I knew what I wanted. He'd once said he wanted it too and now I was going to make it happen.

I climbed off his lap and went down on my knees, grateful I hadn't worn hose. The stones were cool and hard against my knees, but I didn't care. I made short work of his pants, opening them just enough for me to get what I wanted. I didn't bother teasing him, I wanted him too much for that. I lowered my head, taking as much of him into my mouth as possible. I moaned around his cock as his flavor exploded across my taste buds. I'd almost forgotten how good it felt to have him in my mouth, and it had only been a week. I couldn't wait to find out what it felt and tasted like to have him come.

Up and down his length I stroked him, reveling in his taste and the moans coming from his throat. I sucked hard, then softened, teasing my tongue around and over him. His hand came to rest on my head and I could feel the tension in his legs as he fought not to thrust hard into my mouth. I shoved a hand into his pants, cupping his balls and he moaned what sounded very much like my name.

His hand tugged at my hair and I knew it was a warning. I didn't care. I wanted this, wanted him. I sucked harder, hollowing my cheeks, suctioning him into my throat. I wanted all of him and relaxed my throat until I met my goal, my mouth stretched wide enough to hurt.

"Fuck!"

The word was muffled and I was pretty sure he had his free hand in his mouth, but I didn't look up, as the warmth of his orgasm filled my mouth. I took it all, swallowing then swallowing again, gladly accepting his body into mine. I drew back slowly, letting the last of his seed spill across my tongue. When he finally slipped from between my lips, I'd made a solemn promise to do that as often as possible.

He was breathing hard as he looked at me, his eyes so black I couldn't see the difference between his pupil and iris. He reached forward and pulled me to him, crushing his mouth against mine, his tongue plundering my mouth and I knew he could taste himself there. When he broke the kiss, I expected us to be done and told the ache between my legs to wait. Instead, he pulled on my arms until I stood and then pushed up the bottom of my dress, exposing the tiny thong I wore. He pulled it aside and buried his tongue inside me. I swore softly, rocking my hips against his face as he licked me, every pass of his tongue sending me higher and higher until I danced along the edge of pleasure. He flicked his tongue across the top of my clit and I came, clutching his shoulders and pushing myself against his talented mouth. He stayed there as I rode out my orgasm, moving back only when my body stopped convulsing.

"Beautiful," he whispered, pressing his lips against my hip.

I looked down at him, running my fingers along his cheek and down to his lips. It wasn't until he sat back and started to pull me with him that I realized he was hard again. My pussy tightened as I realized there was more to come.

I settled on his lap, holding myself just above his thick shaft until our arms were wrapped around each other, our faces barely an inch apart, and then I sank down slowly, letting myself enjoy the stretch and burn of him entering me. Skin slid against skin as my body welcomed him and my muscles began to tremble with the strain of taking him all in. When we started to move together, everything else disappeared. There was no wedding, no crying bride. No fatigue or jet-lag. We had all the time in the world and there was no one else who existed. How long we made love there, I didn't know, only that I never wanted it to end. It was perfect, and as we came together, his cock pulsing as it emptied into me, I'd never felt more complete.

I heard a gasp and raised my head. Pale blue eyes accused me and I didn't know if they were Brock's or his sister's, only that we'd been caught...

My head jerked up, almost colliding with the face of the smiling flight attendant who'd woken me.

"We're about to land in Philadelphia, Miss." She didn't seem at all perturbed by my sudden and almost violent waking. "You need to put your seatbelt on."

I let out a shaky breath as I buckled myself in. The remnants of my dream clung to me and I couldn't brush them off. It was far from the first sex dream I'd ever had, and not even the first one to star Reed. I'd had those before we'd slept together. But, there was something about it that disturbed me more than I'd imagined possible.

I told myself it was because I'd had it in public and I glanced around, hoping I hadn't moaned – or worse, actually climaxed. My panties were wet and sticky, but I was sincerely hoping it was just arousal. As embarrassing as it was, I knew it wasn't the reason this dream was bothering me.

The logical reasoning was because it had happened at the wedding. My subconscious made me do something to some poor girl that no woman should ever have done to her. I'd made her get left at the altar and then I'd fucked the man she was supposed to marry. Surely it made me a horrible, awful person.

That wasn't why I felt guilty though. I'd had dreams where I'd killed people, dreams where I'd stolen things, and I'd never felt guilty or disturbed. I'd also had dreams where I was flying and one particularly strange one where I'd been an ice cream sundae being chased by a giant banana. Okay, that one had some serious Freudian leanings, but for the most part, I knew that dreams were dreams. I never felt responsible for what happened in them. So what made this one different?

As the captain announced our descent, it hit me.

The knot in my stomach, the guilt that was almost choking me, I was feeling all of it because, despite everything Reed had done, deep down I wanted him to choose me.

Chapter 3

The hotel room Brock had rented for me for the weekend was amazing. It wasn't the most expensive room the Hilton had to offer, but it was still the nicest one I'd ever stayed in. I didn't count passing out in Reed's suite.

The car he'd sent to pick me up had also been nice. The only thing that had bothered me was the driver's face was completely expressionless as he'd opened the door for me, and he hadn't said a word the entire drive to the hotel. I'd never been driven around like this before, so I hadn't known if this was professional or if the driver was just so used to escorting various women around for Brock that he didn't find the need to interact.

I'd told myself it didn't matter if Brock flew hundreds of girls in for various events. This was only a sort-of-date. He was apologizing for his behavior and giving himself a companion for the wedding at the same time. It wasn't like I expected anything of him. He wasn't my boyfriend and neither one of us was saying anything about a commitment of any kind. I had no reason nor right to be jealous.

When I'd arrived at the hotel, I'd been immediately escorted to my room, informed to call if I needed anything, no matter how small, and then left to explore the room that was almost as big as my apartment in Vegas. It was technically just one room and a bathroom, but the main room had a love-seat, table and two chairs, microwave and mini-fridge as well as the usual bedroom furniture. I could essentially live here and not need anymore space.

I put my bag down on the queen-sized bed and started to unpack, then noticed an envelope on the pillow, which my name written across the front. Curious, I opened it and found a card. Not like a greeting card but a plastic rectangle. A gift card. Also in the envelope was a note.

I recognized Brock's handwriting right away.

"Piper, I'm so pleased you agreed to join me. I hope you enjoy your room. I wasn't sure if you had something to wear to the wedding tomorrow, and since I'm busy at the rehearsal tonight, I thought you might like to have some fun. Use the card to get yourself something to eat as well as something to wear for tomorrow. I'll be at the hotel to pick you up at ten. Brock." At the bottom was scrawled something else. "P.S. I think you'd look hot in purple."

At least I knew what color dress he wanted me to buy. Purple was one of those colors that would look either really good or really bad on me, depending on the shade. With this card and all of downtown Philadelphia at my feet, I was sure I could find something.

When I went on my little shopping trip, it was all I could do to keep from humming Roy Orbison as I walked.

Granted, I wasn't a hooker and I was definitely wearing appropriate, though inexpensive clothes, but the looks some of the saleswomen gave me said they weren't entirely sure why I was checking out pricey dresses in their stores.

After I found the one I wanted – on sale no less – I treated myself to a matching panty and bra set as well as shoes. By the time I returned to my room, I was exhausted, but happy and feeling more confident about tomorrow. The only bit of anxiety I was experiencing at the moment was concerning what would happen when I finally fell asleep. I didn't want a repeat of what had happened on the plane.

Fortunately, my sleep was dreamless and when I woke the next morning, I felt better than I had in a long time. I took my time getting ready, enjoying a shower that didn't have squeaky pipes or hot water that ran cold when the neighbor downstairs washed dishes.

By the time the knock came at my door, I was ready. Still, I gave myself a last look in the mirror. I needed to look perfect today.

I'd found the right shade of purple that complimented both my eyes and my hair, and best of all, it had been in a dress that showed off my body. Low cut, but far from trashy, and short enough to be stylish without being scandalous. I'd stayed away from the ones with the low backs. They'd made me think too much of my dream and the feeling of Reed's hand on my bare back. I kept my make-up and jewelry simple, understated. If I hadn't known anything about me, I'd never have guessed I didn't belong with rich, upper-class people.

When I opened the door, Brock let out a low whistle. "Wow, you look amazing."

"Not so bad yourself," I replied truthfully. When I'd first met him, I'd known he was good-looking, but I hadn't really let myself register anything specific since I'd been so hung up on Reed. Now, in his tux, I could fully appreciate just how hot my date was.

He was shorter than Reed, just under six feet, but his shoulders were broader, his chest more muscular. His features were more masculine and there was nothing soft about his mouth or eyes. He looked like the kind of guy who'd kiss you because he knew you wanted it, even if you never said a word.

Brock held out his hand and I took it, letting him lead me to the elevators. We made small talk on the way down and out to where a limo was waiting. For a moment, I nearly panicked, was terrified the entire wedding party was in there and I'd be stuck in a limo with Reed and a bunch of his friends for a very uncomfortable ride to the church. I nearly trembled with relief when Brock opened the door and I saw it was empty.

"It's technically for my family," he explained as he followed me into the back. "But I kind of borrowed it to come get you." He flashed me what I could only describe as a bad-boy grin. "I wanted to impress you."

"Because a plane ticket, hotel room and dress wasn't enough to do that?" I teased. I didn't mention the other money. I'd let him approach it. I'd already gotten a gorgeous outfit out of the trip. I wasn't going to force my hand, especially if there were strings attached.

"So it worked?" He grinned at me.

"I suppose so." I returned his smile.

"When we get there, I have to go make sure everything's cool with Reed," Brock said. He reached over and took my hand again. "Best man duties and all, but I'll make sure the ushers keep an eye on you."

I raised my eyebrows.

"They're my thirteen year-old cousins." He squeezed my hand. "I'll have them put you just behind my family." He paused, and then added, "I'll introduce you before I go, but I didn't think you'd want to sit with them."

I shook my head. He was right.

"Meeting the family on a first date is intimidating. I figured sitting with them at the wedding would be a bit much." He raised our hands and pressed his lips against the back of mine. "Just so you know, I told them I was bringing someone I'd met on a trip, but I was vague. I thought it might be awkward if I said you were one of the strippers we'd hired for the bachelor party. You know, with Reed being part of the family after today and all."

"Good call." At least I didn't have to worry about my occupation becoming known. My previous connection to the Stirling family, however, might become a topic of conversation if Rebecca decided to run her mouth. I could only hope she'd decide the wedding was too interesting to mess with me. If she did, I'd cross that bridge when I came to it. Right now, I was thinking about how Brock had said this was a first date. That implied there would be more, and I wasn't sure how I felt about that.

The church wasn't the one from my dream, but it was huge and old and very ornamental. I remembered seeing it the times I'd come into the city before I'd moved. I'd never been inside though. The architecture was just as beautiful in as it was out and I felt a twinge of envy for anyone who was able to get married in a place like this.

Brock led me over to an older couple standing by the guest book. The woman was tiny, but formidable looking. She had pale blue eyes like Brock, but the resemblance stopped there. Brock was almost identical to his father. I was willing to bet a picture of Mr. Michaels in his twenties would've been identical, save the eyes.

"Mom, Dad, this is Piper."

I held out my hand to Mrs. Michaels first, a polite smile on my face. "It's nice to meet you."

She looked down her nose at my hand, pursed her lips and then shook it. Mr. Michaels didn't do any of the theatrics but I could sense his reluctance as well. Neither one of them looked pleased to see me.

"This is a beautiful church." I kept my voice pleasant, not letting them see that I knew they didn't like me.

"Yes, well, our family was one of its founding members," Mrs. Michaels said, her tone clearly indicating I couldn't possibly understand the importance of that fact.

"So, I have to go check in with Reed." Brock sounded a bit uncomfortable, but he didn't say anything directly to his mother.

I didn't mind. If we'd been dating for real, or this was heading into a relationship, I might've wanted him to stand up for me, but I could take a few snide comments. I was used to them.

Brock led me over to a pair of identical blond boys who had the gangly look of teens who'd hit a growth spurt and the rest of them hadn't caught up yet. "Piper, this is Jason and Jackson. I told them to keep an eye on you." He winked at them. "Make sure no one hits on my girl."

I laughed and hoped he meant that as lightly as it sounded. With a final squeeze to my hand, he left me with the twins and headed off. They took me into the sanctuary and, for a moment, I was confused as to why they sat me on the bride's side, but then remembered I was here as Brock's date, in spite of the fact I knew Reed. The place was only about half full, so I took advantage of the time I had before the ceremony started and looked around.

I felt a surge of relief when I saw the colors were a dusky rose color and gold, different than my dream. I was admiring the floral arrangements when I heard a sharp intake of breath.

I looked up and saw Reed staring right at me. His face was pale and he almost looked like he was going to throw up.

"Piper?" he said it so softly that I almost couldn't hear.

"Oh, hey man." Brock appeared behind him and clapped a hand on Reed's shoulder. "I forgot to tell you that I asked one of the girls from Vegas to be my date." He walked over to me and brushed the back of his hand against the side of my neck. "But don't worry, I didn't tell anyone how we met."

The anger I'd felt at Reed before came back, tightening my stomach. I reached up and took Brock's hand, pressing it against my cheek. Reed blanched and his lips flattened into a line.

"I'm looking forward to meeting Britni," I said evenly. I kept my eyes on Reed's face. "You don't need to worry though. I'll keep your little secret."

"Gotta go," Brock said. He bent down and brushed his lips against my cheek. A muscle in Reed's jaw jumped. "We just came out to see if Danny was out here. I'll see you after the ceremony."

"I'll be here."

Reed held my gaze for a few seconds longer and I saw dozens of emotions flicker across his eyes, but then he broke away without a word, going to do whatever it was he

111

had to do. That was fine with me. I'd at least gotten a reaction out of him.

When he came back out at the start of the ceremony, he didn't look my way. Brock, however, did and the smile he was wearing made me smile too. If he hadn't kept glancing at me, I would've just thought he was happy his sister was getting married, but his eyes clearly said I was some of the reason too.

The bridal march started and my chest tightened, the memory of my dream flooding over me. I swallowed hard as I joined the rest of the congregation in standing. This time when I turned, however, I could see Reed's wife-to-be for the first time. She was about my height, but slender. Her hair was the color of coffee and, unless she had extensions, long. Her eyes were light, like her brother's, though they appeared to be more gray than his. Her features were her mother's, delicate and fine. She was a beautiful young woman and I felt a pang as I thought about how she and Reed would look together.

I turned as she reached the front and couldn't stop my gaze from sliding over, wanting to see the expression on Reed's face when he looked at the woman he was marrying. Except he wasn't looking at her. He was facing her, but his line of sight was just to one side and his eyes met mine. I flushed and tore my gaze away.

What kind of bastard would stare at another woman while his fiancée was walking down the aisle? I tried very hard not to scowl. That would be rude.

For the rest of the ceremony, I kept my eyes glued on the priest and a fake smile pasted to my face. Once it was done, I could relax.

Chapter 4

One of my favorite places in Philadelphia was The Free Library. At least every two weeks or so, I'd walk or take the train or bus when we had a little extra money, and I'd always come home with a dozen books or more. Then, when my mom had gotten sick, it had become a haven, a place I went to when I couldn't take another minute at the hospital.

When I stepped into the lobby, those memories washed over me, and with them also came the sense of awe I'd always felt when I looked up at the high ceiling, the beautiful architecture. And then there was the smell of books. It didn't matter if it was a single ratty paperback or a massive collection, there was something about the scent of a book that felt like home.

I was thinking all of this while the bridal party was posing on the marble steps that led up to the second floor. Brock had insisted I come with him even though it meant standing off to the side and trying not to look anything other than happy for the bride and groom. That was difficult when I knew the truth behind the vows they'd recited. I might not believe a word Reed said about how he felt about me, but I didn't think he was lying when he'd said he didn't love Britni. Guys who cheat don't really love the person they cheat on, no matter how many times they say they do. I might've been his choice, but I had no doubt he would've found someone else to fuck if I hadn't been there.

"Bored?" Brock came up behind me and put his arms around me.

I almost stepped away, but then I saw Reed glance at us and that hurt part of me urged me to take a step back and lean into the embrace. Brock wasn't touching anything he shouldn't have been and it was nice to feel someone's arms around me and know I didn't have to worry about meeting his fiancée – or wife – later.

"Are you okay?" Brock's voice was low in my ear.

I nodded. "Just a bit of jet lag."

"Did you know there's a map upstairs that shows how you can get around downtown Philly underground?"

I nodded without even thinking about it. "Yeah, it's up by the History section."

As soon as I said it, I realized what I'd given away.

"You've been here before," Brock said. There wasn't any accusation to his tone, but I wasn't going to risk him thinking I was hiding something.

"I grew up here." I kept it vague.

He let go of me and stepped around so he could look down at me. "Seriously?"

"Quick version: grew up on the poor side of the city. Scholarship to St. George. Moved to Vegas instead of going to college. You know how it goes from there." I knew I had to throw in the school thing because if he told anyone I grew up here, there'd be awkward questions and it'd look like I'd been hiding my prior connection to the Stirlings.

"So you knew Reed before." He made it a statement.

"He was three grades ahead of me, but I knew who he was." I glanced at the bridesmaids.

"Oh."

I could hear the understanding in a single word.

"You were in Rebecca's class." He reached down and took my head. "Enough said. She's hot, but she's a bitch."

I would've laughed if his statement hadn't reminded me of Reed saying close to the same thing. Dammit, why didn't everything seem to point back to him?

The photographer called for the men and Brock hurried away, leaving me alone with my thoughts, which wasn't much of a comfort. The women came down the steps, huddling together as they went. Even though none of them looked my way, I knew they realized I was there. How I knew was simple. They were talking about me in a way that made it very clear I was meant to hear their conversation.

"I honestly don't know why I expected anything else from Brock. I mean, I know he doesn't do the whole relationship thing, but hiring an escort to be his date to my wedding is just tacky."

Any prior sympathy I'd had for Britni Michaels-Stirling vanished as I heard her speak. Then came Rebecca.

"It's no surprise that's what Piper does. I mean, coming from her background, it was almost inevitable."

I took a few steps to the side so I couldn't hear them anymore, but I didn't say a word. I wasn't going to let the opinions of some high society snobs bother me. I knew who I was, and I knew there was a line I didn't cross. I didn't intend to have sex with Brock. I was his date for the wedding, nothing else. Besides, it wasn't the first comment I'd overheard today regarding my character. Mrs. Michaels hadn't even tried to lower her voice when she'd told Mrs. Stirling that at least Reed didn't have to worry about gold diggers anymore and how happy she'd be when Brock finally settled down with a decent girl. I'd ignored her too. I'd had practice. Didn't mean I enjoyed it, but I was a long way from walking out.

Before my 'fans' could make any more disparaging comments, the photographer called the entire wedding party up for the next few shots and by the time he was done, it was time to head to the reception and Brock was coming my way. He'd already told me he'd insisted we take the limo with his parents so I didn't have to be alone since I was from out of town. I'd hoped that when he found out I knew the Stirlings he hadn't assumed I'd be fine on my own. He hadn't and the two of us settled in for a short, but still uncomfortable, ride to the reception hall.

The beginning of the reception passed rather quickly, which surprised me since I was sitting at a table with people I didn't know. They were all older couples, which made me stand out, but since none of them knew me and obviously hadn't heard the gossip, I didn't mind. As soon as all the main event things, like the first dance and the cake cutting was done, Brock came down and claimed the empty seat next to me.

"Would you like some champagne?" he asked.

"Yes." I'd already finished two glasses, but wasn't feeling much beyond a little buzz. I watched him walk away and thought about how attentive he'd been tonight. He was really taking this whole idea of showing me that he wasn't a drunken douchebag seriously.

A ruggedly handsome and, judging by the smell of him, extremely inebriated man plopped down in the seat next to me. He gave me a roguish grin.

"Hi there."

"Hello." I'd seen this guy with his hands all over one of Britni's bridesmaids, some tiny little brunette with fake nails and awful pink lipstick.

"I'm Peter."

I wanted to say 'good for you' but I behaved myself and gave him a polite smile.

"So, I was just wondering." He leaned toward me. "How much would it be to hire you for next weekend? None of this going out shit. Just you, me, some condoms and a video camera." He winked. "And I'd be willing to pay extra to forget the condoms."

Every part of me tensed for several seconds as I decided between several possible actions.

Take the nearest glass and dump whatever liquid was in it over Peter's head.

Slap him.

Reach down between his legs, grab his balls and twist.

That last one had definite appeal, but I didn't do any of them. Instead, I stood and walked toward the bar where Brock was getting me a drink. I wanted something stronger than champagne.

Less than forty minutes later, Brock and I were dancing at the edge of the dance floor and I was more than a little tipsy. I wasn't quite to the point of drunk where I couldn't make my own decisions, but I was past the point where it would've been safe for me to drive.

I didn't usually drink very much, mostly because I didn't like not being in control, but Peter propositioning me had been the last straw. After I'd downed Brock's drink – I wasn't entirely sure what it'd been – I caught Reed staring at me while he was dancing with Britni, and I asked for another shot. When Brock had suggested we dance, I immediately agreed.

He was good, and it had felt nice to dance with someone who was looking at me, rather than having someone look at me while he was with someone else. I was ready to cut loose a bit and have some fun. After all, Brock hadn't asked me to come with him just because he thought I was cute.

As we danced, we moved closer and closer, going from the getting-to-know-you inches between us to grinding against each other in an almost-obscene way. I started doing it because Reed watching me was pissing me off, but as the alcohol started to work its way into my system, I started enjoying it for different reasons. Brock's body felt good against mine and I could tell he was enjoying himself. He wasn't being pushy or acting like I owed him anything, which I liked. He smelled good, which was always a plus. But, most of all, I wanted someone to erase the memory of fucking Reed and Brock seemed up to the challenge.

Two more shots later and I knew what I wanted. There was just one thing I had to know. I pressed my mouth against Brock's ear and whispered, "Do you have a condom?" I was drunk, not stupid.

His eyes darkened and he nodded. I grinned, grabbed his hand and dragged him away from the reception hall. My first thought was the bathroom, but even my hazy mind knew it was probably a bad idea since there were kids at the reception. Instead, I went down a short hallway, looking for somewhere we could get a few undisturbed minutes. We passed two doors and then I saw the one that said Maintenance Only. Oh yes, this will work.

I pushed the door open and pulled Brock after me. I didn't want fake and romantic. I wanted fast and dirty, even if I didn't come. I wanted an experience that was the very opposite of my time with Reed, I wanted his memory released from my body and my mind.

Either Brock understood what I needed or he was as turned on and eager as me. I didn't know, didn't care. Before the door even closed behind us, he was pulling me into his arms, crushing his mouth to mine.

His kiss was hard and rough, so different than Reed's, which was exactly what I was looking for. I pushed my tongue into his mouth and he did the same to me. We bit and nipped at each other's lips as he pushed me back against the door. His hand squeezed my breast through my dress and it was almost too rough, but I moaned as the pleasure and pain combined. I slid my hand between us, down to the front of his pants and cupped the hardness there. He growled and spun me around, I put out my hands, catching myself before my face hit the door.

I heard a zipper, then the tearing of a packet. A moment later, I felt cool air on my ass as he pushed up my dress. Then my panties were coming down. He left them at my knees and I felt his cock nudging against me. I arched my back and spread my legs as much as I could with my underwear still around my ankles. It was enough.

"Fuck." I groaned as he pushed inside. He wasn't quite as big as Reed, but I hadn't been prepped at all and the intrusion was painful. It was a good kind of pain though, the kind that promised to wipe out the memories I didn't want, the kind that would leave my pussy sore. I knew the only sex I'd be thinking about would be this.

Brock grunted as he pounded into me, and just when I'd begun to think he was completely oblivious to my own needs, his hand moved around in front of me and his fingers dipped between my legs. There was no gentleness to his touch as he rubbed my clit. In fact, I cried out at the first pass, my muscles tensing up, but then my body began to respond and I let it happen.

When I felt him start to lose his rhythm and I wasn't quite there yet, I slid one hand under my dress and pushed aside my bra enough to get my fingers on my nipple. I closed my eyes and rolled the hard flesh between my fingers, sending shivers of pleasure through me to join with the sensations already there.

"Shit!" Brock called out as he slammed into me hard once, then twice and I knew he was coming. He pressed against my clit and I gave my nipple a twist, sending me over the edge.

I didn't make a sound as I shuddered, letting my climax wash over me, sobering me to an extent. Brock pulled out and I heard the familiar sound of a condom coming off. I didn't want to know where he was going to dispose of it. I pushed myself off the door and then bent to pull up my panties. I grimaced at how wet they were as they slid back into place, but at least some of the tension inside me was gone. That had been exactly what I needed.

I kept telling myself that until I almost believed it.

Chapter 5

Brock wanted to go on a date. An honest-to-goodness date. I had to admit, I'd been surprised when he dropped me off at the hotel and said he wanted to see me the next day. I thought for sure he'd invite himself up to get laid again, but he only asked if he could take me out, then gave me a practically chaste kiss and said he'd be by at noon.

I showered and fell asleep almost the moment my head hit the pillow. A queasy stomach and blinding headache had been my wake-up call this morning, but some water, ibuprofen and toast had taken the edge off. By the time Brock knocked on the door, I was dressed and ready to go. My flight was scheduled to leave tomorrow morning, so spending the day with Brock seemed like the perfect way to pass the rest of my time in the city.

"What's the plan?" I asked as I stepped out into the hallway.

"First, a picnic lunch." He held up a basket.

I gave him a dubious look and he laughed, his eyes sparkling.

"Don't worry, I figured you might need something gentle after last night."

Suddenly, I wasn't so sure his words were referring to my hangover. I was a bit sore from last night's encounter, but I didn't regret it.

He stopped in the middle of the hallway and faced me, his expression serious. "I really wish our first time together hadn't been like that. I mean, it was amazing, but I wish it would've been special."

He was getting way too serious. I liked him, but I didn't want him getting all mushy on me. "You mean doing it in a janitor's closet during your sister's wedding reception wasn't special?" I quipped.

A grin broke across his face and I could see a bit of relief in his smile. I wondered if he thought I was going to make things out to be more than they were. He didn't need to worry about that. I chastised myself, remembering how I had said the same about Reed, that I wouldn't have expectations of him either. But that was different because I had known him for so long, I really did think he'd be different. With Brock, I wasn't going to think of the future and since we didn't really have a past, I could stay comfortably in the present.

"Where are we going for our picnic?" I asked.

"To one of my favorite places," he said. The look he gave me was almost shy.

We walked without talking, letting the sounds of the city be the only noise between us. I'd always considered myself a city girl, but there were cities and then there were cities; I hadn't realized how different Philadelphia was than other places until I'd moved away.

When Brock turned, I realized where we were going and smiled. Aside from the library, one of my favorite places to go as a kid had been here. Love Park with its sculpture and fountain was one of the city's favorite romantic spots. Not that I'd come here on dates much. Luc had brought me once, but most of the time I'd come by myself with one of my books and read.

"When Britni and I were kids, our nanny used to bring us here so she could meet her boyfriend," Brock said. "My parents wouldn't let him in the house, so she'd arrange to meet him here. Britni hated it. She didn't like being outside and she used to complain all the time."

That didn't exactly surprise me, but I didn't say it. I didn't want to talk bad about his sister. I had no idea what their relationship was like and, despite what I'd heard, I didn't know what kind of person she was. For all I knew, Rebecca had been the one to tell Britni I was a hooker and I could see someone being upset at their brother bringing a call girl to their wedding.

It was amazing how much perspective one could get after twenty-four hours and a good fuck.

I turned my attention back to Brock.

"On the really hot days, I used to take my shoes off and go wading in the water to cool off."

"Me too," I put in.

He gave me his boyish smile again. "Those are some of my favorite memories from being a kid."

I reached over and threaded my fingers through his. "Mine too."

We picked a spot under a couple trees and Brock spread a table cloth on the grass. I sat down and watched as he opened the basket.

"I moved out last year," he said. "And I'm still getting used to the whole shopping and making my own food thing, so you can't laugh at anything I brought."

I agreed, amused, but not for the reason he probably would've thought. I'd never considered how some things I took for granted as being common sense were only that way because I'd had to do them myself. It never occurred to me that a kid raised with servants doing the shopping and the food preparation wouldn't know how to do either on their own.

He actually managed a decent selection, including some mild cheese, crackers and fruit. He'd also brought plain bottled water instead of trying for something fancy. I appreciated his thoughtfulness. I'd never cared for carbonated water and I didn't think alcohol of any kind was a good idea at the moment. I told him how well he'd done and he beamed at me, as happy as a little boy being praised for being good. Warmth spread through me; I liked that a simple, honest compliment could make him so happy.

We kept the conversation light as we ate and I found myself feeling better than I'd felt since Reed and I had slept together. I was surprised to realize, as we joked about skinny-dipping in the fountain, how much I was enjoying my time with Brock. It wasn't about Reed anymore and paying him back for how he'd treated me, and it wasn't about letting Brock apologize for the bachelor party. This was about two people enjoying each other's company.

"When I asked you here and then said I wanted to take you out, this probably wasn't what you'd had in mind, was it?" he asked as he began to pack up the leftovers.

"No, it wasn't," I answered honestly.

Brock frowned and he looked down. I put my hand on his wrist, immediately understanding how he'd taken my statement.

"It was better."

He looked up, eyes narrowed suspiciously. "You're really saying you aren't disappointed that I took you here with a picnic lunch instead of to some fancy restaurant?"

"Are you kidding?" I leaned closer to him, enjoying the spicy smell of his aftershave. It was different than Reed's, sharper, and I liked it. "That's the sweetest thing anyone's ever done for me."

His face lit up. "Really?"

"Really," I confirmed. "And, besides, why would I want to go to some fancy restaurant where it's obvious I don't belong." I immediately regretted the words as soon as they came out. That wasn't the kind of thing anyone should say at the beginning of any relationship, even one that wasn't going to go very far.

I saw something pass over his face and wondered if he'd ask what I meant, try to pretend he understood or, worse, tell me I was being silly. Instead, he stood and stretched out his hand. I took it and he helped me to my feet. When I was standing, however, he didn't let go, sliding our hands around until our fingers were laced together. I wasn't quite sure how I felt about that, but I didn't pull away. I did like the way his hand felt against mine, the strength in those fingers.

"Come on," he said. "I want to show you something."

We walked in silence and I let myself enjoy being back in the city. It was funny, considering the size of Philly, how much quieter it was than Vegas. Back there, it was always loud with slot machines, entertainers and street performers all night long. People yelling out, trying to draw crowds into the shows. Streetwalkers calling out for dates. There was always noise, no matter the hour or day. In Vegas, there was no difference between Thanksgiving and every other Thursday. Sure, some of the places might close for the day, but never enough to lower the roar to any significant degree.

While Philadelphia had the unavoidable sounds that came with so many people living in one area, it somehow managed to still be quieter than other large cities. Even though there were bad memories here, I had to admit I'd always loved this city. I swallowed a sigh. I wondered if I'd ever get that way with Las Vegas or if I'd always feel like a transplant who didn't belong.

"Here we are," Brock announced.

I looked up. The apartment building was huge, and one of the most expensive ones in the city. I didn't need Brock to confirm he'd brought me to his place and I sincerely hoped this didn't mean he was about to tell me what I had to do to earn the promised ten thousand dollars. Sure, I'd had sex with him once, but the minute he put a price on it, things would change.

"Would you like to see my apartment?"

If he'd tried to be seductive about it, I probably would've turned him down, but he sounded almost shy when he asked, as if he wasn't sure I'd want to go. I was starting to see that his confident swagger was, at least in part, show. I liked strong men, but there was something to be said for a bit of vulnerability as well.

"I'd like that."

He slid his arm around my waist and we headed for the front doors. The doorman gave us a nod and a smile. As we passed, I wondered how many other girls Brock had brought here the same way. I'd wondered the same thing before, how many girls Brock had given this special treatment to, but now it was different. When I'd thought this before, I'd been here as his date for a wedding and that was it. Everything had changed when we'd fucked. It hadn't put us in a relationship, but it had changed the dynamic.

When we got on the elevator, I completely expected him to try something, even if it was just copping a feel, but he remained a complete gentleman. The arm around my waist didn't stray north or south and he didn't try to kiss me. We rode up in silence, me watching the numbers tick past and him casually slouching next to me.

"Penthouse?" I asked as we neared the top.

"Not quite," he said. The elevator came to a stop three floors from the top. "It's about half the size, but still more than enough room for me."

I followed him out of the elevator and to the door on the right of the hall. The one on the left I assumed belonged to the person who had the other half of the floor. When he opened the door, he stepped back and let me walk in first.

Well, shit.

Brock's apartment was bigger than the entire strip club where I worked. It was open and airy, with the kitchen, dining room and living room separated only by the furniture. A pair of French doors led to a balcony and a hallway to my right led, I assumed, to at least two rooms and a bathroom, maybe more.

"You want something to drink?" Brock asked. I raised my eyebrows and he clarified. "I have soda, juice, and more water."

"Juice would be good." I followed after him into the kitchen and took the bottle of mixed fruit juice he offered. I took a sip and waited for him to offer to show me his bedroom. Instead, he surprised me.

"There's a soccer game on I wanted to watch. Do you mind?"

"Soccer, really?"

"I kinda have a bet going about it." He grinned at me as he took a fruit juice. "But if you don't want to, that's fine."

"No, soccer's okay."

We settled on his couch, both in the center and close enough that our bodies were touching, but he didn't try anything. In fact, we sat through the first ten minutes of the game without talking. I had to admit that these silences were surprising me. I'd gotten the impression that Brock was the kind of guy who always had to be talking, usually about himself, but he'd proven me wrong on more than one occasion today.

I looked around the apartment, seeing what I hadn't seen on first glance. There were a lot of electronics, which wasn't surprising. Video games, computers, sound systems, all of that, but there weren't any of the usual things I'd expected from a place an interior designer had decorated. It was a typical guy's bachelor pad, without any of the snooty art a lot of rich kids would've bought just to be pretentious.

"Hey, um, so I talked to Peter this morning." Brock broke the silence. "He told me what he said to you. I put him straight. Told him you weren't an escort and if he acted that way around you again I'd knock him out."

It took me a moment to remember who and what Brock was talking about, but when it came back, I stared at him. Had he seriously offered to punch someone because of something that had been said to me?

Impulsively, I leaned over and kissed him. It was barely a peck, mouth brushing against mouth, but it sent a little jolt through me, reminding me of what it had felt like when we'd kissed the night before.

His eyes darkened to the color of faded denim as he set our drinks aside. As he leaned toward me, I knew he wasn't interested in the soccer game anymore. When he took my face between his hands, all I could think about was the heat from his palms against my skin.

His lips were gentle this time and they moved with mine, slow and easy. It wasn't until I slid my hand up his arm and across to his chest that I realized he was letting me set the pace. I slid my tongue into his mouth, twisting around his and drawing it back into my mouth. I sucked on it and he made a sound in the back of his throat. Apparently that was a signal he'd been waiting for because he pressed me back on the couch, bringing our legs up to twine together as we stretched out on the leather softness.

In the background, I could hear the soccer announcers, but they were fading, lost behind the sounds of Brock moaning into my mouth. I slid my hands under the back of his shirt, enjoying the feel of his muscles bunching as his own hands explored.

I'd worn jeans purposefully so I'd at least have to be a bit more conscious about them coming off, but that didn't stop Brock's hands from cupping my ass and squeezing. I arched against him and he groaned as I pressed against the erection I could feel growing there. One of his hands found its way under my shirt and brushed against the side of my breast. I hooked my leg around his waist, reminding myself that whatever happened it was because I wanted it, not because of any money he'd promised.

Then, suddenly, he was pulling away. His face was flushed, his breathing heavy, but he didn't look upset or concerned. He just pulled me up with him, tucked me against his side and went back to watching the soccer game.

"When does your flight leave?" he asked the question casually, like he hadn't just been groping me a couple minutes ago.

"Tomorrow."

He was silent for a moment and then asked, "I was wondering if maybe you'd like to stay a bit longer."

"Stay?" I pushed myself up so that I wasn't leaning on him anymore.

"In Philadelphia." He looked over and smiled at me. "I'd like us to spend some more time together."

It was on the tip of my tongue to refuse, to tell him I had to get back to Vegas and I couldn't afford to stay, but I didn't. The idea of staying in Philadelphia for a little while longer was actually appealing, which surprised me. I supposed I had Brock to thank for that.

"I'll pay for the hotel room, of course, as well as anything else you need." He reached over and took my hand. "I understand if you're not comfortable with it, but I'd really like you to stay."

"I'll have to see if I can get my roommate to cover my shifts," I heard myself saying. I was rewarded with a wide and beautiful smile.

Chapter 6

Rosa was actually glad to take my shifts, saying that her mother needed to have some tests done and any extra money she could make would be very helpful. She also warned me to not take off too much or else they'd find another girl to replace me. I wasn't sure what that said about the state of the economy if a place like The Diamond Club could so easily replace a stripper.

The second call I made that night when I returned to the hotel was to Anastascia. She was ecstatic, at first, to hear I was back, but when I told her why, her tone changed completely.

"Piper, that boy is a womanizing creep who's got more pussy than a cat shelter."

I would've laughed if her words hadn't held an edge of condescension. "He's not like that, Anastascia," I protested.

"Oh, no? Then why is it every time I've seen him, he has a different woman hanging on his arm? He didn't go to St. George with us, but our families move in the same circles. And, trust me, in our circle, Brock Michaels has a reputation for fucking and dumping."

My jaw tightened. "Just because we don't move in the same circles doesn't mean I'm an idiot."

"That's not what I meant."

"Whatever, Ana," I snapped. "I called because I wanted to let you know I was in the city for the week and see if you wanted to get together, but if you're just going to act like you know better, then it's probably not a good idea."

I hung up the phone before she could say anything else. My stomach hurt. I hated fighting with her, rare as it was. This time, though, it was more than just the argument. It was the fact that, for the first time in our friendship, she'd acted like there really was a difference between us because of money.

Her comments stuck in my head as I showered and curled up into bed. It took a long time for me to get to sleep. I kept remembering sex with Brock, and then how different it had been to make out with him. The feel of his hands on my body. And then I'd hear Anastascia telling me that he did this to a lot of women and how he was known in 'her circle.' By the time sleep finally claimed me, it was well past one in the morning.

I slept late, not waking until almost noon, and finally felt the last of the jet-lag slip away. Brock had already told me he had something to do during the day, but that we were going to go out tonight. I decided to take advantage of the lavish hotel and dug my bathing suit out of my bag. It was older than I would've liked, but I looked good in it and it still wore well.

I headed down to the pool and spent the next few hours doing laps, losing myself in the cool water and the rhythm of swimming. I'd always been a dancer, but swimming had been my second favorite way to stay in shape. I didn't get much of that in Vegas. There were plenty of hotels with pools, of course, but shabby apartment buildings like mine were lucky if the air worked.

By the time I went back to my room, I was hungry. Ordering room service, then lounging around until it was time for Brock to pick me up sounded like a perfect afternoon.

He said we were going to a club, but hadn't mentioned if it was one of the elite ones with a dress code. Since I didn't really have a lot of options, I went with what I'd worn to my audition at The Twilight Room. A short black miniskirt almost too short to be decent and a halter top that showed off my cleavage. With a pair of heels and the right make-up, it rode the line between hot and slutty. It was funny, I thought as I put the last dab of lip-gloss on, how much of my wardrobe rested on a fine line between something appropriate and something scandalous.

Brock grinned when I opened the door. "Damn, you look good."

"Right back at you."

He was wearing a pair of tight jeans that hugged his ass and drew attention to the bulge in the front, and his short-sleeved shirt made his eyes stand out, not to mention the way it showed off his muscular torso. I had no doubt that wherever we were going, he'd be getting quite a bit of female attention.

Anastascia's words came back and I frowned.

"You okay?" he asked.

I nodded. "Yeah, let's go."

The club was close enough for us to walk, though I suspected we'd take a cab back later tonight. It was closing in on nine o'clock so the street traffic was switching from the work force to those heading out for fun. We followed others in our age bracket, all dressed for various forms of entertainment, and soon turned down a street I recognized. A couple streets down, I saw a rainbow-flag and knew where we were going. It was the last straight club before we hit the section of town where all the clubs and bars were gay. Anastascia and I had come down here a couple times growing up.

"Here we are," Brock said, leading me down some steps and through a set of glass doors.

Pulse-pounding music greeted us as we went through another set of doors, these designed to keep the noise inside. The place was dark, lit only by the brightly colored lights that moved in time with the music.

"Do you want a drink?" Brock leaned close to shout the question in my ear.

I nodded. "Nothing too hard," I shouted back. I didn't want a repeat of the wedding reception. Well, at least not a repeat of the hangover part of it. I wasn't sure I'd mind a repeat of the sex.

We finished our drinks as we observed the scene, deciding where we wanted to go. I hadn't been big into the club scene, but two years working at a strip club would get anyone familiar with how things worked. Granted, The Diamond Club didn't exactly have a dance floor, but the concept was similar enough that I actually felt comfortable here.

"Ready to dance?" Brock yelled.

I nodded and he led me onto the floor. I was a bit surprised when he headed straight for the center, but went with it. As nervous as I'd get around a bunch of rich kids, put me anywhere with music playing and let me dance, and I was the most confident person in the world. It was the one place where it didn't matter how much money someone had. Either you could dance or you couldn't. And I could.

Brock put his hands on my waist and the two of us began to move together. Our bodies fell into a rhythm immediately and it didn't take long for the two of us to start getting admiring looks from the other people dancing around. One song blended into another and we kept going. The people around us changed, but we didn't even slow down. We lost ourselves in the music and, by the time we decided to take a break, it was close to midnight and we were both dripping with sweat. Brock ordered another round of drinks and then asked if I wanted to leave. Gazing into his eyes, it was clear he wasn't asking if I was ready to call it a night.

I thought of Anastascia and what she'd said. I thought of his note and the promise of ten thousand dollars. I found myself once again on the brink between my own desire and the moral standards that had once meant so much to me.

He hadn't said I had to have sex with him if I wanted the money. Hell, the first time we'd been together, I'd initiated it. Now, he was giving me a choice. If I said yes, what we did would be my decision. I would do it because I wanted to, not because of the money.

I also didn't want to be with him to prove Anastascia wrong or because, in the back of my head, I knew that Reed was probably having sex with his wife right now and not thinking about me at all. I'd done well over the last two days and I didn't want to ruin it now. Sex with Brock had done been a soothing balm before, why couldn't it be again? Besides, he was a nice guy and I liked him. That and how worked up I'd gotten from dancing seemed like good enough reasons.

"Let's go."

He took my hand and we went out to get a cab.

We didn't talk or even do much touching on the ride to his apartment, only holding hands, but I felt like the cabbie's eyes were on me, accusing me. I kept my head down but in reality, I was used to being judged by those who didn't know me, it had happened my entire life. I reminded myself that I really did like Brock and I'd be doing this even if he hadn't made the offer of extra money. I didn't listen to the voice that asked if my hotel room and food for the week wasn't payment enough.

By the time we reached the elevator, I was sick of the voices in my head and just wanted them to shut up or at least quiet down. As soon as the doors closed, I stepped into Brock's arms, pressing my body close to his. As he wrapped his arms around me, I tilted my head and he leaned in, responding to my wordless request. When his tongue teased at the seam of my lips, I opened my mouth in invitation. He wasn't rough, but there was an edge that told me he wanted me and I pushed myself up on my toes to deepen the kiss. I wanted someone who wanted me. Only me.

One hand moved down to my ass, squeezing as his other hand fondled my breast through my shirt. I nipped at his tongue and he ground his hips into mine. Desire burned even hotter inside me and I reached between us to cup his erection. He spun us around so that my back was against the wall and the hand on my ass moved between my legs, shoving up my skirt until he could reach what he wanted.

I moaned into his mouth as his fingers pressed against me through the silk of my panties. I spread my legs as he rubbed the damp material, getting it more wet by the second. My eyes closed and I tried to concentrate on the way his tongue was thrusting into my mouth and the feel of his strong fingers through the silk. I only wanted to think of the physical. The way my arousal was spiking. The little ripples of pleasure that were radiating out from the center of me.

Then the doors were sliding open and he was pulling away, leaving me to tug my clothes back into place before following him out of the elevator. As soon as we were in the apartment and the door was closing behind us, he pulled me toward him for another kiss. I ran my hands over his firm chest and then down his stomach, enjoying the way the muscles twitched beneath my fingers.

"Baby," he gasped as he broke the kiss. "I have to feel that velvet mouth around me."

I grinned as I went to my knees, my hands working open his jeans, pushing them down until his cock was free. I shivered as I remembered how it felt to have that thick shaft pushing into me. I wrapped my hand around the base and then put my lips around the head. I tasted the salt from pre-cum as my tongue circled him. When I moved forward, he put his hands on my head, giving me gentle, guiding pressure. I took him as deep as I could without gagging, then started to pull back. His fingers tightened in my hair, but he didn't try to stop me.

"Fuck, you feel so good," he moaned.

I increased the suction until I was at the tip and then started all over again. My hand covered what my mouth couldn't reach and it didn't take me long to get a good rhythm going. Little words of encouragement fell from Brock's mouth along with the moans I took as an indication I was doing something right. When his hands tightened this time, I pulled back completely. He nearly snarled in frustration as his dark eyes looked down at me.

"Can't end the party too soon, can we?" I teased as I got to my feet.

With a growl, he picked me up and threw me over his shoulder. I laughed as he carried me toward the bedroom, his pants still undone, his cock jutting out in front of him, leading the way. I bounced when he tossed me onto the bed and before I'd stopped, he was looming over me, his hands searching for the zipper on my skirt.

"I got it," I said, quickly locating the zipper and shimmying it down my legs.

Brock pushed himself up on his knees and pulled off his shirt. Damn he was built. I let my eyes roam over him as I took off my top. Our clothes were on the floor in a matter of moments and I spread my legs in deliberate invitation. The hungry expression on his face was making me hungry too. He'd seen me naked before, but it was different this time. As for me, I was enjoying having my eyes explore every inch of his body.

He dropped between my legs, his hands curling around my hips as he yanked me closer to him. My squeal turned into a full-out wail when his mouth covered my pussy, his warm tongue sinking deep inside. He took long, strong licks from the center straight up to my clit, leaving fire in his wake. Each pass brought me closer to release and I rocked my hips, trying to get more friction where I needed it, but he held me fast and continued his torment.

Just when I thought I'd get there anyway, he stopped.

"No," I protested as he rose to his knees.

A wicked gleam came into his eyes as he reached into the top drawer of his bedside table and pulled out a condom. He slid it on, rolling it slowly down his length, taking his time, enjoying this bit of tease.

Well, two could play at that game. I ran my hand down my stomach and between my legs, parting my folds with my fingers. My slick fingers slipped easily over the little bundle of nerves, while my other hand went to my breast, rolling my nipple between my fingers. I gasped, I was close, so close. I needed him inside me. Now.

His smile widened as he stroked himself, making sure everything was on just right. Before I could take myself over the edge, he was there again, knocking my hand out of the way. The moment he pushed inside me, I came.

Crying out, my body tightening and rising at the same time, forcing him further inside even as my muscles contracted.

"Fuck!" He swore as our bodies came together. His arms slid around my back, pulling me up enough that he could lower his head and wrap his lips around my nipple, filling me with sensation everywhere.

The orgasm that had been fading roared back, crashing into me with enough force my nails dug into his shoulders. Without moving, he increased the suction on my breast, drawing a line of pleasure straight through as another wave of pleasure washed over me.

Finally, he let it slide from his mouth, his teeth scraping over it as it went. I moaned as pleasure morphed into pain then cried out as he began to move inside me. He thrust hard and fast, but his strokes were evenly paced, nothing erratic or uncontrolled about his movement. These weren't frantic, like someone close to the edge, but rather of someone intending I remember every moment of this in the morning.

And that was exactly what I wanted too.

It was almost painful, how hard he drove into me, but I encouraged him nonetheless. This wasn't some drunken quickie in a storeroom. I'd made this choice and wanted to feel every instant of it. His angle kept the pressure off of my clit and I was determined to get off at least one more time. I was riding high on sensation and not climaxing would leave me far too frustrated to even consider.

"So fucking hot," Brock grunted. One of his hands left my hip to grab my breast, his thumb teasing across the nipple before pinching it between his fingers.

"Fuck!" My entire body jumped at the jolt.

"Hmm, sounds like you liked that." He pinched me again as my fingers pressed against my clit, rolling and pressing to increase my pleasure.

This time, electricity shot straight through me, a bolt that cut right down into the building inferno, connecting those two points in an explosion that made me cry out. I sank my teeth into my bottom lip, stifling the name I had almost called out, realizing it didn't belong to the man who was still fucking me. I rode out my orgasm, bringing my focus back to the moment, to this man thrusting in and out of my body. I watched his face as he gazed down at mine, his struggle to hold back his own release. He couldn't. One thrust and then another, he came.

His body dropped onto mine and I gasped as he weight pressed heavily down on me. I felt a moment of panic. I couldn't breath and tried to push against his shoulder to get the dead weight off of me. After a minute, he sighed and rolled onto his back, sliding out, leaving me empty. I closed my eyes and tried not to think about how, even when I'd been experiencing an amazing climax, I'd been unable to completely stop thinking about Reed.

"Piper."

I rolled onto my side so I could face Brock. He turned his head, his eyes meeting mine.

"Move back."

My eyebrows shot up. "Excuse me?"

"Move back to Philadelphia," he said. He rolled toward me and propped himself up on an elbow. "I want to be with you."

I stared at him, unable to believe what I was hearing. He couldn't be serious. He'd seen how his parents had been at the wedding. There was no way he could tell anyone we were dating. I was already Reed's dirty little secret, I didn't need to be anyone else's. It didn't matter if I thought he was sweet. I'd be a joke, and then I'd be something worse.

I had no doubt the Michaels family would hire a private investigator who wouldn't have to look far to find out what I was. Once they did, it'd all be over. Just because he knew what I was didn't mean he wanted anyone else to know.

"Hey." He brushed the back of his hand across my cheek. "I don't care what anyone says or thinks. I want to be with you."

"I don't know," I said, uncertainty in my voice. How could someone like him want to be with someone like me?

A determined light came into his eyes as he correctly read the reason behind my hesitation. "Then I'll prove it to you."

Chapter 7

"Say that again?" I stared at Brock.

He was propped against a stack of pillows, stark naked, and grinning down at me where I was stretched out, recovering from our second round of vigorous sex. I tried to move, and felt the aching in my muscles. I was definitely going to be sore tomorrow.

"We're having a family dinner tomorrow evening to welcome back Reed and Britni. I want you to come with me."

Part of me wanted to ask why two very wealthy people had only gone on a short honeymoon, but I refrained. It wasn't any of my business, and I really didn't want Brock getting the idea I was overly interested in his brother-in-law. So, I focused on the part of those two statements that concerned me.

"Why in the world would you want me to come to your family dinner?"

Brock moved so that he was laying on his stomach, his feet on the pillows and his head next to mine. His face was uncharacteristically serious. "I told you, Piper, I want to be with you. Part of that means I'll want you to come to boring family functions and keep me company so I don't go insane."

I gave him a skeptical look.

He reached over and took my hand. Raising it to his lips, he kissed my knuckles. "Piper, what's it going to take for you to believe I want us to be together?"

I didn't answer because I didn't know. All of this was happening so fast. It was supposed to be a simple weekend. Let Brock apologize for something I didn't remember, buy me some things, get some money, enjoy making Reed squirm and then go back to Vegas. Nothing was supposed to really change. And I certainly wasn't supposed to end up staying longer to hang out with Reed's brother-in-law.

Brock's fingers tightened around mine and for a moment, I had the crazy thought that he knew what I was thinking. I leaned forward and brushed my lips across his.

"Look, it's all just a lot to take in." I moved closer so that the lengths of our bodies were touching. "You asked me to come out here as a date to apologize for..." I let my voice trail off for a moment. "I wasn't expecting this."

"You weren't expecting me to like you?" Brock asked.

I shook my head. "I wasn't expecting me to like you." I flushed. He was asking a lot of me and deserved to know at least this part of the truth. "I thought you were..."

"Like every other guy who hires strippers for bachelor parties?" he finished the sentence. "Or like the assholes who come to The Diamond Club?"

I hesitated. How was I supposed to tell him that's exactly what I'd thought?

"I was one of those assholes who went to The Diamond Club," he admitted. "And when I asked you to be my date, I did it because I was sorry. Also because you're gorgeous and we'd look good together at the wedding." He gave me a childish grin. "It didn't hurt that I knew it'd piss my sister off that I brought someone I met in Vegas. She keeps trying to set me up with Rebecca." He made a face. "That's weird, right?"

I nodded. "Definitely."

He grew somber again. "Then we hung out together and I realized I was enjoying spending time with you." He brushed hair back from my face, letting his fingers linger on my cheek. "And our little encounter in the janitor's closet proved we have great sexual chemistry."

"So that automatically means I should come to dinner at your parents' house?" Now I was getting nervous. When he said everything like that, his actions seemed completely logical and my brain wanted to know why I was arguing.

"No," he said with a smile. "That means you should move back here so we can be together. You should come to dinner for two reasons. One, it'll annoy the hell out of my sister and Rebecca. Two, I told you I'd prove to you that I wanted to be with you. What better way to do that than for me to introduce you to my parents as my girlfriend."

I was pretty sure I looked like a deer caught in headlights. How had we gone from wedding date slash apology to girlfriend? Okay, we'd fucked, but somehow Brock didn't strike me as the type who required someone to be his girlfriend before he'd have sex. According to Anastascia, he preferred not to have any strings attached.

"Or I could say we're dating and leave the label alone." The look he gave me said he understood what I was thinking. "Either way, I want them to know that you aren't some one-date fling."

I sighed. He was being very persistent and charming, a dangerous combination. I threw out my last protest, which, now that I thought about it, I probably should have used first since it was entirely practical.

"I don't have anything to wear." I realized how whiney that sounded and clarified, "I brought a couple changes of casual clothes for the trip and the outfit I wore to the club. The only other thing I have to wear is the dress from the wedding."

"Well then." He grinned and sat up. "I guess that means we're going shopping."

I didn't really believe he intended to take me shopping until we were walking into Macy's. I'd been there before, of course, but only to stare at the elaborate architecture and imagine what it must be like to be able to shop there. I'd heard the pipe organ play once and had never forgotten it, the sheer number of pipes surrounding the upper floor still astounded me.

"This way," Brock sounded amused.

"I forgot how amazing this place was," I said as we walked toward the section of the store that would have the appropriate clothes. Though I wasn't entirely sure what constituted appropriate for meeting – or re-meeting – the parents of the guy I was sleeping with but not exactly dating even though he wanted me to move back to Philadelphia so we could be together. The run-on sentence made my head hurt.

"How can we help you?"

A pair of women approached us as soon as we were within a few feet of the right section. The one who'd spoken was a tall blonde. The other was a shorter redhead, though her hair was more auburn than mine. Both of them were staring at Brock like he was something good to eat. It was on the tip of my tongue to confirm that he was, indeed, delicious, but something stopped me.

This was a chance, I thought. An opportunity to see if what Anastascia had said was true. If Brock was the kind of man my friend said he was, his behavior here would show it.

"My girlfriend needs something for our dinner tonight with my parents." He pulled me closer and slid his arm around my waist. "We want it to be something special."

The women both turned toward me, the expressions on their faces thinly disguised jealousy. It took me a moment to realize they were jealous of me, of the fact that Brock hadn't given either of them a second look. Something warm and pleasurable squirmed in my stomach. I'd never had anyone be jealous of me before, especially not over a guy.

"Let's get you some things to try on." The blonde offered me a fake smile.

I nodded, then glanced up at Brock, a mischievous streak rising up. "Do you want me to model them for you?"

He gave me a roguish grin. "In that case, can we get some lingerie too?"

I playfully smacked his arm and followed the women to the dressing rooms.

What followed felt like something out of a movie montage, minus the bubbly pop song and quick intercuts.

The saleswomen gave me snazzy business suits that would've been great if I'd been trying for a job interview. Those were followed by dresses that screamed jail bait, and even a couple that would've been more suited to a cougar than someone in their twenties. Each of these poor choices was met by scoffing laughter from Brock and a demand that they try harder. I wasn't sure if I was the only one who thought they were deliberately trying to make me look frumpy in front of Brock, but what I did know was he didn't respond to any of the subtle or not-so-subtle flirting being sent his way.

When they finally started giving me good outfits, I noticed a minute change in their approach. They were no longer trying to make me look bad, but rather asked questions about Brock and me. How we'd met. How long we'd been dating. Was it serious? I could sense their frustration when I kept my answers intentionally vague. I'd spent too much time over-hearing the girls at school talk about how they would get friendly with a crush's girlfriend, using her to find out information they'd then use to steal the boyfriend away. If they were going to seduce Brock, they would do it without my help.

I came out of the dressing room in a cute little black dress, feeling like this was the one. When Brock's eyes lit up, I knew I was right. He stood and came over to me.

"I don't know, babe. I might not be able to make it through dinner without tearing that off of you."

I smiled. "If that's the case, I might need to get some lingerie after all."

"No modeling," he said as he pulled me toward him, his hands on my waist. "Not here anyway. Let's save that for when we're alone."

His gaze was fixed on me, lust and desire burning in his eyes. I didn't see a trace of deception on his face and he hadn't even looked twice at the saleswomen. Maybe, I thought, just maybe, this could work.

Chapter 8

I wasn't regretting that Brock wanted to bring me to family dinner, and I certainly wasn't thinking about how Reed and his new bride would be there, all aglow and shit from their strangely short honeymoon. But I was nervous as hell when Brock opened the door to the town car we were taking to his parents' place. I was still asking myself why I'd agreed to this when we pulled up in front of a huge house that looked like it had been around since the city's founding. I didn't need anyone to tell me that it cost more than my entire building in Vegas. Brock took my hand as we walked up the front steps, but he didn't say anything and I wondered if he was as nervous as I was. If he was, he didn't show it.

He greeted his parents with a warm hello and asked if they remembered me. When they were too shocked to answer, he walked right past them, taking me with him. The Stirlings were already there, with the exception of the guests of honor, and they didn't look any more happy to see me than the Michaels had been. Rebecca looked downright put out, which pleased me and made the anxiety worth it.

We made small talk as we waited, but Brock always made sure it steered clear of anything I might be uncomfortable answering. I waited for Rebecca to get in a few pointed barbs, but she appeared to be saving them for later and contented herself with glaring at me while she sipped on a glass of wine.

Before things got too awkward, Reed and Britni arrived. I caught a glimpse of surprise flashing across Reed's eyes before it was gone again, but it made sense that he was able to hide it so quickly. I already knew he was a good liar.

Britni recognized me too and gave me a glare so angry I wondered if Reed had told her about us. A quick glance at him said he hadn't, and her anger was probably because she thought her brother had brought a prostitute to family dinner.

As we made our way into the dining room, I unintentionally discovered the reason for the short honeymoon.

"I really wish you would've taken the extra time off of work." Mrs. Stirling didn't even try to conceal the disapproval in her voice as she spoke to Reed. "It was your honeymoon, after all."

"You know my company's at a critical stage right now," Reed answered in a tone that suggested he'd offered this explanation a million times before. "I can't leave for a whole week or more until it's stable. Britni and I discussed it and decided that, rather than postpone the wedding, we'd put off the honeymoon for a couple months."

Mrs. Stirling pursed her lips. "I hope you intend to take your wife someplace nice then. No woman is okay with giving up her honeymoon."

Most women wouldn't be okay with marrying someone who didn't love her either, I thought, but Britni had done that. Maybe it was a rich person thing. I just didn't get it.

We took our seats around the dining room table and I tried not to stare when someone in a starched white apron came in to serve us. Anastascia's family had a housekeeper who would clean their place a few times a week, but they'd cooked for themselves and she couldn't imagine them having someone serving their meals.

"This must be quite a change for you," Rebecca broke through the quiet murmurings that had been the conversation through the first course of the meal. I didn't even have to look at her to know she was talking to me. She continued without waiting for a response. "Aren't you used to being on the other side of the table?"

"Rebecca." Mrs. Stirling's heart didn't seem to be in the chiding.

"Did she tell you, Brock, that she grew up here? Poor." She practically sneered.

"Actually, yes," he answered without a pause. "Piper told me everything."

Either he believed I hadn't left anything out or he was a better actor than I'd given him credit for. He answered her without batting an eye.

"You must be enjoying this then," Mrs. Michaels interjected smoothly. "The chance to see how the other half lives."

I didn't need her to say the other part of the statement. I knew it already. Before you go back to where you belong. I remembered a movie I'd watched as a teenager. Poor boy saves rich girl's life and gets to have dinner with the important people, most of whom are determined to make sure he knows his place. He'd gotten the girl for a little while, but the story hadn't ended well for him. I just hoped that wasn't going to be the case here.

"You have a lovely home." I gave the Michaels a polite smile. "So much space."

"I suppose you and your dozen half-brothers and sisters all shared a one room apartment, right?"

My smile tightened and Brock put his hand on my back. Across the table, Reed stiffened, though I couldn't tell if it was because of his sister's comment or Brock's touch.

"Our apartment had two bedrooms," I replied stiffly. "And it was just my mother and me before she died."

"I'm sorry to hear she passed," Mrs. Michaels said.

I wasn't sure I believed her.

"That's unusual," Rebecca continued. "Isn't it? Someone like your mother not having a dozen kids from different men."

My hands curled into fists.

"Then again, you're following in her footsteps, aren't you? And you don't have any kids." She smirked. "That we know of."

I stood. "Excuse me."

I heard Brock say my name, but I didn't acknowledge it or stop walking. I wasn't sure where I was going, but I knew it was away from the dining room. As soon as I saw a set of French doors leading outside, I went through them. I didn't care if they went to the front or back of the house. I wanted fresh air and solitude.

I stepped out into what looked like a garden. Leave it to rich people to turn their backyard into a garden rather than keeping it somewhere kids could play. I supposed the Michaels could've done it after Brock and Britni had grown up, but I doubted it. They seemed like the kind of people who wouldn't want to deal with the mess that came from outside play.

I took a deep breath of the warm early summer air. It was well past seven, closing in on eight, but dusk was only just settling. If I hadn't been escaping from a room of horrid rich bitch snobs, I might have enjoyed it.

"Piper."

Brock's voice came from behind me but I didn't turn to face him. His arms slid around my waist and I leaned back against his chest.

"I'm sorry."

I shook my head. "It wasn't your fault. Rebecca's a bitch. Always has been. Usually, I can take it, but..." My voice trailed off.

"But this was about your mother," he finished the thought for me.

I nodded.

"It might not be my fault, but I'm still sorry you're hurt." He kissed my temple.

I turned around in his arms and put my hands on his shoulders. "Do you see now why I can't move back here?" My eyes met his. "Why this can't work?"

"I don't believe that."

"They're never going to see me as anything but trash, even if they never find out how we really met, although you know they will." I ran my fingers through his hair. "It doesn't matter how I dress, or if I learn all the nice buzz words that people in your social circle use. I'm not one of you, and I never will be."

He kept one hand on my waist while the other cupped my chin, holding my face in place as he spoke, his voice intense. "Fuck them. I don't care what my parents think and if they try to make me choose, I'll choose you. I'm not going to let their close-minded prejudices make me miss out on the chance for happiness."

My heart constricted almost painfully. He was choosing me over family. How could I not at least try to see if this could be something? I touched his face, trying to see if he words were real. "Okay." I gave in. "I'll consider moving back."

Brock's face lit up and he lowered his head. The kiss was rough, his mouth moving against mine almost forcefully. It was more than just wanting. This was needing. A hunger I felt myself catching. I slid my arms around his neck and pulled myself closer, pressing my body against his. The hand on my waist dropped to my ass and the one holding my chin moved around to bury itself in my hair.

When we finally broke apart, we were both panting and I was feeling much better.

"I'm glad you're thinking about coming back," Brock said. He wrapped a lock of my hair around his finger and his eyes took on a teasing light. "Who knows if I'd ever find someone else as good in bed as you?"

I rolled my eyes and opened my mouth to retort, but before I could, someone behind us cleared his throat. I looked over Brock's shoulders and saw Reed standing in the doorway, his face an expressionless mask.

Well… this had all just gone to hell.

Chapter 9

"May I have a word alone with Piper?" Reed's voice was flat.

Brock looked down at me, the question in his eyes. I nodded. My stomach was in knots, but I knew if I protested, Brock would wonder why. Right now, for all he knew, Reed wanted to make sure I didn't tell Britni I'd been the stripper at his bachelor party. As much as I like Brock, I wasn't about to let him know any differently.

"I'll wait inside." Brock kissed my cheek. "If you want to leave when you two are done talking, we'll go. I won't ask you to stay."

"Thank you." I watched him walk back into the house and close the doors, giving Reed and me privacy. Only after Brock had disappeared from my sightline did I turn toward Reed. I folded my arms and waited.

"You slept with Brock?"

I lifted my chin, refusing to acknowledge the blush staining my cheeks. "Not that it's any of your business, but yes."

A flash of hurt crossed his face. "How could you?"

My jaw dropped and I stared at him, unable to believe he was actually asking me that question. "Are you kidding me?"

He took a step toward me. "I told you how I felt about you and that I wanted to be with you, and then you show up with Brock? You fucked him? Was that all I was? Or are you just trying to make your way through the richest guys in Philly?"

My fingernails bit into my palms as they curled into fists. "Who the fuck do you think you are?" I crossed the distance in a few angry strides, stopping when I was barely a foot away. "You slept with me when you were engaged, then told me it was over so I'd fuck you again, then treated me like a whore. Now you're pissed because I found a guy who likes me and doesn't care who knows it. He brought me to meet his parents, for god's sake. He wants me to move here so we can be together, not keep me in Vegas like his dirty little secret."

"It wasn't like that!" Reed snapped. "You don't know the whole story."

"I don't need to know. There's nothing you can say–"

"My parents threatened to cut me off."

That stopped me, but only for a second.

"Oh, so you didn't want to have to make your own way like a grown up. That's so much better." My entire body was flushed and it was everything I could do to keep from slapping him. I couldn't believe the nerve he had.

"My business is just getting started. If my parents cut me off, it'd go under and thousands of people would lose their jobs. People who put their trust in me."

My eyes narrowed. It sounded like he was saying he'd sacrificed what he'd wanted to save thousands of jobs, and I was supposed to accept it.

"I don't love Britni." He reached out his hand and I took a step back. "I want to be with you Piper, and I know you want me too. Brock is a distraction. A rebound. I get that. We can still make this work."

"You don't love your wife."

"No." Relief flooded his face and he stepped closer. "I don't."

"You didn't sleep with her, then, on your honeymoon?"

He stopped mid-step.

I moved closer this time. The desire I had for Reed was burning away, my anger taking over. "Tell me, Reed, did you fuck your wife on your wedding night? A woman you don't love. Did you tell her you don't love her while you were inside her?" I watched the color drain from his face. "Did you tell yourself that you had to do it once, to officially consummate the marriage? Was that the only time? Did you turn away her advances or give in so she wouldn't notice? Or did you initiate, giving yourself some excuse that would let you stand there with that self-righteous look on your face acting as if I'm the one out of line for sleeping with someone I actually like? Someone who wants to be with me regardless of what it'll mean to his family."

He didn't say a word, but the shell-shocked expression told me everything I needed to know.

"Go back to your wife and your loveless marriage. Fuck her, because you're never getting near me again. It's too late." I walked past him and didn't look back, not even when he said my name.

I still didn't know if I wanted to move back to Philadelphia and I wasn't sure if what I felt for Brock could become something more, but I did know one thing for sure. I was done with Reed Stirling.

I was out of the house and halfway down the front steps when a hand closed around my arm, stopping me. For a moment I thought it might be Reed, and was filled with both relief and disappointment when I turned and realized it was Brock. I cursed, confused by my reaction. I didn't seem to know what I wanted.

"I know you like Reed," Brock said softly.

I started to protest, but he talked over me.

"I don't care." A determined expression came over his face. "I can make you forget him."

He took my face between his hands and pressed his mouth against mine. The kiss was gentle, not what I'd expected and it startled me into allowing it to last for a few seconds before I pulled away. I started to tell him this wasn't a good idea, that I didn't think it was fair to him, but then movement over Brock's shoulder caught my eye.

Reed stood in the doorway, his jaw clenched, face pale. His hands were curled into fists and he looked like he was fighting the urge to come down here and punch Brock. If he had, maybe I wouldn't have made the decision I did.

I didn't want someone who wasn't willing to fight for me, to fight for what he wanted. Brock said he'd choose me over his family. He knew I liked Reed and didn't care, almost saw it as a challenge. I looked up at him and wrapped my arms around his neck.

"I don't want him," I promised. "Only you."

I pulled his head down for another kiss, but I didn't let this one be gentle. I pressed my body against his and pushed my tongue between his lips. His groan vibrated through him and he pulled me tighter against his body. His tongue curled around mine and I buried my hands in his hair, fisting the thick strands between my fingers.

When we finally broke apart, we were both gasping for air. After I'd caught enough breath to speak, I said, "Take me back to your place. I'll show exactly how over him I am."

End of Vol. 2

Sinful Desires Vol. 3

Chapter 1

It was mid-July in Las Vegas, which meant I actually wanted to be at work. Kind of. The Diamond Club may be one of the sleaziest strip joints in the city, but its air-conditioning was always on full-blast, unlike the ancient unit in the apartment I shared with Rosa, a fellow stripper. We'd been lucky to keep it down to ninety over the Fourth, and it was even worse today.

Now, as I walked through the club to get to the dressing room, I was starting to wonder if the air was even worth it. The heat outside was oppressive and even though it was cool inside, something about the heat made the men behave even worse than usual. It didn't help that some asshole had busted the hinges off of the back exit so that the only way we could keep the door shut was to chain it.

That meant we had to come in and leave through the front, giving the men extra time to ogle, comment and try to cop a feel.

"Hey there, pretty thing." A guy with a thick drawl and a cowboy hat to match pushed himself off of his barstool and into my path.

"I have to get backstage." I kept my voice professionally polite as I tried to sidestep around his massive bulk.

"Don't be like that." He grabbed my arm. "Why don't you give me a private dance?" His dark eyes ran over me. "I'd love to see you take it all off."

"I don't do private dances." I twisted my arm against his thumb, breaking his grip.

The cowboy grinned at me. "I know the owner. All the girls do private dances for me."

I glared at him. "Not me." I'd already compromised myself once by doing a party with Rosa and that turned out to be the biggest mistake of my life. Well, that's not true, I reminded myself, twisting the silver necklace Brock mailed me just the other day. It had led me to him, after all.

The cowboy was laughing as I walked away, calling out that he'd talk to his 'buddy' and I'd be bending over for him before the end of the night. I ignored him. If everyone who claimed to know the owner actually did, then no one would have to pay for anything.

I barely missed having a beer spilled on me as I tried to avoid a drunk with wandering hands, so by the time I finally made it backstage my mood was foul, even worse than when I'd first arrived. The only saving grace was the nice cool air. No guy wanted to see a girl sweating on stage because it was too hot. I inhaled a huge breath of cool air, hoping it chill my nerves.

"The cowboy tried to get you to give him a private dance?" Rosa grinned at me as I stripped off my tank top and shorts.

I made a sound of disgust. "Who is that douchebag anyway? I haven't seen him before."

"Bobby Ray."

I gave her a look.

"Seriously." She grinned as she zipped up the rubber suit she used for her number. "Bobby Ray from Texas, a cattleman who comes up every six months or so."

I couldn't help but laugh at her attempt at a southern drawl. "That's an awful lot of information to get about some audience member who's here maybe twice a year." I buttoned up my too-tight white shirt.

Rosa didn't even bat an eyelash. "He tips good during private shows." She reached for the mask she wore during the opening number. "Better than those Philadelphia boys."

I scowled as I picked up my mask. I didn't want to think about the bachelor party. That just made me think about Reed and how I'd thought, for a few shining hours that I was going to be able to leave this place behind. Oh, he'd offered me a way out alright, but it was more *Pretty Woman* than *Cinderella,* and I had too much self-respect to do that. I know, I know, I rolled my eyes at myself. Most people wouldn't believe it since I took off my clothes to pay the bills, but there were lines I wouldn't cross.

An annoying little voice in the back of my head whispered Brock's name but I quickly pushed it away. Brock was different. He asked me to move back to Philadelphia to be with him. He took me to a family dinner. He actually wanted to get to know me. Sure, we'd had sex and he'd bought me nice things, but I didn't sleep with him because of that and he never treated me like I had to. Despite what Anastascia said, Brock was the real deal. A sweet, handsome, charming man who liked me for me.

I glanced at my phone.

"Your boy toy ain't called yet?" One of the other strippers, a tall brunette named Charlene, smirked at me.

"He called earlier," I snapped. Charlene had overheard Rosa and me talking when I'd gotten back from Philadelphia a couple weeks ago and now all the girls knew about the rich boy in Philly who was trying to be my sugar daddy. It hadn't done any good to tell them that things weren't like that between Brock and me. They had their ideas firmly in their minds, and nothing could make them think any different. It didn't help that Rosa believed Brock was not doing anything but stringing me along.

"Did he say when he's coming out?" Rosa asked.

I shook my head. Ever since I told him I'd consider moving back to Philadelphia, the decision had been hanging over my head. It was bad enough being a poor stripper in Vegas. At least here, the only people I was around were others like me. In Philadelphia, with Brock, I'd be among the richest of the rich and I'd probably be scraping by waitressing and having to stay with Anastascia until I could afford a place of my own.

I wouldn't let myself think about the ten thousand dollars he'd promised me before the wedding. I still wasn't sure what I thought about that, especially since our relationship had evolved so much.

Brock told me last week that he planned to come out and try to convince me to go back with him. He'd said that since I'd spent time in his world, he was going to spend time in mine.

Rosa wasn't buying that line either, saying it was what guys like him said to girls like us when they wanted to make sure we know our place. We were good enough to visit for a fuck, but it was always on the man's timetable and we were just expected to sit around and wait, grateful for their interest and attention. I'd told her a million times that Brock wasn't like that, but she kept insisting she knew his type.

Fortunately, I was saved from having to argue with her again when we heard the manager call for us to get into

173

position for the opening number, and it was all business after that. The only thing I liked about my job was that it was at least similar to real dancing. I could either think about other things and let muscle memory carry me through the routine or, like today, lose myself in the music and forget where I was and what I was doing. Inside my head, I would be nowhere and everywhere.

I kept myself lost during my individual routine as well, barely registering the men groping my ass as they stuffed bills into my g-string. Even when the cowboy squeezed my breast, I didn't do anything other than move further back on the stage, so I was out of reach. Part of me wanted to wipe that smug smile off his face, but the rest of me just kept moving to the music and reminding myself to enjoy the cool air and think of the tips I was making.

I couldn't allow myself the luxury of thinking about other things, other paths my life should have taken. No matter what Brock said, I knew he'd eventually get tired of me and I'd be back here. I had to be realistic. This was my life.

Chapter 2

My maudlin mood stuck with me as I made my way home later that night. Rosa wasn't with me as she'd accepted the cowboy's offer of a private dance back in his hotel room. She'd told me not to wait up, which usually meant she'd be back around dawn, fall into bed and get up only before her next shift started. I wanted to confront her and ask how she could act all self-righteous about Brock when she was going to fuck the cowboy, but I didn't because I knew what she'd say. She wasn't deluding herself into thinking that Bobby Ray was a white knight, sweeping in to save her. She thought that's how I viewed Brock.

I frowned as I started up the stairs. That wasn't how I saw Brock at all. I knew he wasn't Prince Charming and I was definitely no Snow White. I wasn't looking for happily ever after, but I believed that what we did have was real, however long it lasted. I didn't have to pretend to like him touching me, kissing me. My stomach tightened at the memory of our last night in Philadelphia together and how he'd made me come so many times I'd nearly passed out. Sure, there wasn't a deep emotional connection there, but the sex was amazing enough without it.

The apartment was cooler than the hallway, but not by much. It was bearable, nothing more. I pulled off my shirt and shorts as I walked back to my room and tossed the clothes into my hamper. I still wasn't quite comfortable enough to parade around the apartment naked when Rosa was here, but being down to my panties and bra when I was alone wasn't a big deal at all, especially when it was this hot.

I pulled a carton of ice cream out of the fridge and was just getting ready to settle on the couch and marathon a few shows to unwind when my phone buzzed. It was Brock, telling me he wanted to Skype. A few seconds later, the beat-up laptop that Rosa and I shared dinged, saying I had an incoming call. I quickly shoved the ice cream back in the freezer and then answered the video chat. We 'borrowed' our internet from our neighbor's Wi-Fi, but since we worked different hours, he hadn't seemed to notice. I'd appreciated it more over the last couple weeks.

"Who's there with you?" Brock's tone was immediately accusatory.

"What?" I asked as I sat down.

"You're in your underwear. Who's there with you?"

I rolled my eyes. "It's insanely hot here, Brock. I'm alone. Rosa's not even here."

"Really?" His mood shifted immediately, and I recognized that glint in his eyes. "So it's just you?"

I nodded, my stomach tightening. I really hoped he was going to take this where I thought it was going. I could use the release, and it would be more fun this way than to spend some extra time fantasizing in the shower.

"Take off your bra." He leaned back in his chair, giving me a nice view of the way his t-shirt clung to his torso.

I gave him a seductive smile as I stood. Taking off my bra was a little more difficult than stripping in my work clothes, but I still managed to make it look sexy. By the time I kicked aside my panties and returned to the chair, Brock was already rubbing himself through his shorts.

"You are so fucking hot, you know that?" His voice was low. "I'll bet all the guys at The Diamond Club are all over you, wanting a piece of that ass."

I stiffened. Brock and I didn't normally talk about my job, especially not like that.

"Play with your nipples."

I shifted in my seat, still a bit shocked by his words. The arousal I'd felt before had waned with his mention of work, and now he was sounding more like he was giving orders than fooling around with his girlfriend. Rosa's comments came flooding back and, for the first time, I wondered if she was right.

"Come on, baby, let me see them get hard." His words took on a smoother tone and he winked at me through the monitor. "Please."

I couldn't help it; a grinned at his little boy plea. He looked so cute when he pouted like that; all puppy dog eyed. I cupped my breasts and brushed my thumbs over my nipples and was rewarded when Brock growled low in this throat. I watched his hand move from the outside of his shorts to under the waistband. I smiled, feeling innately female knowing he was touching himself in reaction to watching me. Heat unfurled in my stomach, and I rolled my nipples between my thumbs and forefingers, feeling a rush of pleasure as my skin grew more sensitive.

"Are you wet for me?" Brock asked. "Touch yourself, baby. Tell me."

I kept one hand on my breast as the other moved between my legs. My fingers parted my folds, sliding in between. I wasn't as wet as I'd thought I'd be, but there was enough to slick my fingers as I moved them back up to spread the moisture and put pressure on my clit.

"Are you wet for me?" he asked again. "Come on, talk to me. Tell me, if I was there, could I slide right into that tight little cunt of yours?"

"Yes," I hissed out the word as I slipped a finger inside.

"You'd like that, wouldn't you?" Brock's breathing was getting heavier and I saw his hand moving faster. "You like it when I take you hard and fast, fuck you until it hurts."

It was no longer a question and I wasn't sure what he wanted me to say. My fingers moved back to my clit, trying to move myself along. I was hoping to turn my arousal into an orgasm and release some of this pent-up energy and stress. At least it didn't seem like Brock needed me to say much of anything. He was doing just fine on his own. I let his words wash over me, trying to use what he was saying to further turn me on.

"If you were here, I'd have you ride me. Watch those titties bounce. Love that."

I moaned; no other response seemed necessary.

"Are you fingering yourself?" he asked suddenly. "Playing with yourself?"

With a start, I realized his eyes were closed.

"Yes." I was still touching myself, but my movements slowed. I didn't know if it was just the whole over-the-computer thing or the way Brock was talking, but I wasn't really feeling it anymore.

"I wanna see you come." His eyes opened. "Make yourself come for me."

I stared at him for a moment, but he didn't seem to notice my hesitation as he pulled his cock from his shorts. His hand was stroking faster as he waited. Suddenly, I just wanted to be done so we could talk. I leaned back and spread my legs, giving him a good view of what I was doing. I might not have been the kind of person who was comfortable with casual nudity, but when it came to sex, once we'd already been together a couple times, something like this wasn't exactly embarrassing. Besides, I thought as

I began to slide my finger in and out of my pussy; it wasn't like I was really making myself vulnerable here.

I began to moan and breathe faster, twisting my face into faux ecstasy.

This was as much acting as what I did on stage at the club.

I made myself go long enough to be believable before calling out his name. He wasn't far behind me, grunting as he came. He gave me a lazy smile as I excused myself to clean up and I assumed he'd do the same. When I returned, I was prepared to tell him I wouldn't be making a choice about Philadelphia until he came to see me in Vegas, proving he was the kind of man I could trust to keep his word.

He was gone.

I considered calling him back, but my heart wasn't in it. My pussy ached from not being able to relieve my tension, and I was starting to get a headache. I'd had a horrible day at work, and I was still fuckin' miserable from this heat. All in all, I decided it was best to chalk the day up to a total loss, take a cold shower and go to bed.

Chapter 3

I didn't think Brock realized that the whole computer sex thing hadn't been as good for me as it was for him, and I wasn't about to tell him. Not when he'd called the next day to say he was flying in Friday night and staying the whole week. Rosa just rolled her eyes when I told, refusing to believe that Brock really was a good guy, and I was a little worried about how she'd be if Brock wanted to see the apartment. But before I'd been able to decide if I needed to talk to her about it, she'd announced she was heading down to Mexico to visit her mother, leaving me an empty apartment for the week.

With that headache out of the way, I went to work Friday night. I'd wanted the weekend off to spend with him, so asking for Friday as well had been out of the question. Brock had been very understanding when I'd told him and said he'd just have a taxi take him to his hotel and we'd meet up in the morning.

He'd been yawning and seemed really tired, so I never dreamed he had something else in mind.

The lights on stage were also blinding during the first number, leaving the audience faceless, so it wasn't until I went out for my first solo routine that I saw Brock. At first, I thought I was seeing things, but then his eyes met mine and I knew my mind wasn't playing tricks on me. It was Brock, sitting there smiling at him; and he wasn't alone.

Next to him was a young man who looked to be around Brock's and Reed's ages. He had a thinner face, with intelligent, bright blue eyes and thick black hair that looked like it could use a good haircut. I didn't need an introduction to know he was Julien Atwood. The Atwood family had been one of the most well-known families at St. George's, and even though Julien was four years older than me, he'd still been notorious even after he'd graduated. He was the family's black sheep, always doing things his own way and not conforming to the usual rich kid pitfalls like drugs and drunk driving. I hadn't realized that he and Brock had known each other or were still friends.

As the pair made their way to the end of the stage, I was suddenly grateful for my training. I didn't need much concentration to keep dancing because seeing Brock here definitely would've thrown me otherwise. As it was, my face flushed as he slid a bill into my g-string, his hand sneaking around my side to quickly pinch my nipple. I glared at him and saw Julien give him a startled look. I managed to finish my routine without further incident and hurried off stage to regain my composure.

What the hell had all that been about?

I leaned against the wall in the corner of the dressing room, ignoring the questioning looks the other girls threw my way. I closed my eyes and rested my head on the wall. It said something about the state I was in that my clothes were still in my hand, and I was standing there wearing only the tiniest piece of fabric the club could get away with. Usually I was pulling on at least a shirt as I walked off stage.

It took me nearly five minutes to pull myself together and regain my composure enough to pull on clothes and head back out into the club. Generally, between sets we were required to at least stand off to the side so that patrons could praise our work. At least that's how the bosses put it. Basically, it was a chance for the men to ogle us in skimpy clothes and make offers for public lap dances out here or private ones in the back. We were encouraged to mingle and most girls did although it wasn't a requirement. It was the best way to make tips.

It wasn't money that made me venture out into the crowd. I'd spotted where Brock and Julien were sitting and began to work my way toward them, pushing aside hands that got a little too friendly.

"Hey, babe!" Brock jumped to his feet as soon as he saw me and grabbed me in a hug.

I let him linger for a moment before giving him a gentle push back. "Can't have everyone else getting ideas." I smiled at him to show that his attentions weren't unwelcome, just not here. I didn't want the rest of the club thinking they could put their hands on me too.

Fortunately, Brock didn't seem to mind. "Piper, this is Julien Atwood. Julien, my girlfriend, Piper Black."

"Nice to meet you." I held out a hand and Julien shook it. His handshake was firm and he met my gaze, which I appreciated. Too many men under similar circumstances would've either looked away, embarrassed and uncomfortable or they would've been staring at my chest, remembering what was under my tight shirt.

"Brock told me his girlfriend was gorgeous, but wow." His smile was warm and admiring, but not leering. "You're way out of his league."

"According to you, everyone's out of my league." Brock punched the other man's shoulder.

Julien shrugged. "I call it like I see it."

I laughed and signaled to one of the waitresses walking by. After she took their drink orders and left, I said, "I can't hang around too long. The boss tends to get mad if we're paying too much attention to a single person or group unless they're paying."

"In that case." Brock grinned playfully and I had a feeling I wasn't going to like what he was going to suggest. "How about you give me a private dance?"

I knew it wasn't a good idea, but one look at those pale blue eyes and desire was coiling inside me. It had been so long since I'd seen him and memories of our last night together floated into my mind. I'd missed him, more than I imagined was possible. And I wanted him, even after that disastrous computer chat.

"What the hell," I muttered. I held out my hand and Brock took it, grinning at me foolishly. It was impossible not to grin back and my mood had lifted tremendously by the time I glanced at Julien. "It was nice meeting you."

"You too." He smiled. "Enjoy your dance."

"I intend to." Brock winked and let me lead him back toward the private booths where we could entertain a client with something a bit more up-close and personal. How far we went was up to us, though we charged per song. Based on the expression on Brock's face, I doubted he'd be satisfied with a single-song private striptease. At least I hoped he wouldn't, because I wanted our first time together to last. Either way, I wasn't about to make him pay. That would be putting me too close to stepping over the line I'd drawn for myself when it came to sex and money.

We went to the private 'room' in the furthest corner. Separated from the other sections by curtains, it was in the corner which meant it actually had two walls, offering us a bit more privacy than the other sections. Some of the elite clubs had individual rooms where clients got to hear special songs, but the music here, while different from the main room, was the same for all the private dances.

Brock released my hand and took a seat on the massive chair that sat up against one of the walls. I adjusted the curtains and then turned back toward him, frowning when I saw he was holding out a credit card.

"What the hell, Brock?" My arousal was immediately tempered by the gesture.

"You're at work, babe. I don't want you to get into trouble."

His logic made sense and, in a way, it was sweet, but my stomach still twisted as I took the card from him. He was right; my boss would be seriously pissed if he found out I was back here with my boyfriend instead of make money and serving 'real' clients. I was already on thin ice because of the time I'd taken off; I couldn't afford to be reprimanded again.

I ran the card through the scanner.

"Don't set a limit."

My mouth tightened. That he knew we could set an amount or a song limit told me this wasn't the first time he'd been back here. He hadn't lied; I told myself as I gave him back his card. He'd been honest that he'd been here before. I'd just never asked if he'd spent any extra time with any of my co-workers. I really didn't want to know.

He crooked his finger at me, the grin on his face as bright as a little boy. I reminded myself that it didn't matter what either of us had done in the past. He'd picked me and I'd picked him. Neither one of us wanted to be with anyone else, and that was the only thing that counted.

As a new song started, I began to sway in time with the beat, losing myself in the rhythm. Brock's eyes were dark in the dim lighting, watching my every move. Seeing how I affected him, I felt a rush of power. I'd never considered that, when I was doing this because I wanted to, I was the one in control. I'd always consider what I did to be degrading, and while I could still see some of that quality in it, I now realized that there was more to my dancing than I'd ever realized. It was a rush, seeing how much Brock wanted me. Was I going to be all 'women power' and think this was the best job in the world? No fucking way. Was I even going to like it? Probably not. But, for the first time, I could understand why most of my co-workers enjoyed this line of work.

When I got down to my tiny thong, I didn't even hesitate. I turned so that my back was to Brock and bent, slowly shimmying out of the tiny scrap of material.

"Damn, that's hot."

I straightened and looked over my shoulder, giving him a wink before slowly turning around. A third song began as I walked toward him, watching as his eyes flicked from my breasts to the juncture between my legs and then back again. I was surprised he wasn't touching himself yet, but the bulge straining against his zipper left no doubt to whether he was enjoying himself or not.

I went to my knees and pushed his legs apart, sliding my hands up his thighs. I kept my eyes on his as my hands went to his waist and made short work of his button and zipper. I didn't look down until I started to tug his pants and underwear down. He lifted his hips but offered no other assistance. I didn't mind. All of my attention was focused on the erection that had sprung free and was now bobbing against his stomach.

He groaned as I took him in my mouth, letting him slide over my tongue as far as I could before drawing back again. As my mouth and hand worked over his cock, my other hand was between my legs, finding me slick and wet with my arousal. It took a bit of concentration to keep a steady rhythm going with both hands, but I managed, fueling my own desire as Brock swelled and moaned under my ministrations.

His hands went to my head, fingers twisting into my hair. Little pinpricks of pain went through my scalp as he tugged which only added to my arousal, merging with the pleasure I was taking with my fingers. I wasn't into pain, but a little hair pulling and some light pinching, that I didn't mind.

I started to pull away and Brock's hands pushed me back down again, holding me as his hips began to rock, forcing him further into my mouth. For a moment, panic spiked and I was afraid he would hold me there while he fucked my mouth, then his hands were gone and I was able to lift my head. I glared at him as I coughed, but then he was pulling me towards him, his eyes so full of desire that my body couldn't help but respond.

His mouth covered mine as he pulled me onto his lap and I felt a hand between legs. I moaned around his tongue as his fingers pushed into me. He started with two, roughly thrusting them in and out, and I whimpered, thankful I'd already stretched myself.

His teeth tugged on my bottom lip and I ground down against his hand, seeking more friction, more inside me, more of everything he could give me. Then his fingers were gone and I felt his cock nudge against me. A voice in my head screamed at me.

"Wait." I pushed back, rising on shaky feet.

"What the fuck, Piper?" Brock snapped. His cock was in his hand, flush with blood and ready to go. Except for one little thing.

"Condom." I reached into his pants pocket, knowing he'd have at least one in there. If he'd brought one to his sister's wedding just in case, I knew he wouldn't forget when he was going to see his girlfriend at a strip club.

"Seriously?" He sounded annoyed. "Aren't you on the pill?"

I looked up at him; my voice cooling. "Yes, but still."

"What are you trying to say?"

I held up the condom and tore open the package. "I'm saying that if you want to keep going, this is how we do it."

He didn't look happy, but he didn't argue either so I took that as a sign and rolled the condom down his length. He shuddered as I touched him and I realized how close he was. I climbed back onto his lap and positioned myself over his cock. Slowly, I lowered myself onto him, moaning as he entered me inch by inch. His hands gripped my hips, fingers digging into my flesh. A string of swear words poured out of him and I could see the strain as he fought not to come. When he was fully inside me, I stopped, letting him regain control as I rubbed my fingers over my clit. I didn't think he was going to last very long and I fully intended to climax this time.

"Move, dammit." Brock's voice was tense.

I rocked my hips back and forth, riding him, creating the friction I needed to push closer to the edge before giving him the up and down movement he needed.

His eyes zeroed in on my breasts and his hands followed, squeezing and working my nipples between his fingers. I kept my hands on his shoulders, using them for leverage as I moved. The pressure inside me kept building as all of the pent up tension from the last weeks came together inside me. I pushed myself up straight and let my head fall back. I forgot about my annoyance, forgot that I was at work, forgot about everything except the thick shaft inside me and the hands on my breasts. I slipped my finger between my folds and found the throbbing bundle of nerves that was there. I didn't need much extra stimulation before I was coming, my back arching, my body tightening.

"Fuck!" Brock cried out as I squeezed him, my insides gripping him as I came. He pulled me toward him, driving into me with enough force to send a shock of pain through my pleasure, intensifying it rather than extinguishing my flame. He crushed me to his chest as his hips jerked against me twice more before he came, my hand over his mouth to stifle his shout.

He held me as we waited for our breathing to return to normal and I could feel him shrinking inside me. He stroked my hair, then ran his fingers down my spine and back up again, sending a shiver through my exhausted body.

"God I needed you," he said, breaking the silence between us.

I nodded, then reluctantly pushed myself up, feeling his softened cock slip away. Aside from the fact that the way I'd been sitting was making my thighs hurt, I couldn't stay here much longer. I was at work.

My face flushed as I realized the full weight of what I'd done. I'd prided myself on not being like the other girls, at keeping my distance from the men in the audience. Everyone knew I didn't do private dances and I sure as hell didn't fuck on the clock.

I reached over to the card reader and stopped the timer on it. Granted, it hadn't been like I'd been with some random guy, but the truth still remained that I'd just gotten paid to have sex.

"I know you have to get back to work."

Brock's voice drew my attention. He was standing and tucking himself back into his pants. I suddenly remembered that I was naked and started looking around for my clothes.

"Julien and I are going to head back to the hotel and get some sleep. You said you're off tomorrow, right?"

I nodded as I pulled on my thong.

"How about you swing by the hotel like around four or five?" He leaned over and kissed my cheek. "We'll have some fun."

"All right," I agreed.

Brock was already heading out before I'd finished saying the words and I watched him go. I wrapped my arms around my middle, as if I found the air conditioning to be too much, though I knew the chill I was feeling had nothing to do with the temperature in the club. This coldness was deeper. I didn't think it would go away any time soon.

Chapter 4

It took me longer than usual to get to sleep after work, so I didn't wake up until early afternoon. Without Rosa bustling about, it was actually fairly quiet in the apartment and I took advantage of it by being a bit lazy and taking my time. Besides, it was my day off and I was going to spend the evening and most of the night with Brock – and Julien, I now realized – so I wanted to savor the time alone. I was glad Brock was here and I wanted to be with him, but I so rarely had the opportunity for guaranteed uninterrupted time to myself that I certainly wasn't going to waste it.

By the time I was on my way to Brock's hotel, I'd already enjoyed a long, slow shower and a leisurely brunch while reading a book: my idea of a great morning. I was feeling relaxed and was ready to enjoy whatever the weekend threw my way.

I'd dressed for the heat in a cute mint green sundress, but in my purse was a wrap that had belonged to my mother in anticipation of the air conditioning on the strip. When I arrived at the hotel, my skin was beaded with sweat, but I'd at least remembered sunscreen so I wasn't fried. Red-heads with fair skin and the desert sun are a dangerous combination without some heavy-duty SPF.

Brock had texted me his room number last night so I didn't bother to stop at the desk but rather headed straight for the elevators. Of course, he was near the top so I endured several floors of canned music before the doors dinged and I was able to step out onto his floor.

Julien answered my knock, his easy grin prompting me to give him one in return. I didn't really know much about him other than the gossip at St. George, but he seemed nice enough. I supposed if Brock had to bring anyone with him to Vegas; Julien seemed like a good choice. Then again, I'd thought Reed was a better man than Brock, and I'd been completely wrong about him.

"He's in the shower," Julien said as I stepped inside a hotel room bigger than my apartment. "He decided to clean out the minibar last night."

"Enough said." I rolled my eyes. We sat on the couch, one on either end, half facing each other. "You didn't indulge?"

Julien shook his head. "I'm not much of a drinker. A beer every once in a while, but I'm too much of a control freak to let myself get completely wasted."

"A control freak?" I arched an eyebrow. "I must admit; that's one adjective I hadn't heard used to describe you."

His grin widened. "Oh, I'm sure I can imagine what you have heard. Brock told me you went to St. George. Rebecca Stirling's class, right?"

I scowled and he laughed.

"I guess that's my answer." Julien pushed his hair out of his eyes. "I know how all the snobs at St. George criticized me because I didn't like their pretentious parties or care about whose daddies had the most money or the biggest yacht."

"That's because your dad always had the biggest yacht." Brock's voice came from behind us.

Desire flared in my stomach as I turned. He was fresh from the shower, wearing only a towel that barely covered everything. I had the sudden urge to lick the droplets of water from his tanned skin.

"I'll be out in a couple minutes." Brock winked at me as he turned, and a moment later I knew why. He tossed his towel back into the bathroom, giving me a clear and mouth-watering view of his tight ass as he walked away.

"About yesterday," Julien said, drawing my reluctant attention back to him. "I didn't know you worked at the club. Brock just said we were going out."

I waved a hand as I turned back around to face him. "It's a job, not like it was my life's ambition or anything. And at least I'm working."

He gave me a curious look. "What was your life's ambition then?"

"Dance." I smoothed down my dress. "Actual dance, not stripping."

He nodded. "I can see it. You have the body and grace of a dancer." He flushed. "I mean–"

"It's okay," I said. "I know what you meant." It was nice to know that all of Brock's friends didn't automatically assume that because I'm a stripper I was an easy lay.

"All right." Brock emerged from the bedroom looking as hot as ever. "Who's ready to have some fun?"

When I entered the casino with Brock's arm around my waist and Julien on my other side, I was surprised at how many people stared at us. Then a man in an expensive suit hurried over and I realized that Brock was well-known here.

"Mr. Michaels, a pleasure to see you again." The man gave a little bow to Brock, then to me and Julien. "Welcome to your friends as well."

"Anything exciting going on tonight, Johnson?" Brock asked as he looked around the room.

I glanced over at Julien and he seemed almost as unimpressed as I was. Apparently, he hadn't come to Vegas for the gambling. I looked around as Brock led Julien and me after Johnson. It was funny, but even after two years, I'd only stepped into a casino half a dozen times, and only ever to apply for a job. I didn't have a problem with gambling, but it had never really appealed to me. Probably because I'd never had extra money at any point in my life.

"Come be my good luck charm," Brock said as he sat at one of the tables. He yanked me onto his lap and then pushed out the chair next to him. "There you go, Julien."

"I'd rather not," Julien said mildly.

"Don't be a spoilsport, man. I know you got the cash. Get some chips and play." Brock's voice had taken on an edge that made it hard to tell if he was just messing around or if he was serious.

Julien sighed and sat down. "All right, I'll play. But I'm not drinking."

Brock rolled his eyes and gestured to a cute blonde who was hovering nearby. "Scotch on the rocks for me and a glass of champagne for my girl."

"I'm fine, Brock," I mumbled. My face was heating up as the other men at the table looked at me. I was fine with a little PDA, but sitting on Brock's lap like some sort of trophy was a bit beyond my comfort zone. I just didn't know how to tell Brock without embarrassing him, so I didn't say anything.

I quickly discovered that I was pretty much decoration. Julien occasionally spoke to me as he waited for the others to play their hands, asking about things like how Vegas compared to Philadelphia and what had prompted me to move, but no one else did. Brock talked at me, calling me his good luck charm and saying how he was winning because of me, but he never asked if I was enjoying myself or even if I wanted to play. If it wasn't for the way his thumb was tracing patterns on my stomach, I'd almost have thought he'd be just as content with a blow-up doll on his lap.

He was four drinks in when he started to lose. It was just a little here and there, not even close to cutting in to his winnings, but I could see the annoyance on his face. I wondered if he didn't want to lose in front of me or if it was because Julien was the one who kept beating him. By the sixth drink, he was past angry-drunk and into goofy-drunk, which actually was a mixed blessing. While I preferred funny to mean any day, I didn't like the fact that he was starting to get handsy.

"We should get him back to the room," Julien finally said after watching me stop Brock from trying to put his hand up my skirt for what seemed the hundredth time.

I nodded, agreeing completely as I pulled Brock's hand away from my breast. At least, thanks to my job, I knew how to handle drunken advances. "Hey, baby." I put my mouth against his ear. "Why don't we head back to your room?"

He turned his head and blinked at me, his eyes bloodshot and his gaze unfocused. "My room?"

I kept my voice low. "You're still ahead, so why don't you cash out those chips and we can take the party back to the hotel?"

"You've already kicked my ass," Julien lied. "Time to call it a night."

"Course I kicked your ass," Brock slurred. "You suck at cards."

The other men at the table laughed, but Brock didn't seem to notice. He pressed the side of his face against my neck.

"You smell good."

I sighed as I disentangled myself from his arms and stood. Julien collected the chips and went to cash out while I worked to get Brock on his feet. He could stand, but apparently didn't want to. All of my attempts to get him up were met with laughter, both his and the rest of the men at the table.

"Crazy drunk," Julien muttered as he returned. He handed me a bag that I assumed carried the combined winnings and then leaned over to haul Brock out of the chair.

"Would you like me to call Mr. Michaels a cab?" Johnson was back, completely professional, obviously used to practically carrying drunks out the door.

I glanced at Julien and he nodded. "Thank you; that would helpful." I sighed; deeply grateful Julien was choosing not to walk. He seemed a bit more equipped to handle – or rather, manhandle – Brock and I hadn't been sure which would have been harder, trying to get Brock to walk back to the hotel in an attempt to sober him up or dealing with him in a cab.

"He doesn't usually throw up when he's drunk," Julien said as he helped Brock walk towards the exit. "So I figured he'd be safe in a cab."

"Good to know," I said. That would've turned tonight from basically boring into out-and-out awful.

"You've never seen him get this plastered before, have you?" Julien asked.

I shook my head. I didn't remember our drunken encounter at the bachelor party, so I skipped that and went to the one time I had seen him drinking. "We both got drunk at his sister's wedding, but it was closer to just buzzed and tipsy rather than full-out drunk like this."

"We were college roommates," Julien explained. "I sometimes think I've seen him drunk more than sober."

"College roommates?" I couldn't say I was genuinely surprised that Brock hadn't mentioned college, but I shouldn't have been surprised that he'd gone.

Julien grinned at me as Brock shouted something that sounded like some Greek letters that I assumed belonged to a fraternity, though I doubted one was actually called "alpo beto soup."

"NYU for a year," Julien said as he shoved Brock into the backseat of the cab and then climbed in after him. After I'd followed, he continued, "Brock flunked out and I dropped out. He went home to Philly to do whatever it is that he does and I went on a tour of Europe."

"You went on a tour of Europe?" I echoed.

"Backpacking, and I mean that in the original sense. A lot of walking, doing odd jobs here and there. Two changes of clothes. Growing a beard."

I laughed at that one. I couldn't picture smooth-shaven Julien with a five o'clock shadow, let alone a beard. I was starting to understand why Julien was the black sheep in his family. When rich kids said they were backpacking around Europe, it usually meant with a stack of their parents' cash and reservations at the finest hotels. The slightly more rebellious ones might stay at hostels to 'experience' Europe, but none of them would even consider having only two sets of clothes and actually working for their money.

"I grew a beard once," Brock announced. "It itched." He scratched his face as if re-living the memory.

Julien and I both burst out laughing and, after a moment, so did Brock though I was sure he didn't know why. With Brock being in such a good mood, it was easier to deal with him when he kept trying to grab my breasts. Finally, I had to hold both of his hands, and even then he was still trying to grope me.

As we arrived at the hotel, I noticed Julien giving me an odd look. "What?" I asked.

"I'm just a little surprised you're being so adamant about keeping his hands off you. I mean, he *is* your boyfriend. It's not like he hasn't touched you before, right?" Julien followed me out of the cab and then leaned over to help get Brock out.

"I wasn't thinking of it that way," I answered honestly. "I was more thinking that I get enough of drunk guys grabbing at me at work and there isn't really much I can do there. I'm not about to put up with it from him."

I knew I sounded like I was complaining, but I was telling the truth. If we'd been in the hotel room, I probably would've let it go, but I was tired of being treated like meat. When he was groping me in public, that's what I felt like.

I yelped and jumped back as Brock threw up all over the sidewalk, narrowly missing Julien's shoes. Suddenly the groping didn't seem so bad. Better dealing with that than spending the entire ride with puke in my lap.

"You're cute, you know that?" Brock threw his arm around my shoulders and leaned against me heavily enough to make me stagger. I grimaced at his stench of his breath.

"Come on, buddy, let's get you upstairs." Julien took Brock's other arm and took most of the weight off of me. Together, we walked passed the blank-faced doorman, through the doors and over to the elevators.

Once inside, Brock leaned toward Julien and spoke in a not-so-quiet voice. "My girlfriend's hot."

Julien looked over Brock's head at me, eyes twinkling.

"Do you think my girlfriend's hot?"

"Sure, Brock." He gave me a wink that said he was only half-kidding.

"You should see her naked," Brock said and then snorted a laugh. "Right, you did."

I felt my expression harden and Julien's eyes darkened while Brock continued to howl.

"Well, not completely naked." Brock turned to me. "Cause you don't show the pussy at work, do you?" He smirked. "Except for me."

"Man, you're going to want to shut up." Julien gave Brock a shake, but it didn't do any good.

"She didn't just show it to me," Brock said. "She sucked my cock then rode me like nobody's business."

My face flooded with heat. If this was how Brock talked when he was drunk, I really didn't want to know how much of our sex life he'd spilled over the past couple weeks. Horror washed over me as I was hit with the thought of Brock and Reed drinking together. Reed knew that Brock and I had slept together, but that didn't mean I wanted him to know the details.

As soon as the elevator doors opened, I walked off, leaving Julien to help Brock alone. I didn't doubt he'd understand. Still, I was close enough to hear Brock as I was walking away.

"Just take a look at that ass. So firm."

I waited by the door, arms folded, head down. I'd thought I'd been mortified when I'd seen Reed at his bachelor party. I thought I'd been humiliated over the years by Rebecca and others like her. Nothing in my past, however, had prepared me for hearing someone that claimed to care about me talk about the intimate details of our relationship in such a coarse manner.

Maybe Anastascia had been right after all.

I set my jaw. I refused to believe that. People weren't always themselves when they were drunk. He'd feel like shit tomorrow when he found out what he'd done and he'd make it up to me I was sure.

I clung to that as Julien opened the door and the three of us went inside.

"You don't have to be here," Julien said as I turned on the light.

"Are you going to be able to get him in the shower and into bed by yourself?" I asked.

Julien gave me a surprised look. "I was just planning on dumping him in his room, making sure he was on his side so he didn't choke if he puked again and then leave him to sleep it off."

"That's not a very nice thing to do," Brock said.

"Shut up," Julien snapped. "You're being an asshole."

"I am?" Brock sounded surprised. "I'm sorry."

"I'm not the one you need to apologize to." Julien dragged Brock back toward one of the bedrooms.

"Bathroom, Julien," I said. "He reeks of alcohol and puke."

"Who do I need to apologize to?" Brock gave Julien a puzzled look as the two men turned into the bathroom.

"Piper."

Brock looked at me, as if surprised to still see me there. He grinned at me. "Piper's sexy."

I rolled my eyes as Julien sat Brock on the toilet and knelt down to pull off his shoes.

"I'll bet Julien thinks you're sexy," Brock said. He poked Julien in the shoulder. "And it's not just cuz it's been a while since he got laid either."

"Fuck you," Julien muttered as he tossed Brock's shoes into a corner.

Brock's face lit up as I tugged his shirt over his head. "I have an idea!"

I was pretty sure I didn't want to hear it, but nothing was going to stop Brock from sharing.

"We should all fuck each other."

Julien and I both froze, staring at Brock. I couldn't see the other man, but I felt safe in assuming that his face was as shocked as mine.

"Well, not *us* fuck each other." Brock laughed as he gestured to Julien and himself before looking up at me. "But we should both fuck *you*." He slid his hand between my legs, his eyes glittering. "You'd like that, wouldn't you?"

The moment his fingers brushed against my underwear, I pushed him back. "Asshole!"

I was furious by the time we wrestled him out of the last of his clothes and got him into the shower. Julien ended up having to hold Brock under the water just to get him

205

rinsed off, so I dried my still obnoxious boyfriend while Julien took off his wet shirt and toweled himself dry. Fortunately, as we were finishing up, Brock's eyes began to close along with his mouth and we practically had to drag dead weight across the hall. We dumped him on the bed stark naked and I yanked a blanket over him even though I told myself he didn't deserve it.

As Julien and I walked back out to the main area, he said, "Well, that was interesting."

"To say the least," I agreed. I wasn't sure I could look at Julien now. Brock hadn't given up his threesome idea. In fact, while we'd finished getting him cleaned up, he'd described the scene in detail surprisingly vivid for someone as drunk as he was.

"I need a beer," Julien said, crossing to the mini-fridge. "What about you?"

Brock had gotten me champagne at the casino, but I hadn't drunk very much of it. A beer sounded good. "Yes, please."

"You don't have to feel weird around me." Julien's back was to me as he rummaged in the fridge. When he emerged with a bottle in either hand, he added, "I'm used to Brock being like that." He handed me a bottle. "I promise, I won't try to picture the three of us in bed together."

I laughed as he smiled and the tension between us eased. I'd been planning on leaving now that Brock was passed out, but as Julien and I each drank some of our beer,

I decided that it wouldn't hurt anything to stay a little bit longer.

Chapter 5

Not surprisingly, Brock spent most of Sunday recovering from his hangover. Not that he was the one to tell me this. No, it was Julien who texted me from Brock's phone to say that he didn't think we'd be going out tonight. I should've been angry that my second day off wasn't going to be spent with my boyfriend, but I was actually relieved. I needed some time to stop being mad at him for being such a jerk. Apparently a good night's sleep hadn't helped with that.

Instead of moping around the house doing nothing, I decided to swap shifts with one of the girls who was always complaining that she never had a weekend off. That way I'd be available Monday night if Brock was feeling better. Even if I was still pissed, I still wanted to see him, sucker for punishment that I apparently was.

I sighed. I needed to know how he handled instances where he behaved like an ass. Would he apologize or just act like it never happened? I liked the guy, but not enough to put up with this every time he drank.

Hopefully, work would give me the chance to get my mind off of Brock and get some perspective. I hadn't counted on being haunted by the memory of seeing Brock and Julien there, and the 'private dance' that had followed. By the time I got home, I was more frustrated than I had been before and my head was pounding from frustration and worry. I took some medicine and let it knock me out until early Monday afternoon.

My phone ringing woke me up and it took longer than usual to push out of the fog and answer it. "Hello?" My voice was still thick with sleep.

"Hey, babe."

I blinked a couple times and pushed myself up so I was sitting. "Hi, Brock." I kept my tone flat, letting him know that I wasn't happy with him.

"About the other night." He immediately started in on it. "I don't really remember anything, but Julien says I was an ass and he's usually right about things like that."

"You were and he is." I felt myself softening. He sounded like he was going to apologize.

"I am so sorry."

I didn't respond. I wasn't sure I should let him off that easily considering all the things he'd said.

"Forgive me?"

I sighed but was still at a loss for words.

"I really need you to forgive me. I don't know why I drank so much, it was stupid and selfish. I wasted precious time being with you."

The iciness inside melted just a little bit. "All right. I accept your apology. And I won't ask that you don't do it again because I know that's not going to happen."

"Piper–"

I interrupted, "But can you at least try not to do it again during this visit. I'd like to spend time with my boyfriend. The nice guy who asked me to be his date to a wedding. Not the ass-hat from last night."

Brock laughed and I could hear the relief in his voice. "Promise. No more ass-hat boyfriend."

The knot in my stomach eased and I laughed along with him. So he was a crude drunk. I could handle that. It wasn't like he'd been acting that way stone sober.

"Let me make it up to you," he said. "And Julien, since I was pretty bad to you both. We're going out tonight." He quickly added, "To eat. Not to drink and gamble. We're going to go to Alize."

Okay, that was impressive. Alize was one of most expensive restaurants in Vegas. Girls like me didn't get in there unless we were being paid. That wasn't cynical. It was the truth. The style of dress alone would be more than most people could afford.

"Do you want to come to the hotel or do you want us to come pick you up?"

I liked that he was giving me the option. He hadn't seen my apartment yet and he was giving me the chance to decide if I wanted him to see it or not. At the moment, I was leaning towards not. I may have forgiven him for his previous behavior, but it had made me realize how much I still didn't know about Brock. Things were moving way too fast.

"I'll meet you at the restaurant," I said. I could sense that he was confused, but he agreed and didn't press the matter. We chatted for a few more minutes before saying our good-byes. I inhaled deeply and then let it out slowly. That had gone better than I'd hoped. I hadn't realized how much I'd believed Anastascia's claim about the type of guy Brock was. Now I knew she was wrong, at least I hoped she was. The fact that he'd apologized and was trying to make things up to me and Julien was certainly positive evidence.

Now, I just needed to focus on having fun tonight, enjoying our evening and, for the love of god, trying to decide what I was going to wear. I panicked momentarily, once again feeling like a fish out of water. Alize was a rich man's restaurant, with dress codes and certain expectations.

When you're on my kind of income, wardrobe choices for dressy events are rather limited. I didn't want to wear the dress from the wedding or what I'd worn to meet Brock's parents since he'd already seen both of those outfits before. I wasn't sure he'd remember, or even care, but I wanted something different. That left the dress Anastascia had bought me for the reunion.

I knew I looked good in it, but it brought back memories of Reed. Was that really something I wanted to have in my head while I was out with Brock? Then again, I reasoned, what better way to no longer associate the outfit with Reed than to wear it again. Give it a fresh start so to speak.

My decision made, I headed off to the kitchen to grab something to eat before I started getting ready. I didn't just want to look okay tonight. I wanted to look so good that Brock would go out of his way to make sure he never acted like that again.

It took me most of the afternoon to prepare. Waxing is time-consuming and not very fun, especially when you have to do it yourself because you're too poor to have it done by a professional. But every rip was worth it.

Then there was all the other enjoyable stuff that men completely take for granted like eyebrow tweezing and taking care of finger and toe nails. I was usually pretty meticulous thanks to my job, but I went above and beyond for tonight. So much so that when I stepped out of the taxi at Alize's, I was rewarded with two completely stunned expressions.

"I'll take that as a compliment." I smiled at them both as I wrapped my arm around Brock's.

"Where did you get that dress?" Brock finally asked.

"My friend bought it for me for my high school reunion."

Brock laughed. "I'll bet Rebecca about had a fit when she saw you in it. You're gorgeous."

I flushed, pleased with his compliment. Julien didn't say anything but a glance told me he was thinking along the same lines. The three of us went inside and I could feel eyes on us as we went. For once, I didn't feel like the attention was focused on everyone around me, but rather that I was at the center of it, flanked by two gorgeous guys in expensive, well-cut suits.

Alize was absolutely amazing. The view of the city through the massive glass walls was like nothing I'd ever seen before. Even the view from the boys' penthouse wasn't this impressive.

Brock ordered wine for all of us and, for a moment I was worried. Then he grinned at me.

"I'll take it easy, I promise. No repeats."

True to his word, he didn't drink more than a glass through the whole meal. And what a meal it was. I'd never really considered myself a fan of French food, but every single thing we ordered was scrumptious. I almost didn't have room for dessert but when Brock insisted that we all try the chocolate truffles, I had to agree.

As we waited for the final course to be delivered, the topic of conversation shifted to Britni's wedding, which Julien had missed. I squirmed uncomfortably in my seat as I waited for Brock to share about my involvement in Reed's bachelor party. Instead, he glossed over that part of the night and made it sound like the two of us had met during one of his visits to The Diamond Club. It wasn't like Julien didn't know I was a stripper, but I didn't want Brock to talk about the bachelor party and how I passed out and ended up staying the night. I still didn't remember all that happened that evening but it wasn't something I wanted to relive.

"So everything's going well for Britni and Reed?" I hoped my voice didn't sound as falsely bright to the guys as it did to me.

Brock nodded as the waiter set the truffles in the center of the table. He picked one up and held it out to me and I suppressed the urge to roll my eyes. Wasn't your boyfriend feeding you supposed to be all sweet and romantic or something? I'd never really gotten that. For me, it always sounded awkward, and now it felt that way too.

My eyebrows shot up as the chocolate melted on my tongue and I moaned, leaning to savor the flavor before sipping from my water. Brock gave me the rest of the piece which was as mouthwatering as the first before answering my question.

"Yeah, they're doing great. A little on edge because of the whole heir clause thing, but that's not really a surprise." Brock popped a truffle into his mouth as Julien helped himself to a second one.

"The what clause?" I asked. I didn't really want to hear more about their farce of a marriage, but I was curious.

"The heir clause." Brock glanced at Julien who looked just as confused as I was. "Wow, I thought everyone knew about this."

"Why don't fill us in?" Julien asked.

"Well, you know how there was this business deal that went along the marriage?" Brock looked from me to Julien. I took my cue from Julien and feigned ignorance. I didn't want Brock wondering where I'd heard it if Julien didn't know. "Anyway, it's a common thing. Families bound in marriage also make business contracts tying everyone together." He shook his head. "Don't ask me. I don't get it." He ate another truffle. "So, Britni and Reed's marriage also joined some of the Stirlings assets to my family's assets."

"Still not getting the whole 'heir clause,'" Julien said.

Unfortunately, I was beginning to think that I did understand.

"Basically, the clause states that they need to have at least one pregnancy in their first year of marriage, and a baby within three."

"Are you shitting me?"

I was glad Julien said something that drew Brock's attention because I was having a difficult time keeping my expression blank. A forced pregnancy, I'd never heard of such thing. Not in the twenty-first century anyway.

Brock shrugged. "The Stirlings put it in actually. Something about making sure their name was carried on, since Rebecca's a girl and obviously will take her husband's

215

name. I guess Mr. Stirling is the last one in his family line or something like that."

"So Britni and Reed..."

"Fucking like bunnies would be my guess." Brock made a face.

I really hadn't wanted to hear that, and I certainly didn't want to be thinking about Reed and Britni having sex. I reached for my wine, tipped it up and drained the glass. Brock didn't notice, but Julien gave me a puzzled look. I didn't mind. I was more concerned with getting those images out of my head.

Reed's body moving over hers.

Her riding him.

His face between her legs.

Her name on his lips when he came.

"Piper?" Brock touched my arm.

"Hm?"

"You okay?"

I nodded and forced a smile. "Fine. I was just thinking about how delicious the food was." I leaned over and kissed his cheek. "Thank you."

He grinned. "And the night's just getting started." He slapped Julien on the back. "We need to get my friend here some action. Let's hit a club."

"Please tell me you mean a dance club," Julien said.

"Hell no." Brock laughed. "One of the best things about Vegas is their strip joints." He glanced at me. "We'll head to Ruby's."

Ruby's was one of the high-end strip clubs. They catered to high rollers, rich guys like Brock, but they revealed as much as The Diamond Club strippers did. Basically, the only difference was how expensive the dances were and the fact that the guys used fifties and hundreds instead of ones and fives. I really didn't want to go, but I couldn't think of an excuse that didn't sound like I was whining so I kept my fake smile plastered across my face and nodded in agreement. If I was lucky, maybe Brock would think I was bored and we would go somewhere else. At least I wasn't alone in not wanting to go. One look at Julien's face said that he was humoring his friend just as much as I was.

Chapter 6

I'd been in Ruby's once before, but that had been to drop off my application. I'd figured if I was going to take my clothes off, at least I could make decent money doing it. When I'd given it to the busty blonde at the front, she'd given me a quick once over, a polite smile and informed me that she'd file the application but not to hold my breath for a call. Apparently, the girls at Ruby's had to be at least a 36C to be considered. I didn't quite make that cut.

I could feel heat creeping up my cheeks the moment we walked in and I was thankful that the lighting was dim in the audience. Brock was close enough that he would've seen my skin turning red if he'd been looking at me, but his eyes were firmly fixed on the brunette currently gyrating on stage.

We made our way over to a pair of armchairs on the far side of the stage. Brock immediately sat down but Julien gestured toward the other, offering it to me.

"Come here, babe." Brock tugged me towards him and I gave Julien a smile to let him know that I appreciated the offer.

I sat on Brock's lap, leaning back against him as he wrapped his arm around my waist. I wasn't enjoying the show, but even when I was annoyed at Brock, my body responded to his affections. The heat from his arm burned through my dress, spreading warmth across my skin.

I glanced over at Julien and saw him looking at me. He gave me an awkward smile and then turned back to the stage where the brunette was down to her g-string. I couldn't say for sure, but it looked to me like Julien wasn't enjoying the show as much as most men would be. Then a thought occurred to me and I took another peak at him to see if it could possibly be true. Maybe the reason the whole threesome thing had freaked him out hadn't been embarrassment on my behalf but was rather because Julien was gay and no one knew.

When the next act came onstage, I found myself watching him out of the corner of my eye. A couple times, he looked my way and I wondered if he wasn't looking at me but rather at Brock. It would make sense that he'd stay in the closet. As 'open-minded' as some of the wealthy families claimed to be, I doubted they'd approve of a gay son. It might have even been the reasoning behind his black sheep reputation. Better to be the rebel child.

I was still contemplating my theory when Brock flagged one of the dancers to come over. She was a redhead, like me, but the resemblance stopped there. She was a good four inches taller and top-heavy. Based on the rest of her build, there was no way those things were natural, but they still seemed to mesmerize Brock and the other men.

"A dance for my friend," Brock called out over the music.

Julien turned pale and he shot me a look of horror.

"Brock, come on," I spoke quietly in my boyfriend's ear. "I don't think he wants a dance."

"Of course he wants a dance," Brock said, not bothering to keep his voice down. He dug into his pocket and pulled out several folded up bills. "Here you go, sweet thing. Make my buddy here happy."

Based on the woman's smile, I was pretty sure Brock had given her at least twice her normal rate. When she began to move, Julien's entire body tensed. His eyes were on her, but he didn't appear to be enjoying himself. The closer she got to him, the more uncomfortable he looked.

"Get up close and personal with that rack, Julien," Brock teased. "Those things probably cost a pretty penny."

The red-head ran her hands over her breasts as she leaned over Julien, her pale nipples brushing against his lips. I was just about to intervene when I saw Julien reach down and adjust himself. Apparently he *was* enjoying the show. When his eyes darted over to me, I could see guilt in them and understood. Julien wasn't gay. He was trying to be a gentleman. He knew I didn't want to be here and he felt bad that he liked what was going on. I gave him a small smile, hoping he'd take that as permission to enjoy himself. If Brock had already spent the money, Julien might as well have some fun.

The stripper straddled Julien's lap and began grinding down on him. Her mouth was moving and I wondered what she was saying to him. The music was too loud for me to hear any of it.

"You don't really get to see it from this side, do you?" Brock asked, his mouth against my ear. The hand on my waist slid a bit higher until his fingers were brushing the underside of my breast.

I shifted away from his hand on the pretense of answering his question. "Not really. I don't go out and watch the other girls dance."

"I liked watching you dance with Rosa at the bachelor party." One of Brock's hands settled on my knee.

I flushed at the memory. I'd been pissed at Reed and had taken things further than I usually did. Rosa and I hadn't kissed and we'd kept our hands above the waist, but we'd done a little touching.

"I kept wishing you guys would take it further," Brock confessed.

I could feel him hardening against my ass. The hand on my knee slid up my thigh.

"You have an amazing body and I'd love to see it with another woman." He pressed his mouth against my throat and I felt a chaste kiss turn into something open and wet. When he started to suck, I turned so that our lips were just a few centimeters apart.

"No hickeys. I have to work tomorrow."

He nodded, but I saw something dark in his eyes. He didn't like being told he couldn't do something. He cupped the back of my head and pulled me toward him. His tongue pushed between my lips, and his lips were hard and demanding against mine. I leaned into the kiss, not minding the bit of PDA considering where we were.

Then the hand on my hip moved up to my breast. I kept kissing him as I removed his hand, putting it back on my leg. His fingers flexed against my thigh and started to move higher, inching under my skirt.

That was it.

I pulled back, glaring at him and I shoved his hand away. "We're in public, Brock."

"Look around, Piper." He gestured towards Julien. The red-head was grinding on his lap. "Doesn't seem fair that I came to a strip club and can't get even a little action."

I climbed off of him, hands clenching into fists. "I'm not letting you feel me up because you decided you wanted to bring your girlfriend to a strip club with you."

He stood, holding his hands up, palms out, in a gesture of surrender. "Okay, fine." He reached for my hand. "We can take this back to my room." His eyes flicked over to the red-head who was finishing up her dance. "Let me see if she wants to come too."

For a few seconds, I actually thought he was thinking of Julien and wanting his friend to have a good time. Then Brock spoke again.

"You two can dance for me and Julien." He pulled me against him. "Get us all worked up and ready for what comes next."

I took a step back, distancing myself from him. "I just want to go home. Alone."

Anger flashed across his eyes. "You have to be joking. After all I've done–"

"You're going to want to stop there." Julien was suddenly up and standing between us. "Don't say something you'll regret."

Brock opened his mouth and Julien grabbed his friend's arm.

"Trust me, man. You wanna shut up right now."

I couldn't see Julien's face, but there must have been something in it because Brock backed down.

"Fine." He glared at me. "Let's go."

Julien walked with me toward the exit while Brock strode on ahead, not even bothering to look back to see if we were following. My stomach was in knots, tightening with each step I took. I'd excused Brock's behavior on Saturday because he was drunk. Tonight, he'd had a single glass of wine. Was something wrong or was this how Brock really was? Had the guy I liked been just a mask?

I continued to think about it on the taxi ride back to my apartment. Julien and Brock had taken another cab back to the hotel. Brock hadn't even said good-bye. I closed my eyes and leaned my head against the window. The cool glass felt nice against my overheated skin.

Did I make a terrible mistake accepting that first date?

Chapter 7

I stared up at my bedroom ceiling, debating whether or not I was going to do what I wanted to do. Well, part of me wanted to do it. The other part kept saying that making the call meant giving in, admitting that I'd been wrong.

But I had been wrong, hadn't I? The claims I'd made, the righteous indignation about a comment that had truly been innocent. All of that had been based on my certainty that I was right.

Now, I wasn't so sure. Growing up, I'd had to rely on myself a great deal, and after my mom got sick, that self-reliance had only increased. After her death, I'd made all the decisions on my own, and any of them that didn't seem to end well, I'd talked myself into believing they'd still been the right things to do. Moving to Vegas was a perfect example of that. I'd made the choice, thinking that it was the best way to rid myself of painful memories and give myself a new start. When I'd discovered that the grass in Los Vegas was just as brown and dry as it was in Philadelphia, I didn't consider moving back or even moving somewhere else. The stubborn streak that had kept me moving at St. George dug in and I told myself that I was building character, that every artist had to pay their dues. All sounded like good reasons, but I knew they were lies.

Now I needed to know if I was lying to myself about Brock. Was he just another bad decision that I was justifying? I needed to talk to someone and with my mom gone, there was only one person I trusted enough to ask the tough questions.

And it was time I apologized to her.

I picked up my phone. It was two-thirty here, which meant Anastascia would've gotten home from work a couple minutes ago. I tapped her number on speed dial and listened to it ring. She answered on the second one.

"Piper," her voice was cool and cautious, but not forbidding.

"I'm sorry, Ana." I knew those words had to be said first. "I know you didn't mean those words how I took them."

"I meant the ones about Brock." Her tone had warmed, but she still sounded wary.

"I know," I said. "But that's you looking out for me. I knew that all along. I just didn't want to hear it, so I used your comment about social circles to pick a fight."

"It's forgotten," she said, and I knew it was. We didn't hold grudges. "So, tell me what's been going on since we last talked."

I sighed and felt hot tears prick at my eyelids. I hadn't realized until that very moment just how lonely I'd been. I'd told myself that I didn't need anyone, that I could take care of myself, and I had been doing just that. But now I realized how much I missed having someone to talk to.

"Hon, talk to me." Now she sounded worried.

"It all started at the reunion." I knew I had to tell her everything. She had to understand all of it. "Remember when I went out for a walk?"

The words poured out of me. I told her about running into Reed and sleeping with him. About how he'd asked when he could see me again and how I'd intended for it to be just a one-time thing. Then I went on about the bachelor party and how he'd ended up taking me to dinner and confessing that his marriage was a business transaction. I sobbed so hard I could barely speak when I told her how he said he wanted to be with me.

I had to take a break, sip some water and blow my nose but I wasn't finished. I had to tell her it all.

Tears slipped out from under my eyelids as I told her I'd slept with him again only to find out he wanted me as a mistress, nothing more. I moved from that into Brock's wedding invitation, skipping the parts of that story she already knew, and then continued with what had happened after our fight. When I finally concluded with the disastrous night at the strip club, I was crying freely, all of the pain and anger I'd been storing up coming out all at once.

"So, when I called you that night, you didn't answer because you were fucking Reed Stirling?"

"Really? That's the first thing you say?" A laugh bubbled out, slowing my tears.

"Hey, it had to be said."

I could almost hear Anastascia smiling.

"I am so sorry he turned out to be such a bastard," she said. "I know you'd had a thing for him since high school."

I rubbed at my cheeks. "What are you talking about?"

"You didn't hide it as well as you thought you did." She sounded amused. "At least from me. I don't think anyone else realized it." Her voice hardened. "I'd even thought about setting up some sort of meeting for you two. I thought he was one of the good guys."

"So did I." I sniffled, but the main storm had passed.

"You did the right thing, not falling for his bullshit about how he had no choice. Everyone has a choice."

Some of the tension inside me began to ease. I'd needed to hear someone say that I'd done the right thing. I'd spent too much time the past two years around women who would've jumped at the chance to be a mistress to someone like Reed, especially after his whole sob story about his business.

"I mean, does he really expect you to believe that a bank wouldn't loan him the money to keep the business going until it started gaining traction? He's a Stirling. Any bank in Philly would be falling all over themselves trying to give him money."

I blinked. I hadn't even thought of that.

"Thanks, Ana. I needed to hear that." I sat up and ran a hand through my hair, grimacing as my fingers caught on a tangle.

"Don't thank me yet," she warned and I knew what was coming. "I'm about to share a few things you aren't going to want to hear."

I didn't bother to protest. I knew it wouldn't do any good. Besides, I might not want to hear what she had to say, but I knew I needed to hear it.

"You need to end things with Brock." Her statement was firm. "I know he came across all sweet and Prince Charming-like, sweeping you off your feet and everything, but he is not your white knight. That was the act. What you're seeing now, this is the real Brock."

"The one time he'd just had too much to drink," I couldn't stop myself from cutting in, defending him.

"Still doesn't excuse his behavior. If he knows he's a mean drunk, he should be responsible enough not to drink that much."

Her stance on that matter didn't surprise me. She'd never had patience with people who did things when they should've known better.

"As for taking you out for an expensive dinner to apologize, because I know that's what you're going to say next, think real hard about it. Did he take you out because he felt bad, or had he already planned on going out and he just called it an apology? How long does it take to get a reservation at that place?"

My heart sank when I thought about what she was saying. Alize wasn't the kind of place people could just waltz into without a reservation and get a prime table. Brock might've had some pull at some of the high-class restaurants in Philadelphia, but I didn't think that'd work here. Vegas had too many high rollers. Unless he was a regular at Alize or had some big business connections, I was pretty sure he'd have to make a reservation like everyone else. I might've been wrong, but my gut, combined with Anastascia's unwavering conviction told me otherwise.

"And, honey," she said gently. "He took you to a strip club."

"You'd be surprised at how many guys bring their wives and girlfriends to see a show." I wasn't intentionally being argumentative, but I wanted to find other logical reasons for Brock's behavior. I didn't want to believe that I'd rebounded from one jerk to another. I hadn't dated a lot, but I liked to think that my taste in men wasn't that bad, that I wasn't that naïve and stupid.

"Did he ask you if you wanted to go?"

"Yes," I answered immediately.

"Piper, did he say that he wanted to go and then made it sound like he'd reconsider if you said you didn't want to, or did he actually ask you if you would enjoy going to a strip club?"

I didn't answer, but Anastascia knew anyway.

"That's what I thought." Her voice softened. "Believe me, I wish he was as great as he seems, but it wasn't just one person I'd ever heard talk about him. This is his MO, and he'll just keep pushing until you finally snap. And I know you. You're stubborn and you don't like to admit when you're wrong. If you wait until he pushes too far, you're going to get hurt."

I remained silent, but this time, she didn't interrupt. Even after the time we'd spent apart and the fights we'd had, she and I were still close enough that it sometimes seemed like we could read each other's minds. She knew I needed a few minutes to process.

"You may be right," I admitted reluctantly. "And I may be showing that stubborn streak, but I'm going to give him a chance to explain himself."

"You know," Anastascia said with a sigh. "For a girl who's been kicked in the teeth so many times, you sure are willing to forgive people a lot."

"Maybe I'm just trying not to turn into cynical old you," I teased.

She laughed and the mood lightened. "Now, you need to tell me everything about Julien Atwood, because the stories I've heard..."

I rolled my eyes even though she couldn't see me. I would give Brock the opportunity to fix this, but there'd only be this one time. No more chances after this. And if things went south with him, I would be swearing off guys for a while. They weren't worth the heartache.

Chapter 8

I had to work Tuesday night, so I missed Brock's call, but the voicemail he left was apologetic. He didn't try to make excuses for his behavior, but simply said he'd been out of line and rude. He asked to make it up to me the following night on a date. Just the two of us. Julien was going to entertain himself so Brock and I could have some alone time. I agreed, telling myself that his behavior would determine whether or not I broke up with him tomorrow or not.

When my shift ended, I headed back to the dressing room and found a dozen red roses lying on the make-up table. The card held a simple message.

"Piper, thank you for the second chance. - B."

The other girls were curious and I could feel the eyes on me as I changed, but no one asked. One of the things I did like about The Diamond Club was that we all respected each other's privacy for the most part. Now, if you advertised everything, all bets were off, but if you were like me and kept your private life private, no one pried. In a place like this, too many people had secrets.

I carried the roses home, raising them every few minutes to breathe in their scent. It took me a while to find a vase that could hold them all, but once I did, I put them in the center of the table where I could see them from every place in the main area of the apartment. A little smile played on my lips as I made myself something to eat and it stayed through my shower. I was still smiling when I fell asleep.

I was scheduled for a 'morning' shift the next day so I'd set my alarm for just a couple hours of sleep. Morning shifts at The Diamond Club started at ten and went until seven. They were better in some ways, worse in others. Generally, there were fewer customers in the middle of the day since most people used the daylight hours for other activities, so things were more easy-going. That also meant that the men who were there were usually repeat customers and some had a bad habit of getting overly friendly. Especially the ones that felt like since they watched a girl take her clothes off a couple times a week, there was some sort of intimate relationship going on. Every girl at The Diamond Club had at least one of those customers.

I had two. And, somehow, they always seemed to know when I was working the early shift. Since things were a bit more lax, the customers sometimes got away with more than they did at night. The last time I'd worked a morning when my admirers were there, I'd almost gotten fired for slapping them both. The only thing that saved my ass was that they'd both told the manager that the slaps had been worth the feel they'd copped.

Even those two couldn't completely take away my anticipation of the upcoming date. Another bouquet of roses had been waiting at the club when I'd arrived and every time Paul or Leon let their hands linger a little too long, I'd think about my roses. I knew two dozen hadn't come cheap and I appreciated Brock's effort to apologize even while I still questioned his sincerity.

While I danced, I started to consider a third option to the two contradictory schools of thought on Brock and his seemingly double personality. Perhaps it wasn't as simple as him being bad or good. Maybe Brock was *trying* to change. He could have been the kind of guy Anastascia thought he was, but now he was trying to be different. For me. It would explain how he could go from being so sweet to a total ass. He wanted to be a good guy. He was just working at it and kept falling back into his old self.

I had this set in my mind as I got ready for our date hours later. While Brock hadn't said where we were going, he'd told me to dress casual-dressy. That was good because I was pretty much out of actual-dressy. I paired a black miniskirt with a simple green sleeveless blouse and pinned my hair up to keep it off my neck, then I spent the next ten minutes debating the merits of heels over sandals. The sandals won out when I saw that I'd somehow managed to scuff my heels the other night. I frowned as I tossed them back into the corner of my bedroom. There was something else to add to my list of things I needed to buy whenever I actually had the money to do it.

By the time Brock was due, I was pacing in front of the couch. He'd texted this morning to ask if he could pick me up and I'd agreed. He'd already seen where I worked. It seemed pointless to keep him from seeing the apartment. He knew I didn't have money and I saw it as a test to see how accepting of me he really was.

When he knocked on the door, I became really nervous, looking around at my clean by shabby apartment. I'd spent all my extra time picking at little things like they were going to magically transform this place into a palace. It didn't, nothing short of a magic wand would make a difference.

I closed my eyes and took a deep breath before I moved to let him in. He had another huge bunch of flowers, more than a dozen this time. The scent was intoxicating.

"For you," he said as he stepped inside.

That seemed like a pretty obvious thing to say, but I wasn't going to argue. I stretched up to kiss his cheek and then went into the kitchen to find something big enough to hold all of the flowers.

"Next time, I'll make sure I get a vase too," Brock said as he looked at the table where my other flowers were sitting in the only vases Rosa and I owned.

I came out with a water pitcher. "That might be a good idea." I smiled. "They're beautiful. All of them. Thank you so much."

"Well, I owed you a big apology. Astronomical, I believe was the word Julien used."

"Julien?" I couldn't hide my surprise.

"Yeah, when we got back to the hotel the other night, he proceeded to lecture me for about twenty minutes about what an idiot I was and how, if I didn't fix things, I was going to fuck up the best thing that had ever happened to me." Brock stuck his hands into his pants pockets and gave me a sheepish grin. "So, again, I'm sorry."

I nodded as I fussed with the flowers until I was sure I could speak normally. Brock's additional apology, along with his repeating of what Julien had said had gotten me flustered.

"What's done is done," I said. "Apology accepted."

Brock beamed. "Great!" He held out his hand. "Let's go."

"Go where?" I asked as I took his hand.

"It's a surprise."

Considering Brock's last great idea, a surprise made me a little nervous. My face must have expressed every emotion I possessed because he laughed and held out his hand, saying, "Trust me."

I narrowed my eyes at him in mock disbelief but didn't press the issue. If I'd truly forgiven him, I needed to try to trust him. This wouldn't work if I couldn't do that.

Several minutes later, a taxi dropped us off at the Venetian. As we walked toward Empirio D'Gondola, I may or may not have squealed. Whatever sound I made, Brock laughed and kissed the back of my hand.

"I'm guessing that means you like my surprise?" he asked.

I nodded. "I've always wanted to ride them, but never had the extra money."

"Well, tonight, money is no object." He paid for a private ride for just the two of us and helped me onto the gondola. I settled in against his side and he wrapped his arm around my shoulders. I didn't mind that it was almost too hot for the contact to be comfortable, I was too enthralled with the setting.

The gondolier started off and I stared at the Grand Canal Shoppes as we passed. The water was smooth and a much clearer blue than I'd expected. The buildings around us were all fabulous. I'd seen them from far away, but unlike some of the Vegas attractions, they maintained their beauty up close.

The trip was only a quarter of an hour, but I quickly decided it was the best date I'd ever been on. When we left, I leaned against Brock, my arm around his waist. I was right. I so desperately wanted to be right. He may have been that womanizing kind of guy in the past, but he didn't want to be that way anymore.

I hadn't realized we were heading somewhere specific until Brock stopped and we were in front of Lake Como at the Bellagio. He brushed back a few strands of hair that had come free and asked, "Have you seen the dancing fountains?"

I nodded. "A couple of times, it's been awhile."

"Well, you can actually see them over and over again without seeing the exact same thing twice." Brock gestured towards the water as a Debussy piece began to play.

He fell silent then as we both listened and watched as the jets of water shot into the air. Debussy gave way to Andrew Lloyd Webber, then another classical piece that I thought might be Chopin began. The entire experience was lovely… the music, the majestic fountain, his thumb rubbing the back of my hand. We laughed and made small talk, completely at ease with each other.

I remembered how, when we'd gone on our first true date to Love Park, there had been these long periods of silence between us and how comfortable it had seemed. Perhaps that's what Brock needed, to get away from the fancy dining and all of the things that he'd become used to over the years. Keeping things simple seemed to transform him into the guy I cared about.

"This was a wonderful date," I said as the third song faded.

Brock cleared his throat and looked down at me, his expression nervous. "I was hoping we could maybe go back to your place. I didn't get to see much of the apartment when I was there earlier."

I raised an eyebrow, knowing exactly what he was hinting at and feeling my body respond. "The only rooms you missed were the bathroom and the two bedrooms."

"Well, see, there's the most exciting part." That charming smile was back, the one that had convinced me to give him a chance in the first place.

"My roommate's bedroom?" I teased.

We started to walk away, enjoying the easy banter before finally hailing a cab to take us back to my apartment. As we rode, Brock's hand settled on the nape of my neck, his fingers gently massaging the tense muscles there. I closed my eyes and let my head fall forward. Only biting my lip kept me from moaning.

"Your entire neck is knotted up," Brock said as his strong fingers worked at the knots. It was; I could feel it and a long, drawn out moan drew a laugh from him. He kept rubbing and as the tension eased away, it was replaced by a heat that spread down through me. I'd been pretty sure we'd end up in bed from the moment I'd forgiven him. Then when he'd asked about coming back to the apartment, I was sure of it.

By the time the cab pulled up in front of the building, my panties were damp and I was writhing in my seat. Not that I was going to tell him that. He needed to work a bit for it.

The smell of roses greeted us as soon as we came inside. I kicked off my sandals and Brock took off his shoes. I didn't care about the ugly beige carpet, but it was always easier to get completely undressed without shoes.

"Should I bring rose petals to sprinkle on the bed?" Brock broke the silence, his eyes twinkling.

I rolled my eyes and took his hand. "Come on, we need to get this full tour over with." I gestured with my free hand. "Kitchen slash dining room slash living room." We headed down the hallway. "Bathroom, my room, and the one you're the most interested in, Rosa's room."

I let out a yelp of surprise as Brock scooped me up in his arms and pushed open the door to my room.

"Wrong room," I laughed. "I thought you wanted to see Rosa's room."

He took two steps and dropped me onto my twin-sized bed. I looked up at him and, for the first time, wondered how we were both going to fit on the bed. Then his shirt was coming off and I didn't care if our feet hung off the end. I wanted him.

I scrambled out of my clothes as he finished undressing, tossing my panties and bra onto the floor while he watched. His eyes were dark with desire as he crawled onto the bed.

"I've been thinking about this all day. You, naked, spread out for me." He leaned his body over mine, his cock hard and hot against my hip. He pressed his mouth against the side of my neck, lips and teeth worrying at the skin there until I knew he'd leave a mark. I'd need to make sure I covered it tomorrow before work. One hand held his balance as the other went to my breast. His fingers played with my nipple until it was a point and the skin was tingling. When he moved his head lower and took the hardened flesh into his mouth, I moaned.

I closed my eyes, giving myself over to the hot suction of his mouth. His hand slid over my ribcage and down between my legs. I cried out as he pushed one finger inside me and then another. I was wet, but still tight enough that it didn't move easily. After a few strokes, I began to move against his hand, wanting friction a little higher. Instead, he pushed himself up off of me.

"Condom?" he asked.

I blinked, trying to clear away some of the fog. I pointed toward the table next to my bed. He opened the top drawer, tore the wrapper and rolled the condom on without a word. It wasn't until he was spreading my legs apart and settling between them that he spoke.

"You're gorgeous like this, you know." He bent his head and flicked his tongue over one nipple, then the other. "Nipples hard, face flushed."

He reached between us and the head of his cock nudged against my entrance. I told my body to relax, but there was still a pinch of pain as he plunged inside. There hadn't been nearly enough foreplay and, as he continued to push forward, I slid my hand between us, my fingers finding my clit and beginning to rub. The familiar circular motion helped me relax and allowed my body to stretch to accommodate him.

"Your cunt is so tight." He groan as he bottomed out. "Feels so good around my cock."

Before I was ready, he started to move and I gasped, my free hand grabbing onto his arm. "Wait, wait."

He made an impatient sound, but did as I asked. My fingers worked over my clit until I began to feel heat spreading through me and then I nodded. He drew back and then thrust forward, drawing a half-moan from me. Another half dozen strokes and he moved to his knees, his hands grasping my hips. This time, when he drove into me, I was open and ready. There was no pain, just the pleasurable rubbing of him against me, filling me, adding to the electric sensations coming from where my fingers were still playing over that swollen bundle of nerves. I'd gotten a later start and knew it would be a little while longer before I was at the edge, but I could already see Brock's climax approaching.

"Slow down," I said. "I'm not there yet."

His pace didn't lessen. He leaned over me, putting his hands on either side of my waist and the change in position pressed his pelvic bone against where my fingers had been moments before. My eyelids fluttered as my body flooded with pleasure. That was what I needed. Every time he surged forward, he hit that spot just right and sent a jolt through me.

Just as I'd started to feel the pressure inside me building, Brock's hips jerked against me and he let out a sound that was half-way between a groan and a grunt. He slumped over me for a moment and I looked up at him, surprised. My pussy throbbed as he slid out of me and rolled onto his back. My entire body was tense with build-up, my teeth gritted with frustration.

Brock tipped his head to look at me. "Damn that was good."

My eyebrows went up. Was he serious? I wasn't stupid enough to think that every encounter was going to be good, but he hadn't even made an effort to make sure I got off.

"Did you come?" he asked, almost as an afterthought. When I didn't say anything, he gave me a sheepish smile. "I'd like to watch you finish."

If my body hadn't been screaming for release, I might've told him to go to hell, and as it was I was seriously considering it. Instead, I leaned back, closed my eyes and slid my hand down between my legs. It didn't take much, just a few minutes of attention and my muscles tightened.

With my climax came physical pleasure, but there was something missing. Even though I'd had sex with Brock and he was still right there, I felt the same way I did after masturbating alone. I opened my eyes and saw Brock watching me.

"That was fucking hot." He ran his finger down my arm. "You want me to stay? Give me an hour and I'll be ready for another round."

I sat up and shook my head, suddenly annoyed. "I have to work tomorrow. Double shift." That much was true, but it wasn't the real reason I didn't want him to stay. "Sorry."

"No worries," Brock said. He stood and began gathering his clothes. "So that means I'll see you Friday?"

I nodded and stood as well. I smiled up at him and he leaned down to kiss me. It was a good, thorough kiss, leaving my knees trembling. His hand cupped my face and he was looking at me so tenderly.

"Text me on your breaks?" Brock asked as he tucked hair behind my ear.

"I will."

I walked him to the door where he gave me another kiss, another one that nearly melted my knees. Where was this man ten minutes ago? The one kissing me so passionately, so thoroughly, taking his time?

After he left, I headed for the shower to think about what had happened. I didn't exactly have a lot of experience with guys and I knew from my experience with my ex-boyfriend that it wasn't exactly uncommon for the guy to orgasm before the girl, but at least Luc had been concerned about whether or not I'd come. I'd lied to him, not wanting him to feel bad that he'd never been able to make me climax, but considering how attentive Brock had been before, I honestly thought he'd take care of me with his fingers or mouth, especially considering how little foreplay I'd gotten.

He said he'd been thinking about me all day, I reasoned as I stepped under the hot spray. Maybe he'd been embarrassed that he'd come so quickly, or maybe he'd really just wanted to watch me do it myself? I sighed, once again at war with myself and the feelings I had toward this man. Could I really judge him based on one lukewarm sexual encounter? Was that really a good reason to be annoyed with him?

I frowned as I squirted some floral-scented shampoo into my hand and then began to work it through my hair. No, I decided, that wasn't why I was annoyed. Sex with Luc had been mediocre at best, but it hadn't really affected how I'd felt about him. It was that feeling I'd had just after I'd come tonight, I realized. That lack of connection. I liked Brock, but there hadn't been any of that spark between us. What I didn't know was if it had been that way before and I just hadn't noticed because at least then, the sex had been good. Was it possible that we hadn't truly connected any of the other times we'd slept together and I'd only been fooling myself?

I rinsed my hair and then reached for my conditioner. The question was, did a connection like that really matter? Reed and I had a connection from the first moment we'd touched. A lot of good that had done us. At least with Brock, I knew who he really was, and the connection would come with time. When like turned into love, we'd have I; I was sure of it, but for that to happen, things couldn't keep going the way they were now. Something had to change.

Chapter 9

I didn't really have the money to spend on fancy food, but I managed to find room in my budget to make a lasagna from my mom's recipe. A loaf of Italian bread and a bottle of cheap wine, and I was going to be eating Ramen noodles for a while. Still, it meant I could have Brock and Julien over for a home-cooked meal on their last night in Vegas, and I was looking forward to it. I owed Julien a thank you for sticking up for me after the strip club incident, and I wanted to make sure Brock knew I wasn't angry about how things had ended up the other night.

I had given our relationship a lot of thought and when I looked at everything we'd had together, the positives far outweighed the negative.

The first batch of roses Brock had given me were starting to wilt, so I put those aside to dry and set the newer ones as a center piece after moving from the water pitcher to the nearly empty vase. I'd spent the entire day cleaning so that when the guys arrived, my shabby little place actually didn't look too bad. Of course, I'd had ulterior motives for the excessive cleaning since Rosa would be back tomorrow evening and I was going to have to break some news to her.

"That smells fantastic," Julien announced as he entered the apartment. "What are we having?"

"Lasagna," I said as I accepted the wine he offered. It was much better than what I had. I felt a stab of embarrassment and pushed it aside. I'd give the cheaper stuff to Rosa. A parting gift.

"We're starved," Brock said as he kissed my cheek in greeting. "We had a guys' night out and didn't get in until like seven this morning, so we pretty much slept the day away."

Julien glanced at me. "We went to a fight and then hit a couple casinos."

I nodded as if I hadn't been picturing the two of them covered with half-naked strippers. I started for the kitchen. "Make yourselves comfortable. This'll be done in a few minutes."

I was surprised at how well dinner went considering the awkwardness that had happened when we'd been together before. The three of us hadn't managed a single meal without it turning into something embarrassing and rude. Tonight, however, the conversation was kept light, with Julien regaling us with stories of some of the crazier things he'd done in his early twenties.

After we'd finished, I brought out the last thing I'd bought with the last of my tip money: a cherry pie. I confessed that pie making was beyond my skills and Julien revealed that he actually knew how to make an excellent pie crust.

"Okay, this I have to hear," I said as I served out a slice to each of us.

"Well, remember how I said I spent some time in France?" He took a bite of his pie and then nodded in approval. "Well, I met this pastry chef in Milan and she spent a couple months teaching me everything she knew."

"Everything?" Brock asked, wiggling his eyebrows.

Julien rolled his eyes. "She was in her forties."

Brock grinned. "For all I know, you got a thing for cougars."

"Jerk," Julien muttered.

I took a drink of my wine. We were getting to the end of the meal and I didn't know where we were going to go from here, which meant if I wanted to make my announcement, it needed to be soon. As the conversation hit a lull after Brock's comment, I figured now was as good a time as any.

"I've been thinking." My voice sounded loud in my ears and I twisted my fingers together. "And if you still want me to move back to Philadelphia, I will."

Brock's eyes lit up as he leaned over and kissed me. The enthusiasm caught me off guard and he deepened the kiss, sliding his tongue into my mouth. I kissed him back, but broke away as his hand slid down my arm and moved to my breast. My face was burning and I couldn't look at Julien. I was comfortable with *some* PDA, but I knew how it felt to be the third person in a room where a couple was making out. It was awkward to say the least.

"If I make some calls, I might be able to get you a ticket on tomorrow's flight," Brock said. "Julien and I can help you pack tonight."

I held up a hand. "Whoa. I can't leave tomorrow. I have to wait to talk to Rosa and get things settled here. At the very least, I'll need a week."

"Okay," Brock nodded. He was beaming. "I'll start looking around for apartments."

I suppressed a sigh. I was glad he was happy, but we were going to have to have a serious talk before he left tomorrow. He didn't quite seem to get the fact that there was no way I could afford an apartment in the city. Unless... my stomach flipped. Was he going to give me the ten thousand dollars he'd mentioned back at the wedding? I still wasn't sure how I felt about that.

I stood. "If you'll excuse me, I have to use the restroom."

Brock stood as well, grabbing me in a tight embrace before I walked away. "I'm so glad you're coming back. You won't regret it."

I gave him a tight smile.

"I bet when we first met, you never thought you'd be moving back to Philadelphia because of me."

I shook my head. "No, I definitely did not." I didn't add that if I'd thought of moving back at all, it would've been with Reed. I excused myself again and headed back to the bathroom. Before I closed the door, I heard Julien speak.

"You know, you never did tell me how the two of you met."

I flushed, closing the door quickly. I'd assumed that Julien had already known the story. I didn't want to hear it. After I was done, I opened the door, but didn't go out into the hallway. I wanted to make sure Brock had already finished sharing before I went back into the main area.

"So, you just decided that this stripper you'd hired for your brother-in-law's bachelor party was hot and it was a good idea to ask her to come with you to your sister's wedding?"

As I listened to Brock laugh, I became curious. Aside from not wanting to be there when he told Julien about our meeting, I now realized this was a good way for me to find out Brock's original motivation behind his invitation.

"No way," Brock said. "I thought she was hot and wanted to fuck her."

No surprise there, I thought. He'd been pretty drunk that night.

"Okay," Julien sounded puzzled. "How'd you go from that to wedding date?"

Brock laughed again and there was a new edge to it. "Never planned that part of it. I only did *that* because Reed caught me trying to fuck her and I figured I'd better make an apology look good or he'd be pissed."

My stomach roiled and I suddenly felt like I was going to be sick.

"I don't understand. Why would it matter to Reed if you were trying to sleep with the stripper?"

"Because," Brock said. "She wasn't exactly conscious at the time."

He laughed and I shuddered, the pure evil in his voice vibrating deep within my bones.

"She wasn't like the other one, willing to fuck for some extra cash, so I gave her some incentive by way of a roofie in her water." He paused, then added, "Bitch never knew what hit her."

End of Vol. 3

Sinful Desires Vol. 4

Chapter 1

"She wasn't like the other one, willing to fuck for some extra cash, so I gave her some incentive by way of a roofie in her water." He paused, then added, "Bitch never knew what hit her."

I couldn't breathe. My chest was tight, the pressure on it nearly unbearable, but there wasn't anything I could do. I wanted to move, but I was frozen to the spot, forced to listen as my boyfriend continued.

"Still has no clue that the guy she's been fucking drugged her. Dumb cunt actually believed the story that she was pass-out drunk."

The memory swirled back to me… waking in Reed's room the next morning, him claiming I'd been drunk and had passed out. At the time, I knew it couldn't be true, but hadn't questioned it. I'd been too flustered from being in Reed's bed.

Anger flared inside me, hot and bright. It burned away my paralysis and I stormed from the bathroom, crossing into to the main room but froze as I watched Julien land a solid right hook to Brock's jaw. Brock dropped to his knees.

"You fucking bastard!" I heard Julien say, but barely registered the words.

Still on his knees, Brock looked straight at me as he massaged his jaw. I noticed a drop of blood from the side of his mouth but all I could think about was his words: "Bitch never knew what hit her." I felt tears in my eyes and pushed them back, blinking furiously. I didn't want Brock to think I was crying over him. I wasn't. These were tears of rage; I'd never been more furious.

I took a step toward him. I didn't know what I was going to do, but I knew I wanted to hurt him, wanted to tear him apart. It didn't matter that he was bigger than me and probably didn't have any qualms about hitting a woman. He'd been prepared to rape me. Who knew what else he was capable of? He probably didn't see it that way. I was just a stripper after all. Nothing more than a whore who sometimes didn't put out.

A hand closed around my wrist and I struggled against it for a moment before I realized it was Julien.

"He's not worth it," Julien spat the words out. His bright blue eyes were shining with something I hadn't seen in them before. Indignation. Not annoyance or even just the disgust he'd had the other nights Brock had done something stupid. Julien was beyond pissed and it transformed his normally easygoing features into something sharp and fierce. If he hadn't been on my side, I'd have been a little frightened.

"You're seriously going to ruin years of friendship over her?" Brock's hand was still at his jaw as he struggled to his feet. "You don't even know her."

"But I know you," Julien countered. He was still holding my wrist, but now I was the one holding him back. He was pulsing with anger and I could feel his muscles contract with the need to hit Brock again. "I know about the girls in college who claimed you got a little too friendly. Never quite crossed that line with them, did you?"

Brock didn't even look at me. "Come on, Julien. She's a good lay, but she's not worth breaking ties with me."

I ground my teeth together, too furious to even speak.

"Get out, Brock," Julien said. "And I don't just mean out of the apartment. Get out of Vegas. I don't want you to be in the hotel when I get back."

"You can't—"

Julien took a step forward, his eyes narrowed. Brock stumbled backwards. "Remember what you said about my dad always having the biggest yacht? Well, it's still true. You might be a big-shot in Philly too, but my family's got ties everywhere. You don't want to cross me."

Brock sneered. "Never thought I'd see you start throwing around the family weight."

Julien didn't answer, but I supposed the stony silence was enough. Brock just looked at him for a few seconds longer, then left, slamming the door so hard that the faulty latch didn't catch and it banged open again.

I didn't care about that though. The enormity of what just happened hit me full force, and I felt my knees start to buckle beneath me. Julien caught me before I could fall and held me up, wrapping his arms around me. I stiffened for a moment, but relaxed as soon as I realized he wasn't using this as an excuse to feel me up. I couldn't take another fight.

"I am so sorry." There was no pity in Julien's words, only sympathy.

I pressed my face against his chest and tried not to cry. How stupid was I? I'd not only slept with a nearly-married man – twice – but I'd fallen for someone who'd tried to rape me. Not only fallen for him… but fucked him. Made love with him. Cared for him. I was even planning to move closer, had allowed myself to dream of a future.

I swallowed hard, imagining how he must have been laughing at me the entire time. Trying to see how gullible I was? How far I'd go?

My stomach heaved and I was pretty sure I was going to be sick. If I was, I didn't want to do it in front of Julien.

"You can go to the cops about what he did," Julien said, his voice soft. "I'll come with you and say how he confessed in front of me."

I shook my head but didn't look up. I didn't want to see if the pity that wasn't in his voice was in his eyes. "Doesn't matter what you say. No one cares about an almost-assault on a stripper. I wasn't hurt. Don't even remember it."

"He shouldn't be able to do something like that and get away with it." There was heat to Julien's voice now.

"He got a sore jaw out of it." I tried to make the words light. If I didn't, I was going to crack and, as nice as Julien was being, he didn't deserve that. "Thank you, by the way."

"Should've castrated the bastard," Julien muttered darkly. "Maybe that would've taught him a lesson."

Now there was a pleasing image. I pressed my lips together tightly. Julien's comfort was welcome, but I needed to regain my composure enough to see him out before I could let go of everything I was holding in. I was just getting ready to take a step back when I heard a voice speak.

"Well, looks like you're really working your way through the Who's Who of Philadelphia society."

For the second time in just a few minutes, my mind and body were frozen in place by the sound of a male voice. Only, this one wasn't Brock. This was the one voice I didn't want to hear again, but also the only one I secretly longed for.

Reed.

What was he doing here? That question was immediately followed by one prompted by my recent discover. Had he been in on it the whole time?

That thought gave me what I needed to move. I took a step back, breaking free of Julien's embrace. He let me go and stepped off to the side. I wasn't sure if it was because of what Reed had said or if he was able to tell I had someone else to be angry at. I didn't care. All I knew was that now I could see Reed standing in the doorway.

His expression was tight and his eyes guarded. I thought I could see a hint of hurt in them, and rather than feeling sorry for him; it just made me angrier.

"Did you see your buddy in the hallway?" I spat at him before remembering. "Oh, sorry, your brother-in-law. Did he tell you the game was over? I know."

"Oh, so Brock was here too?" Reed snapped. "Were you having a threesome, or did Brock go first?"

I felt Julien take a step forward and knew he was going to come to my defense. I put a hand out. "Could you give us a minute?"

Julien hesitated and I could see him pulled by indecision. Warmed by his need to protect me, I touched him arm and said, "Please."

I waited until Julien closed the apartment door behind him and then turned on Reed again.

"Listen to me, you arrogant bastard." I crossed the space between us until I could've reached out and touched him. I didn't though. I didn't want to touch him ever again. "I'm not sleeping with Julien. He was comforting me. Besides, you have no right to act all holier-than-thou considering what you've done." My hands were shaking and I curled them into fists. "Was it all part of some kind of game? Fuck me, hire me, then see how far Brock was willing to take things? Play the hero and step in so I'd trust you? Or were you just waiting to take your turn?"

Genuine confusion crossed his face. "What are you talking about?"

The fact that he so obviously didn't know what Brock had done should've softened me, but I didn't let it. Besides, I told myself, I knew he was a good actor. Maybe he was faking this, too.

"I'm talking about Brock putting something in my water at your bachelor party," I said. "I hadn't been drinking. Since you kept watching me, I figured you must've known that."

"I didn't know where you were all the time," he countered. "For all I knew, you were out on the balcony doing shots before I came out there."

"Yeah, because that's my thing," I snapped. "Get wasted and hook up with some random guy."

"Wasn't like you hadn't done that before," Reed retorted, his almost-black eyes flashing. "For all I knew, I'd just been a warm-up to see if you could fuck someone else like me."

My stomach twisted again and I had a feeling, at some point very soon, I was going to lose my dinner. I was determined to get my say in before that happened. "Someone like you? You mean an arrogant prick? It's not that hard. Guys like you don't exactly have any sort of integrity to begin with."

He took a step back, a shocked expression on his face.

I kept going, advancing on him, backing him up another step. "You're all the same. Guys like you and Brock. You don't mind slumming it when it means you're getting laid, but that's all girls like me are. Mistresses, whores, not really much of a difference."

Reed held up a hand. "What the fuck are you talking about? I had no idea Brock put anything in your water," Reed insisted. "Had I known, or even suspected it, I would have killed him."

"Yeah, right. My hero."

Reed's eyes narrowed at my sarcasm but I continued, "Don't bother." I crossed my arms. "Wouldn't want you to do something that might jeopardize knocking up the wife you don't love."

"Who told you..." he started to ask, then answered his own question. "Brock." His hands became fists. "Now I'm really going to kill him."

"Oh, was that supposed to be a secret?" I asked. "Were you thinking I'd be a nice piece of ass while Britni was pregnant, but I wasn't supposed to know the reason?"

"It's not like that."

I hugged out a breath, not believing he thought me so gullible. "I know about the heir clause, Reed. Did you think that was going to be your out? Your way to excuse the fact that you say you want to be with me, but you're still sleeping with your wife?" I could feel the little bit of control I had slipping away. "If that's what you came here to say, don't bother."

"That's not why I came here." He tossed an envelope at me and I caught it reflexively. "I came to apologize for my behavior."

I stared at him, then looked down at the envelope, rage building inside me again. "What's this?" I held it up. "Money? Surprise, surprise. That's how men like you 'apologize' to girls like me, isn't it? Buy us off with cash or jewelry." I walked over to the table and grabbed the roses from their vase. It tipped over, spilling water across the dishes I hadn't yet cleaned up. I didn't care. "Or flowers. That's always a good one. I should be so grateful that someone like you would buy me flowers that I should just forgive you." I shoved the flowers into the trashcan, keeping my back to Reed so he couldn't see the tears that had finally managed to escape.

"No," he snapped. "It's not money. It's a place at Madam Emilana's Dance School in Philadelphia."

Shock broke through my anger enough to make me turn, but he was gone. I took a step toward the door. My mind was spinning. This was too much. I was still reeling from Brock's confession and Reed's accusations, and now I had a hundred questions about the envelope I'd tossed onto the table when I'd grabbed the roses.

The first one was the most obvious. Why? Why had Reed pulled strings to get me a place at one of the elite private studios in Philadelphia? There had to be some ulterior motive. Some reason beyond wanting to apologize.

The door opened and my heart gave a wild leap. An unwanted flash of disappointment poured through me. It was Julien.

"Are you okay?" he asked immediately. He glanced at the trashcan where broken stalks stuck up. The scent from the crushed petals was nearly overwhelming.

I started to nod, but it quickly became a shake as my composure cracked. I put my face in my hands and pressed my lips together, desperately trying not to completely break in front of Julien. He placed his hand on my shoulder and the kind touch undid me. I let out a strangled sob and he pulled me against his chest.

All of the frustration of the past couple months, combined with everything that had happened tonight was too much. I could barely breathe as I cried, taking gulping, gasping breaths before letting them out again in choking sobs. I didn't try to explain what I was feeling and Julien didn't ask. He didn't say anything, in fact. He just held me and let me cry.

At some point, we moved to the couch, but his hands stayed on my back the entire time. Not once did they venture anywhere they shouldn't be and I realized I felt safe. I trusted him, and though I knew that might've been the emotional vulnerability talking, I didn't have the energy for anything more introspective.

Finally, I pulled back, brushing my hands across my cheeks. I felt hollow and empty inside, but it was better than everything else I'd been feeling. And I didn't think I was going to throw up now, which was a definite plus.

"Do you want to be alone?" Julien broke the silence with his softly-spoken question. "Or do you want me to stay on the couch?"

I appreciated the way he worded it so there was no doubt as to his intentions. I looked up at him, promising myself that if I saw the least bit of interest, I'd ask him to leave. All I saw was compassion and a hint of anger.

"I'll get some sheets." I sniffled as I stood.

"Don't go to any trouble," Julien got to his feet as well. "This is better than half the places I slept in Europe."

"It's no trouble," I said. "It's the least I could do."

When I came back from the bathroom closet, Julien was clearing the table. I didn't protest because I knew it wouldn't do any good. Instead, I put the sheets on the couch and then went to help him.

After we finished, I showered and finally climbed into bed. I was so emotionally and physically exhausted that I didn't have any problem falling straight to sleep.

Chapter 2

When I woke up, it took a minute to remember why my eyes were swollen and dry, and why I had that hollowed out feeling in my chest. Everything came rushing back all at once and I pressed my face into my pillow to stifle my pained cry. The betrayal, the anger at myself for being so stupid, all of it was still there, though just a bit less fresh than it had been the day before.

I laid there for several minutes, letting the pain wash through me and over me. I knew the only way to deal with it was to let it have its way and learn to breathe around it. This wasn't the worst pain I'd ever felt, and since I'd survived before, I knew this ache would be bearable. It wasn't pleasant, but it wouldn't drive me over the edge. I was stronger than this.

I sat up, my eyes still dry. I wasn't going to let this stop me from living my life. And that meant I had a decision to make.

I'd picked up the envelope from the table last night while Julien and I had been cleaning up, and I'd brought it into my room to dry. I hadn't opened it since it hadn't looked like the water from the vase had soaked through.

Now, I reached over to the table next to my bed and picked it up. It was one of those manila envelopes, so I didn't have to unfold the papers inside before I could see what they said.

The one on top was a welcome letter stating that I'd received a grant from an anonymous donor to attend classes at the studio. The grant was renewing, so as long as I maintained attendance and met the qualifying guidelines, I would be able to continue attending. My place was probationary, based on my performance at my formal interview as well as my progress for the first ninety days.

That actually made me feel better. Reed hadn't just bought them off. I still had to earn my way in. That meant I wouldn't be accepted if I weren't good enough. Most people would've thought that would put more pressure on me, but it was that requirement that made me consider accepting the place. Sure, his money had opened the door, but it hadn't guaranteed me anything more than a shot. I hated the idea of owing him something, but it wouldn't be as big a debt as I'd first thought. And, realistically, I had to consider that it might be worth it in the end.

After the introductory letter were several other papers that appeared, at first glance, to be forms I needed to fill out. I didn't look closer at them, however, because at that moment I heard something, a noise from the kitchen. I stiffened, then remembered that Julien had stayed the night on the couch. Unless Rosa had decided to come home early from visiting her mother, it was him. I heard a man's voice utter a low oath and I smiled. Julien.

I climbed out of bed and headed into the bathroom. I wasn't going to primp, but I also wanted to at least run a brush through my hair and get rid of my morning breath. My stomach rumbled as wonderful smells wafting down the hallway. Julien must be making us breakfast; it smelled like bacon and eggs. But I knew that couldn't be the case. I couldn't remember the last time I'd had enough money for bacon. Toast was the usual go-to for breakfast on the rare occasion either of us ate it.

My stomach growled again. Apparently I was hungrier than I'd thought. The previous night's insanity must've taken its toll. I finished washing my face, pulled my hair back into a lopsided ponytail and headed out of my room and to the kitchen.

"Hey," Julien said as I came out of the hallway. He was sucking on the side of his finger like he'd burnt it. "I was craving bacon and eggs so I went out and got some. Hope you don't mind."

I shook my head, appreciating the fact that he wasn't pointing out what was missing in my kitchen. I'd spent basically my entire food budget on the previous night's dinner.

I frowned as I thought of it. Such a waste.

"So…" Julien's tone told me he was going to ask something of a slightly personal nature. "What was in the envelope?"

My head jerked up. That hadn't been what I'd expected. I'd been thinking more along the lines of wanting to know how I was doing or something like that.

"If you don't want to tell me," he hurriedly added.

"No, it's okay," I assured him. "I was just surprised you'd noticed it, that's all."

He shrugged as he scraped the scrambled eggs onto two plates. "It wasn't there when we were eating, but it was when we were cleaning up. Doesn't take a genius to figure out Reed brought it for you." He glanced at me and then scowled down at the bacon. "Is he trying to buy you off?"

I took a deep breath, wondering if I should share Reed's offer or not. I shook my head. "Not exactly. It's a chance to get into Madam Emilana's Dance School."

Julien brought the plates over to the table while I carried two glasses of water. Other than what was left of last night's wine, water was all we had to drink. He didn't complain though and we ate in companionable silence for several minutes. The food settled well and Julien was a much better cook than I would've thought a rich kid would be, especially after I remembered how Brock had joked on our first date about barely knowing how to shop for himself.

"Can I ask you something?" Julien broke the silence. "And please feel free to tell me to go to hell if I'm out of line."

After everything he'd heard last night, I wasn't entirely sure what was left for him to ask. I nodded. "I'll do that."

"Did you and Reed date when you were at St. George's?"

I nearly choked on my bacon. "You think Reed Stirling would've dated me? A scholarship kid from the wrong side of the tracks?" I laughed.

Julien's expression remained serious. "I think I saw something between the two of you last night that said you have a history." He leaned back in his chair and raised his hands. "Like I said, tell me to go to hell if I'm out of line."

I was quiet for a moment, debating whether or not I wanted to talk about what had happened. Anastascia was the only other person who knew about Reed, but after last night, she was back to not knowing the whole story. Julien knew the end. The question I had to ask myself was if I wanted to tell him the beginning.

I decided on a compromise. "Reed and I never dated, but we hooked up twice." I looked down at what was left of my scrambled eggs. "I'm the one who ended it."

"And he never got over that."

I shrugged. I wasn't going to out-and-out lie, but if Julien wanted to infer that this hook-up had taken place years ago, I wasn't going to correct him either.

"Did Brock know about it?"

"Not exactly," I said. "He knew there was something there, kind of like you did."

Julien hesitated; like there was a question he wasn't sure he should ask.

"Go ahead," I prompted him. "I won't answer if it bugs me."

"Did he really offer you ten thousand dollars to go to Reed's wedding with him?"

I pressed my lips together as heat rose in my cheeks. I briefly considered not telling him or lying. In the end, I settled for another half-truth. "He paid for my plane ticket, hotel room and dress. The note said he'd give me ten thousand dollars, but I assumed he was joking. Since he never gave it to me, I figured that was the case."

I wondered if Julien could tell I wasn't being entirely honest. If he could, he didn't say anything. He ate the last of the bacon off of his plate and then stood. "So what are you going to do?"

I blinked. "About what?"

He picked up my plate and flashed a grin at me. "About the dance grant. I'm guessing since you aren't walking around all smiles, you're still deciding if you should accept it or not."

My eyebrows went up. "You're way more observant than I gave you credit for."

His smile widened as he carried our plates to the sink. "That's the advantage to having a reputation like mine. Most people assume I'm a screw-up, and therefore stupid."

"I never thought that," I countered as I joined him at the sink.

"I'll wash, you dry," he offered. When I gave him a surprised look, he laughed. "Worked my way across Europe, remember?"

I nodded and pulled the dish soap from under the sink.

"Anyway," he continued. "The dance studio, that's back in Philadelphia, isn't it?"

I sighed. "It is."

"And the way you were talking before, it sounded like you hadn't really wanted to go back."

I shook my head. He really was observant.

"Is the grant something you want?"

I considered the question before answering right away. I was younger than Julien, but I wasn't a kid anymore. If I had dreams, they couldn't be the fantasies of a child. I knew I loved to dance, but did I really want to go to school for it? I was twenty-three, and for a dancer, that was almost too old for where I was. If I didn't take this now, I wouldn't have another chance. There was no probably or maybe about it. This was it.

"I want it," I admitted and my heart squeezed at the possibility. "All I've ever wanted to be is a dancer." I looked around the apartment. "And this isn't what I had in mind."

If I took the offer, I could leave this place, quit my job. I wouldn't have to strip anymore. Granted, it meant I was going back to a place with a lot of painful memories and I'd have to find a new job there, but I'd be pursuing my passion and not taking off my clothes for creepy old guys and leering twenty-somethings.

"Look, I know this whole thing isn't any of my business," Julien said as he handed me a plate to dry. "But based on everything you've told me, and knowing there's a lot you haven't, you've been through a hell of a lot."

I couldn't really disagree with that. True, there were a lot of people who'd had a rougher life than me, but it didn't mean mine wasn't hard, just that theirs was worse.

"The way I see it," he reasoned. "You deserve to have something go right for once."

I exhaled, and then breathed that thought back in. Maybe he was right, I thought as I put the dishes away. It wasn't like I'd asked Reed to do this for me, and he'd said it was an apology. That didn't sound like it came with any strings attached except possible forgiveness. And this wasn't like Brock's offer of money, which would've helped me of course; but it wouldn't have changed anything, not really. And it definitely wasn't like Reed's offer to keep me in Vegas as his mistress. This was an opportunity to change things, to move forward with my life.

Julien leaned back against the sink and glanced at his watch. "Well, my plane leaves soon, so I need to go get my stuff." He straightened, his expression sobering. "Are you going to be okay?"

I nodded. "I will. And thank you for being here. I don't know if I would've been okay yesterday without you."

"You have a pen?"

I looked at him, puzzled, but pointed toward the refrigerator where Rosa and I had a pen with a magnet so we could write things we needed on a notepad. Julien scrawled something on a piece of paper, tore it off and handed it to me.

"My number," he explained. "Call me when you make a decision or if you just need to talk."

I waited for the inevitable addition, wondering if it would be a "look me up if you're back in Philly" or "I'll hit you up the next time I'm in Vegas," but it never came. He put his hand on my shoulder and squeezed, but the touch was as platonic as it got. "Hopefully I'll see you back home." He smiled at me. "You deserve it."

"Thanks," I said. "And I will... call you, I mean."

I kept looking at the door even after it closed. I hadn't just been polite, I realized. I really was thinking about calling Julien if I went back to the city. I'd enjoyed the time we'd spent together over the week. Well, the moments Brock hadn't been ruining by being an ass. And then there was the way he'd behaved through this whole shitstorm.

He'd defended me more than once to Brock, ending with a punch, and then he'd held me while I'd cried without trying to take advantage of the situation.

I hadn't truly realized how rare something like that was in a man until yesterday.

As much as I'd been grateful for his help, comfort and advice, I wasn't about to trust a huge decision to a ten-minute conversation with someone who was practically a stranger. I needed a second opinion – well, third if mine counted as the first – and there was only one person who I could trust to be completely honest.

Besides, she deserved to know that she'd been right about Brock, no matter how much I hated to have to go through it all again.

It was close to nine, which meant Anastascia would be at the gym, so I finished cleaning up and even took out the trash. I didn't want to have a single thing in my apartment that reminded me about this disastrous week. By the time I finished cleaning and took a shower, it was close to noon and I knew Anastascia would be home again.

She answered almost immediately. "What'd he do?"

"What?" I was so startled I didn't even think to just answer her question.

"You already told me some of the shit that boy was up to. Now, if he was as good as you said he was, you'd still be snuggling with him in bed instead of calling me."

"Damn." I flopped back on my bed. "You're good."

"I know," she said. "Now, spill."

Spill I did. I picked up from the last time she and I had talked and told her everything that had happened, the good and the bad. When I got to the part where Brock confessed what he'd done and tried to do at the bachelor party, she started cursing so loudly that I had to hold my phone away from my ear. The language turned into the many painful ways she wished to torture and kill him, not the least of which involved stripping him naked and tying him outside during the coldest night in winter and letting bits of him freeze off.

When she finally ran out of horrible things to say about Brock, she said something that nearly rendered me speechless.

"I'm so sorry, Piper."

"For what? You warned me about him," I said when I found my voice.

"If I'd known he'd try something like that, I wouldn't have let up until you dumped him."

"You know me," I said. "It wouldn't have done any good. I would've kept it up, just to prove you wrong."

"True," she admitted.

"And before you start in on Brock again, there's more."

"You're joking."

"Oh, no. That was just the start of my crazy night."

By the time I was done, Anastascia was unusually quiet. I waited for a few minutes, and then couldn't take it anymore.

"So?"

"So what?"

I scowled at the phone. "So what am I supposed to do?"

"Shh," Anastascia shushed me. "I'm trying to figure out if I should redecorate the guest room. You like taupe, right?"

Chapter 3

Anastascia did indeed redecorate her guest room, but she'd decided on a dusky rose color instead of taupe. She'd said I should help choose since I was going to be her roommate, but I'd insisted that the arrangements were just temporary and that she do it herself while I was tying things up in Vegas. She'd pressed the issue until I told her that if I was going to move back and try this whole dance thing, I wanted to make a completely fresh start, including living on my own. It was just something I had to do. After that, she'd moved on to other topics related to my arrival.

It had taken a couple weeks for me to get things in order since I hadn't wanted to leave Rosa in the lurch. I didn't care quite so much about a two-week notice at The Diamond Club, but since I'd been waiting for Rosa to find a new roommate, I picked up as many extra shifts as possible so I'd have at least some money while I looked for a job in Philly. The kind of jobs a high school graduate with experience stripping and waiting tables could get weren't exactly the kind you could find online and send in a resumé for. Anastascia loaned me the money for my ticket, but I hadn't wanted to borrow any more off of her while I was waiting to get a job.

I arrived in Philadelphia on a Friday evening in mid-August and spent the weekend walking the streets and putting in applications despite Anastascia telling me to take it easy for at least a couple days since I started classes on Monday. The only concession I made was to come back early so we could have dinner together.

Now it was Monday morning and I was standing outside a small studio only a few blocks away from Anastascia's place. That had been another reason I hadn't argued too much about staying in her guest room until I found a place of my own. If I could get a job nearby, it would be perfect. There were plenty of cheaper apartments in Fishtown that, eventually, I'd be able to afford.

That was for later though. Right now, I needed to focus on dance. Technically, I wasn't starting a class today. I was observing three different level classes and then would be tested to see where I fit. If they wanted to, they could say that I didn't qualify at all, but I had enough faith in myself that I'd, at the very least, get in on the bottom level.

Concentration was the key.

As I entered the studio, I found myself in a tastefully decorated space. It was clearly the work of an interior designer and the budget had been vast, but it wasn't ostentatious. I introduced myself to the woman at the desk, endured her disapproving glare as she looked at my obviously worn clothes. Moments later, I let myself enjoy the way she pursed her lips when she had to wave me back toward the changing room.

As I walked into the changing room, I once again found myself wondering how Reed had managed to pull this off. This wasn't the kind of studio that everyone in Philadelphia knew of, because Madam Emilana was extremely particular about the students she accepted and she didn't advertise. There always had to be some sort of personal connection, a referral. Had he donated funds to the school on top of establishing the grant that would pay my tuition? Or was she one of his business contacts, the kind of high society person whose favor-for-favor exchange was generally in the hundred thousands to millions?

I pushed the thoughts out of my mind as I headed into the main studio area. The biggest downside to coming back here, I'd discovered, had been my thoughts constantly going to Reed. I told myself the reason was that I hadn't thanked him for the gift because that meant having to address what had happened the last time we'd seen each other.

I'd been wrong that night, and I knew it. This whole thing with Reed and Britni was a mess, but no matter how I felt about that, I knew, deep down, that Reed would never let any woman be taken advantage of. If he'd known what Brock had done, he wouldn't have let it go. Accusing him of not only being culpable, but also wanting to participate had been out of line.

I just didn't know how to tell him all of that.

"You must be Miss Black."

A woman's sharp voice brought me back to myself. She was tall and slender, but muscled. With a graceful neck and perfect posture, I knew instantly she'd been a ballerina.

"I'm Janine Weathers, Madam Emilana's assistant." She smoothed down her already-perfect bun. "I teach the remedial and intermediate levels. Madam Emilana teaches the advanced class as well as private sessions for those students who she believes have the talent to go further."

I nodded. That was my goal then. Private lessons.

"Today, you will sit in on both of my classes and then in Madam Emilana's. Once those are completed, you will perform in front of us. We alone will determine your placement." She glowered down at me. "Any questions?"

"Is there anything you want me to do with the classes?"

A muscle in her jaw clenched. "That won't be necessary. The point of you sitting in the classes today is so that when you place lower than you believe you should be, you'll have a reference point to see what we expect."

I stared at her as she started toward the front of the studio.

"Don't mind her."

I looked over as a girl in her mid-teens grinned at me. "Miss Janine is like that with everyone. She says it's a way to weed out the weak; that if you can't handle her being harsh privately, then you'll never make it out there."

I smiled at the girl and headed for the bench against the sidewall while she went to the rail to stretch out. While I still wasn't fond of the attitude, I understood it now and could appreciate the sentiment behind it. Miss Janine was right about how hard it was out there. The competition for this particular field was intense. I didn't know what the specific stats were, but I did know that the number of girls who made it was well below half.

I studied each of the moves as Miss Janine put the girls through their paces. I had a basic routine in my head that I was going to do, but I'd purposefully left gaps so I could see what the students did first. I figured if I put in and nailed at least two or three things that each class was working on, the better shot I had at being placed higher.

I was relieved to see that the remedial class wasn't working on anything I didn't know. It had been a long time since I'd done real dancing, and while I'd been practicing the last couple weeks, I hadn't been sure where I'd compare to the other students. When the intermediates arrived, I saw that the majority of them were around my age. Most of them smiled at me as they walked past, and the ones who didn't, had expressions on their faces that said when they were here, they never smiled at anyone. I understood that too. Focus was important.

I could see the difference between the classes immediately. These were young women who were looking toward a possible career in dance, whether as an instructor or on stage. From what I saw, I believed I could hold my own with them, maybe even be better.

As they exited, I noticed a couple linger behind, watching the door. When a striking older woman with silver streaks in her dark hair entered the room, the students' reactions told me that this was Madam Emilana. She glanced at me once, nodded and then turned her attention back to the new young women who were stretching. They ranged in age from about fifteen to at least several years older than me, and even watching them at the bar was evidence that they were the advanced class. These were the ones who had a shot of making it. Some maybe only in local troupes, but they'd be doing what they loved.

I was completely entranced as the class worked. I hadn't truly acknowledged how much I missed this. When I'd first started stripping, I'd tried to keep my style and had been told that if guys wanted to see that, they'd go to a show. If anything kept me from being in the advanced class right away, it would be the rough edge I'd unintentionally gained while in Vegas.

When the class ended, some students filed back to the changing room while others left directly. Madam Emilana didn't acknowledge my presence until the last woman left, and then she walked over to me. I stood and held out my hand. Her grip was firm and her eye contact steady. She didn't look down at me or frown like the other two women had and I wondered if that was because of her personality or if she didn't know where I came from. I assumed the other two did.

"Miss Black." Her voice had a hint of an accent I couldn't quite place. "Once Miss Janine joins us, we'll begin your audition."

I nodded. "Thank you for the opportunity."

"Of course." She gave me a smile that said once work ended, the tough teacher went away too. "Any friend of the Stirling family is welcome here."

I managed a tight smile. Okay, so that answered one question.

"Reed mentioned that you didn't have any formal training," she said.

"That's true. A few classes at the local youth center when I was a kid, but that was it."

"And you think you'll be able to keep up with our classes after a few classes as a kid?" She sounded doubtful but not cruel.

It wasn't until that moment that I realized what I should have known before. They didn't know what I'd been doing in Vegas. No one here did. This really was my chance for a fresh start.

"Let's see what you have prepared," Madam Emilana said as she and Miss Janine moved to stand at the front of the studio.

With the weight that had been lifted at the idea of a clean slate, the routine went even better than I'd hoped. I added in each of the elements I'd selected from the three classes, nailing the first ones with ease, the second set without a problem and almost completing the last ones perfectly. A little bobble on one and another that looked a bit rough, but still recognizable. The other parts had been brought in from various forms of dancing I'd done over the years, though the ones from the last two years were much more sanitized versions. All in all, when I finished, I was beyond pleased with what I'd done. I just hoped the judges slash teachers felt the same way.

When I first looked at them, my heart sank because they were turned toward each other, having what appeared to be a low, heated discussion, though their faces were basically blank.

"Miss Black," Miss Janine turned toward me first. "You stated that you hadn't had any formal training."

"That's right." I sounded more winded than I wanted to, but there wasn't anything I could do about that now.

"Then may I ask how you included elements specifically taught in dance classes, one of which is exclusively taught here?"

I wasn't sure if she was angry or not, but I figured honesty was the best way to go. "I watched the classes and chose elements that would fit into the spaces I'd left in my routine."

Miss Janine's eyebrows shot up. "You're telling us that you came here with a half-completed piece, intending to fit in unknown elements that you'd never practiced before?"

I tried not to shift my weight from one foot to the other, but the questions were making me nervous. I wasn't sure if I'd done something wrong or what the correct answer was, so I stuck with the truth. "Yes."

"How did you know you'd be able to do anything we were teaching?"

Madam Emilana still hadn't spoken. She was simply watching the conversation volley back and forth, her face an impassive mask.

I shrugged and immediately regretted it. A shrug was about as far from elegant as a person could get. I straightened my posture. "If I couldn't do at least what the remedial class was doing, I didn't belong here. If the other levels would've been too hard to even try, I would've only added ones from the first class."

Now Madam Emilana spoke and she sounded almost smug. "I told you that was what she was doing."

Now I was just confused and let it show. Neither of the women explained though.

"Excellent work," Miss Janine said, and it didn't sound grudging at all. Maybe she wasn't so bad after all.

"Yes," Madam Emilana said. "You will begin in the advanced class starting tomorrow and should you prove to be as hard a worker as I believe you to be, your private lessons with me will start at the beginning of the upcoming year."

I was still beaming when I walked outside fifteen minutes later. I was also pretty sure that, if I hadn't been a grown woman standing on a city sidewalk, I might have skipped a bit. I was still debating going for it when I heard a familiar voice call my name.

"Piper! I was hoping I hadn't missed you."

I turned as Julien jogged across the street. He was grinning at me and, for a moment, I thought he would hug me, but he didn't. He stopped within arm's reach and stuck his hands into his pockets. It was a hot day and he was wearing shorts, showing off athletic legs that were a bit paler than the rest of his visible skin.

"I called the studio to ask what times they normally held their auditions so I could get here in time to see how you did."

I was so touched at his thoughtfulness, of his remembering my big day. I was smiling so big I thought my face would crack. "Great!" I nearly yelled, "I'm in the advanced class with a chance to have private lessons."

Moving back to Philadelphia now seemed worth it.

"That's wonderful!" He gave me a slightly awkward one-armed hug and then backed away. "Hungry?"

"Starving." I hadn't been able to eat much today. Too many nerves.

"Then let's celebrate," Julien said. "My treat."

I smiled. "Where do you want to go?"

"Your choice. It's your celebration."

"Trolley car?" I suggested.

"Breakfast for dinner." He chuckled. "Bacon and eggs?"

I laughed too. The fact that he'd made me breakfast without expecting anything in return had made that one of my few positive memories of that week.

I was surprised at how smoothly the conversation flowed as we walked back to his car and then drove out to Germantown Avenue. He was still really easy to talk to. I suppose I'd thought our conversations before had been a fluke brought about by the need to be less awkward with Brock being a jerk, or by alcohol. That last conversation we'd had wasn't like this at all, so I didn't count it. Now, I could see it wasn't any of that. Julien was one of those rare people with whom it was comfortable to talk. One subject flowed into another and never ventured into anything uncomfortable or too personal. Over pancakes with maple syrup and cinnamon buns with creamy frosting, he told me what he'd been doing since we'd last seen each other, and then he asked how the job search was going.

I frowned at my pancakes. "I think I covered half the diners and restaurants in Fishtown, but none of them are actually looking for help. They were all really polite and let me fill out an application, but I doubt I'll hear anything from them." I tried to lighten the mood by leaning across the table and taking some of Julien's frosting. "Too bad Brock never made good on his promise. That ten thousand dollars would come in handy right about now." I flushed as I realized how that sounded.

Fortunately, Julien was polite enough to ignore it and kept going with the original conversation. "Are you definitely wanting a job around Fishtown then?" he asked as he stabbed a piece of my pancake, giving me a dazzling smile as he ate the food he'd stolen.

I nodded. "That would be my preference. I'm staying with Anastascia right now and I don't have a car. I could borrow hers, but she's already doing so much for me." I stopped suddenly, pressing my lips together. We were venturing into overshare territory. "It'd just be nice to be able to walk from her place to work and then to the studio, and not have to worry about trying to get a ride." I glanced up at the sun. It was already starting to get darker earlier. "At least until winter comes."

"Yeah, I'll bet that'll be one thing you'll miss about Vegas," Julien said. "No one wants to walk in Philly during January."

I nodded even though I knew I'd be one of the ones doing just that. First priority was to find a place of my own. It may have seemed like I should've worried about a car first, but unless I was forced to get a job somewhere that having one was absolutely necessary, being in my own apartment came first. Walking would help keep me in shape. I'd dealt with walking in Philadelphia winters before. I could do it again.

"I know a few people in the area," Julien said. "I could make some calls." He held up a finger before I had the chance to say anything. "I won't do it if you don't want me to. I know some people don't like taking help." The twitch at the corner of his mouth said he remembered our conversation a few weeks ago regarding that exact thing.

He was right. I didn't like asking for help, but I was getting better at it, especially since I knew once I got hired somewhere, they wouldn't regret it. I was a hard worker, and after two years of stripping, dealing with obnoxious restaurant customers was going to seem like a vacation. Besides, it was either this or borrow money from Anastascia in a week or so when what I had left from the club finally ran out. I'd refused to let her pay for my food and I'd had to get clothes for dance class. That had taken most of what I'd brought with me.

"Thank you," I said sincerely. "I'd appreciate that."

He nodded. "All right then. I'll get back to you as soon as I hear anything." He held my gaze for a moment, and then smoothly transitioned to another subject. "So, tell me what you're going to be looking to do with your dancing. Theater? I'm not even sure what all the options are."

I liked this, I thought. Good food. Good conversation. And a nice guy who wasn't trying to get into my pants. It was refreshing.

Chapter 4

The first week at Madam Emilana's was amazing. Granted, by the end of the week, my muscles were protesting every little move, but it was hard to describe how wonderful that actually felt.

Other things were going well too. Wednesday, Julien had called and given me the name of a tiny little family-owned restaurant two blocks over from the dance studio. I'd gone in before school the next day and was warmly greeted by an elderly Italian man who'd instantly proclaimed me 'Bella' and hired me on the spot. I might've thought Julien paid him if the man hadn't been so honestly excited. We'd set up a schedule that included letting me work split shifts around school and then agreed that Saturday afternoon would be my first day.

I was thinking about how well the move back was going when a car pulled up to the curb and honked. I jumped and nearly flipped off the driver when I heard Julien laughing.

"Didn't mean to scare you," he said as I walked over to the driver's side window.

"You keep showing up here when I'm walking home and I'm going to start thinking you're a stalker," I teased.

"You caught me," he joked back. "I have my camera in the backseat."

I rolled my eyes. "What's up?"

"I want to show you something."

"What?"

He gave me an enigmatic smile. "It's a surprise."

My eyes narrowed. "I'm not really that fond of surprises."

"It's a good one," he said. "I promise." He made the childhood gesture of crossing his heart.

"Promises, promises." I walked around to the other side of the car and climbed in. "Let's get this over with."

"Wow," he said as he pulled the car back into the correct lane. "You'd think I was taking you to get a tooth pulled or to meet my parents or something."

I shot him a sideways glance. "I wasn't aware that we were at that point in our relationship." The horrified expression on his face made me laugh. "Relax, Julien. I was kidding." He still looked tense, so I added, "We're way past that. You've already seen me naked and slept over."

He chuckled and the tension eased. I breathed a silent sigh of relief. I liked what we had and I didn't want it to change. I needed a friend and stability right now. I didn't even want to think about anything else.

"Where are we going?" I asked as he turned away from Anastascia's.

"You'll see," he promised. "It's not far."

We went one more street over, which meant the restaurant where I was going to be working was now halfway between school and wherever we were. He parked next to a church and climbed out. I followed, but couldn't imagine why he'd brought me to a church. He'd never said anything that made me think he was very religious.

"This way." He led the way down one of the cobblestone side streets. We went about a third of the way down and he stopped.

Like the other apartments on this street, it was more of a row house than the kind of apartment I'd had back in Vegas. Red brick with concrete steps that led up to a door with chipped and faded paint, it was a bit more run-down than the buildings on either side of it, but it was still vastly larger than the place Rosa and I had shared. Still, I didn't understand why Julien had brought me here.

"It's not officially on the market until tomorrow, but the owner's willing to take less if he doesn't have to advertise or wait. It needs some work, so I got him to accept a pretty cheap offer for the first year's rent."

It all began to click in my head now. "Wait…what? For me?"

"Of course for you. What do you think?"

Think? My eyes widened. I didn't know what to think. I seriously hoped he wasn't about to offer to pay my rent. I really didn't need another person offering to give me things and money. He'd never made a move on me, so I was going to give him the benefit of the doubt that there was something I was missing.

"Julian," I started then had to pause and look back at the building and its surroundings. "I can't afford to live here. Especially when I haven't even started work yet."

Julien handed me an envelope. "Actually, you can."

I had taken the envelope automatically but now just looked at it in suspicion. "What's this?" I asked, an eyebrow raised in question.

"The money Brock promised you."

My jaw dropped.

Julien's eyes shone with a hard light. "I went to see him yesterday and told him that if he didn't pay up, he'd have to leave the state to get a date. Everyone would know what he did."

I threw my arms around him without thinking and he staggered back as I caught him off guard. "Thank you." I had to whisper the words because I wasn't sure I could say them without crying. This wasn't prostitution money. This was more like the settlement I would get if I'd gone after him for assault. That, I didn't feel guilty about taking.

I pulled back, but didn't completely step away, which meant I was still in Julien's arms when I looked up at him.

Our eyes met and, for a second, I thought he was going to kiss me, but then he was letting me go and the moment faded away. He ran his hand through his hair and I thought he looked a bit shaky. I wasn't the only one who'd felt the almost-kiss then. What I didn't know was how I felt about it. I'd just gotten out of a bad relationship that had begun due to a rebound from something that hadn't even been a break-up. I groaned at how stupid that sounded in my head. Besides, I didn't even like Julien that way. Unbidden, Reed's face came to mind and I shoved it aside.

"I'm glad you're happy about it." He gestured toward the apartment. "Should I get the paperwork drawn up? You can come by and see inside tomorrow, either before or after work. I should have a key for you by then."

I nodded. My head was spinning. This was all too much.

"Thank you so much, for all of this." It was hard to talk around the lump in my throat. "I'll never be able to repay you."

"Well, there is one thing you can do," Julien said. "There's this charity event next weekend and I really don't want to go alone. My mom keeps trying to set me up with her society friends' daughters. I'd rather take a friend I can talk to and have a good time with."

If he hadn't thrown in that part about taking a friend, I wasn't sure what I would've said, but since he'd made it clear we weren't going as a couple, I couldn't say anything but yes.

Chapter 5

I probably should have saved everything I had leftover after paying back Anastascia for the plane ticket and putting down the first two months' rent on my new place, but there was one purchase I knew I had to make. I wasn't stupid. I knew that the charity event Julien had asked me to would include the Michaels and Stirling families. By now, I was sure they all despised me even more than they had before, and they weren't going to be happy with me showing up with Julien Atwood. I had to make sure I didn't do anything else to embarrass my friend.

That meant finding something graceful and sophisticated to wear. And if anyone knew how to pull off that look, it was Anastascia. She'd been a bit disappointed to learn I'd be moving into my new place right away, so having her go shopping with me had been a perfect way to show my appreciation for all she'd done while not giving in to her pleas that I stay longer.

We'd gone Sunday, after my shift at the restaurant had ended, and then spent the rest of the day packing my things. Fortunately, I hadn't brought much, so we'd finished in record time. The rest of the week was spent working around my job and school schedules to get me moved into the building I was still having a hard time thinking of as my place.

Compared to the other apartments I'd lived, it was huge. A separate living room and kitchen downstairs, two bedrooms and a bathroom upstairs. Just having stairs was mind-boggling and I ran up and down them a few times just for fun. The only thing I was still missing was furniture. Anastascia told me she planned redecorate her place, so she'd hand down anything she replaced. When I'd protested, she gave me that look and asked if I'd prefer she just throw everything out. How was I supposed to argue with that?

I bought a mattress, which sat directly on the floor as I couldn't also justify the cost of a bed-frame. Anastascia surprised me with a television as a house-warming gift, but that was pretty much the extent of my furniture at the moment. Despite how bare everything looked, I loved it. The rooms already felt more like home than any place had since my mom died.

Julien was coming to pick me up shortly and I just had a few more final touches before I was ready to go. I'd considered pulling my hair up, trying for one of those elaborate styles high-society women always seemed to spend hundreds of dollars on, but in the end, I decided to go along with what Anastascia and I had chosen for my dress. Simple. So the hair stayed down. It fell in waves a few inches past my shoulders, brushing against my skin. The halter style left my arms and back bare, but only offered a hint of cleavage through a diamond-shaped cut out on the front. The skirt was floor-length, and only a pair of five-inch heels kept it from dragging on the ground. The slit in the side stopped just above my knee, offering enough leg to be enticing, but still elegant and appropriate for a formal event.

I kept the make-up at a minimum as well. Not that I wore much to begin with, but tonight, I swept on just a hint eye shadow and mascara and stuck with plain lip gloss. I didn't want to give Julien any reason to regret inviting me. I knew there'd be talk once people realized I was the same woman who'd gone to Britni's wedding with Brock. I shrugged. It couldn't be helped.

I jumped when someone knocked at the door. "Coming!" I called out as I hurried down the stairs. I still wasn't used to being so far away from the door. When I opened it, Julien was already smiling. His grin widened as he saw me and I smiled back. He looked amazing in a black tux that had obviously been custom made to show off his broad shoulders and athletic build.

"You're gorgeous." He held out a single flower in a thin, simple vase. It was a rose, but unlike the ones Brock had given me, this one was white. "Thought you might want a bit of decoration."

"It's beautiful," I said as I held it to my nose and stepped back, motioning for him to come inside. "I don't have anywhere for you to sit."

"That's okay," he said, looking around as I went into the kitchen to fill up the vase.

I wanted to put the flower in the living room so I could see it when I first came in, but the downside of not having furniture meant the only place I could put it was on the counter in the kitchen. When I came back in the living room, he was standing at the front window, looking out into the street.

"No curtains?" he asked.

"They're a little low on my priority list." I picked up my purse and draped a wrap over it. Anastascia had insisted on the piece of matching hunter green silk. It was the first weekend in September, so it was still warm, bordering on hot, but there was always the chance of a chill.

He offered me his arm at the top of the stairs even though it was narrow and I took it gratefully. The shoes were new, which meant I was still getting used to them. The last thing I wanted to do was face-plant coming down my steps.

When we reached the end of the street, a car was waiting. That wasn't surprising, I hadn't been thinking we were going to walk to the event. Instead of it being Julien's

BMW, however, it was a limo. I glanced at him and he shrugged.

"Easy way to make my parents happy."

As we climbed into the backseat, I finally asked the question that had been popping up in my mind since he'd asked me to go with him. "If you don't mind me asking, why are we going to a charity event? I thought you were the black sheep of the family." I kept my tone teasing. "All about being against the system."

He smiled at me as he settled into his seat. He stayed far enough away that we weren't touching, but not so far that the distance was insulting. "Most of the time I am, but my parents and I have an understanding. They support a few charities that are important to me, and those are the events I'll go to without question, and I'll play the good son. This is one of the few mutual ones we support."

"So what's the event for?" I felt bad that I hadn't asked before. It honestly hadn't occurred to me that there might be a cause that Julien thought was important.

"Autism awareness."

"Really?" I couldn't hide my surprise. I'd fully been expecting something like saving whales or cancer research. Those were important, but I hadn't thought of autism as being something on Julien's radar.

"Did you know I had a younger brother?"

I shook my head. I'd always assumed he was an only child.

"Steven," he said. "I was ten when he was born. He was diagnosed with autism when he was two. It was pretty severe. Doctors said he'd never be able to function in society, that my parents should put him in a home. By the time he was five, they couldn't handle him anymore. His meltdowns were violent. He couldn't bear to be touched, but he also couldn't do anything for himself. Mom wanted to hire in home help, but my dad insisted that they look elsewhere."

I reached over and took his hand.

"They found a place for him in upstate New York, the best money could buy, of course." He gave me a bitter smile. "But the money didn't do any good when the place caught on fire two years later. Two nurses died trying to get him out, but they weren't able to save him."

"I'm so sorry." My heart ached for him. Losing my mother had been difficult, but to lose a sibling under such tragic circumstances... I couldn't imagine it.

He squeezed my hand and then let it go. "Thank you." He cleared his throat. "My parents don't like to talk about him." His mouth twisted. "My dad pretends like Steven never existed, like he wasn't the one who pushed to send him away. My mom... it hurts her too much and I know she blames my dad." The tone of his voice told me that it wasn't just Julien's mother who blamed his dad. "Steven's a very private part of our lives."

I heard what he wasn't saying. Not many people knew about his brother. I wasn't sure how I felt about being one of the few who did. It connected us, created an intimacy I wasn't ready for us to have. But I realized how selfish that was and patted his hand, giving it a squeeze.

"I also support one for the arts, and another for underprivileged youth." He brought the conversation back around before I could overanalyze things. "Though my idea of art and my parents' ideas of art aren't exactly the same."

I chuckled, as I was clearly meant to do and the strange tension between us eased. "Now I need to know what you consider art, because some of that abstract stuff, I just don't get."

I may not have been rich, but I'd gone to a prestigious enough school that our art classes were more about Monet and Van Gogh than about actually getting our hands dirty with the art work ourselves. One of the few things I'd enjoyed about St. George was their insistence in taking the students on as many trips to museums and galleries as possible. My passion may have been dance, but I appreciated many forms of creativity.

Our art discussion kept us engaged until we reached the event venue. I couldn't stop myself from staring like a little kid. The Mansion at Noble Lane was the kind of place where a kid like me would've daydreamed about getting married. Once an actual home, the mansion sprawled out in front of us and it was hard to imagine that people had actually lived here long ago. While it was mostly known for being a wedding venue, I supposed that, with enough money, it could be rented for other events as well. With twenty-two acres, it wasn't like it had a shortage of room for a massive number of guests.

"I didn't realize we were coming here," I said as Julien took my hand to help me out of the car. "I've always wanted to see it up close."

"Well, now you can say you have," he said as he hooked my arm through his.

We followed several other couples who'd also just arrived, walking along a well-lit path that lead around to the back where massive tents had been set up. The weather was perfect, the air cooling off a bit as the sun started to go down. The surrounding trees offered a breeze that was neither too strong nor too weak. I didn't think they could've gotten a better day if they'd been able to pay for it.

"You've got to be kidding me." Rebecca's voice easily carried across the lawn.

I turned toward her, a plastic smile already on my face. She glared at me as I gave her a little wave. Her knuckles whitened around the stem of the champagne glass she was holding and I secretly hoped it would snap. Any amusement I got out of that was lost when my gaze locked on to movement behind Rebecca and saw Brock standing there. Our eyes met for a moment and then he quickly looked away, his cheeks turning a dark enough shade of red that I could see it from where I was standing.

"I'd like you to meet my parents," Julien said. One corner of his mouth quirked up in a half-smile. "But, don't worry, I already told them we were just friends."

I loved his thoughtfulness; that I didn't even have time to get anxious about what they'd think before he was setting my mind at ease. I'd been a bit worried that it'd be uncomfortable going to this thing with Julien, concerned that it'd put some sort of expectation on us both. I wasn't feeling pressure at all.

As he led me past a small knot of people, I heard a sharp intake of air and knew, without even looking, that it was Reed. I kept my head facing front and didn't even hesitate in my step. I was planning on talking to him later if I could get him alone and thank him for my gift. It was the least I could do since it was changing my future, but now wasn't the time.

Julien's parents were friendly enough, though that was probably more because I wasn't trying to snag their son than it was them actually liking me. As long as they didn't start acting like I was a gold-digger or call girl, it was a step up from previous times I'd met parents on this side of the continent.

"Let's find our seats," Julien said as his father excused himself to officially start the event.

Tables had been set up in a circle around a large space I could only assume was a dance floor. We made our way to one of the tables closest to the podium and I saw Julien's name and a plus one. Unfortunately, I also saw Britni and Reed's names at the same table. Suddenly, the evening wasn't looking like much fun.

Fortunately, the other people at our table were nice enough and they either didn't sense the subtle tension or were too polite to comment on it. Reed and I did our best not to speak or even look at each other and Julien helped with that. Once the meal portion of the evening was over, Britni excused herself to the restroom and the other couples wandered off to mingle or whatever it was rich people did at these things. That left Reed, Julien and me alone at the table.

I glanced at Julien. I might not get another chance to tell Reed I was sorry, but I wasn't sure how to ask Julien to leave, especially since he knew there was history between us. Julien caught my eye and nodded, understanding in his gaze. It amazed me how well he could read my emotions and thoughts.

"If you'll both excuse me. I need to visit the restroom." He smiled down at me. "I'll be back in a few minutes."

I looked over at Reed and saw that he was already watching me. I couldn't read his expression though and in the dim lighting, his eyes were jet-black.

"I owe you an apology," I began. His eyebrows rose, but that was all the reaction I got. I kept going. I'd practiced this speech ever since Julien had invited me tonight. I knew it was the only chance I'd have to say it. "When you showed up at my place in Vegas, I'd literally just found out about what Brock had done and I took it out on you. I shouldn't have done that."

His face softened, and he leaned toward me.

"No matter what else had happened between us, I should have known better than to accuse you of something like that. I did know better. You'd never force yourself on anyone. I was out of line, and I'm sorry." I twisted my fingers together as I waited for a response.

"I'd never hurt you like that, Piper." His voice was more intense than it should have been to simply accept an apology. And it definitely shouldn't have made my stomach clench with desire.

He continued, "I'm sorry I lost my temper. I came there to apologize and made things worse."

"Well, I think we're about even now," I tried to joke, but one look at those near-black eyes and my mouth went dry. I hated that my body responded to his that way.

"So you accept my apology?"

There was a hopeful note in his voice that I tried to tell myself wasn't there. "I do," I said cautiously. "And I want to thank you for the gift."

"I'm glad you accepted it." He reached across the table and curled his fingers around my hand. "And I'm glad you're back in Philadelphia."

I pulled my hand away as quickly as I could without being rude. I didn't want to start another fight, especially not here where Britni could be back at any moment. My skin tingled where it had touched his and I rubbed my hand on my leg under the table, wishing I could scrub away the feeling. "After I graduate from the studio, I hope you find another dancer to extend the grant to. There are a lot of talented people who don't get the chance to fulfill their potential simply due to a lack of funds." I could hear the stiffness in my voice and hoped he understood that I was closing off the personal part of the conversation.

He opened his mouth to say something, but I never heard what it was because at that moment, Britni returned. She glared at me, but I gave her a polite smile and sipped at my champagne. It was Reed's decision to tell her about the grant. As far as I was concerned, he and I were done. We might see each other at events like this, but I would make a point of not being alone with him again.

My stomach twisted as I thought of it. Sure, I'd told myself that I wanted to be free of him, but in truth, his touch was almost enough to make me forget everything that had happened.

It was crazy, I knew, but I couldn't help the way my body reacted when he was near. My brain said to quit being stupid and my heart agreed, but other parts of my anatomy were still asking why I hadn't kept holding his hand. And it wasn't helping that, even with Britni at his side, he was still watching me.

"Would you like to dance?" Julien's voice came from my left and I nodded quickly; grateful for any excuse to look away.

I slid my hand into Julien's, feeling the heat of Reed's gaze on the back of my neck. "I'd love to."

He led me onto the dance floor and I slid my arms around his neck. His hands started on my hips, but I stepped closer and let him slide them around to the small of my back. I needed to stop thinking about the unattainable and focus on what I had. Julien was a sweet guy who'd never tried to be anything more than a friendly ear. I needed to focus on my friendship with him and not get bogged down with all that emotional, romantic shit.

The only thing was, now that Reed had touched me, it was like a switch inside had been flipped and I wasn't able to turn it off. I kept feeling the way the warmth had spread through my hand and then remembering what it had been like when he'd touched me other places. I wondered what it would be like if he was the one I was dancing with.

"Don't break your brain," Julien said, cutting into my thoughts. I glanced up at him, unsure of what he meant and he laughed. "You seem to be thinking about something awfully hard."

I flushed as I realized what I'd been doing. How could I be angry at Reed for watching and thinking about me while he was with his wife when I was thinking about him while I was with someone else? Granted, Julien and I weren't even dating, but it was still rude and unacceptable. And dangerous.

"Sorry," I said. "Won't happen again."

He smiled his easy smile. "Don't mention it. If you knew how often I daydreamed at these things, you'd think I was even more of a rebel than you already do." His eyes were sparkling with good humor. "That is, if you think I'm a rebel at all and not just a bored rich kid with too much time and money on his hands."

My body began to relax as we talked. Other people danced around us, but they were nothing but peripheral shapes moving in the background. The only ones I saw clearly were the faces I knew. Brock dancing with some petite blonde who didn't look like she was going to need any extra encouragement to fuck him tonight. Rebecca leaning against a handsome young man whose smile probably cost more than my apartment. And, of course, Reed and Britni. No matter how Julien and I moved, Reed was always there, at the corner of my eye. I kept my face at an angle, not wanting to look at him full-on. It was bad enough that I could feel him watching me. I didn't want to have to acknowledge it when his wife was right there in his arms.

Julien spun me around as another song began to play and I laughed as I whirled away from him... right into someone's waiting arms.

I hit the muscular chest and caught a whiff of subtle aftershave, confirming what I already knew. I looked up into those obsidian eyes and was lost.

Chapter 6

"Piper," he murmured my name as his arms closed around me and it was all I could do not to lean into his embrace.

I could see the truth in his eyes. He really did want to be with me. It wasn't just lust I was seeing there, but something deeper I wasn't sure I wanted to name. It connected to a point inside me, a flame of hope I thought I'd extinguished, and it latched on, drawing me to him. His hands were on my bare back, the heat from them setting my skin on fire.

It felt like the moment lasted a lifetime, but when I found the strength to step back, only a couple of seconds had passed.

"Thanks for stopping me from falling." The words sounded stiff and wooden, but I hoped they'd be enough to satisfy any gossipers.

"Dance with me." Reed took a step toward me, seemingly oblivious to the people still dancing around us.

I shook my head and went another step back. "You should dance with your wife." A sharp pain went through me, but I knew it had to be said. I couldn't keep doing this.

To me or him. "You're starting a family. You can't dance with me. You can't see me."

I hurried away before he could protest. Julien didn't try to stop me, though I did catch a glimpse of him coming after me. I followed the discreet signs and ducked into the bathroom before he could catch up and then went into a stall. I leaned against the wall, taking deep breaths and trying not to cry. I'd told Reed all this before, but somehow, this time felt more final.

When I was sure I wasn't going to do anything completely embarrassing, I flushed the toilet and stepped out to wash my hands. While I was still at the sink, the door opened and I automatically glanced up. I stiffened as I saw Britni enter. I'd never spoken to her one-on-one, only general comments in a group setting. Since she was striding toward me, I knew that was about to change.

"Piper." She stopped about a foot away and folded her arms.

I nodded in acknowledgement as I dried my hands. I didn't indicate that I had any idea of why she wanted to talk to me. For all I knew, she was there because of Brock. Sisters could be protective.

"Listen to me, you little bitch."

I clenched my jaw and reminded myself that it wouldn't be a good idea to knock her out.

"I don't know what kind of game you're playing here, with my brother and my husband and Julien, but whatever it is, Reed's not a part of it anymore." Her eyes narrowed. "Brock told me what you did for a living in Vegas, and I know that you're dancing at Madam Emilana's now."

I wasn't sure which revelation shocked me more, though I was leaning toward the dance studio. How had she found out about that? And if she knew I was there, did she know that Reed was paying for it?

"If you don't stay away from my husband, I'll make sure everyone knows that you're not just a gold-digger, but that you used to be a stripper. The only reason I'm not announcing it right now is because you're with Julien and the Atwoods are a very influential family." Almost as an afterthought, she added, "And most everyone here knows you were dating my brother, and I don't want to spread it around that he sank that low just to get laid."

My hands clenched into fists. I wasn't going to do or say anything that could ruin Julien's family's event. I owed him that much. Still, it took all of my self-control to let Britni walk away thinking she'd sufficiently cowed me. I closed my eyes and took a deep breath, counting to ten. When I was certain I wouldn't go after Britni and at least knock out a couple teeth, I walked back out to the tents.

I didn't have to go far to find Julien. He was standing at the edge of the canopy, anxiously looking in my direction.

"Are you okay?" he asked as soon as I was close enough to hear.

"Do you have anything else you need to do here?" I ignored his question and asked my own.

He shook his head, a puzzled look on his face. "No, why?"

"Because I want to go home."

He didn't ask for an explanation or offer some excuse as to why he couldn't go. He simply slipped his arm around my waist and started toward the path leading around to the front of the building.

Chapter 7

The few weeks following the charity event helped me establish a routine. My work schedule varied a bit, but it was more or less consistent. I'd go to work, class, then back to work. Home, then rinse and repeat. Whatever time I had off was generally spent on the apartment since it did, as Julien said, need some work; but I enjoyed it. There was definitely something satisfying about cleaning and painting and doing repairs on a place that was mine. The guy who leased it to me had said that as long as I wasn't tearing out walls, I could pretty much do what I wanted without having to ask permission.

At least once a week, Anastascia stopped by. Sometimes she brought dinner for us both, other times she came to help. Julien came by more often, though the two of them rarely crossed paths since they were on different schedules. Most of the time, he liked to stop by before class if I wasn't working.

It was one of those mornings during the second week of October when Julien and I were working on stripping the finish off of an ancient table I'd found at a thrift store. Well, I was stripping off the finish and Julien was attempting to help. He'd done something to his hand over the weekend, though he refused to tell me what. It was slow going with his left hand, but I appreciated the help nonetheless. The windows were all open and we had a fan going, but the smell was still strong enough that, by mid-morning, I had the front door open too.

Because of the fumes, neither Julien nor I were talking, so when someone knocked at the door, I jumped.

"Piper Black?"

I turned to see a pair of policemen standing on my front step. They were in street clothes, but I could clearly see the badges on their belts. One was an older man, probably in his mid-fifties, with gray hair and one of those perpetual scowls that people get from working a job that dealt with idiots most of the time. The other cop was a woman. She had short blonde hair and a severe-looking face that softened only when she saw Julien, and then only for a second.

I was suddenly very self-conscious that I was wearing grubby clothes and had a handkerchief on my head, holding back my hair so it didn't get in the varnish remover. My face was flushed and I was sweating. Julien on the other hand, was shirtless and looked good glistening with sweat.

"Are you Piper Black?" the male cop spoke directly to me this time.

"Yes, sorry, that's me." I scrubbed my hand on the cleanest spot of my jeans I could find and held it out as I walked over to the cops.

"I'm Detective Jabowski. This is my partner, Detective Kinsman," the man introduced them as he shook my hand.

Saying that it was nice to meet them seemed a bit strange, so I went with something else that I thought was equally polite. "How can I help you?"

"May we come in?" Jabowski asked.

"Of course." I stepped back to let them come in. "Sorry about the smell."

"No problem." Detective Kinsman's eyes flicked to Julien and then back to me. "We have a few questions to ask that may be of a... delicate nature."

I glanced back at Julien and he crossed the few feet to stand next to me. There was a shadow in his eyes, but I didn't ask about it. It could wait. "It's okay," I said. "He's a friend. You can ask your questions." It was nice, knowing that Julien already knew about my history and that I didn't have to try to hide anything from him.

"All right," Jabowski said. "Do you know a young man named Brock Michaels?"

I stiffened and Julien put his hand on my elbow. "Yes," I said. "We dated for a few weeks."

"How did you meet?" Jabowski asked.

"Can I ask what this is about?" I asked.

Kinsman ignored him and asked me the question again, "How did you and Mr. Michaels meet?"

"I was a stripper in Las Vegas," I said bluntly. I'd dealt with people like them before. They wanted to know if I'd lie because I was ashamed or tell the truth because I was proud. For some people, those were the only two options. "I danced at a bachelor party."

"Who hired you for the party?" Jabowski asked.

"I assume Brock did since he was the best man." I crossed my arms.

"You assume?" That came from Kinsman.

"My roommate in Vegas was the original dancer who got the job offer and she needed a second person. I never talked to anyone about arrangements or anything like that."

"What was your interaction with Mr. Michaels at the party?" Jabowski asked.

Julien's fingers tightened around my arm and I knew he was telling me to be honest. I wanted to lie, but I had a feeling they already knew the answer to most of the questions they were asking.

"I did a general dance for all of the men there, and then danced with some of them more closely. I didn't single anyone out. A few hours into the party, I went out onto the balcony for some fresh air. Brock came out and offered me a bottle of water. That's where things get fuzzy." I worked to keep my voice strong. "I have glimpses of someone touching me, but nothing clear. The next thing I knew, I was waking up in a bed."

"Whose bed?" Kinsman asked.

"The groom's. He told me that Brock and I had been drunk and that he'd stopped us before anything had happened."

"The groom's name?" Jabowski asked.

"Look, I don't understand what–"

"How much did you have to drink that night, Miss Black?" Kinsman cut me off.

"I didn't." I almost snapped at her, barely managing to restrain myself at the last moment. "At first, I'd thought maybe I'd done a couple shots and blacked out, and that's what I didn't remember. I found out later that Brock had drugged the water and tried to rape me. If Reed hadn't come in and stopped him, he would've succeeded."

"Reed?" Jabowski's eyebrow went up.

"The groom." I sighed. "Reed Stirling. I used to go to school with his sister." I wasn't about to volunteer any extra information in that particular connection.

"How did you find out that Brock drugged you?" Kinsman asked, her voice clearly saying that she was skeptical of my story.

"He confessed it to me," Julien smoothly interrupted.

"Excuse me?" Jabowski looked surprised.

"When Brock and Piper were dating, she was still living in Vegas. He and I went down to see her, and the last night we were there, while she was in the bathroom, he told me what he did."

"I overheard it," I added. "That's how I found out." My stomach was churning. I didn't like to think about that night.

"And then I hit him." Julien put his arm around my shoulders.

I suddenly thought of something that hadn't occurred to me until just then. "Why do two Philadelphia detectives care about an unreported assault in Las Vegas?"

"That brings up a good question, Miss Black. Why didn't you report it?" Kinsman neatly dodged my question.

"Because there wasn't any proof that anything happened," I said. I was really getting sick of her attitude. "And, like pretty much everywhere, if a stripper in Vegas cries rape, there better be damn good evidence to back it up. Plus, what happened to me hadn't even been a rape. I didn't think anyone would take what happened seriously."

Julien looked from Jabowski to Kinsman, his expression clearly saying he didn't like how they were handling things. "Maybe I should have Piper call my family's attorney. He plays golf with your boss."

The cops exchanged glances that said they didn't know who Julien was.

"Sorry, I forgot to make introductions," I said sweetly. "This is Julien Atwood." I waited until the last name registered on both faces before adding, "And, yes, those Atwoods."

"You want to tell us what's going on?" I asked again.

Kinsman and Jabowski looked at each other before Jabowski answered, "We're trying to establish a pattern of behavior."

My stomach twisted again as I realized what they meant. Brock had tried to do to someone else what he'd done to me. I glanced up at Julien, but his face was unreadable.

The detectives asked a few more follow-up questions regarding the time Brock and I were dating, but I could tell it all basically boiled down to the same thing: why had I dated a man who'd drugged and tried to rape me? When they realized my answer was always going to be that I hadn't known what he'd done until afterwards, they seemed satisfied. Jabowski gave me his card and said that someone would be in touch.

As soon as they left, I sank down on the floor. What had just happened?

Julien sat down next to me. "Are you okay?"

I shrugged. I didn't know. I thought I'd put it all behind me and I wouldn't have to think about it again. I'd accepted that the closest I was going to get to justice was the money Julien had gotten for me.

"Shit."

"What's wrong?" Julien put his hand on my shoulder.

"The money, Julien." I looked over at him. "If the cops start digging, they're going to find out that Brock gave me ten thousand dollars. It's going to look like hush money." My stomach lurched. "Or like he paid me for sex."

He took my hand. "I'm not going to let that happen, Piper. Brock gave me the money. I gave it to you. I'll tell them you didn't know where it came from. You thought it was just from me."

I shook my head, barely hearing him. Now that I was getting over my initial shock, I tried to process what had happened. How had they found out about what happened in Vegas? Not many people knew about it.

"Reed," I said softly.

"What?"

I looked up at Julien. "Something must've happened to make Reed tell the cops what happened to me. He was furious when he found out what Brock had done." My heart gave a crazy little skip. "He must be worried about how I'd take it." I started to stand. "I have to go see him."

"Piper, wait." Julien's hand closed around my arm, keeping me seated.

I looked over. His face was flushed and he couldn't meet my eyes. Concern for my friend took priority, no matter how I felt about what Reed had done. "What is it?"

"It wasn't Reed," he said. His eyes flicked to mine and then down again. He let go of my arm and folded his hands together. "He didn't tell the cops about Brock. I did."

"You?" The word fell flat between us. "And you didn't think it was a good idea to ask me first? Or, I don't know, at least tell me they'd be coming?"

"Those weren't the two I talked to," he said. "The detective I spoke with said he'd give me a head's up before he came over so I could tell you."

I crossed my arms and reminded myself that I'd been ready to go see Reed to tell him I wasn't mad about what he'd done. How could I not offer Julien a fraction of that same forgiveness?

He held up his hands, palms out. "Let me explain, please."

I motioned for him to continue.

"You remember on Saturday when I mentioned a fundraiser I was going to with my mom because my dad was too busy?"

I nodded.

"Well, it was at the Michaels' house and as soon as I got there, I saw Brock all over this one server. She was barely eighteen and looked like she was too scared to tell him to go away. I didn't say anything when he kept talking to her, but when I saw him give her a drink, my gut said he was drugging her. I kept watching and, sure enough, about five minutes later, he had his arm around her and they were leaving. She was having a hard time walking."

My hands curled into fists and I felt my nails biting into my palms, but I ignored the pain.

"I tried going after them, but by the time I managed to get across the room, they were gone. It took me almost fifteen minutes to find him in a spare room." The expression on Julien's face went from concern over what I was thinking to fury over what he was remembering. "What he was doing to her..."

I felt like I was going to be sick. I looked down at his hands and things clicked into place. My annoyance at him faded as I reached over and gently took his injured hand in mine.

"You stopped him," I said softly. It wasn't a question.

"But I didn't get to him before he raped her."

Now I could hear that some of the anger in his voice was directed at himself.

"You still stopped him from hurting her even more," I said firmly.

Julien looked up at me, his eyes glittering. "I beat the shit out of him, Piper. Knocked him out and kept going. I don't know what would've happened if a couple of guests hadn't heard the commotion and pulled me off of him."

I started to unwind the bandage he'd clumsily wrapped around his hand, ignoring him when he started to protest. "Tell me what happened next," I prompted.

"The cops had already been called, and there were enough guests around that the Michaels' bodyguards couldn't really do anything to me since I wasn't putting up a fight. They also couldn't completely cover up what had happened because too many people had already seen the girl."

I could feel Julien's eyes on me as I finished taking off the bandage. I caught my breath as I saw the damage. His knuckles were swollen and bruised, crisscrossed with angry red cuts.

"You should've gone to the hospital and gotten this checked out," I said and then stood. "Come on, let me take a look at it."

He followed me into the bathroom and sat on the edge of the tub while I got out my first aid kit.

"What happened when the police got there?" I asked.

"I didn't want to tell them why I'd been suspicious of Brock, but I knew as soon as one of them started talking about how 'boys will be boys' when they have too much to drink that I couldn't keep you out of it. They needed to know that he'd done it before and this wasn't a case of her being too drunk to consent and him being too drunk not to notice."

I knelt in front of him and began to clean his wounds. He winced at the sting, but didn't pull his hand away.

"I'm so sorry, Piper. I didn't know how to tell you."

I focused on applying anti-bacterial cream to his cuts. "It's okay, Julien. I understand why you did it." I placed his palm flat on mine. "Can you move your fingers?"

If he was startled by the change of conversation, he didn't show it. "Some." He moved each finger. "I don't think anything's broken."

"You need an x-ray," I said as I re-wrapped it with a fresh bandage.

"I'm fine," he insisted.

I looked up at him now, a new anger rushing through me. "You're not fine!" I snapped, startling him. "You could have serious damage to your hand, Julien. What the hell were you thinking?!"

"I was thinking that I hadn't been there to protect you and I'd fucked up protecting that girl. I kept thinking of his hands on you..." His voice trailed off and he looked away, like he'd revealed more than he'd intended.

"You didn't know me when it happened." My stomach was twisting again, but this time it was for a different reason. I'd suspected Julien felt something for me that was more than friendship, but he'd never acted on it or even talked about it, allowing me to push it away and not have to deal. Now it was right there.

"Doesn't matter," he said. He pulled his injured hand away.

"It does matter," I insisted. I reached out and put my hand on his cheek, turned his face back to mine. "Thank you."

"For what?"

I didn't answer as I leaned forward and brushed my lips across his. His entire body stiffened at the contact. It was brief, chaste, but I couldn't deny the way my skin tingled the moment it had come against his. I stood before either of us could start overanalyzing what had just happened.

"Come on," I said.

"Where are we going?" His voice was unsteady and warmth spread through me as I realized an innocent kiss had done that.

"To the hospital," I said. I'd try to figure out what all of this meant later. Right now, Julien needed a professional to look at his hand.

Chapter 8

Once I'd let it sink in, I'd been worried that what I'd done would change everything, but it didn't. Julien didn't let it. Our friendship remained as solid as ever. If anything, we were closer than before. We just didn't talk about the kiss. Sometimes I wondered if maybe I'd read him wrong and he didn't feel that way about me after all. But other times, I'd catch him watching me and I was sure it was more than just platonic affection in his gaze.

Then there was the way I was starting to feel around him. I couldn't deny the way I'd felt when I'd kissed him, but I did try to play it off as gratitude for what he'd done and said. That worked for about a week and then I had to give it up because I was tired of lying to myself. I didn't think I was in love with Julien, but what I felt for him was absolutely more than friendship.

The day I first admitted that to myself, I spent hours trying to talk myself out of it. Over the last six months, I'd made two very bad choices when it came to men, one of which was a direct result of letting myself rebound into a relationship just because I'd been hurting. By the end of the night, I decided I was going to be smart this time. I wouldn't push anything. I would let our friendship grow naturally and see where things went. I wouldn't try to figure out exactly how I felt about him and I wouldn't initiate again. If Julien decided that he wanted to make a move, then I'd deal.

That worked really well for a couple weeks. We continued doing home improvement stuff around my place. We went out to eat and to movies together. We even went to see a live musical at the theater. Front row tickets that Julien said he'd won, but I suspected he paid full price for. The more time we spent together, the more we shared and the closer we became. When I talked to Anastascia, I could hear the questions in her voice, wondering if Julien and I were dating, but I didn't go there. I loved Anastascia, but for the time being, I wanted to keep whatever this was to myself.

We avoided parties and events that those of his social circle would attend, steering clear of Brock and Reed both. I'd given my official statement a few days after the police had questioned me and they said they'd call if they needed me.

Brock had immediately been released on bail, which wasn't surprising. Julien kept trying to prevent me from seeing coverage, but I couldn't get away from it. Britni's support of her brother was loud and her opinions of both the server and myself scathing. She never quite managed to get our names out there, but a few of the students at

Madame Emilana's had said things that told me they suspected.

Reed's media presence was suspiciously absent. He made no public statements and I never saw a single picture of him with Britni. My feelings for him had quieted, but I wasn't sure if they were completely gone yet.

By mid-November, Julien started hinting that he wanted me to spend the holidays with him and his family. Fortunately, Anastascia had already invited me for Thanksgiving and Christmas was implied. I knew things were strained at the Atwood house, especially since the whole Julien and Brock incident. The Michaels family had apparently been partners in one of the Atwood businesses and lines were being drawn. Julien hadn't said it, but I was pretty sure one of those lines had been his father taking Brock's side.

The Friday before Thanksgiving, I got home from work late, exhausted from a double shift – one before dance and one after – and barely had enough energy to take a shower before falling into bed. I was asleep almost instantly.

I'd only been asleep for a couple hours when I heard someone knocking on my door. I started toward the door when I realized that I hadn't bothered putting on anything when I'd crawled under the covers. I grabbed my robe and hurried down the stairs.

"Hello?" I called as I neared the door. It was a little after one-thirty in the morning and while I had a few new acquaintances, my number of friends in the city was limited to pretty much two.

"It's me."

I easily recognized Julien's voice and let him in. The moment I saw him, I knew something was wrong. His was pale, his hair a mess. He had dark circles under his eyes and his face was drawn. He looked like he hadn't slept since I'd last seen him two days ago.

"What's wrong?" I shivered as I closed the door. We'd had a couple flurries this week, but nothing had stuck. I had a feeling that would change soon.

He sank down on the couch Anastascia had given me after she'd bought a new one for herself. I sat next to him, knowing he'd speak when he was ready.

"My dad." He said the words like he didn't know what they meant. He looked at his hands. "Um, he and my mom were arguing. About Steven. I was just supposed to be picking something up and going back to my place, but they were fighting and then he collapsed and Mom screamed."

A feeling of dread filled me, telling me that this story wasn't going to have a happy ending.

"He wasn't breathing when I came in. Mom was panicking. I started CPR while one of the staff called for an ambulance." He shook his head. "The paramedics kept doing CPR but I could see it on their faces as soon as they

331

touched him. The doctors pronounced him dead at the ER. They said it was a heart attack or aneurysm or something like that. Nothing we could've done." He looked over at me, his eyes wild. "He's dead. My dad's dead."

"Oh, Julien." I wrapped my arms around him. Tears stung my eyes, but they weren't for Mr. Atwood. I hadn't known him. My heart was aching for my friend. "I'm so sorry."

Julien was stiff in my arms, as if he wasn't sure how he was supposed to respond to my embrace.

"My uncle's at the house with my mom. He's her closest brother. I couldn't stay there."

"It's okay," I assured him.

"I'm going to have to call the boards tomorrow," he said. "They need to know. I guess I'll step in for him until they can find a replacement."

I put my hand on Julien's cheek and found it cold and clammy. He was definitely in shock. I picked up the afghan from the back of the couch and wrapped it around us both.

"Shh," I said. "Don't worry about that now."

He looked at me, a puzzled expression on his face. "I'm sad, but I don't understand why."

Some people might've been freaking out, wondering why he wasn't crying, why he sounded so cold. I got it. Everyone processed grief differently.

"Why does it feel like there's this hole inside me, Piper?" His voice trembled. "I haven't loved my dad since before Steven was born. I've hated him since Steven died. Why should I feel anything but relief that he's gone?"

"He's your father," I said simply. "He's the one who taught you how to ride a bike when you were eight. He took you fishing when you were six and pulled you out of the ocean when you fell in." Those had been the only positive stories Julien had ever told me about his father, and they were enough to break through.

Julien buried his face against the side of my neck and sobbed. The sound broke my heart and I ran my hands along his back, trying to soothe him as best I could. For all the grief of my own I'd dealt with, I was never very sure how to handle someone else's.

"I'm so sorry," I murmured as I smoothed down his hair. It was softer than it looked and I stroked my fingers through it as I would a little boys.

I wasn't sure how much time passed before Julien's shoulders stopped shaking, but it was long enough for me to know that I could no longer say that I wasn't sure how I felt about him. Seeing him in pain had broken open the part of me that had been holding back. I was conflicted about what I still felt for Reed and whether or not I wanted to tell Julien how I felt, but there was no conflict anymore about what those feelings were. I'd fallen for my friend.

"You're cold," Julien said suddenly, pulling back. He looked at the clock. "Fuck. It's late and you probably have to work tomorrow." His cheeks were red and I could tell he was embarrassed.

"No, I don't." I stood and held out my hand. "Come on. You go take a hot shower and I'm going to make you some tea."

"Tea?" Julien raised an eyebrow.

"It's what my mom used to make when I was sick or upset."

His expression softened. I'd told him about her.

"Go," I said. "I'll make you some tea and get out the sheets for the couch."

He nodded and headed for the stairs. I put the water on to boil and got the sheets from the downstairs closet. They were cheap, but I'd realized I needed a second pair after Julien had stayed here one night after we'd been painting until three in the morning. I put them on the couch and tried not to think about my epiphany and the fact that the person it was about was upstairs right now, naked and wet.

I wasn't going to screw this up, I vowed. Just because I knew how I felt now didn't change what I'd originally decided to do. I'd made enough of a mess of my life with Reed and Brock. I wasn't going to lose a friend due to lack of self-control.

Once I finished with the couch, the tea was ready and I carried it upstairs. I still didn't have a lot of furniture, so the extra room upstairs was empty. As I walked into my room and set the mug on the dresser, I wondered if maybe I should look into an air mattress or something. Even Anastascia would sleep on that. As it was, she'd stayed in my bed the one night we'd had a late girls' night out, but I didn't want a repeat of that. She still kicked in her sleep.

"Thank you."

I jumped as Julien's voice startled me. My hand bumped the mug, sending a splash of scalding liquid over the edge onto my fingers. I cried out, yanking my hand back.

"Piper!"

"I'm okay." Tears welled up in my eyes in response to the pain, but I refused to let them fall. What was a little burn compared to what he was going through?

"Let me see."

Julien caught my hand as I tried to step past him. His touch was gentle and I swallowed hard. I hadn't realized until now that he was only wearing a towel around his waist.

Fuck.

I'd seen him shirtless before, but this was different, especially since I was now very aware that I wasn't wearing anything under my robe.

I was shocked out of my thoughts as Julian slipped my two burnt fingers into his mouth. His tongue soothed the injured skin and my breathing hitched. His eyes locked with mine. He drew my fingers out and the cool air against my wet flesh eased the last of the pain. Not that I would've felt it anyway. Not with the way he was looking at me.

"Better?" he asked.

I nodded, not trusting myself to speak.

"I know you have the couch made up downstairs but," he tucked a strand of hair behind my ear, his fingers lingering on my face. "I don't think I can be alone tonight."

"You don't have to be," I whispered. I wanted so badly to lean into his touch, but I reminded myself of my promise.

Almost as if he could read my thoughts, he cupped the side of my face, his thumb brushing across my lips.

"Piper."

My name was a groan and almost undid me.

When he began to lower his head, I knew I should stop him. He was emotional and needy and I was here. But I wasn't strong enough. I knew he was hurting and in need of comfort. I could do that for him, be a solace. I wouldn't ask for anything more.

His mouth was cautious against mine, testing to see if it was welcome. I parted my lips, hoping he would take the invitation. A moment later, his tongue lightly touched my bottom lip and I made a soft sound. His hand slid around to the back of my head, holding me in place as he tilted his head, deepening the kiss. With all that he had been through, I'd expected rough and urgent, but this was a slow exploration, as if he was memorizing every inch his tongue explored.

My hands couldn't keep to themselves. They came up and ran across his chest. I may have seen him without a shirt before, but I'd never touched him. He was all sculpted muscles and golden skin. My fingers traced the black ink of the tattoo over his heart. SAA. Steven Andrew Atwood.

When he finally raised his head, his eyes were dark and I could see the desire warring with self-control. I knew what he wanted. I took his hands in mine and placed them on the belt of my robe. This was the turning point. Whatever choice he made, he would decide where things went from here.

Chapter 9

The soft cotton slid off of my shoulders, baring me all at once. No striptease, just flesh. He'd seen me practically naked before, so the near-reverence on his face surprised me. He reached toward me, then hesitated, his eyes flicking up to my face. I took his hand and led it to my breast, moaning as he cupped me. His thumb brushed over my nipple and it hardened under his touch.

"You're so beautiful," he whispered, taking my other breast in his free hand.

I let myself enjoy his touch for a minute, the way my skin hummed against his, and then I reached for his towel. It fell to the floor, revealed the solid, muscled thighs I'd known he had. The deep v-grooves of his hips that pointed down to the dark curls surrounding his cock. He was half-hard and not quite too big to do what I wanted.

I went to my knees, earning a sharp inhalation from Julien. I placed my hands on his hips to steady myself and leaned forward, taking all of him into my mouth. He moaned my name and his hands buried themselves in my hair. He didn't apply any pressure though, letting me move as I wanted. I could feel him swelling in my mouth and knew that soon he'd be too large for me to take completely, so I took advantage of the time I had, applying suction to his full length as I moved my head. When, after a few passes, he was nearly fully erect, I began to run my tongue along the length of him, using my hand to work him until I heard his breathing quicken.

"Too close." He backed away from me and held out his hands to help me to my feet.

I backed toward the bed, pulling him with me. I reached into the night table and pulled out one of the condoms I had left over from my time with Brock. Julien was a bit bigger, but not enough to need a different size. That was good, because I didn't want anything to stop what was coming next.

I pushed aside my blankets and sat down on the edge of the bed. Before I could slide back, however, Julien knelt in front of me, nudging my knees apart.

"My turn," he said.

"It's okay." I brushed his hair out of his eyes. "Just let me take care of you."

He shook his head and leaned forward. "I want this."

I wasn't going to argue with that.

Julien pressed his lips against the inside of my thigh and then held onto my hips as he ran his tongue along the sensitive skin between my legs. I cried out as his lips and tongue began to explore me as thoroughly as they had explored my mouth earlier. I fell back on the bed, letting the sensations wash over me until I came, moaning as his tongue thrust in and out.

My hands fisted in my sheets and my body tried to twist and turn, but he held me in place, sliding two fingers inside me even as I was still quaking with my release. He crooked them, rubbing against that spot inside me, and every muscle in my body tightened. I heard him swear, but I couldn't think clearly enough to understand why.

When I started to come down, he was on the bed next to me, running his fingers lightly up and down my arm.

"We don't have to do anything else," he said softly. "Not if you don't want to."

I picked up the condom packet from where I'd dropped it and handed it to him. He smiled, then tore it open and rolled it on, the hitch in his breathing telling me how close he was.

"I don't know how long I'll last," he said. "You're so tight. Nearly cut off the circulation in my fingers when you came."

I ran my hand down over my stomach and let my index finger slide between my lips. I shivered as it brushed across my still sensitive clit. I spread my legs and looked at Julien. I wasn't going to talk him into it, no matter how badly I was aching for him to fill me.

He rolled on top of me, keeping enough weight propped on his elbows that he wasn't too heavy. I relished the weight of his body as he pressed onto me. He reached between us, his hand brushing against my clit as he positioned himself against my opening. I shivered and wrapped my legs around his waist. My heels rested at the base of his ass and I felt it flex as he pressed inside, slowly entered me inch by glorious inch.

He squeezed his eyes closed as he moved, an expression of almost painful pleasure on his face. My body opened to him, but the fit was tight, causing delicious pressure and friction against every cell. His muscles were trembling by the time he was completely inside and I could feel the strain of him trying to give me time.

"It's okay," I said. "You don't have to wait."

It proved how close he was that he didn't argue with me. He began to move in steady, deep strokes that made me moan. And then, when the head of his cock pressed against my g-spot, I gasped out, "Yes! Right there."

He shifted and his thrusts now included exactly what I needed to start pushing me, fast, toward another climax. My nails raked down his back, not hard enough to break skin, but enough that he hissed in pleasure when I did it. His teeth nipped at my breast before he pulled some of the soft skin into his mouth. Every pull brought blood to the surface and the knowledge that he was marking me spiked my arousal.

As he began to speed up, driven by his own impending climax, I could feel my own approaching. It became a race as I moved my body with his, against his, desperate for us to finish together. Then, as he came with a shout, he ground down against me, giving me the friction I needed to fall over the edge.

I could feel our hearts thudding in our chests, beating in a complimentary rhythm. Our skin was slick with sweat; our bodies still deeply joined as we rode out our orgasms. Even before I started to come down, the thought came to me that what I'd been missing with Brock was right here with Julien. No matter where things went from here, the two of us were connected.

I pulled the blankets around us as Julien slid out of me. I wrapped my arms around him, his head against my chest as he fell asleep. Only when I was sure he was under did I let myself relax enough to fall asleep.

*****

Less than five hours later I was pulled from sleep by loud banging at my door. I climbed out of bed, hoping it wouldn't wake Julien. He turned and moaned but didn't wake. Good, he deserved to be able to sleep. I snatched my robe off the floor, pulling it on as I hurried down the stairs. Who would be at my door at seven-thirty in the morning without calling first?

I yanked the door open without checking, my brain still too befuddled by sleep to completely function.

My jaw dropped.

It was Reed, standing at my door, looking like he hadn't slept much either. He didn't bother with a greeting or anything else, just blurted out what he'd come to say.

"These past two months have been killing me. I told Britni I couldn't do it anymore. It's over, Piper. I'm getting a divorce. All I want is you."

End of Vol. 4

Sinful Desires Vol. 5

Chapter 1

"What the fuck did you just say?" The words popped out of my mouth without me even thinking about them.

Reed's eyes widened.

Moments ago he'd told me that he was getting a divorce and that he wanted me back. I was pretty sure that wasn't the response he'd imagined coming from my lips when he played out this little scenario in his head. There wasn't anything I could do about it now. A gust of cold morning air made me shiver and I wrapped my arms around my middle.

"Can I come in?" Reed asked.

I nodded, stunned and stepped back automatically. He walked into the living room and I took my time closing the front door. I turned, and saw him pacing. He ran his hand through his hair again, a wild, almost feverish look in his eyes.

"You know that this whole marriage is a sham," he said, his words coming out in a rush. "And I thought I could go through with it, for my family. You told me I couldn't see you anymore and I tried to accept it, I really did." He took a step toward me, his hand coming up like he was going to touch me, and then dropping back to his side. "When all this shit happened with Brock and I saw how his family protected him, I realized that I didn't want to be a part of it. How could I defend him when I knew what he'd done to you, what he'd done to that girl?"

I thought about how I hadn't seen Reed during any of the news coverage about Brock. I'd seen plenty of Britni defending her brother, and of Rebecca at her side. I'd seen both the Michaels and Stirling parents offering their support. Reed had been conspicuously absent.

"Britni and I started arguing about it since it happened, how I wouldn't go on record saying Brock hadn't done anything wrong and then, last night, it all just blew up. She accused me of having an affair... with you, and I snapped. I told her that you were an honorable person and that you'd turned me down. Then, she asked if I was in love with you."

Shit. I didn't want to hear this. I started to shake my head. I couldn't do this, not now. Not with Julien in my bed upstairs and my head spinning.

"I told her that I wasn't in love with her, that I never had been, that I wanted to be with you. I said that she and I were done, and I left. I've been driving around all night, trying to decide what I want to do, and I realized that I had to come here and tell you how sorry I was about everything..."

I held up a hand. "Stop, Reed. Please, just stop."

He fell silent.

It was too much. I couldn't think straight, not with him looking at me like that. "I need you to go."

He blinked. "What?"

"This is a lot to take in, Reed. I need some time to think."

Hurt blossomed across his face and I wondered if he'd thought he could show up at my door, confess that he'd chosen me and was leaving his wife, and I'd just welcome him with open arms. One look into his eyes and I knew that had been exactly what he'd expected. I probably should've been annoyed, but I couldn't really muster much in the way of a response.

"We'll talk, I promise," I said, then took a much needed gulp of air. "But you have to give me time to process all that you just said. It's been more than two months since I saw you. I've moved on with my life and then..." Blessed anger finally began to fill me, strengthening my resolve. "Then, life gets rough on your side and you think you can just show up at my house, blurt out this shit and I'll fall gratefully into your arms?"

He closed the distance between us and put his hand on my shoulder. Despite how cold it was outside, his hand was warm through the thin cotton of my robe. "I'm sorry. You're right." His voice was soft, the gentle voice that had drawn me to him in the first place. "I wasn't thinking." He squeezed my shoulder and then stepped away. "I'm going to go meet my lawyer and start getting the divorce papers drawn up. Take all the time you need and call me when you're ready to talk. I'll wait."

He left, letting in another blast of cold air, but I barely felt it.

I walked over to my couch on shaky legs and sank onto the soft cushions. Did that really happen? Or was it simply a dream? I pinched myself and sure enough, reality of my situation kicked in.

Why now?

Why would Reed knock on my door the morning after Julien and I first made love? Was I cursed, being punished by the gods?

I nearly growled out loud in frustration. I knew I'd have a lot to think about today, but I figured it'd be centered on Julien, and how sleeping together could change our friendship; what would happen between us next. I'd never in a million years thought that something like this would happen. I'd been looking forward, focusing on my future… not back.

I sighed, hugging my knees to my chest, trying to curl myself into a tight little ball. Maybe if I were small enough, all of this pain and confusion would diminish as well.

Not too long ago, Reed coming to my door and saying that he'd picked me over Britni would've been everything I ever wanted. But I'd spent my time since that last conversation trying to get over him. I didn't know how well it'd worked.

"Hey." Julien's voice came from behind me.

I jumped up, my face flushing. "Julien, I–"

"You don't have to say anything," he interrupted. He picked up his jacket from where he'd tossed it on the couch the night before. "What happened between us was a mistake."

I stared at him, unable to believe my ears. The words hurt more than they should have.

"Things just got out of hand. It won't happen again." His tone was flat and he couldn't look me in the eye. "I should go be with my mother."

He left before I could argue. Not that there was anything I could've said. 'Hey, I know your dad just died and you want to be with your grieving mother, but I want to talk about the fact that we just fucked' didn't exactly seem like the best thing to do.

I sank down on the couch and put my head in my hands. How had things gotten this fucked up? I'd done the right thing and walked away from Reed. I'd told myself to stay away from romance and had been doing a pretty good job of it. Now, in one night, the nice little world I'd been building for myself here was shattered.

I didn't know what I was supposed to think or do. There was no order to the chaos in my head. I couldn't figure out what to process first. Reed's declaration? What had happened between Julien and me? His abrupt departure? My feelings for Reed? My feelings for Julien? Did I believe Reed? How damaged was my friendship with Julien?

There were too many question marks, far too much for my brain to handle, particularly without coffee. I stood. I needed to call in reinforcements. Anastascia was going to be pissed that I woke her up this early on a Saturday, but when she heard what happened, I knew she'd understand.

My only other option was to go curl up in bed again and try to pretend like none of this had happened. But considering my sheets and pillows probably smelled like Julien now – that subtle musky scent that wasn't cologne or aftershave, just him – I doubted I'd be able to put anything out of my mind. So, no matter how much I wanted to act like nothing had changed, I trudged back upstairs to get my phone and make the call.

Chapter 2

I ended up spending Thanksgiving with Anastascia and her parents. They'd both been happy to have me and the holiday should've been the best I'd had since before my mother died. In Vegas, I always worked the holidays. The tips sucked, but there had usually been a bonus and the girls with families always appreciated it. Being with the Galaways was the closest thing to being with family I'd had in more than two years, but I hadn't been able to fully enjoy the experience.

I'd called Anastascia not long after Julien left and told her everything. She'd agreed that pushing Julien about what had happened wouldn't be right considering all he was going through. Instead, I sent him a text telling him I was here if he needed me, and then waited for him to initiate contact. By Tuesday, without a word, I gave in and called. It had gone to voicemail and I left a stumbling message, telling him I'd seen the funeral announcement in the paper and that I'd be there if he needed to talk. I told myself that I'd had a good reason to call and that, this time, I'd wait until he reached out first.

By Tuesday night, I tried texting. Then another two calls on Wednesday. I texted him on Thanksgiving, but received no response. Not even a cursory return of my 'Happy Thanksgiving' greeting. Friday, I placed two calls, though I'd been tempted to do more. I hated looking like I was needy, but the silence was unnerving. I was worried about him. I missed him. Now, I was walking into the church with Anastascia and had absolutely no clue how I was supposed to handle seeing him again.

"How do you want to play this?" Anastascia asked as we approached the receiving line at the front of the sanctuary.

"Damned if I know," I muttered, biting the inside of my lip.

She and I got in line behind some people that I recognized from the cover of Forbes magazine. I'd only met Julien's parents once and didn't know anyone else in the family, so I kept things simple. A handshake and a murmur of condolences got me up to Mrs. Atwood. I repeated what I'd said before, but my "so sorry for your loss" was more heartfelt as I looked into her sad face. She was impeccably dressed, her hair and make-up perfect, but no matter how expertly it had been applied, I could still see the circles under her eyes. I remembered what Julien had said, how his parents had been arguing when his father collapsed. I could only imagine the guilt she must be feeling.

And then I was moving along and Julien was right there. A million questions came into my head, but I didn't let them out. He looked like he'd aged ten years since I'd last seen him, even though it had been only a week. My heart ached for him. I opened my arms and, after a brief hesitation, he stepped into my embrace.

"I'm so sorry," I said.

I felt a tremor go through his body and his arms tightened around me for the briefest of moments. I inhaled deeply, indulging myself for a few seconds as his scent carried me back to that night. Then he was releasing me and taking a step a backwards, putting distance between us.

"Thank you for coming." His voice was stiff and he didn't meet my eyes. He seemed to be looking everywhere but at me.

"Of course." I was surprised that I managed not to let the words betray the stab of hurt that went through me. He was grieving. I had no right to have expectations of his behavior. I repeated that to myself as Anastascia and I found seats. It didn't lessen the pain and only made me feel guilty. It wasn't only my questions, though. Those were easier than I'd thought to hold back. No, I simply wanted to be there for him. Be his friend, as he'd always been to me. I wanted to put my arms around him and hold him, try to take away his pain.

"Piper."

A low male voice said my name and I turned, starting to smile. The expression froze when I saw Reed taking a seat across the aisle. I forced myself to finish the smile. I still hadn't figured out how I felt about the other morning. Every time I tried to think about it, I started worrying about how Julien was doing. Reed really did have awful timing.

"Hi."

"Can I talk to you?"

I shook my head. "Not now." I gestured toward the front of the sanctuary where the family was moving to their seats.

"Do you know what you're going to say to Reed?" Anastascia whispered as a priest slowly walked across the platform to stand on the other side of the casket.

"Nope, not a clue." I pulled my coat more tightly around my shoulders. Winter had come with a vengeance yesterday, blasting Philadelphia with cold air and flurries of snow too dry to stick. I'd only been in Vegas a couple of years, but the heat had made me forget what a real winter was like. The exterior chill just added to the interior cold I felt. I felt frozen with uncertainty.

Thankfully, Anastascia didn't try to pressure me into anything. She knew what a difficult time I was having and had been very supportive. What she hadn't been able to do, however, was tell me what I was supposed to do. I had a feeling there was an opinion she was keeping to herself for some reason, but I didn't push her on it. I wasn't sure I was ready to know what she truly thought anyway.

I tried to focus on what the priest was saying about Julien's father, hoping I could gain some insight into the family. It didn't take long to realize that the list of platitudes being spouted had nothing to do with the real man Julien had known. My attention wandered, alternating between sideways glances across the aisle to see if Reed was still looking at me – he was – and ones up front to see if I could deduce any sort of emotion from the back of Julien's head – I couldn't. All Julien's hair did was remind me what it had felt like, brushing against my thighs, wound between my fingers.

I squeezed my eyes closed and took a slow breath. Those were not thoughts I needed to be having at a funeral.

The service was nearly twice as long as the one I'd had for my mother and enough different that it barely reminded me of hers at all. That was some small comfort for me, I supposed. I knew Anastascia had been worried about that. I would've been too if I hadn't been so busy thinking about how my friend was doing. I understood the loss of a parent, though mine hadn't been a surprise.

The service ended and everyone watched in silence as the pallbearers helped take the casket down the aisle and out the front of the church. Out of the corner of my eye, I saw Reed trying to get my attention but I turned away from him. I knew I needed to talk to him at some point, but I wanted to figure out how I was feeling before I did.

"I need to use the restroom," I whispered as the ushers started to dismiss people. I slipped out the far side of the pew and headed toward the stairs at the back, hoping to avoid the throng of people in the back. I'd only been in here once as a kid, but I was pretty sure I remembered where things were.

A few minutes later, I had to admit that I was wrong. I was near what I assumed was the priest's study, but didn't see any sign of a bathroom. I sighed. It'd probably be quicker to go back into the sanctuary and wait until we got back to my place than it would be to keep searching.

As I hurried around the corner, I wasn't watching where I was going and ran straight into a wall of solid muscle. Hands closed on my arms and I looked up to see almost-black eyes looking down at me.

"Reed." My mouth was suddenly dry.

"Piper." His voice was soft, a caress over the word that made me remember other, more intimate, times he'd said my name. "I'm glad I finally caught you."

His hands burned through my shirt, heating my skin. I swallowed hard, wondering if he was going to try to kiss me... wondering if I'd let him. He released me and took a step back.

"I wanted to apologize for showing up at your house like that," he said. "I was completely out of line. I never should've sprung things on you like that."

I nodded. "It's okay. You just caught me off guard." I didn't seem to know what to do with my hands. Finally, I settled for crossing them in front of me.

"Look, I don't want to fuck this up again." His expression was earnest. "Go on a date with me this coming Friday. It'll be a real first date. We'll talk. No pressure."

A chance to sit down and talk to him was a good idea. And a week would give me the time I'd need to start putting together a better picture of how I felt about what had happened with him and with Julien.

"No," I said and watched his face fall. "Not a date, but I will have dinner with you… to talk."

A smile broke across his face and I couldn't help but smile back. I might not know whether or not I still cared about him enough to want to try a relationship with him, but I did know that I liked seeing him happy.

He reached out and took my hand, giving it a quick squeeze before releasing it again. "I'll pick you up at seven, and we'll keep it casual."

I nodded and watched as he walked away. I couldn't deny that he looked good in his suit. My stomach clenched as I remembered the way he looked out of it.

"Dammit," I said to myself. "This is going to be a long week."

I smoothed non-existent wrinkles from my dress pants and then started for the stairs. Before I took more than half a dozen steps, I caught a glimpse of someone hurrying by. I didn't need a close look to know that it was Julien. He'd seen me, I was sure of it, but now he didn't even look my way, confirming that he didn't want to talk to me.

I scowled. I really hoped this date with Reed would help me figure out what I wanted and that this distance Julien was putting between us would ease the awkwardness. I just wanted to move on with my life, but I had a bad feeling that was going to be easier said than done.

Chapter 3

The first week of December was just as confusing and miserable as I'd feared. Work was fine, if a little boring, but everyone at Madam Emilana's was freaking out. We would be performing pieces from The Nutcracker for a friend of Madam Emilana. Apparently, he was looking for a few girls for various parts in a new version of Phantom of the Opera that he was producing in early summer. Auditions would begin after the first of the year, and rumor had it that any girls who caught his eye now might be getting a personal invitation.

What should have been an exciting announcement was tempered by the fact that the only person I had to share it with was Anastascia. I'd called Julien and left a message for him, telling him about the opportunity, but that had been three days ago and I hadn't heard anything back.

Then, late last night, Anastascia called. The pipes in her apartment had burst, and then the heat had gone out. The combination meant there was no way she could stay there, especially not in December. I, of course, invited her to stay with me. I loved my best friend and, normally, having her at my place for a couple weeks would be a blast.

Problem was, I didn't want laughter and distraction. I needed to be able to think and, even when she tried to give me my space, I had a hard time focusing on the problem.

At least she'd helped me pick out the perfect 'I'm not saying I'm interested but maybe I could be' outfit. He'd said casual, which I was glad about since it meant I could wear jeans instead of a dress or skirt. I enjoyed dressing up, but I didn't bare leg in the winter without an insanely good excuse. Tonight, I was wearing my nicest pair of jeans – the kind that hugged my curves without looking painted on – and a clingy sweater that made my eyes look almost like emeralds.

When Reed knocked on the door, Anastascia gave me a look that said she expected a full report when I got home and then headed upstairs to my extra room. I took a deep breath and opened the door. Reed's eyes warmed when he saw me and he held out a bouquet of wildflowers.

"Thank you." I motioned for him to come in. I was relieved to see that he'd kept it casual as well. Not that he didn't look good. He wore designer jeans with an expensive cut and a fitted long-sleeved shirt that showed off his broad shoulders and chest. He'd gone with a rich, deep red so we looked like we matched to make Christmas colors.

I put the flowers in a vase and set them on my kitchen table, then headed back out to the living room where Reed waited. His hands were in his pockets and it was then I realized that he was as nervous as I was.

"Ready?" He flashed me a charming smile and gestured toward the door.

His car was sitting at the curb, and I wasn't surprised to see that it was the latest BMW model. He wasn't a snob about the money he and his family had, but he didn't go out of his way to downplay it either. And he did like his cars. I smiled as he opened the door for me before hurried around to the driver's side.

"Since we're keeping it casual, I was thinking about Earth Bread and Brewery," Reed said as he pulled out of his parking space.

"That sounds great," I said. "I love their flatbread pizza."

"And I figured a good beer might loosen things up." He winked at me.

"Good idea." I began to relax as we drove.

He kept the conversation casual, asking how dance was going and my job. I wasn't sure how to ask him questions about work and his life without bringing up his ended marriage or the fact that his parents had threatened to cut off his company if he didn't marry Britni. I was pretty sure their threat would carry over to divorcing, particularly if it was before they had a kid. So, I let him steer the conversation and didn't push when he skirted around the more serious topics. Once we got into dinner, I'd make sure we discussed the things that needed said, but I was glad we were keeping it light for the moment.

The place was packed, but Reed didn't have a problem getting a table rather quickly. I had a feeling the Stirlings rarely had issues pulling strings to get reservations. As we started up the stairs, I could feel Reed's eyes on me as I went in front of him. I wondered what he was thinking. Was he just admiring the view or was he remembering what it had felt like to have his hands on me? Heat flooded me, chasing away the last of the winter cold.

When we reached the top, the hostess smiled at us and asked us to follow her. Not surprisingly, her gaze lingered on Reed a bit longer than me. Even if she didn't know who he was, his looks alone were enough to attract attention. I gave him a sideways glance to see if he was flirting back, but his smile was only polite. He put his hand at the small of my back, not quite touching, but enough to guide me around the tables to a relatively quiet corner.

We each ordered a beer and then turned our attention to our menus. The nearly idle chatter continued until after we ordered and our food arrived. Only after we'd both had a few bites of the vegetarian pizza we were sharing did Reed's expression grow serious. Butterflies fluttered in my stomach. I knew what was coming.

"I'm starting my own business."

Okay, maybe I didn't know what was coming. I leaned forward and he put his hand over mine. My skin tingled where it touched his.

"You were right to make me leave last week. I wasn't thinking clearly. There were things I needed to do." He gestured toward the hand covering mine and I noticed for the first time that his finger was empty. "I hired two lawyers. One for the divorce and one to handle the business aspect of it. I took the papers to Britni two days ago and gave her my wedding band. The engagement ring went back to my mother for safe keeping."

The way he looked at me told me that he had something specific in mind for it and those damn butterflies did another lap. His fingers tightened around mine.

"And I went to both of our parents and told them that I didn't love Britni and I couldn't stay married to her."

My eyes widened. That had taken some serious guts to do that. I just hoped he hadn't mentioned me to them, especially since I wasn't sure how I felt about him anymore. I could only imagine how they'd feel if Reed did this all for me but I rejected him.

I almost winced. The word rejected sounded so harsh.

Reed continued, unaware of my internal conflict. "I knew my parents would try to threaten me with the same thing as before, so I handed in my resignation. I told them that I'd take the money my grandparents had left me to start my own business, and if they couldn't accept the decision I'd made, they could cut me off."

"Reed, I–" I had to say something. He had to know that he couldn't do all of this for me, not when I wasn't sure where we were going to go, how I was feeling.

"I've never felt this free before," he said. "You showed me that I couldn't just keep living the life my parents told me to live. I was suffocating and hadn't even realized it."

I smiled. "I'm glad you feel free." That much was true. I did still care about him. I was happy he'd started standing up to his parents and making his own choices. I loved how happy he looked. I just didn't know if it was enough to get past everything else.

He shifted our hands so that our fingers were laced together. "They may come around; they may not, but I've made my choice." His eyes met mine. "And I choose you."

Oh, fuck. My heart skipped a beat at his words, but I could feel that excitement was only part of it. Almost as significant was worry over what would happen if I didn't choose him.

He sat back, releasing my hand. "I'm sorry. That was too much, I know." He smiled and took a drink of his beer. "No pressure or expectations tonight. I just wanted to let you know where I am."

I nodded and drained what was left of my beer, hoping the buzz would counteract my nerves.

"I know you probably have questions that you've been wanting to ask," he said. "So ask away. Anything you want and I'll answer it honestly."

I took a bite of my pizza as much to give myself a few minutes as anything else. I did have a million questions, but most of them weren't for Reed. There were a few though, that I needed answers to. I picked one thread at random.

"Why now?" I put down the slice I'd been eating. I didn't think I could eat any more. "You said it was because of what Brock had done, but you knew about what he did to me months ago. Back in Vegas, you made me believe that you were going to break off your engagement but went through with it anyway. And…" I was getting riled up now, counting his indiscretions off one finger at a time, "you've been married for nearly six months and keep claiming how much you wanted to be with me even though you didn't make a move to end things until last week. How am I supposed to trust that you won't do the same thing now? Get bored after a while, find some random woman to hook up with and string her along until you dump me."

Reed's expression tightened. "I was afraid," he said flatly. "Afraid to stand on my own two feet. But I'm not now."

I didn't point out that his 'own two feet' included a hefty inheritance that he was keeping. People raised in families like the Stirlings rarely understood what it truly meant to be on their own. The family was always there to cushion the blow.

He continued, "I was terrified that if I risked everything for you, I'd lose you and I'd have nothing."

"And now?"

A new, more grown-up look crossed his face. "You motivated me, but I did this for me too." He started to reach for my hand again but pulled back before our fingers touched. "I know I fucked up with us. Badly. And I know there's a chance this isn't going to work between us. Even if it doesn't, I'm glad I filed for divorce and stood up to my family."

I felt a measure of relief. At least I didn't have that pressure on me. I steered the topic away from choices so he didn't ask me to make one right now. "What type of business are you starting?"

His eyes lit up. "If I can get this off the ground in the next year, I might be able to start bringing over some of the people at my old company who wanted to stick with me."

The atmosphere between us shifted to something much more relaxed as he told me his plans. I could definitely see why his parents were so adamant that he take over the family businesses. It wasn't just that he was their son and they wanted to maintain the family part of things. He knew what he was doing. I didn't have the first clue about what it took to run a business, but even I could understand the way he laid things out.

The discussion took us through the rest of the meal and our check. As we stepped outside, the brisk air made me shiver and Reed put his arm around my shoulder, pulling me to him to share his body heat as we walked toward the car. I flushed, warming up enough that when I got into the car, I wasn't shivering anymore.

"Smells like snow," Reed commented as he started the car. "Real snow."

I nodded in agreement. "The forecast said it'd probably stick tonight. Just an inch or two, but enough that they're going to pull out the salt trucks."

"People forget how to drive on snow after summer," he said.

We discussed the weather until we arrived back at my place. He turned down the one-way street and stopped in front of the house. The street was empty; everyone either tucked inside for the night or already wherever they'd be for the next few hours.

Reed turned in his seat, reaching for my hand. He warmed my chilled fingers between his palms. "Thank you for coming with me tonight."

I nodded, suddenly aware of the silence that reminded me how alone we were.

"I've missed you, Piper." He reached up and brushed his fingers down my cheek, leaving a blazing trail across my skin. He leaned toward me.

I closed my eyes as his lips touched mine. His mouth was firm, but the kiss wasn't forceful. He waited and couldn't help myself. I parted my lips, tilting my head to change the angle. There was heat there, the pleasure of skin sliding against wet skin. Then his hand slid up my waist, his fingers brushing against the underside of my breast and I pulled back.

"I'm sorry," he immediately apologized. "I got carried away." He brushed some hair away from my face, a small smile on his face. "I've been fantasizing about kissing you again for a long time."

"I need time, Reed. Time to figure out what I want," I explained. "I can't just jump back into bed with you. That's what got us into this mess to begin with. I want to make the right decision. The smart one." I pressed my hands together. "I need to decide what my heart wants. What's right for me."

He nodded. I saw a flash of hurt in his eyes but he pushed it back. "I understand." He picked up my hand and pressed his lips to the back of it. "I'll wait. I owe you so much more than that."

"Thank you." I could feel tears prick my eyes as I took my hand back. "I'll call you once I figure things out. Thank you for dinner."

As I walked up the sidewalk and front stairs, I told myself that my eyes were just watering from the cold. When I was inside, I forced a smile at Anastascia, who was sitting on the couch, but she wasn't fooled.

"Honey, what happened?"

"It was a good evening," I said, pulling off my coat. "He explained things and apologized again. He told me that he served Britni with papers and stood up to his family." I hung up my coat and kicked off my shoes. "He wants to be with me."

"Isn't that a good thing?" Anastascia asked. "Isn't that what you wanted?"

I sighed. "I don't know, Ana. I really don't know anymore." Why couldn't I just have some sort of neon sign flash in front of my eyes and tell me that I wanted to be with Reed? Life would've been so much easier that way.

Chapter 4

The crackling of the fire in the massive stone fireplace set the mood. The flickering flames were the only light to see by, but it was all I needed. A blanket was spread out on the wooden floor, the fleece inviting me to sit as it promised to be the softest thing I'd ever felt against my skin.

I did exactly that, stretching out and letting all that soft warmth caress my back and down my legs. The heat from the fire warmed the front of me and I realized I was naked.

I ran my hands over my flat stomach, feeling the muscles from years of athletics hard beneath my pale skin. Some women tried to fight their natural coloring by forcing tans, but I didn't bother. I had the kind of skin that burned in the sun and looked almost orange when I used the spray or lotion stuff. I'd learned that when my boss back at The Twilight Room had told me I was too pale. When I'd shown up the day after, he'd laughed and given me two days off to get myself back to normal. He'd never asked me to tan again.

"You're beautiful."

A husky male voice attracted my attention as he stepped from the shadows. He, too, was nude, and the firelight played off of his sculpted body, sending a rush of heat through me that had nothing to do with the fire. He stretched out next to me, our bodies less than an inch apart, close but still not touching.

"We have all night," he said. "And I intend to explore every inch of you."

I shivered in anticipation. He raised his hand and let it hover over me, teasing. I could feel the energy pulsing between us, traveling that short distance from all of the places where his body was close to mine. When he finally placed his palm on my stomach, I moaned. A simple touch and he could melt me. There was no doubt in my mind that I loved this man, that I craved him, body, mind and soul.

His hand slid to my breasts, caressing first one and then the other. My nipples were hard before he even touched them, and then he circled them with his fingers, teasing the tips before dropping his hand to my stomach again. This time, it moved down and I parted my legs, eager to feel his touch where I needed it the most.

First his fingers ghosted over my inner thighs, almost light enough to tickle, and when I squirmed, he smiled. My hands came down to move things along and he shook his head. Without the fingers between my legs missing a beat, he used his other hand to gather my wrists and hold my hands still. I could've struggled against him and he would've freed me, but I didn't. Instead, I caught my breath as one fingertip ran the length of my slit, the sensitive flesh there responding instantly to his touch.

He slid his finger between my lips, and I sighed. It teased around my opening, circling it before moving up to gently rub my clit. I moaned, shifting my hips as I tried to get more friction where I wanted it. He chuckled and the sound sent a rush of arousal through me. When he lowered his hand and slid his finger inside me, it went easily. I was tight, but so wet that he found no resistance.

"So hot inside you." He leaned over me as his finger began to move in a slow, steady rhythm. His tongue darted out, flicking against my nipple and I gasped. He did it again and then closed his lips over the pale pink flesh.

"Fuck!" I cried out, my back arching as he began to suck. Each pull of his mouth was a new torture. Each stroke of his finger sent ripples of pleasure through me. When his thumb began to work over my clit, I squeezed my eyes closed and waited to explode.

Then, suddenly, his mouth and hand were gone, leaving me dancing on the edge of agonizing ecstasy. I was so close and he still held my wrists, preventing me from doing anything to ease my own suffering. I opened my eyes, preparing to yell at him to return to his previous ministrations, but then I realized he'd stopped so he could settle himself between my legs.

"Yes..." I hissed the word in anticipation of what I knew was coming. He grinned, blowing on my sex before dipping his head and diving in.

His tongue teased me, gently stroking my flesh before his mouth pressed against the inside of my thigh. When he began to suck on the skin there, I swore. I shouldn't let him do that there. He knew my costume for the recital, though complete with tights, wouldn't prevent people from seeing a bruise-like shadow when I danced. I knew that was why he did it though, to mark me, to make sure everyone knew I was his.

Not that there was really any doubt. From the moment I'd chosen him, he'd never tried to hide that we were together. He didn't care what anyone else thought. Not family, not business associates. Not the arrogant social circles who clamored for his approval.

I wailed as his mouth finally moved right where I wanted it. The sound echoed off the cabin walls and I was grateful he'd brought me here this weekend. No neighbors to disturb. And with the noises coming from my mouth as he licked me, I had no doubt neighbors would've complained.

I didn't realize that my hands were free until I started to move them and found that I could. I buried my fingers in his soft hair, pressing him closer to me as I came. His tongue continued to dip into my pussy, caressing my quivering walls and pushing me into another orgasm before the first had completely faded.

Even as I came down, I found his body over mine, his cock nudging at my entrance. Our eyes locked, and he waiting a moment before he slid inside me inch by glorious inch. The motion was smooth, but slow; allowing me the time I needed for my body to adjust, but without completely letting me up. He changed angles, dragged right against that spot that caused me to catch my breath. In and out he stroked, taking me higher, my body tightening; I was already coming again.

He ground his hips against me, rocked into me, the base of his cock rubbing against my clit until I dug my nails into his back, begging him to stop.

"Too much, please, please." Tears streamed down my cheeks as my senses went into overload. When he stilled, I gave a sob of relief. My muscle spasms around his cock kept me going, but the overwhelming feeling that I couldn't handle what was happening had faded.

"Piper," he said my name gently.

I nodded, answering the question he didn't ask. I needed him to move. I was still shaking, but having him inside me but not moving was its own special kind of torture. I could only imagine how it felt for him.

We found a natural rhythm immediately, our bodies dancing with each other with every thrust. It didn't take much for him to drive me over the edge again, sending me to that place where pleasure bordered on pain. And still he rode me, my name falling from his lips with every stroke. I lay limp beneath him, my body unable to process a single additional thing. I kept my eyes focused on his face as he moved above me, into me, through me. I knew every inch of it, and still, I looked. I had seen this face in pain, angry, joyful. I'd watch his eyes flash with emotion. I loved this face.

I loved him.

The realization jerked me awake even as my partner came inside me. My body was shaking with the aftereffects of the dream. I knew I'd come at least twice, maybe even three times, while I was sleeping, and I'd been in the middle of another climax when I'd woken up.

None of that, however, was at the forefront of my mind. No, what had me gasping and my heart racing was the revelation I'd just experienced while in the midst of orgasm. And I knew that's what it had been. Not a weird coincidence, but my brain telling me to accept what my heart already knew. My neon sign.

I was in love with the man from my dream and I needed to get him back.

Chapter 5

Even though it had come as a bit of a shock to me, Anastascia wasn't surprised at all when I told her I'd fallen in love with Julien. Instead, she told me, matter-of-factly, that she'd suspected my feelings for Reed were only a teenage crush that manifested itself as love due to the heightened emotions surrounding my return home for my reunion. I told her she was going to be a great counselor, but I didn't want to be psychoanalyzed.

She grinned as she finished her eggplant salad. "Well, you know where to find me if you change your mind."

I rolled my eyes, but I knew that I'd probably end up asking for advice before this whole thing was over. As I'd proven over the past six months, I sucked at relationships, and I wanted to make things work with Julien. The problem was, I didn't know what to do next.

All day Saturday, while Anastascia was shopping for holiday decorations for my place, I sat on the couch and alternated between calling Julien and moping when he didn't pick up. I left more voicemails than a sane person would, stopping only when Anastascia came back.

We spent the night decorating my place to meet her high standards of appropriate Christmas decorations, but despite the fun I was having with my best friend, I couldn't quit thinking about the man I loved.

Things didn't get any better as the week began. I limited myself to a single call and a single text per day and then spent the rest of the day checking my phone. I was unfocused in dance and twisted my ankle, making it painful to even walk, much less rehearse. I taped it up and continued to practice on it until Wednesday when Madam Emilana told me to take the rest of the week off. That was the last thing I needed, more time to think, but she was insistent and I knew she was right. If I didn't rest it now, I could injure it bad enough that it'd impair my ability to dance in the future. Dancers were expected to push themselves, but there was a difference between auditioning, practicing or performing on a bad ankle and forcing exercises that I could put off a week. My recital of The Nutcracker would be the week of Christmas, starting with a Sunday performance. I had to be in top shape then.

I wanted to work extra hours since I didn't have class, but my boss saw me limping as well and would've sent me home too if I hadn't told him that I needed the money. As it was, he hovered over me so much that it was almost worse than not being able to dance. He did let me pick up some extra hours on Friday, but that was only after Cecily called off. We couldn't handle our busiest night with just one waitress. He needed me and I was glad for the work.

Anastascia wasn't any help, but only because I didn't tell her about my futile attempts to make contact. I let her assume that I was giving him room to grieve, and I tried to convince myself of that too… that Julien was just mourning and didn't want to share his grief. I didn't let myself remember how he'd said he hated his dad. To me, that should have made things easier for him to handle, but I didn't understand that part of his situation. I'd loved my mother and her loss was still a gaping hole in my life.

I spent most of the day Saturday on the couch, my foot propped up and on ice. I'd overdone it the night before at work and knew if I didn't stay off it and let it heal, I risked permanent injury. If I wasn't careful, I'd lose my spot in The Nutcracker and worse, the opportunity it presented.

It was the end of the second week in December. The city was full of lights and decorations. Christmas music was playing everywhere that had speakers. People were shopping, their arms full of brightly-colored packages.

I had a Christmas tree up and lights all around the living room thanks to Anastascia. This was my favorite time of year and I should have been thrilled to be spending it in my own place. It'd be the first Christmas I'd have off since before I went to Vegas, and before that, I'd spent the previous three Christmases in the hospital with my mom. But I couldn't find enjoyment in the decorations or even the specials I spent the entire day watching. If this kept going on, my first Christmas back in Philadelphia was going to turn out to be worse than Thanksgiving.

Then, finally, Sunday morning, he picked up his phone. Instantly, I could tell something wasn't right. It wasn't just the normal sadness that came from the loss of a parent. He sounded distant.

"I was wondering how you were doing." I started there because it was the truth. I was worried about him. I knew how rough it was to lose a parent and how easy it was to just shut people out. If I hadn't had Anastascia when my mom had died, I didn't know what I would've done.

"Keeping busy." His voice was flat. He didn't sound angry with me or cold or anything like that, but he also didn't have his usual warmth.

"That's good." I tried another tact. I really didn't want to have this confession over the phone, especially since we were going to have to deal with what had happened between us the night his dad had died. "I was wondering if you'd like to get a cup of coffee tomorrow morning."

I heard the hesitation, and then Julien spoke, "I'm busy tomorrow."

"Oh." I tried not to sound hurt. "What about Tuesday? Or whenever you're free next."

"Yeah, Piper, thing is, I don't know when I'll have some free time. I've been super busy lately."

I felt tears sting at my eyes and was thankful Anastascia was in the shower. I didn't want her to see me like this. I was pushing too hard, being too clingy. With everything Julien had been through, it wasn't out of the realm of possibility that he wanted some space.

"Look, I have to go." Julien sounded uncomfortable. "I'll talk to you later."

The call ended before I got anything else out. I stared at my phone, unable to believe the way the conversation had gone. Anger cut through everything else. I understand being busy or distracted, but not even giving me a chance to say good-bye? That was rude, and totally unlike Julien.

I dialed him back, debating between calling him out on it and point-blank asking him what was wrong.

I didn't get to do either. This time, the call didn't ring and ring until it automatically went to voicemail. It barely got one ring in before the familiar robotic voice was asking me to leave a message. Julien had deliberately sent my call to voicemail. He didn't want to talk to me.

The tears spilled over as hurt overcame my anger. I didn't understand. I thought he'd cared about me and now he was treating me like I'd been some one-night stand. Horror washed over me. Was it possible that's what he considered me? He'd said what we'd done had been a mistake, but I'd taken that to mean that he didn't want to ruin our friendship. I hadn't even considered that was his way of telling me he'd gotten what he'd wanted and was finished.

"Piper?" Anastascia sat next to me but I didn't look up at her. "What happened? Is it your ankle?"

I shook my head. "My ankle's fine." That, at least, was mostly true. With yesterday's rest and some anti-inflamatories, it was almost back to normal. That should've made me happy, but this thing with Julien made that impossible.

"You finally reached Julien," she said. "What happened?"

I quickly repeated the conversation. Considering how short it had been, it didn't take long. Then, I finally gave voice to my concerns. "Because of what happened with Reed and Brock, did he think I'd be easy and then once he'd fucked me, he didn't want me anymore? I mean, it wasn't like we made promises to each other, but I thought for sure he cared about me."

"I thought so too." Anastascia frowned. "The way that boy was looking at you when he thought you weren't looking. It was clear as day."

"So what happened?" My cheeks flushed as a possibility occurred to me. "Was I bad in bed?"

"Hon, from what you told me, I don't think that was the case." She put her hand on my shoulder.

"Then what is it?" I sniffled. "Do I just attract assholes or something?" I rubbed at my eyes. "It makes sense, I guess. I mean, look at what I spent the last two years doing."

"No," Anastascia said firmly. "You are not doing that. Reed and Brock were mistakes, and Reed even ended up apologizing for the way he behaved."

She had a point, but I couldn't completely agree. I had no idea how Reed was going to deal with the fact that I didn't want to try things with him. I'd been too chicken to call him yet.

"I've seen you with Julien and heard the way you two talked to each other. He's been into you from moment one."

"What?" I raised an eyebrow.

"Honey, guys don't deck their best friends for how they treated a woman unless they care about that woman." She shrugged. "Or at least the ones I've seen don't. You two have been friends, but the only thing that's kept him from trying to make it something more is how skittish you've been." She pursed her lips. "And, it didn't help that you've been pining over Reed this whole time."

I couldn't argue with her there.

"Something had to have happened."

"Something did," I reminded her. "His dad died and then we fucked."

She shook her head. "That's not it."

"He said it was a mistake the next morning."

She waved a dismissive hand. "That's just boy talk for being freaked out." Her eyes widened. "Shit. How long after Reed left did Julien come downstairs?"

"A couple minutes. Why?" I gave her a puzzled look.

She raised her finger, like she was Sherlock solving a mystery. "Julien heard Reed say he was getting divorced and that he wanted you back."

"And..." I prompted, but realized I already knew what she was going to say.

"So, he hears that the man you've been in love with since you were a teenager is leaving his wife to be with you. I'll bet he thought you'd slept with him in the heat of the moment because you felt sorry for him but that you really wanted to be with Reed."

"But..." I breathed. "I didn't even know what I wanted. And I told Reed to leave because I needed to think."

"Piper, I love you, but you suck when it comes to men."

"Thanks," I said dryly. I knew it was true, but that didn't mean I liked being reminded of it.

"Julien was vulnerable. His guard was down. He knew how you felt about Reed and he didn't know you'd started to think about him in any way other than as a friend."

That made sense when I thought about it. After all, I hadn't figured it out, so how could I have expected Julien to? But, I still wasn't sure her explanation was correct.

"Still, I kept calling him. That should've been a hint. It's not like I showed any preferential treatment to Reed or anything..." My eyes went wide as it hit me. "Oh fuck."

"What?"

I sighed. "The day of Julien's father's funeral, when I went to find a bathroom–"

"And Reed asked you to go out with him," Anastascia supplied.

I nodded. "I completely forgot until just now that Julien was there."

"What?!" she exclaimed. "How can you forget something like that?"

"It wasn't like he was standing right there next to me," I said. "But when I was walking back upstairs, I saw him. He must've overheard me agreeing to go out with Reed." I flopped back on the couch. "What am I going to do?"

"You have to explain it to him. All of it," she said. "You have to tell him that you fell for him, that you aren't in love with Reed. Tell him he's the one you want to be with."

Yeah, that sounded good. In theory. "Easier said than done. He's not taking my calls, remember?"

Anastascia stood. "Then you don't call." She held out her hand. "You have to go to him."

"I don't know," I said reluctantly.

"Grow a pair," she snapped. "Do you love the boy or not?"

I answered automatically, "Yes."

"Then you have to tell him." She pulled me to my feet. "Let's get you dressed and then I'll drive you over."

"Oh, yeah, that's going to be great. You sitting outside his loft while I go in and try to convince him of how I feel."

"I'm dropping you off," she said as she led me upstairs. "If things go well, Julien can take care of getting you home." She grinned. "Maybe tomorrow morning."

I glared at her. "And if things don't go well?"

"Then you take a cab or give me a call. Either way, you're going."

Chapter 6

I tried to convince Anastascia to let me drive myself, but she insisted, saying I'd chicken out and not go through with it. I had to admit that a part of me had considered that a possibility. The more I thought about it, however, the more I realized she was right. I needed to do this. If Julien's distance was due to a misunderstanding, then I owed it to him, and to myself, to clear things up. Even if I'd read him wrong and he didn't want to be with me, he deserved to know how I really felt.

I'd kept the clothes simple, mostly because it was cold outside and I'd be putting my coat, scarf, hat and gloves on before I went. It still wasn't the coldest it would get this winter, but I'd missed the last two winters. It was taking me a while to get back into it.

When I was finally satisfied that I look nice even beneath the bulk, I got into Anastascia's car and let her drive me the half a dozen blocks to the loft Julien had bought at the end of October. I'd been there a couple of times and absolutely loved it. It was the entire top floor of an apartment building, with most of the walls knocked out to leave three bedrooms, two baths and then a giant open space that served as kitchen, dining room and living room all at once.

"Good luck," Anastascia said solemnly as I got out of the car.

It was evidence of how nervous I was that I gave her a wobbly smile and thanks rather than flipping her off in an attempt at dark humor. She waited until I was in the lobby before she pulled away. I used the elevator rather than the stairs, not wanting to put the extra strain on my ankle. It was still feeling good, but I knew that any extra exertion could hurt it. But as soon as the elevator door closed, I felt suffocated and then I had six floors of riding to think about all the ways this could go wrong.

I could've misread the signs and it really had been just a mistake brought about by too much emotion.

He could be angry at me for going out with Reed in the first place.

My numerous calls made him think I was some psycho stalker.

He realized he didn't care about me as much as I cared about him.

He was more upset about his father than I'd realized and none of this was about me at all.

When the doors opened, I was struck with the nearly overwhelming urge to ride back down and tell Anastascia that Julien hadn't been home. She'd be able to tell I was lying though, so I knew that wouldn't work.

I forced myself off of the elevator and across the few feet that separated me from the door to Julien's loft. I raised my hand and knocked, the sound loud in my ears.

I heard footsteps from inside, then locks being undone. The door opened and Julien was standing there. It was nearly noon, but he was wearing only a robe, telling me he hadn't been up long. His hair was wet, though not dripping, and hung in his face. I'd told him at the beginning of November that he needed a trim, but it didn't look like he'd done it. His eyes brightened when he saw me and a rush of emotion went through me.

If I'd had any sort of doubt that I'd made the right choice, it vanished when I looked at him. There was a deep, physical reaction to seeing him standing there, his robe belted loosely around his waist, a strip of smooth skin visible. The memory of what his chest felt like under my hands made my palms itch to touch him and see if it was like I remembered. And then there was the way my heart constricted when our eyes met. In that brief moment, I could see into his soul and it was just as beautiful as he was. There was the man who'd defended my honor every time Brock had done something. The man who'd been there to hold me when I'd been hurting and had never asked for anything in return. He'd supported me, helped me without thought of reciprocation. He'd been my friend and then my lover. He was the one I wanted.

I smiled and opened my mouth to tell him all that, to confess everything and then step into his arms. Hope surged through me.

Movement behind him caught my attention and my world came crashing down.

Tall, slender, with perfect skin and wet blond hair, a towel-clad woman walked out of the bathroom and headed for the kitchen.

Instinct kicked in and I chose flight rather than fight. I ran back to the elevator and slammed my hand against the button. I heard Julien call my name and prayed that the door would open before he got to me. I couldn't do this. I was barely holding on as it was. My insides felt like they were being torn apart and I needed to be away from here so I could deal with the pain.

The doors dinged and I darted inside, hitting the lobby button before I'd even stopped moving. I caught a glimpse of Julien's confused expression before the doors closed and down I went. I ran as soon as the doors opened in the lobby. I didn't want to take a chance that he'd gone down the stairs and could be only a minute or two behind me. I couldn't talk to him, couldn't even look at him right now.

I stumbled, twisting my bad ankle enough to send a flare of pain shooting through it, but I didn't stop. I needed to get away. Somewhere. Anywhere I could hide and think without risking Julien finding me.

As I ran, it began to snow. Fat flakes that stuck to my eyelashes and got in my mouth while I was trying to breathe. They forced me to slow down and when I did, I looked around to see where I was. I wasn't too far from home, but Anastascia was there. I couldn't face her. Not yet. But, there was a place I could go.

The church service was just letting out, so it was easy enough to slip inside without anyone noticing me. I took a seat in a back corner pew, obviously meant for latecomers or maybe some people from the church who watched for troublemakers. Either way, it was warm and dry, and if I bowed my head and closed my eyes, people should leave me alone.

I could hear people around me, but I tuned them out as I gave myself over to the agony trying to claw its way out of my chest. With my scarf pressed to my face, I was able to cry unnoticed, and my hands covered my mouth, muffling the sounds.

Everything in me hurt. My heart felt like it was being ripped out of my chest and stomped on. It was worse than what I'd felt with Reed, or with Brock, because what I felt for Julien was so much stronger. He hadn't been a rebound or some guy I'd had a crush on for years. I'd thought I'd known him. We'd spent time together, talking. We'd shared things about our lives.

And I'd been just another conquest to him. A notch in his bedpost.

A bitter thought came to me. Maybe he and Brock had planned the whole thing, using what Brock had done as a way to get me to trust Julien. Was all of this just some sick joke?

My stomach lurched and it took everything in me not to throw up. I'd trusted him almost as much as I trusted Anastascia, and I could see how that had been a mistake. She'd proven herself to me over the years and we'd become friends when we'd been younger and a bit more innocent. I should've known better than to let my guard down with anyone, especially someone from one of those kinds of families. People like me were just playthings to them.

As my tears subsided and the pain turned into a steady ache, my head began to clear. I'd come back to Philadelphia despite what had happened with Reed and Brock because Julien had convinced me that I should follow my heart and my heart was in dance. I loved working with Madam Emilana and I loved my job. I just needed to decide if staying here was worth the new painful memories. I wasn't even sure I could sleep in my room since it reminded me of Julien and our one night together. For the first time since I'd returned, I was back to feeling like I didn't really have a home.

I had so many memories of Julien in my place, not just that night. He'd helped me do so much renovating that we'd joked the place should've been half his. Now, everywhere I looked, I'd see all of the different things he'd done. Leaving, though, felt like I was giving up.

I didn't want to leave Philadelphia again, I decided. Anastascia was the closest thing to family I had. I'd tried running from the memories before and that hadn't worked. I'd ended up alone. At least if I was dealing with things here, I'd have her. I had a shot at making my dreams come true, and I couldn't let some asshole ruin it. No matter how much pain I was in, I could still dance.

I winced as I shifted, a new pain telling me that if I wasn't careful, I could lose that too. I needed to go home and get my ankle taken care of. Now, more than ever, I was determined to succeed. I stood and took a calming breath. Maybe it would be better this way, I thought as I slowly limped toward the door. Without Julien to distract me, I could focus on dance alone. That would be my only love from here on out.

Chapter 7

It took me longer to walk the short distance home than it had to get from Julien's place to the church, but I wasn't going to push it. Now that I'd come to grips with the fact that the only thing I could trust not to betray me was dance, I needed to take care of my ankle. It also didn't help that it was still snowing, leaving the sidewalks more treacherous than usual.

Despite my layers, I was cold by the time I made my way up the front steps. I pushed opened the door and blinked the snow from my eyelashes. Anastascia was standing directly in front of me, a wide smile on her face. I nearly groaned. I didn't want to do this right now. I could tell by her expression that she thought things had gone well and hashing this all out was going to make me even more miserable than I already was.

"Ana, I don't–"

"You have a visitor," she cut me off.

I paused in the middle of taking off my scarf. She couldn't be serious. The only person I could think of who'd come to see me would be Reed since I hadn't called him yet, and I'd told him to wait until I contacted him. I sighed and finished taking off my scarf. Maybe it was better to get all of this over and done with in one day. I could spend the rest of the day curled up in bed then and not have to deal with anything.

"It's Julien."

I didn't say a word or even waste the energy glaring at her for letting him in. I turned and walked back out the door. I didn't know where I was going and I didn't care that it was cold and I'd left my scarf inside. All I knew was I didn't want anything to do with Julien Atwood. Not anymore.

"Piper!" Anastascia yelled my name, but I kept going.

I was at the sidewalk when I felt a familiar hand on my shoulder. Tears burned in my eyes. Fine. If he wanted to talk, we'd talk, and he'd learn he sure as hell didn't want to hear what I had to say. I let him turn me around and then shook his hand from my shoulder.

"Come back inside so we can talk." His voice was soft.

I didn't look at him, unable to stomach the thought of what I'd see on his face. No matter what it was, it'd be a lie. "If I go inside, it'll be alone." I crossed my arms. "You're not welcome in my house anymore." I saw the flinch and wondered just how good of an actor he was.

"Piper." Anastascia appeared at my side. Her expression was stern. "I'm going to pick up some groceries. Go back inside with Julien and talk."

I opened my mouth to argue.

"It's freezing out here." She cut me off before I could say anything. "And you need to get whatever this is," she gestured between Julien and me, "worked out."

I glared at her, but I knew she was right. "Fine," I snapped. I pushed past Julien and stormed into the house, ignoring the pain shooting up my leg.

I heard Julien following me, but I didn't turn to look at him. I pulled off my snow-covered boots, sucking in a breath at the new flare of pain in my ankle. That wasn't good. Still, my anger was stronger than the pain. I hung up my coat and then crossed into the living room, determined to keep at least several feet between Julien and myself. I crossed my arms, holding them tightly across me, as if I could physically pull myself together.

"What's your problem?"

I spun around, surprised by the accusatory question. Now, I could see anger flashing in Julien's eyes and my own temper flared to match.

"Excuse me?"

"You kept calling me, leave dozens of messages, show up at my house and now you're acting like I did something wrong." He took two steps toward me. "You don't talk to me, don't bother saying whatever it was you kept calling to say. You just stand there for a minute and you fucking smile at me before running away. What the hell is your problem?"

I stared at him, unable to believe he was actually trying to make this out to be my fault. "I am so sick of you lying, cheating bastards."

His eyes widened and a stab of vindictiveness went through me. I'd shocked him. Good. It was about time someone called him on his shit, and I was tired of letting guys like this walk all over me.

I pointed an accusing finger at him. "All you had to do was say you had a girlfriend and I never would've let things go that far. Or when you said it was a mistake, you could've been a bit clearer. You wouldn't have heard from me again."

"Girlfriend?" Julien looked puzzled.

"Oh, that's better." I rolled my eyes. "Not a girlfriend then. Just another conquest like me. What, once you fucked me, the challenge was gone? You men are all alike." I saw something like understanding flicker across Julien's face.

"Calm down, Piper. It's not what you think."

I laughed. "I saw her, Julien. I'm not an idiot, no matter how dumb I feel for trusting you. You were in a robe. She was in a towel. You'd both just taken a shower. It doesn't take a rocket scientist to figure it out."

He took another step toward me but I held my ground. His eyes were bright, but I couldn't read them.

"Yes, I'd taken a shower. Before Megan and Gary shared theirs."

Confusion took the edge off of my anger.

"Gary's my cousin. He lives in Chicago with his girlfriend, Megan," Julien explained. "They're going to DC for Christmas with her family and decided to make a trip out of it. They got in late last night and are staying here for a few days."

"Your cousin," I said the words as my brain struggled to understand. "And that was his girlfriend."

"Yes." He dug his phone from his pocket and tapped a few icons, then held it out to me.

The picture on the screen was of Julien and two other people. I recognized the blond, though she was wearing actual clothes rather than a towel. And she was sitting on the lap of a handsome man who, while resembling Julien, was definitely not Julien. Judging by the possessive way the guy's arms were around her and how she was kissing his forehead, Julien was telling the truth.

He put his phone away. "I'm sorry I didn't answer your calls," he said. His expression was blank. "I've had to take my father's place on some different boards and get caught up on all the business things. Then there's looking for people to take my spots and getting them up to speed." He angled himself away from me. "It's going to keep me busy, so I don't know how much I'll be around."

I frowned. What the hell? I may have been wrong about who Megan was, but I wasn't imagining this. He was trying to blow me off.

"It's good that you have Reed," he continued. "He can be there for you now."

Things clicked. He wasn't blowing me off. I closed the distance between us and put my hand on his arm.

"What happened between Reed and me is over."

"But I heard him say he was getting a divorce; that he wanted to be with you." Julien looked down at me, confusion in his eyes.

"He is and he did say that," I agreed. "But I realized that I don't want to be with him anymore." I took a deep breath and then put my heart out there. "I don't love Reed. He was a high school crush that I thought was what I wanted. He's not. You are. I'm…" I took a deep breath and then let it flutter out of my mouth. "I'm in love with you, Julien."

I watched emotions play across Julien's face and curbed my impatience. I couldn't tell what he was thinking, but I knew if I rushed it, any chance the two of us had would be gone.

"Piper."

I met his gaze and felt a pang of sadness at the guarded expression in them. Had I done something to hurt him? Sure, there'd been a misunderstanding with his cousin's girlfriend, but that had been an honest mistake. What had I done that would make him think he needed to keep his shields up with me?

"I can't be the rebound guy." He looked away.

I blinked, completely caught off guard. Was that what he thought? I reached up and put my hand on his cheek, turning his face back toward me. "You're not," I said firmly. "You're the guy."

"But you went on a date with Reed..." His voice trailed off.

Now I understood. "You think I'm saying I'm not in love with Reed because he ran off to Britni again. That I'm vulnerable and willing to fall for the first guy who's nice to me. Like I did with Brock."

"That's not what I meant," he said.

"It's okay," I interrupted before he could start feeling bad. That hadn't been what I'd intended. "That is what happened with Brock. I was in a bad place, feeling sorry for myself for what had happened with Reed. Feeling used by him. I hated my job and my self-worth had taken a serious hit." I brushed back some of his hair. "You were my friend through a lot of that, and you never asked for anything else. I didn't fall for you right away, not like that. It snuck up on me." I smiled. "I was falling in love with you before Reed showed up here."

Hope flared in Julien's eyes and I watched him reign it in.

"I didn't sleep with you that night because I was trying to get over Reed or Brock, and I didn't do it out of pity either."

A muscle in Julien's jaw twitched and I knew I'd struck a nerve. That was what he'd thought. It made sense. If he'd been convinced I was still on the rebound, it was no wonder he considered our night together a mistake.

"I wanted to comfort you," I admitted. "But more than that, I wanted you." I put my hands on his chest and he sucked in air. I was laying it all out on the line now, risking everything on the hope that he felt for me the same way I felt for him. "I wanted to know what it was like to kiss you, touch you." My body was just a couple inches away and longed for more contact. "To feel you inside me."

"Fuck, Piper," he breathed the words before his mouth came down on mine.

I slid my arms up around his neck as he pulled me against him, his grip almost painful. His lips parted mine as he kissed me and I could feel his need, his want. Months of angst and desire poured into me and my entire body throbbed in response.

He broke the kiss, but didn't let me go. His forehead rested against mine as we caught our breath. When he could speak, he said, "I am so sorry for avoiding you." He put his hands on my cheeks, his skin burning against mine. "I thought I could handle it, being just your friend, and then we slept together and I was lost. I couldn't be around you if you were with someone else. It hurt too much."

I brushed my lips across his, needing to do something to ease the pain I heard in his voice.

"These past couple weeks have been torture," he confessed. "I couldn't get you out of my mind. I'd stare at the same page for an hour but not know what it said. I haven't been able to sleep much, and when I do, you're there too."

I remembered my dream the night after I'd gone out with Reed, the one that had made me finally admit how I felt about Julien. "I dream about you too," I said.

The smile that broke across his face made things tighten low inside me. I waited for him to kiss me again, to slowly strip off my clothes. His lips and tongue to taste my skin. My nipples hardened at the thought of his mouth on them, sucking and nibbling. The ache between my legs grew as I remembered what it had been like to have his head down there, devouring me. The stretch of him filling me...

He took a step back and I nearly stumbled. He put out a hand to steady me, but didn't take me in his arms again. Rejection washed over me. I didn't understand.

"I want to do this right," he said, his expression saying he'd correctly read my feelings. "As much as I want to take you upstairs and ravish you." His eyes sparkled at the word. "I want to take it slow."

Was he kidding? I knew my mouth was hanging open and snapped it shut when he chuckled.

"Trust me, Piper. I want you." He took my hand and threaded our fingers together. "I've wanted you from the first moment I saw you."

My eyebrows shot up.

He nodded. "It's true. You walked out onto that stage at The Diamond Club and I wanted you. Brock didn't tell me who you were until the end of the dance and I felt horrible that I'd been ogling my friend's girl, but I couldn't quit thinking about your body. Then I met you and you were even more beautiful in person. I couldn't figure out how an ass like Brock had managed to snag someone like you." He brought our hands up to his mouth and brushed his lips across my knuckles. "I tried to fight it, even after I saw the way he treated you, but once I heard what he'd done, I knew I couldn't deny it anymore."

"And all that means you don't want to take me to bed?" My question was half-teasing.

"It means that I already started things out wrong when we slept together before. You deserve better than how I treated you."

A lump formed in my throat. Of all the men in my life, Julien was the only one who hadn't done anything wrong and he was the one apologizing.

"So," he said. "I want to take you out on a proper date. Not us hanging out here with pizza and beer, or even us going out as friends. I want this to be a real first date. Will you go out with me this Saturday?"

I smiled. "I'd love that."

He gave our hands a yank to pull me toward him, but the sudden movement made me step wrong and I couldn't hold back the pained cry as my ankle nearly buckled. Julien caught me.

"What's wrong?" His face was mere inches from mine, but I could see that kissing was the last thing on his mind.

"I twisted my ankle," I confessed. "Came down on a jump wrong."

"And you were running around on it?" He sounded annoyed. He scooped me up in his arms, ignoring my protest. "You need to get off of it."

"I'm fine," I said as he headed for the stairs. "I can walk."

"Nope," he flat-out refused.

As he started up the stairs, I put my arms around his neck to help with balance. I had to admit it was nice not having pressure on that ankle and more than nice to be in his arms. He set me down on my bed and gently disentangled my arms. His eyes darkened as they slid across the sheets and blanket. I knew he was remembering that night and the warmth radiating from his eyes spread through me.

He bunched up an extra blanket and placed it under my sore foot. "I'm going to get you some ice," he said. "And then I'm going to call Anastascia and tell her it's safe to

402

come back." He pointed at me. "Don't even think about getting up for the rest of the day."

"Are you going to stay and take care of me?" I asked, blinking prettily. I placed my hand on my stomach and ran it up to cup one of my breasts through my shirt.

Julien made a sound in the back of his throat and his hands flexed. "If I stay, you're not going to get much rest."

I smiled. "I'm okay with that."

He glared at me. "Anastascia is going to make sure you behave and I'm going to call you off work for the next two days." He held up a hand to start to protest. "It's either that or I drag you to a doctor and he makes you give up dance for a few weeks."

I looked at him, to see if he was serious. He narrowed his eyes and mine widened in response. "Okay," I said, pouting. "Your idea's better."

"Good," he said. "Now I'm going to get that ice. Don't move."

I watched as he walked out, amazed at how things had turned out. I pulled my phone out of my pocket and placed it on my nightstand. There was only one more thing I had to do, but I'd wait until Julien left to do it.

Chapter 8

A part of me had wanted to take the easy way out and do this over the phone, but I owed it to myself to do things right. I'd forgiven Reed for what he'd done, but if I didn't meet him face-to-face, I'd feel like I was being vindictive, purposefully being rude for past grievances. And despite what had happened, I truly felt Reed was a good man and deserved better.

I'd wanted to meet him right away, but Anastascia had put a stop to that, reminding me I wasn't supposed to be up and around. So I'd reluctantly put it off until Wednesday and resigned myself to feeling guilty until then. Fortunately, Anastascia took Monday and Tuesday off to make sure I didn't do anything other than go to dance, so she kept my mind off of things.

Nothing, however, could keep me from being nervous as I walked into the little café where I'd arranged to meet Reed. This was going to be hard, not because I doubted I'd made the right choice, but because I didn't know if Reed would be angry for all of the things he'd given up to be with me. I really didn't want to cause a big scene in public.

I rubbed my hands on my jeans to dry them, took a deep breath of icy air and stepped inside. The rush of heat made my cheeks tingle even though I'd only been outside for the couple minutes it had taken to walk from where I'd parked Anastascia's car to the café door. I scanned the room and saw Reed raise his hand from a back booth. I smiled and nodded a greeting. I doubted I'd be able to eat breakfast, but some coffee was a necessity if I was going to get through this.

After I got my order and took a sip to make sure they'd gotten it right, I made my way around the maze of tables and slid into the seat across from Reed. The hopeful look in his eyes made my stomach clench. I wasn't sure which would be easier, easing into it or using the band-aid approach and just saying it outright.

"So..." His fingers tightened around the cup in his hands.

I couldn't bring myself to keep him waiting anymore. Band-aid approach then. I kept my voice as gentle as possible, knowing it probably wouldn't soften the blow. "This isn't going to work between us, Reed."

Hurt flashed across his eyes and he reached for my hand, taking it between both of his. "Please, Piper. I know I fucked up. Let me make it up to you. I promise I can be a better man."

I gently pulled my hand away. "I'm sorry." I shook my head. "What we had." I struggled to find the right words.

405

"It was too intense, based purely off of emotion and physical attraction. I'd had a crush on you and we were both vulnerable. The sex was great, but whatever connection was there, it wasn't real."

His mouth tightened. "Things could be different this time. I've changed."

I nodded. "I know you have." And he had. The fact that he'd stood up to his parents was huge. "But I've changed too. I've learned a lot about myself and done some growing up. One of the things I realized was that we aren't right for each other."

I watched as it sunk in and waited for a blow-up. His fingers flexed on the table.

"Is there someone else?"

For a brief second, I considered lying to him, but then realized I'd be doing exactly what I'd accused him of doing. It'd hurt for him to hear the truth, but it would be worse if he found out I'd lied.

"There is," I confirmed.

A shadow passed across his face. "Who?"

"It doesn't matter." He'd find out soon enough. I had no doubt the gossip mongers would have a field day with this one. "But I know he and I are supposed to be together." I wanted to apologize again, but refrained. I hadn't cheated on Reed or led him on. I felt bad that he was hurting, but he pain couldn't become my responsibility.

After another minute of silence, he let out a slow breath. "Okay," he said. His eyes met mine. "I hope he knows how lucky he is."

I smiled. I couldn't help it. "We both do."

He drained his coffee while I tried to figure out something to say. Unfortunately, I blurted out the first thing that came into my head without thinking about whether or not it was appropriate.

"Are you going to try to work things out with Britni?" I slapped my hand over my mouth. "Shit. I'm sorry. That was completely out of line. It's none of my business. I'm so sorry."

He held up a hand, the corners of his mouth twitching with humor. I had a flash of memory about what it had felt like to have those lips on mine, moving over my skin. There was fondness to the memory, but no heat, confirming what I'd told him. My feelings for him were platonic.

"It's okay," he said. "And the answer's no. I'm through letting other people dictate my life." He gave me a sad look. "It's already cost me too much."

He didn't have to tell me what he was thinking at that moment because my mind was already there. How different things might've turned out if he'd made that decision earlier. If he'd broken up with Britni before his bachelor party, would he have forgotten about me and our little tryst, or would he have tried to find me? If he'd followed through with it when we'd been in Vegas, would he have asked me to come back to Philadelphia with him? Would I, instead of planning a date with Julien this weekend, be looking forward to spending Christmas with the Stirlings, perhaps wondering if it was too early to be thinking about a ring?

I didn't like where that train of thought was taking me. I asked another question, "What about the family business?"

"Rebecca," he said. "My parents are pissed enough at me that they're going to let her be in charge, even though they'd always said she wasn't cut out for business. I just hope the people in the company aren't going to suffer because of what I did. Punishing me is one thing..." His voice trailed off and he forced a half smile. "I'm not going to let it change my mind. Whatever Rebecca does will come back on them."

"What about you?" I asked. "Do you think she'll do a good job?"

He rolled his eyes. "Piper, you know my sister. What do you think?"

I smirked. "She flunked economics and, rumor has it, did some 'extracurricular work' to pass her computer class. Social media was the extent of her computer knowledge."

"So you can understand why they haven't let her do anything before."

"Maybe they'll change their mind about the whole Britni thing to keep Rebecca out of the board room," I suggested.

He shook his head. "They aren't the kind of people who'll go back on a threat. They'll put her in charge to punish me. But I'm not going back there."

"Right." I suddenly remembered. "Your business idea."

He spun the empty coffee cup between his fingers. "I'm thinking now I might put things on hold for a while."

Guilt welled up inside me. So I had screwed up things.

"I need to clear my head," he continued. He glanced up at me. "About a lot of things, not just this." He gestured between the two of us. "I need to figure out where my life's going and what I want from it. I'd never really given it serious thought before. It'd always been understood that I'd take over the family business, and I didn't have anything that was pulling at me, some other passion I needed to explore."

"Where are you going to go?" I asked. I couldn't imagine never having dreams of my own. As poor as I'd grown up, my mother made sure I'd known, with enough hard work, I could accomplish what I wanted.

"Europe," he said. "I have a few friends from college who live there. One is in Germany, another in France. I haven't seen them in a while. I'll look them up." He tried for a wider smile. "Besides, rumor has it the women over there are easy."

I forced a laugh and he did the same. I could tell he was trying not to show what he was really feeling. "And I've heard they like Americans."

He smiled at my attempt to go with his joke. He glanced out the window and stood. "I really should get going."

I stood as well. We looked at each other for a moment before exchanging an awkward hug.

"Be careful," I said.

He nodded and turned toward the door.

A question popped into my head. I didn't want to ask it, but I knew I needed to. "Reed, about the dance grant." He stopped and turned. "I need to know when it expires."

"It doesn't." His voice was quiet. "You have talent, Piper, and you deserve every opportunity to use it. It was a gift to you; no strings attached." He paused, and then added, "And I'm taking your suggestion about making it a permanent thing for low-income families. Once your studies are complete, you'll get to help select another person to help."

"Reed, I don't know what to say."

"Nothing," he said. "I just expect some good seats when you make it to Broadway."

And then he was gone, leaving me standing in the café wondering if it was possible that things had actually just gone better than I'd ever imagined.

Chapter 9

I'd fully expected to be nervous when Julien picked me up for our date, but I wasn't. Not that I was exactly calm. Excitement hummed along my skin and the anticipation made my heart beat faster the closer the time got. Anastascia had gone back to her place yesterday, so I didn't even have her around to distract me. In fact, her parting words about why she hadn't stayed out the weekend had been about giving Julien and me space to do what we wanted, where we wanted. Not exactly the words of encouragement I could've used.

Would we end up back here? How long did he want to wait? The question kept circling in my head even as we walked to his car. I reminded myself that Julien and I were going to do this right. If we had sex tonight, it would be because the timing was right, not because I had no self-control when it came to him being naked.

I was surprised our conversation came as easily as it had when we were nothing more than friends. I'd anticipated an awkwardness that never came to be. We didn't struggle for topics or rehash the discussions we'd had before. If it hadn't been for the little things, it could've been any one of the dozens of times we'd hung out together as friends. Little things like Julien taking my arm as we walked down the concrete stairs to the entrance of The Tavern or how he placed his hand on the small of my back as our waiter led us to a table by the wine cellar.

The cold and threat of snow had kept people away and the place was relatively empty. We could hear the piano and singing from upstairs and it added a nice background to our easy conversation. He told me about what he was doing with all of his father's businesses and I told him about the different aspects of dance I was working on. We discussed the possibilities of ways he could use his family's companies to better the community, as well as having a lively debate over which Christmas special was the best.

By the time the check came, what we were doing felt as natural as breathing. When he reached for my hand across the table and threaded our fingers together, little sparks of electricity danced across my skin. It felt right, like we'd been made to fit together. His thumb traced circled across the back of my hand.

"We didn't talk about where this night was going to end," Julien said softly. His eyes met mine. "I should take you home, give you a kiss good-night and then call you tomorrow."

I swallowed hard, my stomach clenching as I willed him to give a second option. I knew we'd only been on this one date, but my body remembered his too well and craved it. He'd said he wanted to take it slow, but I wasn't sure that was the best option.

He continued, "Or, you could come back to my place. My cousin and his girlfriend left this morning. We could watch a movie and see where things go from there."

"I'll take option number two." I didn't even need to think about it.

Relief showed on Julien's face and his eyes sparkled. "I was hoping you'd say that."

The energy between us on the ride from The Tavern to Julien's loft was almost palpable. If it hadn't started to snow, I probably would've leaned closer, run my hand over his thigh, but the roads were slick despite the salt trucks and I didn't want him to lose control of the car. Talking to cops or being in the ER was not how I planned on finishing out tonight.

Both of us were coated with fat, wet flakes by the time we got into his building and we laughed as we brushed them off. Even that laughter had an undercurrent of sexual electricity and only the presence of an elderly woman in the elevator kept us from starting things up right there. Instead, we stood next to each other, our fingers linked, and pretended we weren't both thinking about ripping the other one's clothes off.

I saw Julien's hands shaking as he tried to get his key in the door and I flushed with pleasure at the realization that I could do that to him. When he got the door open, he pulled me in after him and was on me before the door finished closing.

His mouth was hot and greedy, his tongue pushing between my lips even as he worked to remove some of the layers between us. Laughter bubbled up, escaping in a little burst at one of the points when our mouths parted. He pulled back, a puzzled expression on his face as he dropped his coat to the floor.

"I was just wondering if we were skipping the movie."

He rolled his eyes and smiled, leaning down to take my mouth again. This kiss was no less intense, but the near frantic nature was gone. This was slow and thorough, one of those deep, wet kisses that movies always seemed to show but real-life never lived up to... until now.

My coat joined his on the floor, the snow melting into puddles next to our boots, but neither one of us cared about that at the moment. Without breaking the kiss, he picked me up and began to walk back toward his bedroom. I took advantage of my new position to tear my lips from his and begin working my way over the side of his neck and up to his ear.

He moaned when I tugged on his earlobe and the noise grew louder when I scraped my teeth on his neck. His hands tightened around me for a moment, and then released me, dropping me onto the bed.

I looked up at him as he undressed. His movements were unhurried, sensual as he unbuttoned his shirt. By the time it fell to the floor, my heart was racing. His pants were next, but he didn't just pull them off. It wasn't until he started on them that I realized what he was doing. He wasn't dancing, but it was stripping just the same. The tease, the leisurely reveal. As he kicked aside his pants, he was left in just a pair of gray boxer-briefs, tight enough to reveal how much he was enjoying what he was doing. Those came off at an excruciatingly slow pace, the expression on his face saying he liked taunting me.

Once he was done, I reached for the hem of my sweater, ready to return the favor. His hands covered mine, stopping me. Without a word, he moved my hands aside and pulled my shirt over my head. His eyes locked on mine as he peeled off my pants, ending up on his knees in front of the bed. He parted my legs, dropping his gaze to the dark green silk I was wearing.

"Damn," he swore softly. "You're soaked through."

I sat up and wrapped my hand around the back of his neck, pulling the two of us together until my mouth covered his. I took control of the kiss, my tongue sliding between his lips to explore the hot recesses of his mouth. His hands skimmed over the bare skin of my back, fingers finding the hooks and making short work of them. I moaned as his hands moved along my ribs, around to begin to work their magic on my breasts.

I arched into his touch, our mouths parting. His lips trailed fire down my throat, pausing every so often to shower a bit of extra attention. Not so much that I'd have to worry about covering it up, but enough to know that's what he wanted to do. When his mouth reached my breasts, I buried my fingers in his hair, loving the long, silky strands.

"Don't ever cut your hair," I whispered.

I wanted to close my eyes as he lavished attention on first one breast, then the other, but I wanted to watch him more. He looked up at me, his eyes darkening with each gasp and moan. Then his fingers were hooking around the elastic of my panties and they were sliding down my legs. They caught on my right ankle, but neither of us paid any attention. I was too busy watching him kiss his way down my stomach.

He sighed as his fingers slid between my folds, parting them and making way for his tongue. He licked one long stripe, making me fall back on my elbows.

"I've been dreaming about this," he said, glancing up at me. "Making love to you this way."

He hooked my legs over his shoulders and stretched his hands on either side of me so that our fingers locked. This time, when he buried his face between my legs, I called out his name. My fingers tightened around his as his lips and tongue went to work. Pleasure washed over me as his talented mouth sent every nerve singing. But it was when he looked at me from under those thick lashes that everything else faded away. I could see into the depths of his soul and something inside me reached out to something inside him.

As a child, I'd always been a romantic, believing in true love and happily ever after. Life had quickly taught me that those things didn't exist. When I'd first hooked up with Reed, I'd felt those parts of me wanting to come back, but I'd thought his betrayal had killed the last of any real romantic notions. Now, I found they hadn't been killed, but rather had just been dormant these past few months. I knew there'd be work and it wouldn't be easy, but in that moment, I knew I'd found my soul mate.

My orgasm burst over me as the realization hit me and I cried out, my back arching, hips rising, sex clenching around his tongue. He held me, kept me grounded as I came, and then his hands were on my hips, moving me further onto the bed. I heard a familiar ripping sound, and then he was stretching out over me, his cock nudging at my still quivering core.

"I love you," I said, reaching up to press my palm against the side of his face.

The smile that spread across his face brought tears to my eyes. "I love you, too." He brushed a stray hair off of my cheek, then leaned down to kiss it.

I raised my hips even as he surged forward and we came together in one firm thrust. His mouth covered mine, swallowing the half-scream that came from the sudden, nearly painful stretching. The feeling of being too full didn't stop me though. I began to move against him, with him, our bodies falling into an instant rhythm, the kind of dance that said we'd been partners for years.

He pressed against all the right parts of me and, as his hand slid over my hip and down my thigh to my knee, I knew we had been made for each other. He pulled my leg up and I keened as the change in position drove him even deeper than he'd been before. He was a part of me, connected in every way a person could be.

The room was hot, in stark contrast to the weather outside, and our bodies glistened with sweat. Our labored breathing mixed with the sounds of flesh coming together, punctuated by the pleasurable moans that escaped between kisses. It was just us, here in this room. The world outside didn't exist. Nothing and no one beyond the two of us. Time ceased to matter. We could've been there, riding the edge of passion, for minutes, hours or years. All I knew was that when it crashed over us, I didn't know if we could survive.

And then it was there, rushing, covering us with a flood of pleasure so intense I saw stars flash in front of my eyes and across his beautiful face. I heard Julien call my name and I was vaguely aware I was digging my nails into his back, but I couldn't get my muscles to obey me and release him, so I held him more tightly and rode it out.

Afterwards, our bodies lay entwined, trembling, and I wondered if either of us would have the strength to cover us with a blanket before we fell asleep. I put my arm across his stomach and pressed against him, not wanting to sink into oblivion. I knew it was irrational, but the last time I'd fallen asleep with him; he'd freaked out and run the next morning.

"I'm not going anywhere," he murmured as he pulled me more tightly against his side. "Not this time. You're stuck with me."

I kissed his chest. "Stop reading my mind."

I was still smiling over our unusual connection when I drifted off.

When I woke the next morning, he was gone. My hand went to the place where he'd been and found the sheets still warm. Before I could panic, he spoke, his soft voice coming from behind me.

"You've got to see this."

I rolled over and saw him standing at his window. I wrapped a sheet around me as I climbed out of bed. He was fortunate that the window was high enough to prevent anyone from seeing that he was naked, but I had to cover myself. As I reached his side, he took a step back and pulled me in front of him, his arms curling around my waist.

I gasped. I didn't need to worry about anyone seeing us in the window; there was no one to see us. The entire city was covered with white. The streets of Fishtown were buried under several feet of snow. It was clean and white, pristine.

"The news is saying everything's shut down for the day," he said as he kissed the top of my head. "No one's supposed to be out unless it's an emergency."

"So," I said slowly, leaning back into his warmth. "What you're saying is, I'm stuck here for who knows how long."

"Seems like it." He nuzzled my ear. "Oh, what will we do to pass the time?"

I reached behind me and found my prize already starting to swell. He gasped as I took him in hand. "I can think of a few things."

We laughed and he nuzzled me, the heat of his breath against my neck. "I can think of dozens."

As we returned to bed, the laughter shifted and became something equally as joyful. We didn't rush and we didn't second-guess. We had the day and we were going to make the most of it. Tomorrow would come and we'd face whatever it brought, but for right now, we were going to enjoy today.

Chapter 10

As the first day of summer passed, I realized I'd been back in Philadelphia for almost a full year. Sometimes, it seemed like just yesterday that I'd returned for my high school reunion and my life had been turned upside-down. Or should I say, right-side-up. Other times, the memories of those days were so distant that they seemed like they'd happened to someone else. The one thing that never changed was that I was happier now than I'd been since my mom had gotten sick. Things weren't perfect, of course, but life was good.

Julien and I didn't spend much time with the high society types, but we were around enough, along with Anastascia, to keep up on the latest news. News such as the speedy dissolution of Britni and Reed's marriage, and her quick recovery with the heir to the McCord fortune. They announced their engagement at the beginning of June with plans for a spring wedding next year. I wondered if this was another business transaction, especially after Anastascia said she'd seen Britni's fiancé frequenting a couple of gay bars in the city, but I didn't dwell on it. That marriage wasn't my business.

The one aspect of Britni's family that was my business, however, ended up with a neat and tidy resolution. Brock was two months into an eighteen-month sentence for assault and would then be on probation for another three years with mandatory counseling and no alcohol. He probably would've gotten a lot worse if he'd gone to trial, but his victim preferred the plea over having to take the stand. I didn't really blame her. I could understand what she was going through. I would've testified if I'd been called, but I hadn't been looking forward to sharing everything with complete strangers. We'd heard rumors that the Michaels family had settled with the victim in the civil case as well, paying her medical bills on top of a nice chunk of money. I hoped she would be able to go somewhere new to rebuild her life.

It hadn't been just the Michaels who had kept me and Julien's relationship from being the headline society news. Reed had left for Europe a week after he and I had talked, and two weeks later, Rebecca had been named head of the marketing department, Reed's old position. Within three months, she'd messed it up so much that the shareholders had stepped in and forced Rebecca out to save the rest of the company. The Stirlings had been furious, but that had been small compared to what had happened next. Less than a month after Rebecca's humiliating departure from her family's company, she'd been caught in a compromising position with a married man. And not just any married man, but the father of one of her high society friends. From what Anastascia had heard, Rebecca reputation was beyond tarnished. Yeah, karma could be a real bitch.

As for Reed, he was still in Europe. He'd sent me a picture of him in front of the Eiffel Tower back in April and had told me he was doing well. He said he was grateful I'd had the guts to do what he couldn't. Julien had heard that Reed's parents were trying to get him to come back and run the rest of the family business after the Rebecca disaster, but Reed was hardly taking their calls. I was happy to see he was sticking with his decision to be his own man. I really did wish him all the best.

After all, it was thanks to him that I was currently standing backstage in one of Philadelphia's most beautiful theaters, getting ready to take part in my first official production. Granted, it was only the chorus line for a new version of Phantom of the Opera, but it was still a part I'd been personal chosen to play. This wasn't some sort of recital for the dancers from Madam Emilana's. This was a legitimate production, with auditions and casting.

My time at Madam Emilana's was going better than I ever dreamed. I hadn't been able to perform in The Nutcracker thanks to my ankle, but she'd set up a private audition for me with her friend. After getting cast as a chorus girl, I started my individual lessons with her in January. We decided to move away from a ballet focus into more modern styles of dance as I realized where I wanted to go. At her suggestion, I'd begun taking voice and acting lessons with a goal of being on Broadway—not just as a background dancer but as one of the stars. The producer of Phantom had already promised me at least a few auditions for his future shows. After this past week of rehearsals, he'd taken me aside and said he wanted me to try out for a lead in an original piece he was working on.

I took a deep breath and cleared my head. I couldn't afford to be thinking of all that, not when I had a show to perform right here, right now.

The music began and my body took over. I followed the other girls out onto the stage, smiling at the bright lights and the audience I couldn't see. Somewhere in that audience, I knew, was Julien. Anastascia was there too, probably sitting next to my boyfriend chatting about her crush on the young man who played Raoul. I danced for them, the people who'd supported me through everything. I danced for Reed and the kids from the wrong sides of the tracks who would also benefit from the grant he'd set up. I danced for my mom, who'd sacrificed so much but had never gotten to see my dream become real.

By the time intermission came, I knew with absolute certainty that this was what I wanted to do with my life. It had been an idea—a dream—before, but now I knew I wanted it to be a reality. It wouldn't be easy, but I felt certain I could do it, especially with Julien and Anastascia in my corner. When I went back onstage in the second act, it was with a new purpose, to show everyone in the audience what I could do.

After the curtain call, I headed toward the dressing room with the rest of the chorus girls only to be stopped by the producer.

"You were amazing!" he gushed. "Absolutely mesmerizing!"

"Thank you." My face was flushed with gratitude.

"My understudy for Meg just informed me that she's pregnant."

Pregnant? I held my breath.

"Her doctor told her that she's high-risk and not allowed to dance." He handed me a script. "I want you to be the new understudy."

I stared at him. Meg wasn't a leading role, but she was a supporting character and had a song with the lead. "I-I..." Words failed me.

"I'll take that as a yes and a thank you."

"Yes!" I blurted out. "And thank you!"

He beamed at me. "Excellent! We'll discuss more details on Monday during rehearsal. Enjoy the rest of your night."

I was practically walking on air as I made my way through the chaotic backstage, smiling and exchanging compliments as I went. I barely registered a single face until I saw him standing outside the dressing room door.

Julien set the large bouquet of white roses down on a nearby chair as he embraced me, holding me tight.

"You were amazing," he said. "I couldn't take my eyes of you."

His hands slid over the rough lace of my costume, heat blazing through the thin fabric. I shivered.

"Thank you." I kissed his cheek. "And the roses are beautiful."

He released me and reached into his pocket. "And they're not your only gift."

I wasn't sure which I wanted to do first, share my news or open the present. Then I saw the way Julien's eyes were shining and decided the gift would come first. It was a small, flat box without any writing to tell me where it was from. I was still trying to decide if it was earrings or a necklace when I opened and saw it was neither.

A key.

I looked up at him, puzzled. I already had a key to his loft; he'd told me to keep his extra one when he'd asked me to run back to pick up something for a dinner at Anastascia's.

"A key to your loft?"

He picked up the key and showed me the ribbon he had tied through it.

I read the words written on the bit of lace. "'To my heart and our home.'" I stared at the words. "'Our'?"

"I want you to move in with me." He tucked a few escaping tendrils of hair behind my ear. "I don't like us having to figure out whose place we're going to or thinking about whether or not we're spending the night. I want us to be together all the time. I want a home. With you."

Tears welled in my eyes and I couldn't speak around the lump in my throat. He looked at me expectantly, wanting an answer I couldn't voice. Sometimes words aren't necessary and I did the next best thing. I threw my arms around him and pressed my lips against his. The tears spilled over as we kissed and I could taste the salt on my tongue, but it wasn't bitter. These were tears of joy. After years of never knowing where I belonged, I finally had a home. My heart swelled with love and I moved my mouth to his ear.

"Take me home."

He smiled down at me. "Gladly."

- *The End* -

What's next?

** Casual Encounter **

My wedding day was supposed to be the happiest day of my life. Instead, my heart was shattered into a million pieces.

When twenty-five year-old Aubree Gamble is left at the altar by her boyfriend of four years, she isn't sure where she's suppose to go from there.

Her friends try to help, suggesting everything from hiring a professional to setting her up on blind dates, telling her she needs a casual encounter to move on, forget all about her past love.

As things are about to go very wrong, a mysterious stranger comes to her rescue and Aubree thinks that he could be the one person who can help heal her broken heart. What she doesn't know is that her handsome hero isn't exactly the white knight she imagines.

Don't miss the first installment in the *Casual Encounter* series by best selling author M.S. Parker.

Acknowledgement

First, I would like to thank all of my readers. Without you, my books would not exist. I truly appreciate each and every one of you.

A big "thanks" goes out to all my Facebook fans, street team, beta readers, and advanced reviewers. You are a HUGE part of the success of my series.

I have to thank my PA, Shannon Hunt. Without you my life would be a complete and utter mess. Also a big thank you goes out to my editor Lynette and my wonderful cover designer, Sinisa. You make my ideas and writing look so good.

About The Author

M. S. Parker is a USA Today Bestselling author and the author of the Erotic Romance series, Club Privè and Chasing Perfection.

Living in Southern California, she enjoys sitting by the pool with her laptop writing on her next spicy romance.

Growing up all she wanted to be was a dancer, actor or author. So far only the latter has come true but M. S. Parker hasn't retired her dancing shoes just yet. She is still waiting for the call for her to appear on Dancing With The Stars.

When M. S. isn't writing, she can usually be found reading– oops, scratch that! She is always writing. ☺

Printed in Great Britain
by Amazon